OCT 15 2019

P9-CMT-157

Springdale Public Library
405 S. Pleasant
Springdale, AR 72764

WHITE HOT SILENCE

Also by Henry Porter

Remembrance Day
A Spy's Life
Empire State
Brandenburg
The Dying Light
Firefly

WHITE HOT SILENCE

HENRY PORTER

The Mysterious Press
New York

Springdale Public Library
405 S. Pleasant
Springdale, AR 72764

Copyright © 2019 Henry Porter

All rights reserved. No part of this book may be reproduced in any form or by any electronic or mechanical means, including information storage and retrieval systems, without permission in writing from the publisher, except by a reviewer, who may quote brief passages in a review. Scanning, uploading, and electronic distribution of this book or the facilitation of such without the permission of the publisher is prohibited. Please purchase only authorized electronic editions, and do not participate in or encourage electronic piracy of copyrighted materials. Your support of the author's rights is appreciated. Any member of educational institutions wishing to photocopy part or all of the work for classroom use, or anthology, should send inquiries to Grove Atlantic, 154 West 14th Street, New York, NY 10011 or permissions@groveatlantic.com.

First published in Great Britain in 2019 by Quercus Editions,
an imprint of Hachette UK

Published simultaneously in Canada
Printed in the United States of America

First Grove Atlantic edition: September 2019

Library of Congress Cataloging-in-Publication data is available for this title.

ISBN 978-0-8021-4753-0
eISBN 978-0-8021-4754-7

The Mysterious Press
an imprint of Grove Atlantic
154 West 14th Street
New York, NY 10011

Distributed by Publishers Group West

groveatlantic.com

19 20 21 22 10 9 8 7 6 5 4 3 2 1

For Miranda and Benji

CHAPTER 1

Two figures were moving up the hill in the hot afternoon of the Calabrian autumn, silhouetted against the dusty white track that led to one of the abandoned mountain villages that now housed refugees. She recognised the effortless stride of men who had walked across deserts and guessed they were African migrants on the way to the refugee village of Spiadino. There was no other reason for them to be out in these barren hills, yet it was odd they hadn't taken the coast road then headed up to the village. Maybe they encountered less trouble using this route.

She had been holding a phone while trying to get through to Denis Hisami, and she placed it on the dash as she rounded the first of several small bends that lay between her and the two men – on these roads the gravelly surface was as treacherous as ice. The phone began to vibrate then slide towards her. She caught it before it dropped into the footwell and answered Hisami in Palo Alto. It was 6.30 a.m. in California, but her husband was already at a meeting which she knew from his rather abrupt manner the day before to be a critical.

'Hi there! Sleep well?' she said with a smile in her voice.

'Where are you?' She heard him move. 'We thought you'd have taken off by now.'

'They needed someone to deliver a vehicle to Spiadino. Seemed like a good opportunity to see what they're doing in the new centre. *Our* new centre, Denis.'

'Yes, but I'd really prefer you to be here with me,' he said.

'I'll be on the next flight from Naples – promise.'

This was unlike Hisami. In the year of their marriage – they were just two weeks past their first anniversary – she had never known him to be demanding, or to complain about anything. But there was a plaintive note in his voice, which she chose to put down to disappointment.

'I'm sorry. Should've checked with you. Just thought you'd be pleased to hear what good work the Foundation is already doing. We're making a real difference to these people's lives.'

'I know, and I want to hear about it, but right now I would like you to be here with me. I need to talk something over and I'd appreciate your advice.'

This, too, was out of character. Denis never showed any doubt about the course he was taking and seldom consulted her about business. He would occasionally walk her through his dealings, but this was more like a briefing after all his calculations and dispositions had been made. He was the most self-sufficient and purposeful man she had ever encountered. Just then, briefly, and irritatingly, Paul Samson flashed into her mind, but she dismissed the image of him reading in their bedroom on a biting cold morning in Venice and, using the nickname for Denis that had appeared out of nowhere a few months before, she said with some passion. 'Oh, Hash, I'll be with you before you know it. I can't wait.'

Hisami began to say something but she could hear voices in the background and realised he felt constrained. At that moment she reached the two men and slowed down. As she passed them, one turned and raised his hand and grinned at her. She recognised Louis, a wraith-thin Senegalese who bore the mental and physical scars of the journey across the Sahara to Libya, where he had been confined, tortured and eventually kicked out of detention with the same mysterious fury with which he had been arrested and beaten a few months before. Somehow, he'd found his way on to a boat which then capsized just outside Italian territorial waters and he had been pulled from the sea half dead by a ship operated by a German NGO. Louis's first language was Wolof but he spoke good English, though with a hiss caused by a missing upper front tooth that had been knocked out in Tripoli.

'Hold on,' she said to Hisami, 'there are some men on the road out here – I recognise them.'

She brought the car to a halt in a cloud of dust and turned round to see Louis and his companion running towards her, smiling and waving their arms. One had a phone in his hand.

'What's going on, Anastasia?' Hisami demanded.

'These men I know are obviously going to the village. I'll give them a ride. They're perfectly fine. Don't worry.'

She heard Hisami protest, but by now Louis was speaking to her through the open window and saying it was a miracle that Signora Anastasia had come along at just the moment they felt they could go no further – they had been walking for twelve hours straight and were out of water. And, yes, they were going to Spiadino, so that his companion, Akachi, could take up a job as a baker and Louis could maybe help out as a soccer coach and seek work as a carver of wood. There was a promise of a roof over their heads in Spiadino, now known as the Village of a Hundred Nations, and they felt blessed and hopeful about the future.

As this all spilled out, she put her hand up to stop him. 'Hold on, I'm on the phone. Get in and I'll finish up with this call.' Speaking to Hisami, she said, 'Did you hear all that? It's nothing to worry about. I'll be at the village in half an hour, and then I've got a car later to take me to the local airport for the Naples flight.'

'Let me know when you get to the village,' said Hisami.

She hung up and turned to Louis, who'd got in beside her. His smile had suddenly faded into a look of angry regret, as though she were about to compel him to act against his will. He put out a hand.

'Sorry, Signora Anastasia, but you must give phone to me.'

Jerking her hand away from his, she shouted, 'Are you crazy! I don't expect you to steal my things when I offer you a ride. Get the hell out now!'

Louis looked hurt and, shaking his head, snatched at the phone again, while Akachi leaned forward and attempted to pin her arms from behind. She swapped the phone to her left hand and let the car jump forward, causing them both to be thrown back. Akachi struck the side of her head wildly and Louis tried to wrestle the key from the ignition but then took hold of the wheel as they charged towards the bank on their right and collided with it, causing rock and clods of dry earth to cascade on to the front of the car. He was cursing in his own language and his eyes bulged with fear and aggression. He lashed out at her with a backward blow aimed at her face, but she ducked and he missed. Releasing her seat belt, she tumbled out of the door and ran up the track towards a black Mercedes van that had rounded the bend above her. She stopped and waved frantically at the van, but the driver seemed in no hurry to help her, even though it must have been obvious that she was in trouble. Her two assailants had climbed out with their backpacks, yet they weren't bothering to pursue her, nor, she noted in a flash, were they themselves making any attempt to escape from the Mercedes.

About fifty metres up the road from her car, she stopped in her tracks. The Mercedes rolled to a halt and two men got out and began to walk towards her. Both were armed, which for one brief moment reassured her, but then she threw a look at Louis and his friend and saw they were simply waiting by her Toyota, which had come to rest with its front mounted on a boulder. She glanced up the track again and saw the men had now raised their guns and were beckoning her towards the Mercedes. One spoke to her in Italian, using her name, but by the time she registered this she had vaulted over a short length of crash barrier and was plunging down a slope towards dense scrub and a stand of stunted oaks some fifty metres away. Pursued by a small landslide of rocks and dirt, she dived into the scrub and dug into the pocket of her jeans for her phone.

Desperately trying to regain her breath, she dialled Denis and ordered in her mind the details he would need to know immediately – her position, roughly twenty kilometres north of a town called Prianzano, descriptions of the migrants and of the two men in the Mercedes.

The call went straight to voicemail. She swore and waited for Denis to say, 'Leave a message and I'll return your call as soon as I am able.' She spoke calmly but urgently, saying she'd been targeted for kidnap and one of the Italians knew her name. She was still free and was going to try her luck along a gully that went due west from her position, but that might mean she would have to break cover for a few seconds and so give her position away.

She hung up and peered through the bushes. On the road above her, the four men were standing together, looking down the steep bank. She wondered why neither of the two Italians had come down after her. She moved to her right, snaking across the dead leaves and twigs, painfully aware that each slight sound might tell them exactly where she was. Her sweat dripped on the leaves beneath her and her palms were covered in pinpoints of blood from the thorns on the ground. She stopped and decided to make another call, this time to her contact in Spiadino, an Italian-American psychologist named George Ciccone who had set up the Aysel Hisami Therapy

Foundation in the village to treat the many migrants suffering from post-traumatic stress disorder. She got through and told George to write down the same details she'd given Hisami, including descriptions of the men and Hisami's number. 'Have you got all that, George?' she hissed. 'Okay – now call the Carabinieri. Tell them a kidnap is in progress. Get a photograph of me to them and talk to Denis. Now!'

She hung up and called her husband again. It went straight to voicemail so she began describing, in a rapid telegraphese, what was happening on the road and everything around her – the lone white building across the valley, the line of transmission towers that crossed the hill above the road, the cluster of mobile-phone masts on a peak in the distance, the orange streak in the rock above the Mercedes where the road had been carved from the hillside. If she managed to escape, they would need to know exactly where the attempted abduction had taken place to find her. She stopped with her face in the leaves because one of the Italians was calling down to her and using her name again. He spoke a brutal, coarse English. 'Signora Anastasia, you come here or I kill your black friends.'

With the line to Hisami still open, she parted the foliage in front of her to see that Akachi was now held by the straps of his backpack at the edge of the road with a gun to his temple. The stocky individual with the gun forced him to his knees by kicking his legs from under him then pushed his head down and placed the gun at the nape of his neck. Akachi held out his hands in prayer, begging for his life.

'Wait! They're threatening to kill the two migrants,' she said into the phone. 'It has to be a bluff. The migrants who stopped me are in on the act. They have to be.'

Then a shot rang out and she jerked up to see Akachi's body slump and the short Italian who had executed him start casually kicking the body over the edge, as if it were a roll of old carpet. Akachi's body fell with a thud on to the ground and began to tumble down the slope, in the process leaving a pathetic trail of possessions that spewed from his backpack. It came to rest at a thorn bush a dozen metres away from Anastasia, with the man's shocked, lifeless eyes staring in her direction. 'My God, they killed him,' she whispered into the phone. 'They just shot him dead. Jesus, what is this? What do they want?'

Louis was brought to the edge of the road and, wailing about his friend, he, too, was forced to his knees. 'You want to see this man killed also?' shouted the Italian. 'Then I will kill him. One less Africano in our country is not a problem for us.' By the direction he faced, she could tell that he didn't know where she was, so it was still possible for her to escape – the vegetation below her in the gully was dense and difficult for two men to search alone. She crouched and peered through the bushes, biting her lip. 'If I run, they'll kill him,' she said to the phone. 'God, I wish you would tell me what to do.'

Then one of the men started counting down in Italian, calling the numbers out above Louis's wail. Without thinking, Anastasia shouted, 'I'll come if you let him go! I want to see him walking away from you.'

'*Mostrati!*' shouted the Italian – show yourself!

'Let him go, or I'll run and you'll never find me.'

They knew where she was, and one of the Italians began to climb down the slope. If she were going to make a dash for it, she'd have to run now. She knew she was in good shape and could easily outpace the stocky little Italian, whom she noticed flung away a cigarette before lowering himself on to the rubble below the road.

Louis was hauled to his feet, now calling out to Anastasia to save his life and screaming that he didn't mean for her to be harmed.

'You come – this guy walks away!' shouted the man who held Louis.

She looked down to the screen of her phone and turned on the video to 'record', keeping the call open.

'I have to go,' she said simply to the phone. 'I must – I love you, Denis. Know that.' She kept talking, telling him that she was going to find a place to leave the phone on the way up.

She stood and, holding the phone by her side she made her way up the incline, taking care to choose a route that would not require her to use her hands, because she needed to record as much as she could before reaching the men. This necessitated moving to a spot a few metres down the road from where the Toyota had come to rest, but it didn't seem to bother the two men, who now waited calmly with Louis, who she saw had wet himself.

'Let him go now,' she said as she neared the top of the bank. 'Tell him to walk towards me.'

The Italian holding him made a shooing movement to Louis, who picked up his bag and stumbled towards her. The short man followed him, holding his gun with two hands in front of him.

She climbed on to the road and began walking towards Louis, holding the phone beside her so that it would capture the men and the registration plate of the Mercedes. She saw Louis was going to try to pass her without looking at her, but just as she reached him she darted to the right and took hold of him and searched his tear-streaked face. He was utterly distraught. All the hardship and anguish in the young man's life was written in his eyes. She put her hand on his shoulder and slipped the phone into the pocket of his trousers with the other hand. 'Look after this,' she murmured. 'Take it to the police.' She spoke with her head down so the short man approaching them could not hear her or see her lips move. She let go of him, not even sure if he was aware of what she'd said. 'Run!' she said, and he staggered off.

She turned to the man with the gun. 'What do you want with me?' she said, trying to block his way. He grabbed her around the neck with his left arm and held her tight to his chest then fired three times, bringing Louis down with the last bullet. She saw the momentum of Louis's chaotic dash for freedom carry him over the edge of the road with his arms spread out, as though he were about to fly.

CHAPTER 2

There were six in the conference room of Gilly & Co., a law firm on Verona Street, a block away from Alma Street in the heart of Palo Alto. Denis Hisami sat looking out of the window at the firm's exotic grass and cactus garden, pondering the motorcycle that had tracked his car from the gates of his estate on the ocean near Santa Cruz, causing his driver to speed up and take several evasive detours and his bodyguards to place their hands on their weapons. Hisami was sure he was never in any danger because the biker plainly wanted to be seen – he was just another part of the low-level campaign of harassment that had been going on for a few weeks.

Outside, a gardener moved in the shafts of light coming through a big-leafed eucalyptus, tidying and picking up stray twigs from a pink bougainvillea, the only splash of colour in the garden. Hisami got up and nodded to the group of men who had arrived in black SUVs and were now being served coffee and juice.

It was early, even for this crowd, and they didn't engage much, apart from murmured greetings. Micky Gehrig and Martin Reid had flown up to San Carlos Airport from LA on separate jets. The other three – Hisami's lawyer, Sam Castell, the tech investor Gil Leppo and the heir to the giant Waters–Hyde defence contractor, Larry Valentine II – owned homes in the Bay Area. Of the six gathered, five were some of the smartest investors on the West Coast and four of them were not happy to have been summoned to Castell's office that morning.

The two items on the agenda Castell had in front of him came from Hisami. The first concerned the mysterious transfers of large sums of money in and out of the accounts of TangKi, the blockchain start-up they were all investors in, and the second was the disappearance of Adam Crane, TangKi's CEO and the firm's cheerleader, who'd brought many of them in on the deal. But Hisami was at a disadvantage – he was by far the smallest shareholder in the room and because he'd only joined in a later round of funding for TangKi his shares had fewer rights; and he was not on the board.

It was as Sam Castell splayed his hands on the glass table and opened the meeting that Hisami received the call from Anastasia in Italy. He rose, miming apology, and moved to the window to talk. The call was unsatisfactory for two reasons – first, he had expected her home that evening and really needed to talk out his problem with her, because, despite what she said about herself, she thought in straight lines and always had original advice to offer. But, second, and more importantly, he didn't like the idea of her picking up migrants out in the Italian countryside. She assured him they were okay and he heard friendly voices in the background as she prepared to ring off, but Hisami's loss of his beloved sister, Aysel, had instilled in him a mistrust of humanity, particularly of men who found themselves alone with a vulnerable woman in deserted countryside.

He rang off, returned to the table and explained that the caller had been Anastasia.

'I hope you'll give her all our best – she's doing such great work,' said Castell, reaching for his water. 'But from now on, gentlemen, can I ask that you stay off your phones. We have a lot to get through here. Denis, the floor is yours.'

Hisami placed his phone deliberately in front of him and looked around the table. 'We've all known each other a long time,' he said. 'We've been co-investors in some of the best deals of the last two decades, which I guess means we trust and respect each other's judgement.' The men nodded. 'With TangKi, I'm in a far less influential position than you all, having invested only $7 million and at a later moment than you. But that said, I believe I have certain responsibilities, both as an investor and as a citizen, which is why I bring this matter to you personally.

'Some of us have spoken on the phone over the last couple of days about the transactions going on over at TangKi, but I wanted to update you on my findings in circumstances where we can talk freely. Over the last seven months a sum in the region of $270 million has washed through the company. The money goes out and then some of it comes back, but there are no real clues as to the destination or source.'

'Stop right there,' said Martin Reid. 'Are you suggesting fraud?'

'No, I am simply bringing the issue out in the open so you can make up your own minds.'

'That can be done on email,' Reid said aggressively. Reid was true to form. Known as 'the gravel-washer' because he took up the gravel on his drive in Wyoming and had it cleaned after every winter, he was, despite his seventy years, a remorseless, hard-driving bastard, as well as an interventionist right-winger.

Hisami nodded and smiled. 'Hear me out, will you, Martin? I would not have asked you up here without good reason.' He paused. 'So, this money is leaving the company and is destined, as far as I can tell without having access to the account, for Europe. Then it's matched by funds coming from other sources. I have the details of the flow, which Sam will hand out to you now.'

They all looked at the figures. Micky Gehrig flipped his braided ponytail over his shoulder and pulled out a pair of round black glasses from his breast pocket. Micky dressed young and sported a number of charity bands on his wrist. Like Hisami, he had made his first big fortune from an online payment service, then went on to invest in gaming and cryptocurrencies sites. He had put $50 million of his fortune in to send himself and his Russian wife to the International Space Station on board a Russian Soyuz rocket spacecraft and was now a leading space investor. After scanning the figures, he opened his hands incredulously. 'I know about this money – it's all to do with research and development in Europe. Adam told us all about that!'

'Did he?' said Hisami. 'I don't recall that. It's not in any of the company's formal accounts, nor in the investors' letters he sent out regularly.'

'I know it is. I forget precisely where, but the money is there in black and white. Anyway, what's the problem? TangKi's just been audited and it's making good profits. Hell, we're all set for an IPO in the next few years. We are all going to make a lot of money, Denis. What they do with their research funds is Adam's business.'

'And ours.'

'What are you saying?' asked Larry Valentine. 'I'd trust Adam with my family's life. He's a fine man and comes from an impeccable background. Why haven't you invited him to this meeting, or brought it up with the board? I'm sure it would take just a few moments for Adam to allay any fears you have.' Larry was always reasonable and squared away every issue with the folksy wisdom of the barbershop. In reality, he was just as tough as anyone in the room. To retain the family influence in Waters–Hyde, to deal with Washington and the competitors in the defence industries, you had to be. Larry glanced along the table with a look that asked what the hell they were all doing. 'Denis, help us out here,' he said. 'What do you think is going on?'

'If I were to make a guess, it looks pretty much like a money-laundering operation.' He looked down at his phone and saw there was another call from his wife.

'That's a mighty big claim to make,' growled Martin Reid. 'Have you brought that idea to Adam?'

'I tried that, but I got no response. He's not answering his phone or responding to emails. He's gone off grid. Maybe there's something going on here.'

Valentine ran a finger inside his striped golfing shirt. Hisami had never seen him in anything else – the golf shirt, blazer, flappy beige pants and sneakers. 'Then it seems simplest to wait until he returns and you can ask him yourself. This is not a financial emergency – I'm sure he's got a good answer.'

Hisami nodded. 'Of course, you may be right, but let me say that there is absolutely no trace of Adam Crane. It's possible that he has been gone longer than I think, and for a good part of the period someone down at Santa Clara has being trying to pretend he's on site by moving his car in the lot every morning. It took a few days for them to admit he wasn't there.'

Gehrig pushed back his chair. 'Is that all you got – his fucking car is being moved every day? Jesus, what the heck are we doing here, folks?'

But Hisami wasn't listening – his phone vibrated and he saw Anastasia's name on the screen again. His hand twitched as if to pick it up but then withdrew. She was almost certainly ringing to apologise, though he realised now that he had been at fault and had been less than warm when he heard she wasn't already on her way home to him. He'd make it up to her.

He looked up and caught Gil Leppo's eye as Gil slid a conciliatory hand towards Gehrig. 'We're here now, Micky. I think we should do as Denis asks and hear what he has to say.' Gil was a lone-wolf investor with an unfailing touch. His investments in biotech had made him hundreds of millions, but the source of his money – the original stake that had allowed him to make those bets – was a mystery. People mentioned armaments – maybe gun-running. A few years before, Gil had appeared from nowhere, adapted the look of a tennis-club Romeo to something approximating an artist or rock musician, and quickly made it his business to get to know everyone, including some big Hollywood names. Animated at all times, ferociously bright and a big reader, Gil had evolved into quite the society figure and was always found at oligarch conferences like Sun Valley, as well as the parties around Oscar time. He came over to Hisami's place every couple of months to play tennis or backgammon. Afterwards they dined and talked books and business. He was the nearest thing in the room Hisami had to a friend and, given Hisami's own secret background of fighting for the Kurdish Peshmerga, he wasn't too concerned about Gil's history. It took a lot to be in this room and, unlike the other three, Gil and he had made their fortunes from scratch.

When no one reacted to his appeal, Gil Leppo leaned forward and patted the table with his hands. 'Come on, people! Denis is wise – if he says something's going on, I want to hear about it. What else you got, my friend?'

'Thanks, Gil – I appreciate that. These flows of money are kept utterly separate from TangKi's books. There's an account that's run by Adam Crane and no one else has access to it.'

'Then how do you know about it?' asked Leppo, the smile

dying in his face. 'How'd you know what goes in and out of it?'

'You have to take my word for it, Gil. I do know.'

Leppo shook his head. 'That may be okay for now – and I do trust you, Denis, I really do – but if we take this further, which is what you want us to do, we have to have evidence.'

'You have a source in the company,' said Gehrig accusingly. 'How do you know that person is reliable?'

'Let's just say I am sure of the information. I am also certain that, since I started looking into this, I've had some trouble – my car has been followed and there are people watching my property. This is not important, but when, out of the blue, I am approached by a law firm in DC that wants to buy my stock for three times its current value on behalf of a client who wants – and I quote – "to get in the blockchain business", I become suspicious.'

'You're saying these things are connected?' said Martin Reid.

Hisami nodded. 'They sent a couple of lawyers out here and they gave me a presentation on the disruptive powers of political investigation – how it could paralyse my activities and stop people doing business with me. They wanted me to know that I could be targeted in any number of legitimate ways – the IRS was mentioned, the Justice Department and the Senate Homeland Security Committee.'

'Jesus! The Homeland Security Committee!' exclaimed Leppo. 'What could they possibly want with you?'

Hisami shrugged. 'What's important is that the moment I started looking for Adam Crane and trying to track these money flows, someone comes along with a big carrot then a very big stick.' He paused and looked candidly around the table. 'We've all known each other a long time. My first reaction was that I should tell you what's going on and ask if any of you have experienced similar pressure. Maybe you have some idea what this is about.'

The room was silent. Gehrig exchanged looks with Valentine and Reid. 'Maybe I'm speaking for others when I say that nothing you've said persuades me there's a problem,' he said.

Valentine started nodding. 'Micky is right. And by the way, you should raise this formally with the board, then we'll see it's discussed at some point. What we cannot do is form a cabal outside the board and act on unproven allegations. With all due respect, Denis, we have to do this properly.'

'That's what I expected you to say, which is why Sam has already sent a letter to the board on my behalf.'

'Then why the fuck did you get us out of bed today?' demanded Gehrig.

'To tell you personally of some grave concerns I have. It was the only responsible thing to do. I am not seeking to circumvent the board.' This was all true, but he also wanted to look each of them in the eye and assess who else might be involved. Was the whole board in on this, or was it just a delinquent management working in collusion with sinister forces in Washington DC? There was a lot he didn't tell them – the nature of the inside source, or his use of Zillah Dee, the head of America's most youthful inquiry outfit, which she'd founded four years before on an old naval vessel moored in the Potomac River after she, along with two others, were ejected from the National Security Agency.

Zillah had employed Hendricks Harp, the private intelligence firm in London that Hisami had used to try to rescue his sister from inside ISIS territory. They believed they might just have located Adam Crane living in London under another identity.

The men around the table talked on. Hisami watched, occasionally demurring with a shake of the head or seeking to distract by cleaning his glasses, but always with that obsessive, slightly terrifying focus Anastasia had named his 'white-hot silence', a phrase instantly appropriated by Hisami's staff and abbreviated to WHS.

Reid was saying something, but now Hisami wasn't paying attention. He'd glanced at his phone, seen that second missed call from Anastasia again and decided he needed to respond to her. He raised his hand to Castell. 'Forgive me, Sam, but I've got to make a call outside the room. It'll take just a few moments. It could be important. My apologies to you all.' The eyes in the room followed him to the door. As it closed behind him, he pressed the green call button under Anastasia's name and raised the phone.

What he heard in her first message appalled him, but he did not react, merely beckoned to his right-hand man, Jim Tulliver, who had been waiting at the far end of the hall until the meeting came to an end. 'Listen to this,' he said, putting the phone on speaker. Tulliver didn't say anything until they reached the end of the voicemail. 'They knew her name?' he said.

'Yes. She's left another voicemail.'

They heard a rustling and then Anastasia began to talk. This time, she held the phone closer to her mouth and they could hear every intake of breath. She spoke in clear, rapid bursts, describing the landscape around her and giving more details of what had happened. She was still free – that, at least, offered some hope.

He paused the voicemail. 'Text Zillah and get her over here.' As Tulliver typed the message, Hisami looked around the plush offices of Gilly & Co. but saw nothing. The same dread that filled him on hearing the news that Aysel was missing on the front line with ISIS in northern Iraq flooded his whole being. Not again! This time, he couldn't lose.

Neither of them had seen Castell exit the meeting and approach them. 'This is kind of awkward, Denis. They are all pissed that you called them in and that you've left to make a phone call.'

'I need a room – somewhere private. Now! Can you arrange that for me?'

Castell began to protest.

'Now, Sam!' said Hisami quietly.

'Of course,' said Castell, pushing at the door of a room that was essentially a miniature version of the conference room. He returned to the meeting and Hisami placed the phone on the table and played the message.

Now Anastasia was talking about the trees and the slash

of orange in the rock. She stopped. 'Shit, I don't know what they're doing – all four of them are beside the road. There are two white men – they look Italian and they have the two Africans with them. The Italians came in a black Mercedes. They are in their late thirties. They have guns. One is short and stocky. The taller one is younger, maybe early thirties. The two men I picked up are Louis and Akachi from West Africa. Louis was in the camp in Lampedusa. He is from Senegal. I saw him in Sicily, too. Akachi, I have never seen before. They said they were going to the village, they must have known I was going there. This was planned. They knew where I was going and the Italians knew my name! Hold on, they're shouting again. I'm going to take a look. I don't think they know where I am – they're facing the wrong direction. Wait! They're threatening to kill the two migrants.' She stopped for a few beats. 'It has to be a bluff. The migrants who stopped me are in on the act. They have to be.'

A shot rang out – it was unmistakable. A gasp of horror came from Anastasia. Then silence. Shock in her breath: 'My God, they killed him. They just shot him dead. Jesus, what is this? What do they want?'

'They've got Louis – they are going to kill him unless I go up there . . . oh God!' They heard rustling and they knew she must have moved her position. 'They've pushed the body over the edge. The man has rolled down to me. He's dead.' She muttered something in Greek, and there was more rustling. 'If I run, they'll kill him. God, I wish you would tell me what to do.'

'Run, Anastasia. Run!' said Hisami under his breath. 'They're going to kill the other one anyway, doesn't she know that?' Tulliver saw the stricken look on his boss's face and shook his head in dismay.

They heard the noise of a bird singing quite near and someone shouting in the distance. After a few seconds, she said into the phone, 'I'm going to do it. I'm sorry, but I have to go up there. They've already killed one man.' Then she called out at the top of her voice, 'I'll come if you let him go. I want to see him walking away from you . . . Let him go, or I'll run and you'll never find me.'

Hisami gripped the table. 'She's going to let them take her.'

'I love you, Denis. Know that . . . I'm walking towards them now . . . I am filming . . . I'll find a place to hide the phone as I go up . . . getting as much as I can . . . you have to come here and find the phone.' They heard her breathing rate increase as she struggled up the slope. When she reached the top, she whispered, 'It's a Naples plate – NA M01082.'

From the crunch of her footsteps, they could tell she was walking on the road now. 'She's still got the phone,' said Tulliver.

There was a hurried exchange, Anastasia said something, then her voice faded and vanished. There was a sound of rapid movement, three muffled shots and a series of thuds, then absolute silence.

The two men looked at each other. 'What happened?' whispered Tulliver.

Hisami just shook his head. 'She's either dead, or she's been kidnapped.' He gripped his forehead with his right hand and breathed very deeply for a few seconds then called his wife's number and listened. It went straight to voicemail and he heard Anastasia's voice telling him to leave a short message or text her. He hung up. 'Okay,' he said to Tulliver, 'we need to get hold of the Italian police and give them that plate number. Let them have Anastasia's phone number so they can get a fix on those calls. Have the office call the State Department and find out who we talk to at the US Embassy in Rome about liaising with the Italian police. I'll need the plane ready for this afternoon – tell Mike Daniels we're going to southern Italy.'

Tulliver's phone pinged with an incoming text message. 'It's Zillah – she's in the lobby. She was in her car outside because she thought you'd need her at the meeting.'

'Bring her up here, please,' Hisami said.

Tulliver went to find Zillah, while Hisami listened again to the two voicemails. A couple of minutes passed before Sam Castell knocked and opened the glass door with an awkward look. 'I'm sorry to bother you, Denis, but there are people here to see you.' He caught sight of Hisami's expression. 'What's going on? You look terrible.'

'Something very urgent has come up. Can you thank them and make my excuses?'

'I wasn't talking about the meeting. Officers from ICE are here – Immigration and Customs Enforcement. They want to see you.'

Hisami's head snapped up. 'What the hell do they want? How did they know I was here?'

'I guess they're the government,' said Castell. 'You may want me to stay for this.'

He hadn't finished before two men appeared at the door.

'Mr Hisami?' said the first, through the open door. 'We are here at the instruction of the Secretary of Homeland Security to inform you that they have suspended your passport. Written notice has been sent to your home, but we wanted to advise you personally, sir, in case you had any plans to travel out of the United States in the near future.' He was straight out of an old police precinct, with oiled, bristly, short hair, folds of skin over a button-down collar and a mean little mouth. The younger man, soft face with hair that flopped over his right brow, wore an open-necked shirt and a grey jacket. He looked West Coast, whereas the older man was from the East. They both held folders.

'We have a copy of the revocation order here,' said the younger one, withdrawing a sheet of paper from his folder. 'It's straightforward – it requires you to submit your passport to us at the earliest opportunity.'

'As Mr Hisami's lawyer, I'll take that,' said Castell, intercepting the paper. 'What's the reason given by the Secretary of Homeland Security?

'It's all there, sir.'

Castell scanned the document. 'They're claiming you made false statements on your passport application twenty years ago. That's obviously crazy.' He read on. 'It says – "The Secretary has determined that the passport holder's activities abroad are causing or are likely to cause serious damage to the national security or the foreign policy of the United States." This is bullshit. I'll have our team get on to it right away.' Castell looked at the older guy. 'What's going on here? Have you any idea of Mr Hisami's standing?'

'We know who Mr Hisami is, if that's what you're asking. We're just delivering the notice, sir.'

Hisami shook his head. 'This is no coincidence, is it? My wife's been abducted and now you're suspending my passport so I can't travel.'

Castell swivelled to face him with an appalled look. 'What are you saying, Denis?'

'Exactly that. Anastasia has been abducted. I've just listened to her messages. Now, my only priority is to get her back. Can you deal with this, Sam? If you'll excuse me now . . .' He made to pass the two men.

The younger one moved to block his way. 'I don't know anything about your wife, sir, but we will need your passport. You can appeal the decision with State, sir.'

Hisami walked to the window, dialled a number and murmured into the phone. He turned to the two men. 'It will be at my home, just show your ID.'

'We would prefer you to come with us, sir.'

Hisami moved towards them. 'You only have the power to seize my passport – nothing else. You know that, and so does my lawyer.'

CHAPTER 3

On a calm but bitingly cold day three years before, Paul Samson and Anastasia Christakos chartered a boat in the port of Pula in Istria, Croatia, and sailed across the Adriatic to Venice.

Two weeks had passed since the events in the farmhouse in northern Macedonia, where four terrorists had held them, together with a Syrian boy, Naji Touma, his friend Ifkar and the old couple who ran the farm. They had been saved from torture and certain death by the intervention of Denis Hisami, who dispatched three of the terrorists and was aided in the killing of the man named Machete – Almunjil – by the boy Naji, who stabbed him in the heart at the very moment that Denis Hisami fired with the deadly skill of his days with Peshmerga. Hisami vanished immediately, satisfied that the man who had raped his sister, Aysel, and was responsible for her death was himself now dead. Nothing of what had happened could be allowed to get out, if Hisami's position as a pillar of Bay Area society was to remain intact. Credit for the rescue was given to the Macedonian security forces, a story that Samson, Anastasia and Naji had no trouble in maintaining during the debriefing by European intelligence services, who were glad enough to receive the vital information brought to them by Naji. Only the British spies Peter Nyman and Sonia Fell had pressed them on the exact sequence of events at the farmhouse, but this had earned them the scorn of their European colleagues and they'd stopped their questioning.

It took a few days to extract Naji's family from the refugee camp in Turkey and transfer them to the new home provided by the German authorities, which had also guaranteed places for Naji and his equally bright elder sister in a school for the gifted. To Naji's extraordinary joy, a helicopter had arrived in Pudnik, in northern Macedonia, to take him to Skopje airport to catch a German government plane to Berlin. The expense of this was covered in recognition of the extraordinary intelligence on ISIS that Naji had brought to the West on his battered phone, which had survived a dunking in the Aegean and every sort of hazard on his journey through the Balkans.

While Samson was treated at the Skopje hospital for the beating he had received from one of the gang – there was concern that he might lose the sight in one eye – Anastasia flew back to Lesbos to arrange cover for a period of leave that was well overdue. By the time she returned to the Balkans to meet him at Zagreb in Croatia, he had been told that his eyesight was not going to be damaged and had more or less recovered, though the swelling and stitches around his eye were still visible.

The trip to Venice was her idea. Neither of them had been there and it was Anastasia who insisted that they arrive by boat rather than plane. So, they travelled west from Zagreb in a rented car, cheerful but saying little, and dropped it off at the ancient city of Pula, where Samson began to search the port for a boat and skipper, not an easy task, as winter had set in and the charter yachts were being serviced or were laid up on the quays. At length he found the owner of a large, snubbed-nosed trawler who said he was willing to do the journey, but for an exorbitant €3,500 due to the price of fuel. But after his win on the thoroughbred Dark Narcissus at Ascot racecourse two weeks earlier, Samson had no difficulty paying.

They boarded the *Maria Redan*, freshly painted in a dark blue and red livery, at 6.30 a.m. on a Tuesday morning with a couple of holdalls and backpacks. The skipper, a man named Filip, turned out to be more obliging than his manner on the quay had suggested. He prepared a breakfast of rolls with cured ham and coffee, which they consumed as the *Maria Redan* left port and set course to the north-west of the Adriatic. Filip seemed to understand that the voyage held a special significance for them and that they were making a journey towards each other, as well as to Venice.

'You still smoking?' she asked Samson when the land had disappeared in the mist that blurred the border between sky and sea.

'Not much, but I have cigarettes somewhere.' He fished in his backpack.

They went out on deck, perched on the winding gear in

front of the wheelhouse and lit up, but the fine spray coming from the bow soon made it impossible to smoke and they flung their sodden cigarettes overboard. 'You okay?' she said.

'Yeah, I'm fine. I wonder about this. You know – what the hell we're doing.'

'You think this isn't going to work, that it's not meant to be?' she shouted as they crashed into a wave.

He shook his head and wiped the spray from her face. She smiled and licked her lips.

'But that's what you said before we found Naji. Remember? Commitment wasn't your thing. That's what people always say when they're not sure. I've said it myself.'

'How can anyone be sure? What I know is that I love being with you and I think you're a smart, decent human being and I'm attracted to you.' She ran a finger along his lips. 'This is the happiest I've been for years. That's because I'm with you and I can forget the stuff I do every day back in the camp. And forget what happened in the mountains.'

'So I'm a distraction? I guess that's okay.' He looked at her with mock-hurt.

'That's right – you are. But a distraction that I might love for all time. Who knows, Paul? I have no idea about the future. Nothing really makes any sense. We're in a new time and no one can be sure what happens, or where we'll be in a few years. So, I live in this moment with you, on this stinky old boat in the middle of the sea, and I rejoice in it and I'm not going to spoil that moment by worrying about the future or obsessing about the past. You understand that, don't you?'

He shrugged agreement, but she wasn't about to stop. She shifted her bottom on the winch to face him, laid her hands on top of his and looked at him so earnestly it made him smile. 'Paul, we saw each other in a moment when we both thought we were going to die. After that, you really know a side of a person that no one else is going to see. There's a fucked-up intimacy in that, as well as a kind of shame. It's like the ultimate nakedness.'

He nodded. 'That's a good way of putting it.' Samson had seen the worst of Syria on his trips to find Aysel Hisami, but the drawn-out terror in the barn had shaken him more profoundly than anything he'd witnessed in that war.

'When you see people like those men and what they do, it destroys some part of you. That's a problem I deal with every day in the camp – the psychological effect on people who have lost their faith in humanity and humaneness. We both suffered that, and so now we find it hard to be casual and treat this for what it is – fun and companionship. It doesn't have to be meaningful, Paul. My life is too damned serious!'

'You are, obviously, right,' he said sarcastically.

'That's cowardice. Argue with me!' She squeezed his hand. 'Anyway, Mr Spy, you're the guy who lives in the moment – hundreds of racehorses and women.'

'Just a few of both, actually.'

She ducked as the *Maria Redan* thumped into a big wave and squealed as the water trickled down her neck. When she stopped writhing, he gently took hold of her face. 'Stop talking and kiss me.'

'Or what?'

'I will jump overboard and you will have to rescue me.'

She frowned and thought for a second. 'I can't make up my mind which is worse.' Then she offered her mouth, parted with a mischievous grin.

'You taste of the sea,' he said, smiling at the pleasure he found glistening in her eyes.

'So, that's settled,' she said, jumping up. 'We're going to have a mad, irresponsible affair. And we will live for the moment! Come on, I'm freezing. Let's go inside.'

A couple of hours passed. Samson dozed and Anastasia insisted on steering the *Maria Redan*, having assured the skipper that seamanship was in the blood of every true Greek. They spied Venice from about five miles out and Filip slowed the boat so that they could go out and watch as the Campanile, Doge's Palace and the Church of San Giorgio Maggiore gradually came into focus against the smudged backdrop of the Dolomites.

'God, it's so beautiful!' she gasped. 'Wasn't I right about coming by sea? You want to hear something?" She closed her eyes to rifle her memory.

'"The soft waves, once all musical to song,
That heaved beneath the moonlight with the throng,
Of gondolas – and to the busy hum,
Of cheerful creatures, whose most sinful deeds
Were but the overbeating of the heart."'

'You surprise me. Where's that come from?'

'Your English poet Lord Byron. He lived here when he was

in disgrace, having had sex with far too many women!' She gave him a reproving look. 'Byron liked the Greeks, and we like him.'

'You know it by heart?'

'Yes, by my *overbeating* heart.' She winked at him. 'It's the poem that made me want to come here. I did a course at university on the English Romantics.'

'You astonish me.'

The *Maria Redan* made for the port of Venice via the broad Giudecca Canal, the tradesmen's entrance to Venice, used by the riff-raff of refuse barges, muck clearers, builders' launches, delivery boats and, on this occasion, two empty hearses. They disembarked on the first free quay and Filip was made to sign papers because the authorities suspected they had come from outside the EU, and Samson and Anastasia were marched away to immigration, where they were delayed because of their unusual and, therefore, suspect arrival in Italy. They took a water taxi to a small hotel five minutes' walk from the Rialto Bridge. Anastasia had arranged it all – a top-floor apartment with a tiny kitchen and a small balcony that overlooked a chaotic roofscape and from which you could just see the Campanile. There were flowers, a bottle of white wine from the Veneto and a guidebook on the table, along with a note from the manager thanking the signora for her choice.

This scene Samson would later recall with formidable pain – the sight of her dropping the bags, twirling with pleasure on the tiled floor and throwing herself backwards on to the bed with her arms out. To the sound of church bells from a nearby bell tower, they made love, at first with shyness and some amusement, but then, as they moved with each other, never losing the other's gaze, they finally expelled the memory of the mountain barn that smelled of shit and old hay and celebrated life and the absence of terror. The image of her below him, smiling and urging him on and taking her own pleasure, would never leave him. He was enthralled, and afterwards he mused how very different she seemed to when he saw her unblushingly shower in front of him in Macedonia. He kissed her stomach and traced a line with his fingertips from her pelvis to a breast and then to jaw and chin, and was in awe. His grave expression made her giggle and tweak his nose. Whether he fell in love at that moment, or this was simply the summation of all he'd felt since they'd lain together on her bed in the rackety seaside villa in Lesbos when they first met, was moot. It would churn in his mind long after she had left him and he was inconsolable without her. He would try to pinpoint exactly when he fell for her with the bitter hope that, if he identified that moment, he would somehow be able to reverse it and move on with his life. But this was the first real love of a man who'd coolly run his life as he wanted – his first complete acquiescence. As he approached his forties, he told himself that it was pointless to deny it.

Afterwards, as it grew dark, they talked in the light from the illuminated bell tower that permeated the room, casting fantastical shadows on the ceiling, and they drank the wine that was left for them and teased each other, which was how their relationship would be conducted over the next year or so. In

Venice, they spoke seriously about their lives, but rarely afterwards. He was her light relief and he was to discover that he was unable ever to broach the subject of their future together or suggest a change in her rigid terms and conditions because she would cut him off and withdrew into herself.

It was that evening in bed that she began to call him by his second name, because her father had been called Pavlos – the Greek version of Paul – and she admitted that she disliked the name almost as much as she did her two-timing, hypocritical bully of a dad. So, Samson it was. And in his mind, Delilah she became.

They walked out and dined in an old-fashioned restaurant with sparkling glass lamps, starched white table clothes and solemn waiters. It was filled with a noisy local crowd that Anastasia criticised – a little piously, he thought – for their wealth and ignorance of how life was for the people she saw every day. The place had been recommended by her friend Gianni, who, the next day, was to take them on a tour to visit locked churches and monasteries that held seldom-seen masterpieces, and she wanted to be able to say that they'd been. She conceded that the food was for the gods. They drank more wine and stared at each other across the table with pride and disbelief. They told funny stories of their past, taking delight in everything about each other, and at some stage she leaned forward and said she would never find anyone she wanted to fuck more than him. 'You are the lover of my life,' she whispered gleefully. He knew that she was unquestionably something more to him – the love of his life.

Much later, he'd remember that she dropped Hisami into the conversation that evening, not about the intervention that saved them both – they kept off that subject. She told him he had been in touch with her and had offered money – a lot of money – to extend her work on Lesbos, with a proper clinic and more therapists, and she was taken with the way he had acted on their chat in the hotel before the rescue in the mountain farmstead. The money was great, but what really impressed her were his follow-through and his grasp of detail after such a brief conversation. She went on about that, saying it was the mark of a really successful individual. Samson should have seen the threat, but he was no more aware of Hisami's intentions than of his ability with a gun. As they had climbed the mountain to the farmhouse looking for her two weeks before, Hisami had asked him about his interest in Anastasia and, though Samson had thought nothing of it at the time, the man couldn't have been plainer about his own ambition and he was, in fact, already plotting to win her.

Those three days and four nights in Venice changed Samson for ever. As they went about holding hands – something he'd never done before – and were stopped in their tracks one morning by the sun coming through the mist over the Grand Canal and poked about deserted churches with her elegant friend, Gianni, he wrongly assumed their time would have the same effect on Anastasia. But it was in one of the more obscure churches, to which Gianni had gained access by ringing a bell in the priest's house, that Samson saw her take what, in retrospect, seemed to be a firm decision about him.

They were in front of an elaborate baroque stone monument when Gianni called over to the priest hovering in the aisle and asked if he could play some music he believed his friends should hear in a church that had a slight association with the composer Antonio Vivaldi. The priest nodded and wandered over to them good-naturedly, saying that the place needed to be stirred from its slumber. Gianni translated then took out his phone and searched through his playlist. 'This little piece is known by very few people, and yet it is the best musical description of love that has ever been composed.' He raised a finger. 'Only in this recording by I Solisti Veneti is the piece executed correctly by the violinist Piero Toso.' He repeated the title so they wouldn't forget it – *Andante* from the Concerto in B-flat major for violin and double orchestra. Then he played it through the phone's speaker, holding the phone up so that the music sounded in the cold, still air of the church. Samson, who didn't have a particularly developed musical taste, was deeply moved by the two themes circling each other, parting, meeting again and, after a heart-piercing solo by the man Toso, rushing together in triumphant climax. The old priest nodded wistfully, while Samson put his hands together in a single clap. But Anastasia, avoiding his eyes, threw her head back and let out a little mocking laugh then turned on her heels and walked from the church.

He asked what she thought of the piece that evening. Oh yes, it was fine, but wasn't that church freezing and didn't the priest look sad and weren't those paintings gloomy? What she was doing was ruling out the possibility of a serious relationship.

She knew he was annoyed and a little hurt and, later, he was rougher with her in bed than before and she seemed to like it when he held her down with all his strength. It was the sex she was there for, not, it turned out, love, or even romance.

About eighteen months later, after she had told him about Hisami and said their relationship was over, he reluctantly opened his heart to Macy Harp, his racing companion and the owner of Hendricks Harp, the firm that had sent him into Syria to find Hisami's sister, Aysel. Macy looked pityingly at him and said, quoting Wodehouse, his favourite author, that Samson had an 'air of crushed gloom which would have caused comment in Siberia'. Samson should have known better than to damn well fall in love in Venice, which was, to put it bluntly, such a bloody cliché, because it had no more meaning than a carnal fortnight in Majorca. After that, Samson pulled himself together, tried to forget his 'overbeating heart' and grimly applied himself to the business of earning a living, which, after a disaster on the racecourse and his mother's sudden death, was an urgent priority.

CHAPTER 4

Anastasia woke up in complete darkness. She remembered she'd been dragged into the van and that one of the Italians had held her with his hand clamped over her mouth while the other stabbed her viciously in the thigh with a needle, but nothing after that. How long she'd been unconscious, she had no idea. She was aware of a headache and a raging thirst, and her body ached all over. Her hands were tied behind her back and her legs were bound. She wriggled and found she was lying on a wooden pallet. She could feel the slats by brushing her cheek back and forth.

The space was cool and echoed like the inside of a tank, and she thought she sensed some kind of motion, though she wasn't sure because she couldn't see anything and there was no point of reference. But the nausea in her stomach told her she was moving. She held her breath to listen. There was a faint rhythmic hum, like an engine, and inside this space she was in she could smell fuel or engine oil, which might explain why she was feeling sick.

She yelled out, but the sound of her voice just echoed in the tank. She shouted again and again and, because no one came, it made her feel even more desperate and alone.

She needed to calm herself and bring order to her mind. Yes, she had stopped for the two migrants and they had been part of the plan to abduct her, yet they had both been gunned down. But the two Italians hadn't killed her, which they easily could have, and that meant she was probably not in immediate danger, though this was little consolation and did nothing to ease the horror that kept sweeping through her. She had to think. She'd told Denis and George Ciccone where she was and they would act immediately to inform the Italian police. And the registration plate of the Mercedes – had she read it out to Denis's voicemail or merely filmed it with the phone she dropped into Louis's pocket which had gone over the side of the road when they shot him? She couldn't remember. But if she hadn't read the number out – and thinking about it now, she was sure she hadn't – they'd find Louis's body soon enough and they would have a complete record of the car and images of the two men who had kidnapped her. She worried that they wouldn't be able to unlock the phone because Denis didn't know her passcode. She hadn't altered it since changing it in Venice to Samson's damned birthday – 09/10. She told him she was never likely to forget it that way, but of course she had ignored his birthday for the last couple of years and that code was now the only part of Samson in her life.

Those calls to Denis and George at the village were vital. Her kidnappers didn't know that she'd used her phone, so she had that one tiny advantage. The police would be on to it much sooner than they were expecting and Denis would put everything he had into finding her. But what was this about? Money! It could only be money. They knew how rich Denis was. Her husband would pay up quickly and she'd be released very soon – that was the only thing that made sense.

She waited and listened for a long time, wishing she hadn't taken off the hooded jumper she'd been wearing that morning. She shouted out a few times more – but nothing came back except the sound of her voice in a ringing reverberation from the metal walls that surrounded her. No one answered. She had no clue where she was.

She breathed slowly, making her body relax, which was difficult because she was hurting all over, particularly on the right side of her pelvis, where she must have landed when they threw her into the tank. And the binding cut into the skin above her ankles. She worked her toes inside her trainers – thank God they hadn't taken those – and fluttered her fingers to keep her circulation going. She told herself she must take control in some way, however small. She felt her watch biting into her back. Yes, the watch! She must find out the time and date; she desperately wanted to see its luminous face in the dark. Now all she had to do was free her hands. That was going to take time, but she was sure they were bound by rope, and rope, however thick, could eventually be worn away by friction. She began to rub her wrists against the wood of the pallet, changing angles so that the rope did not blister the skin on the underside of her wrists. She worked at this for an hour or more and, by curling her fingers into her palms, began to feel the frayed edges of the rope. In the end, she didn't need to get through it all because the action loosened the knots and she was able to pull her right hand free, then her left. She rubbed her wrists, pushed up to a sitting position and worked her shoulders. It was 5 a.m., the day after her abduction, which meant she had been unconscious for over twelve hours. She swept the bindings on her legs with the tiny light from the watch. She could see almost nothing but determined that there were two lengths of thin cord. She started to pick at the knots with her thumb and fingernails and at last one succumbed, but her legs remained bound together until she wrenched up a slat and sawed at the rope with the rough end of the wood, driving splinters into her fingers and ankle in the process.

After rubbing her calves and stretching, she felt her way along the wooden slats until she reached a metal wall. There were horizontal ridges in the structure and a very small vertical crack through which came a draught. Not only was this fresh air but it smelled of the ocean, and in an instant she understood she was in a sea container on board a vessel that was steaming through the night. That explained the slight motion in her stomach and the distant thrum of the ship's engine. She sank to her knees, appalled. Where was she being taken, and why? If the kidnappers wanted money, it would have been far simpler to hold her in a location in Italy and exchange her for the ransom. But now she was on a boat going hell knows where. She got up, inhaled slowly and moved to her right, feeling for any mechanism to open the door from the inside. Her foot encountered something on the floor of the container and she stopped. She crouched down, reached out and felt a head of hair and before she had time to withdraw her hand she was touching the stubble and cold, dead skin of a man's face. She recoiled with a scream and for several minutes sat hunched and shivering, the wildest thoughts flooding her mind. For some reason she remembered those containers and lorries packed with dead migrants that were discovered across Europe by customs officials, but that couldn't be the case here. No matter how hard she thought, she couldn't work out what was going on.

Her need to survive overcame her revulsion. Was this Louis? Had they retrieved his body? If so, he might still have her phone in his pocket. She moved forward and began to frisk the body, her hands working efficiently while she stared up into the dark, trying desperately to detach her actions from her mind. She quickly determined that it wasn't Louis – the individual was too big and, as far as she could tell, his clothes were different. She moved from the trousers to a light jacket and found nothing, but then her hands encountered some hard objects in the top pocket of his shirt, which had been wrenched round to the man's side – a packet of cigarettes, a lighter. She flicked the lighter on and looked around. Another body was sprawled on the floor and she now recognised them instantly as the Italians who had abducted her. They had been summarily executed, just like the two migrants, probably just after they had dumped her unconscious into the container. But still the thought was there: whoever was behind this wanted to keep her alive.

She frisked the other man, the taller of the two, who had seemed to be in charge on the road, but found nothing except a chunky silver bracelet and his belt, which she tore from the loops of his trousers and fastened around her own waist under her shirt. She didn't know what use she would put the belt to and no idea why she now took the laces from one of the man's trainers and stuffed them in her pocket. It was too much to remove their clothes, although by now she was very cold. Maybe later, when she could bear it no more, she would pull off the man's leather jacket and wrap it around her shoulders, ignoring the caked blood on the collar. It was clear that a bullet to the back of the head had ended their lives. The tops of their heads had been blown off and there was a lot of blood congealed on the floor and splattered on the side of the container. But their faces were intact, their expressions impassive, which suggested that they hadn't had the slightest clue about their imminent death.

She examined the door of the container, using the lighter, and saw there was no way to open it, then crawled back to the spot where she had been left. If they wanted her alive, they would have to feed her, and that meant someone would come. She replaced the ropes as best she could on her ankles and waited, blowing on her hands in the dark.

At around six the first sliver of light came from the crack in the door, and very soon after that she heard voices on the other side of it. She lay down, whipped her hands into position behind her back and shut her eyes. The door was wrenched open with a bang and, through closed eyes, she was aware of a very bright torch-light. There were three, maybe four, individuals and they were speaking a Slavic language, which could have been Russian, though she thought it might be Bulgarian. One of them came to the far end, where she lay in the dark, shone the light directly into her face, muttered then went back to the others. She cracked open an eye and saw that there were only three men and two were preparing to lift one of the bodies out of the container. They seemed worried about getting blood on their clothes. They hoisted the first body, grunting in disgust, and began to shift it out of the container. The third man moved back to let them pass and threw the beam of the torch on to the deck so they could see. Through the open door she caught sight of the beginnings of a pink sky, a green, corrugated deck, lines of containers and a mast at the bow that was festooned with lights.

She couldn't see what they were doing but she suspected they were going to dispose of the bodies over the side. She knew that, once they'd got rid of the second body, the container would be locked and there might not be another chance to escape. She crouched, her ears straining, then slipped to the door. She knew what Denis would do in these circumstances and, for that matter, Samson. Both would seize this opportunity. The ship seemed large. There must be hundreds of places to hide. She would run and take her chances.

Through the crack between the door and the side panel of the container she saw them hoist the body to the railing. One held it while the others lifted some kind of weight attached to a chain. She moved further back into the container, pulled the leather jacket from the second victim, took another look through the gap and satisfied herself that the men were still struggling to weight the body. She took a deep breath and decided it was now or never. She edged out of the darkness of the container, darted to her right and found herself in a narrow, windy canyon between two rows of containers that ran right up to the bow. She needed to get as far away as possible and quickly find a place to hide. There was nowhere forward, except a hatch that could be opened by turning four enormous levers. One attempt, heaving with all her strength, was enough to persuade her that her efforts would be useless. She glanced back. The ship was by no means fully loaded and at the centre of the vessel there were several gaps in the aisles of containers. The men were on the starboard side, so she moved over to port and weaved her way towards the bridge, glancing to her left every time the other side of the boat came into view. She saw and heard nothing. Not even when she sneaked to the point opposite where she thought they would still be dealing with the second body. She put on the dead man's jacket and waited. There were no signs of a search, no alarm or loudspeakers sounding, no floodlights switched on to pick her out in the half-light of the dawn – just the sound of the wind tearing through the containers and the superstructure of the vessel as it ploughed through the Mediterranean, heading to the rising sun and the east.

CHAPTER 5

Paul Samson sat in the office above the restaurant where his mother had been found dead of a stroke by her loyal maître d', Ivan. He shifted his attention from a stack of papers on the partner desk that his mother and father had at one time shared and picked up the internal phone to tell Ivan to give Peter Nyman a drink and keep him downstairs for ten minutes. He turned off his two screens, cleared away a folder containing the documents he had been working on and made a call to Macy Harp's office a few minutes away. Macy rarely used a mobile phone, so Samson had to go through his assistant, who answered immediately in a crisp upper-class English accent. Harp came on the line.

'I'm being bloody haunted by Peter Nyman again. Any idea what he wants?'

'No. Why don't you ask him and call me back?'

'Yes, just wanted to know if he's been snooping around your end.'

'He hasn't. Any news on Crane? Our client is very keen to hear of any more developments.'

'Nothing more than that he has an expensive penthouse in a new block in the centre of London under the name of Ray Shepherd. Haven't been there yet but I've got an email account for him, which is intermittently still in use. But I'm not going any further on this until you tell me a bit more about the client on this one. You know I don't work blind. I wouldn't be happy to give his location unless I was assured that no harm was going to come to him.'

'Rest assured, that won't happen,' replied Macy impatiently. 'I know the client and they're not going to do anything like that. Speak later.'

Samson sat back in his father's old chair and glanced at the wall of photographs from his parents' life, most of them meaningless, now that both were gone. When he had sorted out the debts accumulated in the last three years as his mother struggled to keep the Cedar restaurant afloat he'd do something about the photographs – maybe put them in an album and give it to his sister, Leila. She was better on the family history and their Lebanese heritage than he was, and she was still grieving deeply for their mother, so he thought it might help. He missed their mother too. They'd had good times when Anastasia was with him and his mother became convinced she would eventually marry him – the thing she desired most for her son. Under Anastasia's gentle cross-examination she had talked about her time as a young girl in post-war Beirut, about meeting the dashing young trader who would become her husband. She relaxed with Anastasia and opened up in a way that he'd never seen before, not even with Leila. And when Anastasia married Hisami, she had been dreadfully disappointed and of course blamed Samson for failing to give her the sense that she could build a life with him and so letting her go.

He turned in the chair and buzzed down to Ivan to tell him he was ready to see Peter Nyman.

A little over three years before, Nyman had climbed the stairs to this office above the restaurant to find out whether Samson would take on the task of finding a Syrian boy who had escaped from the camp in Lesbos and was on the road north in the Balkans, pursued by an ISIS hit squad. Samson had not seen Nyman, or his ambitious sidekick, Sonia Fell, since the debrief in Macedonia, when the boy – Naji Touma – had given European intelligence services the access code to his cache of secrets. It had made Nyman, who had doubted the boy's value as a source, look flat-footed and out of touch.

He rose and greeted Nyman, who wore the same lifeless expression and shapeless suit as always, but did not take his hand. Nyman chose a chair without consulting Samson, hovered over it and let himself down so the cushion gasped with the impact.

'Keeping busy?'

'That's the sort of question my hairdresser asks,' said Samson.

'I'll come to the point,' said Nyman, pausing to pat down his pockets for something. Eventually, he produced a tin of mints, took one and proffered the open tin. Samson shook his head. 'Yes, you see, your chap Ray Shepherd has been found dead.

Nasty business. Tortured, then a bullet to the head. Someone wanted something from him. Once they'd got it – or not, as the case may be – they killed him, and left his body for all to see on the balcony of his flat overlooking the park.' He grimaced with distaste. 'An observant schoolboy spotted him on the school's early-morning exercise in the park. He pointed out to his PE teacher that it was odd the man was sitting without a shirt on his balcony on a cold autumn day and odder still that, if you looked closely, he didn't seem to possess a face.'

Samson said nothing.

'You're surely not going to pretend you didn't know of Ray Shepherd?'

'I'm not working for SIS, and I'm no longer at your disposal, Peter. So what I know and what I don't is none of your bloody business.'

'True, but you do have responsibilities as a citizen, and one of them is telling the police everything you know about Shepherd and why you were hired to investigate him. They will no doubt be interested to learn of the very considerable energy you applied to finding out that he owned a penthouse in this expensive block, the one that he was murdered in last night. Might put you in the frame as a suspect. Never know your luck.'

Samson didn't rise to that. 'What's your interest?'

'Well, for one thing, this character Shepherd might have looked the perfect gentleman but his rap sheet includes gangsterism, money-laundering, murder and mayhem. We have kept a watchful eye on him. You knew, of course, that he had snow on his boots.' Nyman smiled to himself. 'That's what we used to say in the Cold War when things were oh so much simpler. But to a member of the younger generation who has no memory of those days, we say he was Russian, or possibly Ukrainian. But besides that, he was an anti-Semite. All in all, a grade-one shit.'

'Sounds like it,' said Samson, shifting. 'Can I get you anything – coffee, water?'

Nyman shook his head. 'I'm sure you don't need your life further complicated by the police crawling through your affairs.' Then he stopped and simulated forgetfulness. 'Of course! I should have said how very sorry I was to learn of your mother's death. She must be a great loss to you and your sister. It can't be an easy time for you.' His eyes swept the room and lingered on the wall of photographs he'd admired three years before. 'It's always a difficult moment, however old you are – becoming the next one on the conveyor belt to oblivion, and all that.' His eyes returned to Samson. 'You've had some problems, I know. Debts you inherited and debts you've made for yourself.'

'My mother has nothing to do with this so please don't embarrass me, or yourself, by thinking you can make some leverage out of her death and my position, which is, incidentally, perfectly secure.' Nyman shook his head, as though this was the furthest thought from his mind. 'It was a great shock and, yes, her death came at a difficult time for us,' continued Samson, 'but Leila and I will continue running the restaurant and, as you saw for yourself downstairs, we are already busy

Springdale Public Library
405 S. Pleasant
Springdale, AR 72764

for lunch and there are two sittings for dinner that are booked out. We've had a lot of support from my mother's regular customers.'

'I'm glad to hear it. But you are doing other work besides ordering in the wine and tahini, yes? And that is because, before your mother's death, you suffered a very big loss on the racecourse – a quarter of a million pounds, they say, on a horse you owned called Legend Run. Sire, Midnight Legend; dam, Deep Run, eight years old and a big, big jumper. I didn't think you touched the jumps, Samson, because everything is, as it were, up in the air.' He smiled at this feeble joke. 'You see, I know all about it. I've read up on it. The horse wasn't running under your name that day at Newbury, as is often the case with owners who like to hide their interest, but it was yours all right and you made that huge bet. I don't need to remind you this was precisely the scenario envisaged by the risk-averse fusspots of the HR department, which is why you were defenestrated.'

'So what do you want from me?'

'I want to stay on the subject of that race for the moment. Why on earth did you make that bet? What in heaven's name induced you?'

Samson wasn't going to give Nyman the pleasure of gloating. 'It was in the racing press – read it for yourself.' It had been a disaster, and it was all due to the setting sun at Newbury Racecourse, which at particular times of the year shines along the line of the five fences on the home straight. The racecourse authorities deem this to be a hazard for the jockeys because they are blinded by the sun and cannot see when to kick their horse over the jump, or where they are landing. After a hurried consultation, the stewards removed the five jumps from the race, placing boards along the top of the fences, leaving just seven fences on the far side of the course. Legend Run loved the air. He gained as much as a length and a half over every fence. On the flat, he was as good as any of his regular opponents and more tenacious at the finish. He was the perfect steeplechaser and at the height of his powers, but the absence of those five fences made all the difference and he struggled to make third. Samson had committed his money long before there was any question that the sun would show itself on that otherwise overcast afternoon. The only good thing about the day was that Anastasia hadn't been there to see his humiliation. By then, their break was complete.

Nyman sucked at his mint and revolved it around his mouth contentedly. 'I suppose the point I'm making, in an oblique way, is that the story about your gambling debts and those that your mother left on this place might explain why you were so interested in tracking down Ray Shepherd and relieving him of some of the enormous funds at his disposal.'

Samson smiled. 'Now you're being silly, Peter. How much money did he have?'

'Tens of millions. We're trying to trace it, which is why we want to know who you're working for.'

'You're going to have to ask Macy about all that.'

Nyman produced his pained look. 'I was rather hoping to keep this between ourselves. I have a problem with private-intelligence companies – I suppose it's the difference between working for the public good and making money.'

'You were happy to resort to the private sector to find Naji in the Balkans.' Samson smiled. 'Look, I told Macy you were here. Anything you have to say to me, you say to Macy. That's the way we work. And let me make a couple of things clear. Please don't try to intimidate me with any financial difficulties you think I have and don't expect me to breach client confidentiality.'

'Ah, I see. You don't know who the clients are?'

'It's not your business.'

'Perhaps I can help you out a little. They're American and they're acting through a proxy named Zillah Dee. She's an interesting person – a very modern person. And I don't just mean young. She leaves the NSA by mutual agreement and looks for all the world like an East Coast debutante. She's the CEO and founder of a company called Dee Strategy, and here I quote from the company's landing page, "Dee Strategy Inc. is an elite corps of former US, European and Israeli intelligence officers. Operating out of Washington and Tel Aviv, DSI provides litigation support, financial investigation and conflict resolution."'

'I've never heard of her.'

'Well, she's very pally with Macy and she's been here twice over the last two weeks. Flies into Blackbushe Airport on a jet – a Gulfstream G550 – and takes the helicopter into Battersea, whence she is conveyed to the offices of Hendricks Harp in Mayfair. I just assumed that, if you were doing the work, you must have met her and that you knew she was using Denis Hisami's company jet.'

Hisami's involvement was certainly news to him, but he showed no surprise. No doubt that was the reason Macy had been so cagey with him.

'If that's all,' he said, rising, 'I should be getting on with ordering the tahini. If you want more, go see Macy.'

A hangdog look was followed by a pout. 'Later, Samson, later,' said Nyman. He clambered from the chair with a little grunt and moved to the door, pausing on the way to look at the photographs. 'You understand that I must inform the police and security services about your connection to Shepherd – as a matter of openness and cooperation.'

'You must do as you see fit.'

'These photographs are so poignant now that both your parents are gone. Must be sad for you to see them in the splendour of their youth. They were a very glamorous couple. Beirut was where they came from, wasn't it? Marvellous place in the fifties and sixties – it's where that drunk Kim Philby lived before he bolted to Russia, you know.'

'An age ago,' said Samson.

'I suppose so, but we've got the same problems now as then, only the people causing them are no longer labelled communists.' With this he gave a curious flick of his hand and vanished through the door to the stairway.

Samson picked up the phone, then replaced it and took one of the five mobile phones on charge in the cupboard on his father's side of the desk and called Macy Harp. 'He says our friend has been killed,' he said. 'Found on the balcony at Hyde Park.'

'You'd better come round.'

It was a minute's walk but Samson didn't make it. He had gone a few paces from the Cedar's entrance when two men emerged from an unmarked Range Rover and intercepted him. One held out a Metropolitan Police ID while the other stood back slightly, as though Samson were going to make a run for it.

'We'd like to ask you some questions, sir,' said the one who'd shown his card. 'It won't take long.'

'Am I being arrested?'

'No, but we'd like you to come with us now, sir. It'll save a lot of fuss if we get this over with.'

'I'm late for a meeting. I'd better phone.'

'We'd rather you didn't, sir, if you wouldn't mind.'

'I'm not under arrest.'

'No, but we do need to talk to you urgently.' The other policeman took hold of Samson's arm and steered him towards the car, where a third man waited in the back seat. He was no more a policeman than Samson was.

CHAPTER 6

At his Mesopotamia Estate in the Bay Area, Denis Hisami had not slept. His eyes were still open when the light showed at the edges of the curtains. He swung his legs from the bed and sat thinking for a few moments before taking a shower and dressing.

Waiting for him when he emerged from the bathroom was a tray with juice, sliced mango, oval breads called *samoon*, and *gaymer*, a thick white cream made from buffalo milk, all prepared by his Yazedi chef. He took the juice and sat down at a small round table with a view out over the ocean. He glanced at the framed photographs of Aysel and Anastasia surrounded by children in a refugee camp, thought for a few seconds and thumbed the numbers of his passcode into his phone.

He hoped a message would be waiting for him but he did not expect it. The coordination of Anastasia's kidnap and the seizing of his passport were proof enough of what they wanted. They didn't need to underline the point with an email, although he had received three in the previous forty-eight hours from different addresses which obliquely suggested he back off and sell his shares in TangKi. The situation was now clear to him. Her abduction had been triggered by news of the meeting in Palo Alto. He had said little of what he knew but now everything he'd found out, all that he suspected about Adam Crane, could not be revealed if he wanted to see Anastasia again.

His eyes moved to her photograph, a black-and-white shot he'd seen on the *New York Times* site before they were together and bought from the photographer. This time, he would not lose, he told himself again, though he had no idea how he could win and that, for Hisami, was a frighteningly new experience.

Downstairs in the Ocean Room, the group of six had already assembled when he entered, so quietly that no one heard him, took a cup of coffee and set it down with his mobile phone beside a high-backed chair facing them. There were three from his company, including Jim Tulliver, and three from Dee Strategy, two of whom were about to leave for Italy. Zillah Dee came in wearing ear buds and clutching two phones. A young man came behind her, holding two more phones. She wore black pants, a loose grey shirt, trainers and her usual string of pearls. The tiny tattoo on the underside of her wrist was just visible. She chose a chair near to Hisami. 'We're ready, sir. Craig, you can go ahead,' she said to the man who'd followed her into the room.

'Before you start, have the Italian authorities had any kind of demand?' asked Hisami.

She shook her head. 'No. Sometimes it takes a long time for them to make the demand. It's all part of softening up the loved ones, sir.' She said this as a matter of fact. It was one of the things Hisami liked about Zillah – no frills, no sentiment.

A big screen set up in front of a fireplace came to life. 'This is an aerial of the place where Mrs Hisami was abducted yesterday,' she said. 'The bodies of the two African migrants used by the kidnappers were found at or near the places marked beside the road. The second body, which we believe to be Louis, was hard to recover because it had fallen down a deep crevice and lay in a small watercourse at the bottom.'

She got up and moved to the screen. 'Here is the track where the Mercedes waited for the interception to take place. We assume the kidnappers needed to know that Mrs Hisami's vehicle had been stopped before they made their move. The Carabinieri believe that this indicates they did not want to attempt the abduction while the car was moving, which means they wanted to make sure no harm came to her. We know that they turned the Mercedes here and headed east, but the important fact is that officers picked up cigarette stubs here, and these are being examined for DNA.'

'What about the plate?' asked Hisami.

'That's interesting – they've tied it to the underworld in Naples. The registered owner is a man who runs a funeral parlour and is part of one of the connected families. He uses the van to collect the bodies from people's homes. The Carabinieri are talking to him now.'

'My wife's phone?'

'No sign of that, sir, and it's going straight to voicemail. We've tried getting a fix, but there's nothing doing. No signal, or the battery is down. We used the phone towers in the area to confirm her position when she was taken. I asked the police to do analysis of other calls made around the time locally and they were already on it. We believe that one of the migrants phoned or sent a text to the men waiting up the track. And if we can trace that, we can get a number for the phone the men were using and track it.'

Hisami nodded. 'What else?'

'I recorded the conversation with the man who is leading the investigation. His name is Colonel Fenarelli. He speaks good English – he did some time on attachment to the NYPD.' She nodded to Craig, who played it through the TV set. 'We'll go straight to the relevant part.'

'We are sure,' said the Italian policeman, 'that this was a well-planned operation which was initiated in Sicily and depended on exact intelligence of Signora Hisami's plans. The two men who took Mrs Hisami groomed these two men, so we are tracing their movements to learn where contact took place. We have a description of the two abductors, which Mrs Hisami gave to Mr Ciccone in Prianzano and Mr Hisami in the voicemail. This is being used by officers in Napoli to find the names of the two men, and we have our own database, of course. We are certain that we will trace them.'

'What do you need from us?' Zillah asked the police officer in the film.

'We want to know when Signora Hisami changed her plans

and when she told her husband.' Zillah stopped the recording and looked at Hisami for an answer.

'She told me in the phone call yesterday morning,' he said. 'I expected her to be on a plane by then.'

'Okay, I'll inform them,' she said. 'But there were others who knew before you. Eight members of the charity's team knew she was going to the village. I'll be giving their names to the police.' She nodded for the recording to continue.

'Typically, how does a case like this go?' Zillah asked Fenarelli.

'Mr Hisami is a very rich man, so we believe there will be a ransom demand. But we must ask ourselves questions.'

'What are those questions?'

'Kidnapping is rare in Italy today. There is too much inconvenience for the criminals. It is complicated to collect the money without being arrested and they risk being sent to prison for many years. Those men who made a living doing this sort of crime now earn millions of euros selling drugs.'

'Go on, please, sir.'

'But the suspects were obviously professional criminals and they were very organised. So we ask ourselves why they are doing this, when they can make more money on a shipment of *cocaina* to Il Porto di Napoli. Did these men kidnap Signora Hisami because she was working with migrants? We cannot answer that for sure, though it does not seem likely.' He paused and they could hear the officer take a drag on a cigarette. 'Is there someone who wishes to harm Signor Hisami? Maybe that is an answer. Maybe this is not about money. Maybe it is about revenge, or possibly someone wants to threaten him.'

'Thank you for sharing your thinking with me,' she said. 'What steps are you taking to trace the Mercedes?'

'There is a national alert on the registration plate.'

'As I made clear earlier, Mr Hisami does not want any publicity about his wife's abduction. He believes it would endanger her life. The US Embassy has contacted you to emphasise that the American government also does not believe that publicity is in the interests of Mrs Hisami. But on the murders of the two African men, will you be telling the media about that?'

'We issued a statement about the two dead migrants,' replied Fenarelli. 'After a little time we will have to say they were shot, and that will be a story for the media because violence against migrants is, regrettably, more common than it used to be. But we will not say anything about a kidnap.'

'We have your assurance on that?'

'*Sí*, Signora, but this decision will be reviewed if circumstances change.'

'The US Embassy would need to be consulted about that,' said Zillah firmly. 'Mr Hisami also.'

She nodded to Craig to stop the recording and swivelled to Hisami. 'Shall we go through the arrangements in Italy?'

Hisami nodded. 'Go ahead.'

'We already have two operatives there. Yossi is setting up in a town on the coast – forty miles from the site where the kidnap took place, which is a short distance to the local headquarters for the Carabinieri. He has been in touch with Fenarelli, and

Pete and Jonathan here are leaving for Italy tonight and will carry out on-the-ground investigations. We need to make sure that the Italians are doing all they can. We've fired up FBI and CIA contacts in Italy and I'm in constant touch with the embassy. They're being helpful.'

After they had talked a few minutes more on the arrangements Zillah had set in place, the room started to empty, leaving only Hisami, Tulliver and Zillah.

'Any news on the passport?' she asked.

Hisami shook his head. He removed his glasses and pinched the bridge of his nose. There was a long silence, during which they heard the distant swell of the ocean. Zillah was about to say something but Tulliver gave her an imperceptible shake of the head. Eventually, Hisami looked up, his eyes burning with a deep inner fury. He appeared to force himself to communicate.

'So you agree this is all connected, Zillah?' he murmured.

'It's a concerted campaign.' She handed him a tablet. 'It's just a question of who's doing it.'

'What's this?' he said, looking down at it.

'That's a story that was published last night by newsJip.com. It's a political-gossip website, Silicon Valley-based.'

Hisami read the headline that was leading the site: SPECIAL FORCES PAST OF HIGH-PROFILE TECH INVESTOR DENIS HISAMI AND A DRAMATIC BALKANS HOSTAGE RESCUE.

Underneath was a photograph of Hisami and Anastasia taken at a charity fundraiser and, more worrying, a blurred shot from twenty-five years before of a young man in fatigues, an automatic weapon hanging from his shoulder, addressing half a dozen soldiers. It didn't look like him and he didn't recognise any of the men in the picture, but he thought the leather flying jacket on the young man in the photograph was almost certainly his.

We interrupt your evening, dear reader, to bring you news of mystery man and billionaire tech investor Denis Hisami, who, it is revealed, stormed an IS terrorist hideout in the Balkans three years ago in an action that resulted in the slaying of four or more terrorists and the rescue of hostages.

Hisami, who made billions of dollars jumping on the social media boom early, is believed to have freed a former British spy who was being tortured by IS terrorists. His name is not known and mystery surrounds the identity of the other hostages, but rumour has it that one may have been his current wife, Anastasia, with whom this tech *éminence grise* set up a foundation to help migrants.

Her presence on that lonely mountainside has yet to be confirmed, but impeccable sources state that it all has something to do with Hisami's sister, who was serving as doctor with Kurdish forces on the front line with ISIS four years ago when she was killed. Hisami tracked down the people responsible for her death and eliminated the squad of trained Moslem killers in a deadly hail of bullets.

At the time, there was no mention of Mr Hisami's role

in the action, though his presence in the area has been established without doubt. The Macedonian authorities took the credit for killing the terrorist squad and for releasing the hostages, but you can't keep a story like this hidden for too long.

Facts have emerged about Mr Hisami's past that suggest he's certainly capable of ruthless action. He served on the front line in Northern Iraq with the Peshmerga forces a quarter of a century ago and as a young man won a reputation as an audacious and skilful commander.

For years, rumours have circulated in the investor community about Hisami, who is famous for his shrewd, below-the-radar operating style. But few suspected that he was so handy with a gun and could, on his own, pull off an operation like this, which, our sources say, was more reminiscent of Rambo than an investor with the old-world courtesy and intellectual tastes of Denis Hisami.

Lately, things have not been going so well for Hisami, who is estimated to be worth over $5.6 billion. It is said that he is under pressure on several large-scale investments, especially one in the Reason TV Channel, which he has been trying to buy into for three years. Other investments have not done so well either, and banking sources say that Hisami is being pressed to sell stock in companies that have yet to make the big bucks. In consequence, the whole complex web of his holdings is now threatened.

But with this kind of resumé, Homeland Security can find a role for him. Watch this space, folks – there's more on this one coming down the pike. Be sure of that!

Hisami handed the phone to Tulliver. 'See if the lawyers can do something about this.'

Tulliver skimmed the story and started shaking his head. 'My advice is to leave it. This isn't worth your time right now.'

Hisami nodded and studied Zillah Dee. 'Okay. Where do you think this comes from?'

'Not sure yet, but someone badly wants to stop you investigating TangKi.'

'And you think they'd kidnap my wife for that and have my passport suspended?'

'Yes.'

'So do I.' He reached for a water bottle and looked out across the ocean, which sparkled in the morning sun. After a couple of minutes of intense thought, he turned to them. 'Only someone in the government can be behind this, or someone who has a very great deal of influence and has access to a lot of information.'

'The CIA knew about the incident in the Balkans,' said Zillah. 'Word gets out about these things, and I guess the story on the website is preparation for someone to leak the news about your passport. Evidently, they're building a case that makes it seem as though you concealed your past from the US authorities when applying for citizenship and that your activities are a danger to US foreign-policy interests.'

Hisami glanced at Tulliver for his reaction. 'I pretty much agree with Zillah's assessment.'

'But to have my wife kidnapped by Mafia types in Italy – even the US government doesn't do that.'

'Maybe there are two separate strands to the campaign – an official one and a dirty one.'

Hisami thought again then opened his hands in genuine mystification.

'Wouldn't it be easier to just kill me?'

'That's maybe an option – they've kept this place under surveillance.'

'It's the obvious course.'

'Maybe you have something that is valuable to them – something they need you to give up,' said Zillah.

Hisami said nothing and stood. 'We have to think of Anastasia – she's all that matters. I appreciate what you're doing in Italy, Zillah, but we all know that there's one person in the world who can find my wife, and that's Paul Samson, and he's already working on the Crane side of this affair.'

'Yes, Mr Hisami, but I thought . . .'

'Samson probably already knows I'm behind the investigation. He's smart – he will have made connections. Talk to Macy Harp. See what he thinks about the idea.'

Tulliver coughed and looked at Zillah. 'As I understand it, he was once close to Mrs Hisami.'

'Yes, he was. That's why I want him to work on the case. There's no better incentive.'

'But is that fair? And maybe he'll have too much invested in the case to do a really good job.'

'Jim, I'm grounded. I can't leave the country. I have to sit here and wait. There's no one I trust more than Samson.' He pinched his finger and thumb in the air. 'He came this close to finding Aysel, and he never gave up, even when we stopped paying him. He will find Anastasia. All that matters is that we get her back, right?'

'Just raising my concerns . . .' Tulliver stopped when he saw the look in his boss's eye.

'I have no choice and, by the way, when Samson hears she has been abducted it's the only thing he'll want to do. Zillah, talk to Macy then take the plane and go and see Samson in London. You will be dropping me off at Teterboro Airport in New Jersey so I'll have just a five-hour time difference with Europe. Tell Samson everything – every detail about TangKi. If he wants to speak to me, that's fine. Jim, I need you to stay here and work on the passport issue and the TangKi board meeting tomorrow. And tell Sam Castell to look at this newsJip website.'

They got up. 'I'll see you on the plane in about two hours,' said Hisami, picking up his phone. When they'd left the room he searched his contacts for Senator Shelly Magee, an old ally and friend, but before he tapped in her number, there was an incoming call from Gil Leppo.

'Hey!' said Gil. 'Just got out of the pool. And I guessed you'd be up. I wondered how you're doing.'

'Thanks for helping out at the meeting yesterday. I was grateful for your support. I'm sorry I had to leave.'

'Yeah, Castell said you had some problems.'

'Gil, I want to ask you something – who's my enemy in that room? Which of them wants to destroy me?'

'No one, as far as I know. I mean, they're competitive people, but they respect your judgement. In our world, everyone can behave like a See You Next Tuesday but, honestly, Denis. I don't think anyone is, like, seriously fucking with you.'

'Word leaked out about that meeting, Gil. Someone told Crane.'

'That's not surprising. They all like him and admire what he's done.'

'So people are in touch with him. They know where he is. Is that Gehrig? He seemed defensive during the meeting. Martin Reid?'

'I didn't say that people are in touch with him, Denis. I just said it wasn't a big surprise that word leaked out. From Micky and Martin's point of view, it looks like you're trying to mount a coup against Adam. They're pissed. They think you're after something.'

'Did you talk to Crane, Gil?'

'Nope. Like you, I haven't heard from Adam in a while.'

'Okay, so if you hear anything from him or anyone else about anything, let me know, will you? I'd appreciate that.'

'Sure thing,' said Gil. 'Say hi to your beautiful wife for me.'

'I'll be sure to do that, Gil.' He hung up and sat thinking for the best part of half an hour.

CHAPTER 7

The crew didn't discover she was missing until several hours after the sun had risen then vanished behind a bank of black cloud that moved south from the Balkans. She had climbed on top of a container and found a place that was shielded from view by stacks three high either side and at the same time protected her from the worst of the wind. She was wearing the dead man's jacket, held close to her body by the belt she had taken. Gusts of wind brought the smell of a heavy aftershave from the material to her nostrils.

She heard voices below her and crawled to peer over the edge of the container. A party of at least five men was methodically sweeping the ship, trying the doors of the containers and looking into the narrow crevices between them. They went up and down the length of the vessel twice then began to check the tops of the lower containers with the help of a metal ladder that was slammed against the container ends. She slunk to the far corner of her box, climbed to the third storey and waited, quite comfortably, pressing her back against one container and resting her feet on a ridge on another. A man made a cursory investigation of the top of her container. She saw a bald head fleetingly but then it disappeared and gradually the voices receded from her part of the deck.

Although the ship wasn't large by the standards of some container vessels, there were many other places they would need to search, so she reasoned she was safe for a while. Her challenge now was to stay undiscovered until the ship reached its destination, and to do that she would need food and water and somewhere warm to sleep.

The ship sailed on and hit the bad weather that had been threatening all day, causing it to pitch and roll in a furious wind that ripped spray from the top of the waves, repeatedly soaking her. This reminded her of the last time she had been at sea, crossing the Adriatic to Venice with Samson. She allowed herself to think of those few days spent exploring the outlying backwaters of the city and finding such delight in each other. And she thought of Samson – hopeless, brilliant and sexy, and kinder than she would ever be. A lover, not a husband.

At dusk the deck lighting began to burn and she decided that it would be risky to break cover – watchful eyes on the bridge could easily pick her out. She waited a further five hours, during which time she saw no movement at all on the deck and heard nothing, but that was understandable, since the weather was atrocious. She often had to throw herself flat on the roof of the container to stop herself from falling off. Then, as midnight approached and the winds abated, she let herself down and moved with great stealth to the shadows of the containers nearest the bridge, where she could see more clearly the layout of the stern of the ship. If she was to steal food, this is where she would have to go. She watched for a full half-hour before satisfying herself that there was no one around – it seemed incredible they weren't looking for her. She wondered if the decks were covered by CCTV but there were no cameras on the lighting masts and none, as far as she could tell, on the bridge that rose above her.

She slipped through the shadows and found a companionway that descended to a deck where there were several doors leading to the bridge and main quarters. She went down, stopping to listen every other step. There was no noise except the churn of the engine. At the bottom, to her right, she saw a row of portholes facing out to sea. No lights shone from them. To her left was another short companionway that led to a door that spilled light on to a gangway. She went down, using the rails, her feet barely touching the steps. Through the door she heard the noise of someone working deep in the heart of the ship's main quarters. She listened hard. It sounded as though they were scrubbing a floor with a brush and a hose. Music was playing in the background. She crept past the door and moved along the passage. The first door was open on to a storeroom filled with cleaning supplies, piles of cloth and drums of cooking oil. The next appeared to be a dumping ground for old furniture – broken tables and chairs, light fittings and coils of fine chain were heaped on the floor; safety netting, lamp torches and some mini traffic cones were arranged neatly on the side. Above them, hanging on a row of pegs, were life vests and high-visibility jackets with the name of the ship printed on the back: CS *Black Sea Star*. She put one on and tucked her hair into the collar. At a distance, in the dark, she might pass for a member of the ship's crew.

The passage led to a large, well-lit space with long stainless-steel surfaces, square ventilation ducts and a tiled floor. She had found the galley, but there was no food in sight. To her left there was a smaller room with two sizable fridges and a door marked 'Cold Store'. It was here that the man was working. He was kneeling down, facing the cold store, chipping away at something on the floor with a knife. The music was very loud – something Latin American – and he did not hear her as she sped past a series of ovens and huge gas rings. She now found herself in a darkened service area. A line of vending machines contained canned drink and snacks; there were tables and chairs and a dark TV set was mounted on the wall. She hunted around under the counter and found a kitchen knife, which she pocketed, then a jar of cereal, a cardboard box full of cookies in wrappers, croissants in cellophane and some little containers of butter and jam, presumably laid out for the crew's breakfast. She stuffed as much as she could into her pockets and retraced her steps, carrying the cereal jar under her arm.

This she nearly dropped when the man popped up from behind a steel cabinet with a look of enquiry on his face. He looked Chinese. He smiled and said, 'Hi.'

'Hello,' she said. 'I'm sorry – I felt hungry.' She was searching his face to see what he would do, but he evidently had no idea who she was or why she was there. 'It's so cold out there,' she said in her most normal voice. 'I needed to eat. Hope you don't mind.'

He shook his head. She wasn't sure he understood. 'Very cold,' she said, making a rather hopeless attempt to mime a shiver.

'Yes,' he said. 'You want drink? I got whiskey and Metaxa 12 star in cabin. We can watch movie and drink Metaxa.' He was undoing his apron and smiling. 'I finish now. We make party. We make good, good party.' She returned his smile. Maybe he didn't know about her and the dead men who had been heaved over the side earlier that day. Maybe this strange little man was aware of nothing outside his spotless, glistening galley.

He beckoned her to follow, which she did because she had no better option and, besides, she reasoned that, if she were with him in his cabin, she might be able to prevent him from raising the alarm. He reached up to switch off the lights and fans in the galley and indicated that she should go through the door first.

'Where is everyone?' she asked.

'Sleeping,' he said simply.

'The men I saw on the deck?'

He shrugged. 'They drink then they sleep.'

It was possible that they had given up the search because they knew there was nowhere for her to flee, but that seemed odd, considering the lengths they'd gone to to snatch her on the road and eliminate all the witnesses to her abduction. None of it made sense to her, but she was too cold and hungry to wrestle with the problem.

The man led her to the end of the row of dark cabins she had noted on the way down to the galley and ushered her into a space with a bed, a TV set, a computer and clothes in two neat piles. On a shelf were a photograph of an elderly Chinese woman and one of a young girl standing in front of a blossom tree. He dropped into a large, revolving office chair and gestured for her to perch on his bed, switched on a small table lamp and reached into a cabinet to retrieve two bottles.

'I need to eat something first,' she said, taking the croissants and cookies from her jacket pocket. 'Where are you from?'

'I'm Chinese from Malaysia, but I no go there for many, many years.'

'You have family?' she said, pointing to the photographs.

He shook his head. 'All dead.'

'You have a home?'

'This my home.' He poured two glasses of Metaxa and handed her one, which she put on the shelf at the end of the bed. 'Now we see movie.' He tapped a key on his laptop and the screen came to life with a still from a porn video. Two women and a man were frozen in a comically ecstatic position.

'That is not my kind of movie,' she said.

He looked amazed. 'This good film. We make party and see them do the fucking.' He giggled.

She had eaten two croissants and was beginning to feel a little better so took a sip of the brandy. 'What's your name?'

'Zhao Liu.'

He took out a very long cigarette and sat gaping at the

threesome, the cigarette hanging unlit from his mouth. The two women were taking turns to fellate the man, a muscular brute who was shaved all over and had a sleeve tattoo.

'Zhao, can we watch something else? I don't like this. It's so ugly.'

'This good part.'

'I don't want to watch.' She found it hard to believe she was having this conversation. 'Have you got a phone? Can I use your email?'

He shook his head and pointed up. 'Internet not work. No phone.'

'The ship must have satellite communication with the internet. I need to speak to my husband. Can you show me where I can do that?'

He shook his head. 'I am chef – I know only cooking but I am good cook.'

'But you could show me where I can send a message to my husband. There must be some place the crew communicate with the shore.' But he wasn't paying attention. 'Will you show me, Zhao?'

He shrugged. 'I have other movie.'

'Anything's better than this. Besides, seems like you know it quite well.'

He had lit the cigarette and was puffing on it excitedly as one of the women came, rather too theatrically to be convincing, and the man groaned.

She tried another tack. 'Or maybe you can send a message. That would work just as well. I'll give you an email address and a phone number. I have to get a message through, do you understand? It's a matter of life and death.'

'*Sound of Music* – Julie Andrews.' He searched the computer and found the download.

'Where are we going – which port are we going to, Zhao?'

He grinned mischievously. 'You give me kiss then I tell.'

She thought for a moment. He might have an interest in porn but Zhao was no rapist. He was just a little guy bobbing on the ocean without friends or family or any place to go. He struck her as one of the loneliest individuals she had ever met. 'A kiss – nothing else.' She leaned forward and placed her lips on his cheek. 'Which port?'

'Odessa. Burgas. Not know.'

'Bulgaria. Is the ship Bulgarian? Who owns the ship? Is it Russian?'

'I not know.'

'When do we get there – how long will it take?'

'Day and half, maybe two days and half. I chef, not captain.'

'I need to get this message through. I need that very badly, Zhao. Will you help me? Can I write down the number that you must call and an email address with a message?'

'You my Julie Andrews,' he said, evidently still swooning from the kiss.

'I am your Julie Andrews if you do this one thing for me.' She reached for some paper and a pen on the desk. 'Can I write it for you?'

She kept it simple – the name of the ship, possible destinations, the nationality of those she had heard speaking, which she now thought was almost certainly Russian, the time she was writing the message, which was almost thirty-six hours after her kidnap. She put nothing of her circumstances, except that the two men had been killed and she had escaped from the container. She ended with 'I love you.' She folded it and placed it on the desk in front of Zhao.

'Drink,' he said.

'Will you do this for me? Will you promise?' She laid her hand on his. 'Please, Zhao. My life depends on it.'

He nodded. 'Drink brandy and we see Julie.'

She took a mouthful and suddenly felt very warm and drowsy. Before Julie had sung 'Do-Re-Mi', she had keeled on to her side and was asleep.

At four, she woke to find Zhao, still dressed, asleep by her side and holding her hand. There was barely room for the two of them on the narrow bed and his leg was hanging over the side. She moved her arm and he stirred. 'I'm going now,' she whispered. 'Don't tell anyone I was here. And Zhao, please, please send that message. Write it out as I have and send it to the email address.'

He mumbled something about his Julie.

His eyes had closed again. She nudged him. 'Zhao, I need you to concentrate. Can you do this today? I will come back later if you do this for me. Do you understand?'

As she pushed herself up to swing a leg over him, she noticed a black cable-knit beanie hat and gloves on top of the cabinet by the door. 'Can I borrow those? It's cold out there.'

He raised his head and nodded.

'Thank you, Zhao. I don't know what I'd do without you.'

She went into his little bathroom, peed, rubbed some toothpaste around her gums and put on the hat, stuffing her hair into it. She flipped up the collar of the high-visibility jacket and looked in the mirror, steadying herself against the movement of the ship with one hand against the side of the cabin. Her skin was grimy but still noticeably pale. She took a can of instant dye for grey roots on the Perspex shelf that she suspected Zhao used, sprayed it on her hands and wiped it all over her face, darkening her skin. By the time she came out, Zhao was sitting with both feet on the floor and a lost, regretful look in his eyes. She touched his shoulder.

'You know, don't you?'

He nodded.

'Why aren't they looking for me?'

He shrugged. 'They find you in morning.'

'Can I stay here?' she said, suddenly realising it would be much safer. She crouched down and looked up into his eyes.

He shook his head. 'If you here, Zhao dead.'

She put her hands on his knees. 'Okay, I'll go now. But Zhao, please send that email for your Julie.'

He smiled and nodded.

She slipped out into cold air, waited and listened for a few seconds before closing the door then climbing the companionway. She made for the stacks of containers, head bowed against the wind, hands thrust into the rib pockets of the jacket, shoulders hunched to bulk up her profile.

CHAPTER 8

Macy Harp phoned early and told Samson to be at Hendricks Harp by 7.30 a.m. There was a lot they needed to go through that they couldn't discuss on the phone. He arrived before time and found Macy reading a copy of the *Economist*. 'Never seems to be time to catch up,' he said, dropping the magazine on to his desk. 'Want coffee?'

Samson nodded slowly. Macy was acting oddly. There was none of the usual affability in his round, red face, and when his eyes met Samson's there was a rather business-like look in them.

'What's going on?' he asked.

'I'll tell you in a moment.' He sat down before buzzing through to the outer office for coffee. 'So, what did the Security Services want to know?' he asked.

'They seemed to know it all. I told them how I tracked Crane through an agency that supplies call girls from France – they knew that. They knew we had got hold of his email address, though they didn't know Naji Touma helped me with that. They knew the exact amount of money we are trying to trace, though they pretended otherwise, and they didn't ask me about its destination, which I take to mean they had all the information they required on that. And I have to tell you, Macy, that Nyman dropped into our little chat yesterday afternoon that the client was using Denis Hisami's plane. So I have a question or two for you. What's this got to do with Hisami?'

'But the murder of Crane – what did they say about it?'

Samson hesitated, just to let Macy know that he wanted answers too. 'They said he had been tortured very badly. They believe that took place at another location because of the mess and the noise. His face was unrecognisable – the exit wound was . . . well, you can imagine for yourself. They know it was Crane because of the DNA match with the articles in the apartment – clothes, etcetera.'

'So Crane was living there as Ray Shepherd, a UK citizen born in Guernsey, but in fact we know he was Russian originally, or maybe even Ukrainian.'

'Correct. They know that too.'

'So what on earth did they want with you?'

'Simply to check what we had found out, then, once they understood I was pretty much in the dark about our clients and what their exact motives were, they sent me packing.'

'And they didn't try to threaten you by suggesting you were a suspect?'

'There's no point, Macy. I didn't have enough information. I didn't even know who our client is.'

'And the Syrian boy – you are still in touch? How old is he now? Where's the family living?'

'He's seventeen or eighteen – I forget. They're living in Latvia – Riga. They left Germany because Naji was offered a scholarship by the Latvian government. They have fast-tracked his education and he's well into his degree and getting through it really quickly. The family had a lot of problems last year in a town near Chemnitz in Germany. We had to sort them out.'

'He must be very able. Can't think of anyone who has done more to help European intelligence services than that brave little fellow.'

'He's almost six foot tall now,' said Samson, not hiding his frustration. 'Macy, you're avoiding the subject because you know I'm angry that you didn't tell me about Hisami's involvement in the Crane case. You betrayed my trust.'

'A touch harsh, Paul.'

Samson never raised his voice but he did now slap his hand on Macy's desk.

'No, you screwed up with this one, Macy. The deal is that you tell me everything about a contract – everything! And because you knew I wouldn't take the job with Hisami in the background, you didn't bloody well tell me.'

'Steady, Paul! It's not like that.' He put up his hand as his assistant, Tina, came in with the coffee, and nodded thanks without smiling, which Tina knew meant she should leave without the usual banter with her boss and Samson. There'd been a long-standing endeavour by Macy, which preceded Samson's raging affair with Anastasia and was not entirely unserious, to put Tina and Samson together. Samson had graciously resisted.

'You and I both know you needed the work,' said Macy, bringing the cup to his lips. 'You asked for a hundred grand and we got you that. I knew it wouldn't be an arduous job, but I didn't mind charging that because I felt Denis owed you for all the risks you took looking for his sister in Syria. So it seemed to me a good contract and I didn't feel remotely compromised by keeping this information to myself. So, there it is, Paul.'

This was intended to close the matter, but Samson wasn't having it. He coolly regarded his racing companion and occasional employer and shook his head. Even if he had wanted to be conciliatory, his nature wouldn't allow it. 'I'm sorry to say it, but this is a deal breaker. I damn well have to be able to trust you, Macy. I can't do these jobs for you if you withhold information from me. And I won't work with you until that is understood between us.' He got up, knowing this might be a permanent break. Macy was too hard-nosed and too damned foxy to give him any such assurance.

'Just sit down, will you, chum,' Macy said quietly. 'We've a lot more to talk about, and I'm afraid I have some bad news.' He picked up the phone and said. 'Is she here?' He waited. 'Then send her in.' He hung up. 'Please sit down, Paul.'

Samson did as he was asked.

'This is Zillah Dee, of Dee Strategy Inc., Paul,' said Macy as a young woman entered with a slim computer case under her arm and a cup of coffee in her hand. 'Zillah is working for Denis Hisami and she has something to tell you.'

'I've heard about you,' said Samson.

She sat down in the other chair facing Macy's desk – no smile, no attempt at pleasantry, although she did offer a hand and gripped his with considerable force. She was striking, well put together, with a kind of irreproachable air. She regarded Samson with remarkably still grey eyes. He smiled but got nothing in return. Hard core, he thought. 'I'm sorry to hear the news about Mr Crane's death,' she said. 'We will doubtless discuss its relevance momentarily, but first I have to tell you that Mr Hisami's wife, Anastasia, has been abducted in southern Italy – Calabria – and her whereabouts are currently unknown.' She said it without drama or the slightest hint of feeling then waited for Samson's reaction. 'You understand what I have just said, Mr Samson?'

'Yes, I do.' He stopped to absorb it properly. An image of Anastasia laughing passed through his mind – it was always the same memory – and he felt dread and hopelessness wash over him. 'You'd better tell me the details.'

Which she did over the next ten minutes, in an account as clear and precise as any intelligence briefing, laying out every known detail of the kidnapping on the country road, the death of two migrants, the car used, the telephone calls to Hisami and a colleague in the Foundation, the Italian police investigation and the reporting systems put in place with the Italian authorities and the US Embassy. She told him no ransom demand had been made and that the police thought the abduction had nothing to do with Anastasia's work with migrants.

Macy glanced at Samson for his reaction. Samson ignored

him. He was shocked but he wasn't going to show it. 'Then what's the possible motive?'

'Over the past few weeks,' Zillah Dee went on, 'Mr Hisami has been investigating the transfer of large sums of money out of accounts run by the company TangKi – we thought there was just one, but a source inside the company now says that four accounts are likely being used. And this is why we asked you to trace Mr Crane for us – we were certain that Mr Crane was at the heart of the operation and that all the money was passing through London on its way to multiple destinations in Europe. There can't be any doubt, sir, that there are parties who desperately want Mr Hisami to desist from this investigation.'

'Who?'

'We're not certain at the present time but Mr Hisami is confident that the suspension of his passport on the day of his wife's kidnap, the degree of surveillance he has endured and, indeed, the seizing of Mrs Hisami are all connected. In the last twenty-four hours, he has also experienced some business difficulties which he believes are part of a coordinated campaign against his interests.' She paused. 'The case you were working on, the disappearance of Adam Crane, is central to the whole affair. It's a blow that he's no longer with us because, obviously, he could help.'

Samson leaned forward. 'What are you doing about Anastasia?'

'As I said, we have people on the ground in Italy, and they are already liaising with Italian authorities and following up leads. In truth, that's why I'm here to see you, Mr Samson.'

'Hisami wants me to find her!'

'That's correct, sir. He has asked me to ask you if you would help. He understands the sensitivity of the situation, but he's had the greatest respect for your abilities since you worked together trying to locate his sister. Would you consider it?'

Samson made a small sweeping gesture to dismiss the question. 'Of course.'

'Are you sure?' asked Macy. 'Can you be objective? Frankly, I wouldn't recommend it.'

'Our relationship was over some while ago. My feelings for Anastasia are friendly but they won't cloud my judgement,' he said, briefly acknowledging the lie to himself. 'You can fix everything, Macy? I'll require an unlimited budget on this. I'll leave for Italy as soon as possible and will need Tina to arrange a ticket.'

'There's no need. I have Mr Hisami's plane.'

'Good, but I must stress that I work alone.'

'Understood, but I need to coordinate with my people and talk to the Italian police. So I will be on the plane with you.'

'I can't have you getting in the way,' he said firmly.

'Yes, but you must appreciate that I'm in charge of this operation and am reporting directly to Mr Hisami.'

'Tell him I'll need to speak to him, because this all seems to be connected with his business dealings. What I want from you now is a detailed briefing on everything.' He turned to Macy. 'And, for that, we'll need a room.'

'We can do that on the plane, sir. It'll save time.'

Samson thought for a moment. 'Yes, but I need to check a

few things here before I leave. I'll meet you at the airport at four. That's Blackbushe, right?'

She nodded.

An hour later, Samson had packed a rucksack and was on his way to meet Detective Inspector Jo Hayes of the Metropolitan Police in a Mayfair Italian coffee bar that had recently upgraded from a basic greasy spoon to offer a breakfast menu with avocado toast and chia seeds. Hayes, who had served in MI5 but was now back at Counter-terror with the Met, arrived ten minutes after him, by which time Samson had read an email from Zillah Dee. The kidnappers had been identified, with ninety per cent certainty by the Carabinieri, as two mid-ranking figures in the Neapolitan underworld. Their names were Salvatore Bucco and Niccolo Scorza. They had served prison sentences for drug offences and fraud. Scorza owned a soccer bar and Bucco was in the vegetable business. They worked as a team yet there was no suspicion that they'd ever been involved in kidnapping before. A nationwide alert for the two men was in place.

Hayes, a vivid redhead with a wide grin which she deployed as an amateur nightclub singer in her spare time, dumped her shoulder bag on the table and said, with her usual breeziness, 'Hello, handsome! Shit, you look awful, what's happened?'

'It's complicated,' said Samson. 'I need your help.'

'I owe you, we both know that.' Three months before, Samson, while investigating the disappearance of a young princess from the Gulf States, had put Jo on to a group that were using artworks to launder money destined for terror groups.

'You heard about the murder of a man named Ray Shepherd in Knightsbridge?' he started. 'Your people had me in because I was involved in tracing this man, who was until recently living in the US under another alias – Adam Crane.'

'I didn't know about the American alias but I'm pretty much up to speed. The victim was tortured at an unknown location then dumped on the balcony of his flat.'

Samson nodded. 'Can you get me into the flat?'

'You've got to be joking,' she said incredulously. 'It's a crime scene. It's still crawling with Forensics. There's no way I can do it.'

'What can I offer you in exchange?'

'It's not a question of that, Paul. If I were on the team investigating the murder, I might be able to help, but this isn't even my beat.' She smiled at him. 'What's the problem? You traced your man. He's dead. You move on.' She shrugged at the simple logic of the situation.

Samson glanced out of the window and breathed in. 'Well, it's about a kidnap in Italy, and this man held the key to it. The thing is, your people and the Security Service know a lot more than I do about Shepherd/Crane, which is the reason they let me go so quickly. They just wanted to find out who I was working for, but I didn't have the first idea.' He thought for a few seconds. 'How about I give you everything I learn about the victim – that's everything from the American side? What your people don't know about is the money. Looks like a huge money-laundering operation.'

'No,' she said definitely. 'No, I am not bloody well doing this – okay?'

'Maybe hundreds of millions of dollars being washed through London, and Crane was at the centre of it all.'

'No, no, no! Get it into your fucking head – I can't do it. Please don't go on asking me.'

'Okay, so I'm going to tell you everything. A woman, a woman I once loved very much, was kidnapped in Italy two days ago, just when Crane was being tortured and killed. It looks like she was taken hostage to deter anyone from investigating Crane's affairs. I have to get into that apartment to check on something. I won't be more than a minute or two.' He saw she was thinking hard whether she could get him in.

'Who is this lucky woman?' she asked. 'I didn't have you down as the falling-in-love type.'

'She's an aid worker. We met a few years ago. She's with someone else now. Married.'

'And you still love her?'

He shrugged. 'It's history.'

'You poor sod!' Her leg started jiggling and she looked away. 'Fuck it. I'll do it, but on the condition that anything you find out you pass to me and that will be over dinner in your mum's place. Always wanted to go there.'

She went out and made a couple of calls in the street, pacing up and down with her finger pressed to her ear. He could tell she was calling in some favours. She came back. 'We're on, but not until half twelve. I'll meet you there.'

★

The apartment was enormous and anonymous, like a very expensive hotel suite, with several large rooms, most of which faced the park and accessed the balcony where Shepherd/Crane was left for all to see. The forensics officer who let them in said, 'We're pretty much finished, but you must wear these.' He handed them blue shoe covers and latex gloves. 'I'm going for a smoke and coffee. You've got ten minutes.'

Samson moved quickly, searching for signs of a computer or laptop. He found nothing, which didn't surprise him. These items would be the first to be removed by the police. Then he went to the bedroom suite and entered the huge white alabaster bathroom and examined a pair of sinks below a bronze-tinted mirror. There were no personal items to be seen, and nothing in the cabinets under the sinks. He searched the wardrobes but found no clothes and nothing in the chests of drawers either. He looked around and noticed right-angle marks on the wall. 'Someone's removed the pictures from the wall!' he called out. 'Looks like they were pretty big. They would need two people to take them down. Have they checked with the concierge when these things were moved? Unless the police moved them.'

Hayes was at the door. 'That's not something our lot would do.'

'Might be important,' he said, going back to the bathroom.

'What are you doing in there?' she asked.

'Just looking,' he said, taking out one of the labelled zip-lock plastic bags he'd brought with him. He crouched down in the shower and prised off the drain-cover cap and saw what he was looking for. With a pair of tweezers, he pulled out several strands of hair caught in the grille and carefully placed them in the bag. He slipped it in the pocket of his rucksack and joined her in the bedroom.

He then strode across the living room, which also showed no signs of individual taste or of any actual person living in the flat, and opened the door on to the balcony. Hayes's phone was ringing. She answered at the same time as trying to signal that he shouldn't go out. Samson seemingly did not see and went out nevertheless.

It was obvious where the body had been propped up. There was blood on thc tiled floor. He knelt as if to check something and, using a small craft knife he'd brought, along with the plastic bags, scraped a dried flake of blood into a bag so quickly that when Hayes joined him on the balcony she had no idea what he had done.

'It doesn't make sense,' he said, straightening up. 'They say he was tortured at another location and then brought here to be killed. Did you see the security in the lobby? How are they going to bring a tortured man into this building – huh? How are they going to avoid the CCTV downstairs and in the lifts? It had to have all happened here, but there are no signs in the bathroom.' He looked at her. 'How badly was he tortured? What were the signs?'

She shrugged. 'I have no idea.'

'Well, it doesn't add up, does it?' This was true. There were some anomalies in the story that he had been told, but they were unimportant to him. Samson had got what he had come for and he wasn't going to press the point with Hayes, who was already looking impatient.

As they travelled down in the lift, she said, 'I'd like to know what this was all about, Paul.'

'The paintings. There were no paintings anywhere to be seen. Crane collected art and he had a good eye. That was one of the ways I tracked him down, a bill of sale from one of the galleries in New Bond Street. So, where are the paintings? Were they stolen, or did someone remove them before the murder, knowing that the murder was going to take place?'

'You're saying the motive was theft?'

Hayes, usually so shrewd, was missing the point. 'Not exactly, but you guys really need to go over the CCTV and find out what was removed from the flat and when.' He raised his eyebrows on the last word.

'I'll mention it,' she said, still looking puzzled. 'Was that all you wanted to see?'

'It was a really useful visit in many ways. I am eternally grateful to you, Jo. We'll do that dinner in a couple of weeks.'

Outside, he grabbed her hand hurriedly and gave her a kiss on the cheek. 'Thanks, you're a star,' he said before hailing a cab to go to Battersea heliport.

Five minutes after Hisami's jet took off from Blackbushe, Zillah Dee undid her seatbelt and reached over to tug a broad attaché case towards her. 'These were sent over by Mr Hisami's office just this afternoon. I had them printed at Hendricks Harp. They show that a total of $271.5 million has passed through TangKi in the last year, and all of it was bound for London. This is the aggregate from all four bank accounts Mr Hisami traced. There may be more, but we will never know, because five people were fired following Mr Hisami's meeting with the board members a couple of days ago. He didn't say as much, but I'm guessing that his source was among them. The company was taking no chances and fired the whole department, and with good pay-outs and NDAs, so that's the end of his information from inside TangKi.'

She looked at him with those remote grey eyes. 'What do you make of it, Mr Samson? By the way, what should I call you – Paul, or Mr Samson?' He caught a glimmer of a smile.

'Paul's fine, but most people call me Samson. Have you analysed these figures? Is there any pattern to the transactions?'

'No, my people are looking at them now, but the interesting thing is where the money's coming from. As far as we can tell, it's all inside the States and that's important. It's really hard to work out whether it's been stolen from TangKi or the company is being used as a channel.'

'Tell me about the TangKi board.'

'You mean, which one of them helped Crane?'

He nodded.

'There was a meeting two days ago. I guessed that Mr Hisami asked those particular four board members for a particular purpose. My company is looking into their lives, so I wanted to see them for myself. That's one of the reasons I was at hand when he got the calls from his wife. All but one could be involved, and that's Larry Valentine – he has problems with a love child of sixteen that his wife is about to find out about, and, besides, this is not his kind of thing. Of the others, Martin Reid is the most likely because he shared Crane's right-wing agenda and has a history of making anti-Semitic remarks, which was always Crane's schtick. Micky Gehrig is Jewish and wrapped up in his space kick but he does have a Russian wife, and that may be important. We're looking into her. Gil Leppo is Denis Hisami's friend, and Denis and he have worked together on several investments. So, I guess it would be Martin Reid, because he also has the power to turn the heat on Denis through the government and the banks. Everyone fears him.'

'So whoever it is gave shelter to Crane while he moved money out of the company and ordered and coordinated Anastasia's kidnap to coincide with the meeting. Does that sound like Reid?'

She looked out of the window. 'You're right, it would be a new departure for him. He's a bastard, but a really conventional one.'

They ate sandwiches and drank diet Coke. She dozed for twenty minutes and Samson's mind wandered to Anastasia. He hoped she'd know that he would do everything to find her. When Zillah opened her eyes and reached for the can of Coke again, he asked, 'What was Crane's life like in California?'

She looked out of the window at the Alps, which glowed pink below them in the late-afternoon light. 'You ski, Samson?'

'No.'

'Crane did. He was a good downhill skier, cross-country, too – Squaw Valley mostly, Aspen also. He made some serious contacts on the slopes and that's how he entered the world of tech finance and start-ups. He had the money and the talk. He also had a charming wife, who wasn't his wife, and two kids that came with her. She literally brought her entire family and loaned it to this operation. That's a remarkable investment of time, money and effort by someone or other to put their man at the heart of Silicon Valley.' She stopped and looked out of the window.

'Do the board members know he's dead?' asked Samson.

'No – the London police are still talking about Ray Shepherd.'

'What's going to be their reaction when they learn?'

'Mr Hisami is waiting for that. He thinks that the people who are in on this – whatever the heck *this* is – will show their hand. It's like Crane is his own little Russian sleeper cell, but then he buys into this company, which is actually a very good idea, and it's now making real money. It's a success, as start-ups go, so you ask yourself, why did Crane go illegal? Why didn't he just stay and run the company and make himself a billion dollars?'

'A higher calling?'

'Yes, but if he'd been something as simple as a Russian spy, they would have kept him in place.'

'How much do you know about the Russian connection?'

'Crane was born Aleksis Chumak in 1973 to a Russian mother and a father who was half Russian, half Ukrainian, in a town fifty miles north of Odessa. There were three boys. His father was a manager in a heavy-engineering works. And get this! He built cranes. The boy was a grade A student at Mechnikov National University in Odessa and was spotted by the embryonic Ukrainian intelligence service, although he was intrinsically part of the Russian culture that Ukrainians rejected. Maybe his Ukrainian second name helped in that. Then the trail goes dead, and the next we hear of him he's in seriously bad company and setting up all sorts of schemes for defrauding his own government as well as Western investors. Turns out he had a gift for criminality.'

They fell silent. At some point the pilot came on the intercom. 'We're just approaching the Adriatic, so we're less than an hour from Brindisi. You might want to look out on the starboard side of the aircraft, folks. There's a wonderful view of Venice in the twilight.' Samson didn't look out and Zillah's eyes were focused on her tablet.

He watched her for a few seconds. He had been struck by how young she looked yet how pragmatic her view of life was. She talked like someone with thirty years' experience of power and politics, yet she couldn't have been older than thirty-five, certainly not older than Samson, who was now pushing forty.

He noticed a trace of satisfaction in her expression – the first sign of anything approaching warmth in her sternly beautiful features – and saw in the window reflection that she was watching a film. He asked what it was.

'Sail boats,' she said. 'They're my new passion. I started my company in a decommissioned naval vessel on the Potomac that was like a houseboat and I took to watching the sail boats going by and realised it was a good way of leaving DC and having some fun on the weekend without getting in the car.' She stopped the film and searched for something, then turned the device towards him. He saw a yacht with a dark blue hull, sails filled and a crew waving at the camera. 'This is *Ariel*. I bought her eighteen months ago. She's a Bjarne AAS fifty-three-foot sloop built in 1952. We all sail it.'

'Who's all?'

'Five members of my staff – we learned together in the spring. We're a pretty good crew now. She's moored alongside the old wreck.'

He swiped through the photographs. 'You have a lot of electronics on board.'

'Can't be out of contact. Actually, we can handle pretty much any communications challenge when we're out on the ocean.'

'Do you still work out of the old boat?'

'No, we have offices in DC. But I kept it on. It can be useful for meetings.'

Samson smiled. 'I have no experience of the sea, but the one trip I took across the Adriatic made me think I'd like to sail.'

'You would,' she said, as though he had no choice, and took the tablet back.

'How did you get into this business?'

'Advertising,' she said.

'That seems like an odd route.'

'I was running a web advertising company in Manhattan and we were playing around with the steganography – hiding code and messages in images – and someone at the NSA got in contact, though I didn't know it was the Agency at the time. They were impressed and a little concerned about what we were doing. They asked for help. I gave it and, eventually, I joined the Agency.'

'But then you left.'

She snorted a laugh. 'Right – the Agency is fine, but I saw an opportunity. And there were maybe too many procedures and a lot of middle-aged guys who weren't the sharpest. We started the company knowing that we were only going to use our generation and younger. I guess one day I'll be made obsolete by a new generation, but then I'll have my boat and money.'

'Where did you grow up?'

'What's this – a background check?' A brief glimmer of a smile. 'I was raised in Kentucky by parents who in their twenties read a book about self-sufficiency – *The Good Life*, by Helen and Scott Nearing. Have you heard of this book, Samson?'

He shook his head.

'Right, my childhood and teen years were spent planting peas and hoeing and plucking chickens and stacking cords of wood and weaving blankets with my mom's faux-I designs of goddam apple trees and doves, and going to a school with kids that were all strictly the end of the gene pool. I guess most of them are now on opioids and giving birth out in the woods. Get the picture? My upbringing was a tedious fucking idyll. Is that enough?' He nodded. 'I know all about you, so no need to reciprocate.' With that she closed the picture of her boat and tried to get on to the plane's wifi again. Samson studied her for a few seconds. He couldn't work out whether she was straight, gay or asexual. Zillah Dee gave out no signals whatsoever: she was, in this respect, an utterly neutral presence.

Ten minutes later she said, 'By the way, I appointed a kidnap consultant this afternoon, an Italian specialist in the field. He may be a waste of money, but I need someone to give us a fix on the police, to tell me when they're bullshitting and when they're hiding stuff. He's recommended by folk in the Agency, so maybe he'll be of use. There's a meeting at the Carabinieri headquarters tonight at ten o'clock – all my people, together with the kidnap consultant, Dr Fabiano. We should just make it. We'll travel together and you can pick up the rental at the police headquarters. You have your driver's licence?'

Samson nodded. Then, after some thought, he said, 'Can you gain access to Crane's home in California?'

'Shouldn't be a problem – why?'

He opened the pocket of his rucksack and withdrew two plastic bags. 'These are DNA samples from Crane's apartment in London. One's blood from Crane's body, the other is hair from the shower next to the master bedroom. I want to see if we can get a match with samples from Crane's place, samples that are incontrovertibly from Adam Crane. I'd like to be certain that the body on the balcony was really his. From what you've told me, Crane is not the kind of man to get himself murdered.'

She took the two bags. 'I'll send them to the States tomorrow and I'll put in train collection of samples from his place now.' After she'd emailed the instructions she looked up and said,

'We'd have to make sure it's a sample from Crane, not the woman and two kids.' She thought for a moment. 'But then, that doesn't matter, does it?'

'You're right. All we need is one match. It would be helpful to establish whether the samples from the shower and the balcony in London are from the same person. That will tell us a lot.'

She nodded, went back into her email and started scrolling through the messages. A few moments later she lowered her second can of Coke, swore, then said, 'This email is from Mr Hisami's lawyer. Mr Hisami's been arrested by the United States Immigration and Customs Enforcement – ICE – on suspicion of lying on his N-400 citizenship application form. They say he failed to disclose his participation in acts of terrorism in Kurdistan and that he is associated with a designated foreign terrorist organisation in Turkey – the PKK. He's being held in the Metropolitan Correctional Center in Manhattan.' She looked up. 'If Crane is dead, who's fucking with Mr Hisami?'

CHAPTER 9

In the middle of the afternoon, on the second day of her voyage, the ship slowed to a few knots so that there was almost no sensation of it moving forward through the water. Anastasia guessed the reason because she had done some calculations while wedged – as before, with her back against one container and her feet planted against another – high up between two stacks of containers. If the boat was indeed headed for the Black Sea, that would entail a voyage of between a thousand and twelve hundred miles. Travelling at roughly twenty knots, which she knew from her time on a migrant rescue boat was the average speed for a vessel like this, the ship would take about two and a half days to reach its destination. She estimated she'd been at sea for between thirty-eight and forty-four hours and so had travelled between seven hundred and sixty and a thousand nautical miles. The ship would probably dock during the night, or just after dawn the next day.

But they couldn't enter the port with her running free. The

captain had probably banked on her being apprehended when daylight broke that day. There had been a lot of activity on the decks around her in the early morning, but she had become adept at working herself from one gap to another when she heard voices near her hiding place and they never came close to spotting her. So, the captain slowed the ship to little more than walking pace to allow the crew to make use of the remaining light.

The ship rolled in a gentle swell that came from the north, which forced her to keep adjusting her feet on the vertical surface in front of her, yet this was easier than the day before, because the containers were not being regularly drenched by the sea and her soles didn't slip. With the absence of any forward motion and the engines barely turning over, she could hear much more than during the first search of the day. Now, it seemed to her, the entire crew was deployed in combing the ship, but for some reason she was less frightened and altogether more determined to evade them. Maybe it had something to do with that odd little man's hospitality the night before and the food she had kept with her and nibbled through the day. She assumed that, for his protection, Zhao must have informed them that he had seen her, though he surely would not have confessed to giving her his bed for some of the night. She didn't dare to think of the laconic email she had drafted for him to send to her husband.

The men were now clambering all over the containers, but they had to do this on their hands and knees to stop themselves tumbling to certain death in the sea or serious injury on the deck. She heard them swearing and calling out to each other, no doubt complaining about the appalling danger they faced. She was far too quick for them. She had removed the high-visibility jacket and stuffed it in the narrow gap between two containers, and her clothing was dark so they never caught sight of her in the deep shadows, even when they were close enough that she could hear them puffing with exertion. The search went on for hours and there was a part of her that enjoyed outwitting them.

Then, as dusk fell and the ship's lights began to flicker and she heard men climbing down from the container stacks, the loudspeakers came to life. It was a poor PA system but she made out her name and that whoever held the microphone was telling her in fractured English that she could not escape because the ship would stay in the middle of the ocean until she was too weak or dehydrated to continue hiding. The voice started by promising her a meal, a shower and a bed. She shook her head in the shadows, muttering an oath in Greek, and went to retrieve her jacket. The ship had begun to get underway again – although at half the normal speed – and a wintry breeze could be felt in the narrow steel canyons.

She had survived another day, and now she had the night to think of a way of making her escape. She began to move about more freely, first checking the position of the ship's lifeboat, the large, orange, bubble-like craft hanging between two cranes on the port side. There was absolutely no hope of operating it on her own. She looked for a smaller craft, a rigid inflatable dinghy, perhaps, but found nothing. Again, the ship seemed surprisingly empty. She saw a couple of men patrol up and down the main aisle between the containers, but they vanished after ten minutes and she was able to continue to dart from shadow to shadow. Around midnight she noticed lights appear to the south – an island a few miles off the starboard side. They must be threading their way through the Greek islands. She could make out the cluster of harbour lights around the port's entrance and the riding lights of small fishing boats that were bobbing about halfway between the ship and the island. The water was still warm at this time of year and she might just be able to swim the distance to the fishing boats, although the thought of diving into the black ocean from such a height and the possibility of being sucked into the ship's propellers were too much for her. But the island gave her an idea. Even the smallest community was served by a mobile-phone mast these days, and the little Greek port that she was watching with such intense longing would be in easy range of a phone on the ship. She would get hold of a phone while the island was still in sight, whatever it took.

She crept back to the container where she had been held, found it unlocked and pulled the door open. Inside, she knelt down, felt for the timber pallet and wrenched free the length next to the one she'd broken the day before. She swung it in the dark then stepped outside.

She would need to move cautiously and pick her target with care. She made for the bridge, walking confidently in the ship's high-vis jacket, and passed a long, wide, sheltered gangway. She heard people on another deck above her but there was no one to be seen at her level. There were lights on, however, and shadows passed across a porthole. Opposite a door of clear glass, she withdrew into the shadows beneath the lifeboat and waited, contemplating the haggard image of herself in the polished metal panel that ran up the wall opposite her. She looked wild and violent. Was she really going to do this – club someone to the ground and force them with a knife at their throat to give up their phone and the passcode to unlock it? Yes, she undoubtedly was. These people had killed two men and dumped them in the sea; they meant her harm and, if necessary, she thought she might kill too. These were thoughts she had never had before. She was a psychologist, for Christ's sake, and she helped people as a matter of vocation. Yet she wasn't surprised at herself. The events in the Macedonian farmhouse, much in her mind since she'd seen the two men killed on the road, made her accept that it was in her to go to any lengths. Her career in psychology was a conscious counter to what she recognised deep down might be a fairly extreme personality. The last two days had brought that to the surface. She was angry as hell.

She waited. The island might be out of range now, but there would be others and she'd climb high up on the containers to see the lights in the night. Suddenly, the door handle was worked and a man carrying a tray with one arm pushed the door open and stepped over the raised metal threshold. He swung left and moved quickly towards the companionway symmetrical to the one she had taken down to galley level on the other side of the shop. He was small and looked like he might be a waiter. He must be heading to the galley with his tray of empty cans and wrappers. He put his hand to the rail to steady himself and proceeded down, watching where he placed his feet.

She moved quickly, gliding down behind him. She didn't hit him with the wood but simply put the kitchen knife to his throat. 'Give me your phone,' she whispered, 'or I will kill you.'

He was very dark – Pakistani or Bangladeshi, she thought. His eyes turned to her, staring with undiluted fear. The whites were streaked with brown veins at the edge. He said something in his own language, then in English, 'Please – no. I have child.'

'Put the tray down and give me your phone. Your phone, dammit!'

He understood and crouched to place the tray on the step. She bent down with him. 'Don't try anything or I will kill you.'

He shook his head and straightened. The knife pressed into his flesh as he felt in his pockets and handed her the phone over his shoulder. 'The passcode!' she hissed. 'The fucking passcode!' She watched his finger as he jabbed at the screen.

'3398 – right?'

He shook his head.

'Is that right?'

He nodded.

She took the phone. 'Go down. Nothing will happen to you if you stay quiet. If you make any noise, I will cut you. Got that?'

He nodded. She prodded him down the companionway to the under-deck and then to the stern of the vessel and an area that contained coils of rope, marker buoys, chains and several cable cylinders standing on end. 'Take off your jacket and shirt.'

Only then, as she saw the pathetic naked torso of the man – all skin and bones, just like the people who'd crossed the Sahara – did she feel sorry for him. 'I'm afraid I've got to tie you up.' He was shivering. 'Turn around and face away from me.' Much of what followed she had planned. She ripped the belt from her waist, made a loop and placed both his arms through it, then tightened it high on his biceps and knotted the length of leather left over around the loop. For good measure, she used the shoelaces she'd taken from one of the bodies to bind his wrists. Then she stuffed his shirt in his mouth and tied the sleeves fast around his head. 'Now get down with your face on the deck.' He sank to his knees and lowered himself forward. She tied the sleeves of his jacket around his ankles then dragged part of a heavy chain over to him and piled it on the back of his calf muscles so there was no hope of him moving.

She left him and fled forward to the dark towers of containers that she now probably knew better than anyone on board. She climbed nimbly into one of her hiding positions, in the lee of the tallest stack, which obscured her from both the bridge and deck, pausing briefly to search for the island's lights. They'd gone, but she took the phone out and looked for a signal. There was one bar. She dialled Hisami's number and waited, rocking slightly and looking up at the stars through a thin veil of cloud, praying he would answer. The call didn't go through. She tried and failed again, and wondered if the man's phone was barred from making expensive international calls. She tried a text. 'Am being held on ship CS Black Sea Star. Position somewhere Aegean heading north. Likely destination Odessa/ Burgas. Russians and East Europeans on ship. Am free and in hiding. Phone this number soonest. Ana x.' The message appeared to leave the phone. She made two more attempts to get a call through then told herself she would wait until she was nearer the land and put the phone in her pocket. Too exhausted to stay awake and wait for another island to appear, she allowed herself to sleep for what she promised herself would be just half an hour.

Much later she woke to the sound of the phone ringing. She'd kept the ringer on in case she fell asleep. She sat up and dug in her pocket to retrieve it before the caller hung up. 'Denis?' she said as she raised the phone 'Denis, is that you?' But no one was there. The call must have dropped as she answered it. She waited, clutching the phone with both hands. It rang again. 'Denis! Denis!' she whispered, with increasing desperation. No answer came, yet the line was definitely open. Someone was at the other end. Then it went dead. She wondered if it was one of those calls when one person can hear but the other can't. After the phone rang for a third and fourth time it dawned on her with horror what was happening, because now she had become aware of some activity on the deck below her. The ringing had led them to her. They must have found the waiter trussed up and then dialled his phone to locate her. Men were scaling the containers all around her.

CHAPTER 10

There were nine in the room listening to Colonel Fenarelli, head of the investigation and, as it turned out, a graduate of both the NYPD and FBI's organised crime team in Manhattan. They were Samson, Zillah, two men from the US Embassy, one a nameless CIA agent, two of her men, Jonathan and Pete, plus two Italian detectives and kidnap specialist Dr Fabiano.

Fenarelli moved to a screen on the wall and signalled to one of the detectives. 'The kidnap victim was taken here.' He pointed to a spot on a large-scale map where Anastasia's car had been stopped. 'The bodies were found here and here. We believe that Mrs Hisami was then taken towards the east, because there are the signs of a car turning at this point – here. But the more important clue found at the crime scene was a hundred metres to the east. Several cigarette butts – and we've matched the DNA on them to Scorza and Bucco. The men were obviously waiting there a long while before the interception took place.'

He turned to his audience. 'This is significant because it establishes, without doubt, that the operation was carried out by the Camorra, not the 'Ndrangheta, the pre-eminent organised crime group in Calabria.'

'Why do you say it's significant?' asked one of the men from the US Embassy.

'Because it's unusual for the Camorra to operate so deep in 'Ndrangheta territory, and for them to carry out a kidnapping in this area is unheard of. 'Ndrangheta – yes! They have many places to hide the victim, in caves and forests all over the region, but the Camorra have no facilities like this. They would have to move the victim a long way to a place they could be sure would not be discovered.

'So, this suggests many questions to us. One, why were the Camorra prepared to risk offending their enemies in Calabria? Is it because Mr Hisami is very, very rich and they expect to win a large ransom for his wife? Two, why were the Camorra operating in Sicilia? We know that Bucco and Scorza were in Sicilia for one week before the kidnapping and that they were using this time to find the two immigrants that Mrs Hisami recognised on the road. There was a lot of intelligence needed for this and . . .' He held up his index finger. 'They had up-to-date information about Mrs Hisami's movements. That takes much organisation. Just these two men, operating outside their familiar territory of Napoli, could not have done this on their own. So, we conclude that the Cosa Nostra of Sicilia helped them. That interests us because that kind of cooperation can only be arranged at the highest level. And then we ask ourselves other questions. What is the purpose of this collaboration? Is it money? Why was she not taken in Sicilia? Why did they wait until she was on the road in Calabria, a journey which she only decided to make ten hours before leaving?' He shook his head. 'You see, this is not a regular case.'

'Any news about the car, Colonel?' asked Zillah, without looking up from her tablet.

'We have put in place national alerts for the men and the car, as you know, but there is nothing. We know that Scorza and Bucco did not return to their families. Our sources in Napoli say that Scorza's wife was expecting him home to take his vows as a godparent for her sister's child. Her sister is married to a Camorra boss, so that interests us. Why has Scorza not come back? We would expect these two men to deliver the victim to other members of the gang and return home.'

'Can you say more about the search operation you have put in place?' she asked.

'We've covered the whole area near this place – *le grotte e refuge di montagna . . .*'

'Caves and mountain shelters?' offered Zillah.

'*Sí*, the caves and mountain shelters, and also abandoned buildings. We have interviewed the people who live within five kilometres of the point of the interception and we are sure she is not being held anywhere near this place.'

Samson cleared his throat. 'Feelings against illegal African immigrants are running high in your country. Is it possible a right-wing group kidnapped Mrs Hisami? Have you investigated extremist groups?'

'It is possible – yes. But, *signor*, if they wanted to stop what she was doing they would have simply killed her with the Africans.'

'Can you tell us anything about the phones?' asked Samson. 'The immigrants on the road must have used a phone to text the men waiting a hundred metres away. Have you recovered that phone?'

'No, but we know the number and the time the text message was sent,' replied Fenarelli.

'That means you know one of the numbers the kidnappers were using,' returned Samson. 'Does it match either of these men's personal phones?'

Fenarelli shook his head; he knew what Samson's next question would be.

'Has there been any activity on that phone since Mrs Hisami was seized?'

'No.'

'Has there been any activity on the men's personal numbers?'

'No, they were all using *telefoni usa e getta*. How do you say?'

'Pre-paids – burners,' said Zillah.

'Does that strike you as odd?' asked Samson.

'No, these people are not stupid. They would not bring their personal phones with them when committing a crime like this. That would make it easy for them to be traced to the scene of the crime.'

'I agree,' said Samson. 'But here's the point. They had no reason to believe that Anastasia had recorded the plate number of the Mercedes and descriptions of them in her voicemails.

That means that, once they left the scene of the crime, they were free to use their phones without risk of being associated with the crime. And yet you say they haven't made any calls to their families, even though one of them is expected at a big family event tomorrow. Seems odd, does it not?'

Zillah Dee looked at him while he was saying this and nodded slowly, but it was the nameless CIA agent, a crisply dressed young man in tinted spectacles, who spoke next.

'Have you asked for satellite imagery? It was a clear day down here, as I understand it. Shouldn't be a problem in making an application to our folks – you can do it through me and I will source the material.'

The kidnap specialist, Dr Fabiano, had said nothing so far. He occasionally made the odd gesture of frustration but had kept his own counsel until the colonel suggested that the investigation was going as well as could be expected at this stage. Fabiano then raised his head and spoke in Italian for a minute or two, then summarised for the room in English. 'They have nothing, *signori*. They are at zero and so are we.'

Samson couldn't disagree with that. Later, when they were outside, he asked Zillah how she planned to prod the Carabinieri into action. 'I'll go through the embassy, but that's kind of hard with Mr Hisami in jail. News of his arrest has just broken and the broadcast media has picked up the online gossip of two nights ago that he used his military training to rescue some hostages in the Balkans.'

'I wasn't aware of that story being used,' said Samson.

'Right, but I guess you knew about it anyway,' she said,

without any kind of inflection. 'You and his wife were both there. People know. Things like that tend to have currency.'

'Maybe we need to focus on the American end of this thing,' he said.

'Yes. By the way, you were right to ask about the phones. Seems like the absence of calls from those men could be really significant. I will ask about satellite . . . we could use some confirmation of what happened out there.'

Early the next day, Samson left the town to visit the place he had imagined so clearly when listening to the two voicemails Anastasia had left for Hisami. There was nothing else he could do. There were no leads to follow and any attempt to talk to the Naples Mafia would be utterly pointless. Whatever the Carabinieri's lack of progress, they were the only ones with sources in the Camorra high enough to make any sense of their involvement.

He needed to start at the place where it had all begun, and this he would admit to no one. He wanted to be where she had been on that unexceptional stretch of road and see what she had seen before she gave herself up to save the life of the man who had betrayed her. He passed through the outskirts of the town, noticing several M5S posters calling for an Italy for the Italians and demanding the deportation of 600,000 migrants. He ignored two calls from Zillah, which followed a text from her earlier asking him to keep her informed of his movements.

As he climbed into the hills, he saw a sign to Spiadino, the village Anastasia had been due to visit, and decided that he would pay a call on her colleagues after seeing the road. It seemed possible that someone in the Foundation, either in Sicily or Calabria, had informed the kidnappers of Anastasia's movements. He needed to talk to the man Ciccone.

There was no police tape marking the scene of two murders and a kidnap. He found the exact spot only after noticing the slash of orange-coloured rock Anastasia had mentioned where the road had been blasted through the mountains and then the residue of paintwork from her car on some boulders. All trace of the tracks in the dirt had been eliminated by the police vehicles.

He parked where the road was wider a little further down the hill and walked back to the boulders in the extraordinary silence of the mountains. There, he crouched and turned. She must have leapt from the car, made straight for the short length of two-rail crash barrier and headed down to the cover, seventy metres away. He stepped over the barrier. Three footprints were still visible in the sand before the slope turned into rubble and waste. They were made by a small shoe and were almost certainly Anastasia's. He let himself down the slope by holding on to a cable, walked through the dead weeds towards the trees and entered the shade. This must be where the calls had been made from, but there was no sign of her having been there in the carpet of dead leaves. He looked up towards the road. It was hard to see anything unless you were on the ground. He knelt down then moved to the right to work out where the first victim's body had been pushed over the edge, at a spot where there was no crash barrier. He sat back on his haunches and looked around. Nothing moved. There wasn't even the birdsong that could be heard on her voicemails.

Below him the vegetation was much denser and lusher. In the shade were some large plants with big, fleshy leaves. If she had gone just a little further down, they would never have found her. He walked towards the plants and noticed it was muddy – water oozed under his feet – and a few metres on there was a small stream. Remembering that in one of the reports sent to Zillah before they arrived in Italy there was mention that the second body had been in a culvert and hard to retrieve, he parted the vegetation and followed the tiny watercourse back up the slope until he found a metre-wide crack in the limestone rock, not obvious until you were on top of it. He looked up. It was just possible that a man shot while fleeing for his life would end up there. Then he noticed strands of rope on the side of the crack, which might indicate that the police had hauled the body up from the crevice. He lowered himself into the dark space and was surprised to discover how deep it was and, once he'd got to the bottom, how wide. Using the light from his phone he searched the silt either side of the tiny stream and found the impression made by the body, also the footprints left by the officers who had presumably secured the body before raising it into the daylight. There was nothing more to be found, so he began to climb, having picked out the holds before he left the ground. The rock crumbled in his hands but he moved quickly from one hold to another until he was nearly at the top, when, pausing for breath, he noticed something flat and grey caught on the edge about a metre to his left. He shifted and reached for the object. It was a phone. It must have either fallen from the victim's body as it crashed to its resting place or dropped from his pocket as the police officers brought him out of the crevice. He slid it into his back pocket and continued to climb.

At the top, he scrambled over the limestone lip, grazing his stomach a little, then jumped up. The phone had run out of power and there was no way of telling what was on it, and he knew that the charger brought for his own collection of phones wouldn't work. He looked around some more, particularly on the bank she must have climbed, but soon realised that the place held nothing more for him. He got back into the car and headed for the village, the phone beside him on the passenger seat.

Spiadino was a pretty hill-top town that was abandoned at the edges, with many houses deserted and falling down, but evidently thriving in the centre. He parked his car in the main square, in the shadow of a run-down seventeenth-century church that reminded him of the empty Venetian churches he had toured with Anastasia.

The Aysel Hisami Therapy Centre was just off the square, in a renovated building that once belonged to the Partito Communista and still bore slogans in relief on the façade. A woman with a pile of braided hair was crocheting at the reception. He said George Ciccone's name and gave his own, then, guessing she was West African, continued in French. He was with a client, she replied with a radiant smile, and would not be available for half an hour. There was a café on the piazza and he could wait there. As he turned to leave, he slapped his forehead and asked, '*Mademoiselle, avez-vous des chargeurs pour les téléphones mobiles?*'

'*Bien sûr, monsieur.*' She lifted a plastic container full of chargers. '*Pour tous les modèles de téléphones.*'

He found one that fitted and asked where he could plug it in.

She pointed to a locked cabinet behind the desk. '*Les clients ne sont pas autorisés à conserver les téléphones pendant leur traitement.*' She opened the cabinet and he saw three phones on charge inside. He handed her the phone.

It was a while since he had smoked but, sitting in the brilliant light of the piazza, with a good coffee, he felt the need of a cigarette. In Venice, they had started smoking a cigarette after dinner every evening and it became a thing with them, smoking out of the window after sex or at the back of Cedar after eating. They never talked in these moments and regarded each other with amusement and, it had to be said, some wariness. It was all part of the silent struggle between them, which, with hindsight, he suspected he had been losing from those first days in Venice.

The waiter gave him a cigarette and proffered an old-fashioned Pearl lighter. 'Where's everyone?' Samson asked in English. It turned out there were workshops producing pottery, leather goods, glass and lampshades on the outskirts of the town. Spiadino had more or less full employment now, plus a choir of twenty, two football teams and a dance group. People were making a great life there. The native townspeople loved the *minestrone* of different cultures and said the annual celebration of Ferragosto had been the best for fifty years. Yet populist politicians were now implementing harsh new policies on migrants and they might all soon face deportation.

A man in sunglasses, tracksuit bottoms, a T-shirt and trainers materialised in front of him. 'Hi, I'm George. Is there any news?'

Samson got up and shook his hand. 'I am afraid not.'

Ciccone sat down and nodded to the waiter for his usual. 'Forgive my appearance – we have soccer training at midday. So, what happens? How does this go?'

'We have to find out why she was abducted. That's the first step.'

'Isn't it just for money?'

'Nothing's been heard from the kidnappers.'

He looked at him intensely. 'You're the man . . . I've seen you before – in Lesbos, in the harbour café one night. You came along and dragged Anastasia from our table to ask about the Syrian kid, remember?' Samson nodded, but he didn't remember Ciccone. 'I worked on her team in one of the camps on the island.' He removed his sunglasses. 'Can I ask you in what capacity you're here? As I recall, you and Anastasia had a relationship.'

'I'm here to find her. I'm working for her husband. Finding people is my job.'

'And you expect to do this without getting emotionally involved?'

'I'll try.'

'I hope so. She's a great woman and she has done immense

good here, and at other places. This centre is turning people's lives around in a way that even I did not believe possible. You look around this town. People seem happy, and that's because they are safe and have a roof over their heads. But they carry dreadful burdens inside, experiences that you and I cannot imagine. They now have the prospect of happiness – or, should I say, a regular life? – because of the therapy we offer them.' He leaned forward. 'You know – we love her. Everyone does. She's taught us all to listen, and I mean really *listen*.'

Samson nodded. This was the part of her life that she had always kept separate from him. He was the entertainment – the distraction – and she rarely talked about her work.

'These two men who tricked her into stopping on the road, did you know them?' he asked.

Ciccone shook his head. 'No.'

'Were you expecting them to join the community in the village?'

'No, and anyway, that's not my job. I run the Aysel centre – that's all.'

'When did you hear that she was coming here?'

'It was my idea. I mentioned it in a call about three or four days before she was taken. I told her about some of the successes we've had and I really wanted her to come. There was a village dinner that night and I thought she would enjoy it. A lot of this is my fault.' He dragged his hand through his hair and looked away across the square.

'But she was expecting to be here for the day only. She had a flight from Brindisi that evening.'

'We were hoping to persuade her to stay,' he said, still with his eyes on the far side of the square. 'I mentioned it to her, and I knew she would. I feel really bad about this. If I hadn't asked her to come, none of this would have happened.'

'You shouldn't feel bad. They would have tried to seize her somewhere else.'

'What the fuck is this about, Mr Samson? I mean, who'd want to kidnap her?'

'We have to think about the feeling against migrants. Do you have any trouble with that here? Any extremist activity?'

'A few incidents – young men driving into town, causing trouble, threatening the women. It was unpleasant, but the community is solid and the majority of the Italian folk love what has been happening here, so the extremists are told to get lost. Local people feel proud of the sanctuary that's been created in Spiadino.'

'Did she encounter any problems in Sicily that she told you about?'

'No, I just asked her to bring the damned car and she was a bit worried about finding her way here.'

'Who knew about these arrangements – anyone here, for example?'

'Just me. I didn't tell anyone because I wasn't sure she was going to make it. At the other end, in Sicily, there would have been more people who knew, maybe five or six employees of the centre.'

Samson's gaze lifted to some brightly coloured hangings that were draped from the first-floor windows of three old buildings. Below these were two children waving a wand that sent a stream of bubbles across the square. Two dogs played in the shadow of the church and an ancient Italian man sat in the shade of the only tree, hands folded on top of his cane. Spiadino was peaceful. Anastasia would have liked it.

'The banners are stunning, aren't they?' said Ciccone. 'That building there has been restored and houses single female migrants. The banners give thanks to the town.'

'When she called you from the road, what did you do?' asked Samson.

'I phoned the Carabinieri and then called again repeatedly because they weren't taking me seriously. Then I had the town's mayor call them and he got a better response, but it took a long time. Eventually, I phoned Denis's office, but by that time they already knew.' He paused as an espresso with a side of milk was set down. 'It must be awful for Denis, and I guess it can't have been easy for him to call on your services.'

There was an edge in Ciccone's voice that suggested possessiveness about Anastasia. Samson guessed he was being cast as the disreputable ex-lover, summoned as a last resort. 'Denis employed me to look for Aysel in Northern Iraq and Syria,' he said quietly, 'the woman your organisation is named after.'

'I didn't mean . . .'

'That's okay, Mr Ciccone. But I want you to know I'm not here as a concerned friend. I have a job to do – you understand? How did you discuss her arrangements – phone, text or email?'

'We spoke on the phone. The broadband is really unreliable in the town.'

'Anyone overhear you?'

'No, I was in my office.'

Samson watched a familiar BMW enter the square and pull up next to his by the church. Zillah Dee got out with one of the men working for her. She spotted him and made for their table.

'And this must be Mr Ciccone. Hello, sir,' she said, offering a hand. 'Zillah Dee, we spoke on the phone. Look, I need a word with Mr Samson. Would you mind?'

Ciccone sat back and downed the coffee. 'Sure.'

They walked into the centre of the piazza, where Zillah stopped and turned to him. 'A body has been recovered in the southern Adriatic by an Italian naval vessel that was heading to Brindisi.' Samson's heart turned over. 'The body was of a male. There was a slip of paper in the back pocket of his pants that suggested the victim was Italian – a receipt for gas bought at the beginning of the week.

'And?'

'The man had been shot in the back of the head. The paper was photographed and sent to the Carabinieri, who checked out the receipt. It was Niccolo Scorza's debit card, one of the two men who kidnapped Mrs Hisami.'

Samson searched her eyes. 'What the hell does that mean?'

'That we are dealing with people who are prepared to eliminate every witness to the kidnap. We must assume that Bucco is at the bottom of the ocean. There were signs that Scorza's body was weighted because a small length of chain was attached to his legs. The weight must have come free when he was dumped. The ship that picked up the body is about to dock at Brindisi, and DNA tests will establish whether it is in fact Scorza. But it seems very likely that it is.'

'How far out was he found?'

'About a hundred and seventy miles due south of the heel of Italy, near Greek waters.'

'Why so far? You don't need to take a body a hundred and seventy miles to dispose of it.'

'Maybe he was alive for a good part of that journey.'

Samson thought. 'This isn't sounding good.'

'None of it's good. Look, Samson, you should have told me you were coming out here to interview Ciccone.'

'Yes, I should have. Sorry. Was there any reason that the Camorra wanted their own men dead? Were they using people who they knew were expendable?'

'The Carabinieri are investigating that line. Now I have some questions for Mr Ciccone, so . . .'

She walked back to the café and Samson returned to the centre to retrieve the phone. Without looking up, the receptionist said. '*Vous avez beaucoup de messages, Monsieur. Le téléphone n'a pas arrêté de cingler.*' Alerts on the phone hadn't stopped sounding. She unlocked the cabinet and fanned her face, as though the phone were hot from activity.

He took it and saw the messages and missed calls listed on the screen. If the phone hadn't still been attached to the charger, he would have dropped it. The missed calls and texts were all from Hisami – this was Anastasia's phone! He checked on his own phone, where he had a copy of the final voicemail, and listened intently to the end of the recording – the moment when she murmured something and her voice became muffled, followed by rustling and the sounds of shots before the call ended. She must have handed the phone to Louis or maybe placed it in his pocket, which was why it had fallen with his body into the crevice, where, of course, there was no reception. That's why the messages and log of missed calls had come through on the phone only once it was charged.

Having unplugged the phone, Samson sat down on one of the chairs, a little shocked. The receptionist shot him a confidential look from over the counter and whispered, '*Vous pouvez garder le chargeur si vous voulez. Nous en avons plusieurs comme celui-là.*' He replied that it would be very helpful to keep the charger since they had so many and thanked her.

He bent over the phone and pressed the home button so the screen illuminated again. This surely couldn't be the same phone she'd had when they were together! He had never taken much notice, so he couldn't tell, but he remembered sitting at the restaurant on the Giudecca and her resetting her password because another device had been hacked. Yes, she said she would make it his birthday so she would never forget it – 09/10. It seemed unlikely that she hadn't changed it by now, but he tapped 0910 gently into the keyboard. A photo of Denis Hisami in tennis shorts and a white cap appeared, with a small dog under his arm.

CHAPTER 11

In prison jumpsuit and loafers, Hisami waited in the interview room of the Daniel Patrick Moynihan US Courthouse for Tulliver and his lawyer, Sam Castell. Detention was nothing new to him. As a young commander, he had been held twice by the Iraqis, both times in circumstances where his captors had no idea who he was or what he did. On the second occasion he escaped before they found out, bludgeoning two guards into unconsciousness, yet for the time he was detained he'd entered a sort of torpor, reducing his metabolic rate and banishing anxiety until his opportunity arrived.

This incarceration was much tougher. In effect, he had been placed in a kind of quarantine that meant that he could take no action to save his business empire and his wife, and now the judge had just denied him his liberty on the grounds that he might be declared an illegal alien and ICE would need to instigate an immediate deportation order.

The team put together by Sam Castell under immigration-law

expert Marcus Phinney argued that there was no substance to allegations that Hisami had lied on his immigration form; that there was no credible evidence he had ever been a part of a terrorist group – on the contrary, he was once a heroic young commander with forces that had been America's allies; and that he wasn't going anywhere, because business deals were in play; plus, he had responsibilities to his investors and the numerous charities that relied on him. Denis Hisami had made his home in the United States, implored Marcus Phinney, and created wealth and many thousands of jobs. This was no way to treat a leading member of the Bay Area community who was doing so much to improve the lives of his fellow Americans.

Conceding all this to be true, the judge had looked over her glasses and addressed Hisami. 'I am afraid, sir, that you will have to spend at least another week in the Metropolitan Correctional Center while the other side assembles its case.' She shook her head when Phinney asked her to consider an ankle monitor and house arrest. 'Mr Hisami, if minded, has the means to do anything he wants, Mr Phinney. Once a terrorist connection has been mentioned, I have no choice.'

There were now fifteen minutes before Hisami was due to be returned to the hellhole of the prison a few blocks away. Tulliver and Sam Castell arrived and told him about developments on the legal side, and about the TangKi board meeting, where his allegations had been raised but more or less dismissed. Hisami listened intently but did not react. There was only one question in his mind. If Crane was dead, who was working the levers? Who had the power and the necessary information about his past to engineer his investigation by the immigration authorities? One of the men in the room who had been with him in Castell's office was responsible, but there was no clue in the investigation he had done on the company as to which of them was Crane's collaborator. He also had to consider that this individual was not merely Crane's wingman but the principal actor, and that this man knew he would be paralysed, even if released, to take any action on TangKi. If Hisami were to use any of the mass of information he had accumulated, this man would ensure Anastasia's death. There had been communications from the kidnappers, and he knew that was the tacit message when she was taken as the meeting in Castell's office began.

No one could know he had been contacted, and that would remain the case as long as Anastasia was held. His silence was probably her only chance of survival, although he was a little relieved that Samson had agreed to work alongside Zillah Dee and thought that combination might just produce results. But then, as they sat there in the interview room, Tulliver received a text message to the effect that the body dragged from the Adriatic was definitely that of one of the kidnappers. Hisami was silent for a few seconds. 'That obviously means she is no longer in Italy,' he said eventually. 'It eliminates the idea that it was for ransom.'

'Zillah reached that conclusion,' said Tulliver.

Castell chose this moment to intervene. 'Can I ask you something, Denis? These people are coming at you from all sides, and they're really getting to you. You got the US government bearing down on you with all its might, the media too. They've put your ass in jail, investors are threatening to pull out of projects you've worked on for years, and they may've taken your wife as a hostage. Why don't you quit pissing off everyone at TangKi, sell your stock and step away?'

'Sam, you should know me better than to ask that,' Hisami replied. 'Besides, it's not that simple. Do you think I'd risk my wife's safety for some principle at TangKi? We're in a situation here which is like a trap – the more I struggle, the tighter I'm held.' He fixed Castell with his eyes, as if willing him to understand. 'You do get this, Sam?'

'Yes, but it's really hard to represent you if I don't have the full picture. I need to know why you're behaving like this. Why don't you just quit?'

'Because it won't make any difference.' Hisami got up. His black loafers looked ridiculous with the orange prison suit. He placed both his hands on Castell's shoulders. 'Sam, all you have to do is find a way of getting me out of jail. Forget TangKi. Forget the board. Just get me out of here. Then at least I'll have some options.'

Castell moved to the door. 'I will get you out, Denis, even if I have to call in every political favour.'

'Be careful who you ask for help – check with Jim.'

Castell shrugged and was gone.

'Have you got my phone?' he said to Tulliver.

Hisami began to go through his emails, dictating replies to Tulliver, who recorded them on his own phone.

In the space of ten minutes, they dealt with the investigation of the missing money, Crane's murder, the back-up finance for a deal with the purchase of a biotech start-up and the response to media requests for information on Hisami's youth and period with the PKK.

Suddenly, Hisami stopped and grabbed Tulliver's forearm. 'Jim, Anastasia's sent an email.' He read it again. 'It's from someone else's account, which explains why I didn't notice it. She's on a ship headed for Odessa . . . or Burgas. She's got one of the crew to send an email to me . . . ship's name appears to be *Black Sea Star* . . . held in container . . . now free and is in hiding.' He handed Tulliver the phone. Tulliver read the email, which was poorly spelled and littered with random characters. Immediately, he phoned Zillah and read it out.

Hisami took the phone back. 'You need to move quickly – looks like this was sent at least twenty hours ago. She may already have reached the Black Sea. The body likely came from the ship, so they have a reason to arrest the captain and search the ship.'

Two large prison guards opened the door and beckoned to Hisami. He handed the phone to Tulliver. 'Find a way of getting me news.'

'Should I have access to your email?'

'Can't do that, Jim. Just not possible.'

'But what if she sends another email?'

Hisami was aware of the sense of what Tulliver was saying but he simply couldn't risk anyone seeing his emails and wished he could explain to Tulliver. 'Just get me out,' he said quietly. 'Do anything! But watch Castell. He's a hothead.'

★

Samson parked on a stony track off the coastal road where there was good mobile-phone coverage and sent the film from Anastasia's phone to Zillah Dee and Fenarelli's team at Carabinieri headquarters. He didn't drive off immediately but watched the footage again. She had held the phone remarkably still as she emerged from the trees and scaled the slope towards the road. And once on the road, she had walked so slowly that the two men and the quaking migrant were clearly visible. Then she jinked to her right and a second later the video ended. But the audio continued, as it had on the voicemail, with the microphone recording the sound of the man running, gun shots and a succession of impacts as he tumbled into the crevice.

He got out and walked away from the car, thinking about Anastasia and what it took for her to risk her own safety with such a slight chance of saving that man's life. An old woman, working in the field nearby, a huge basket of tomatoes beside her, said good afternoon. Samson raised a hand to her and smiled. Yes, he thought, Anastasia wanted a larger, more meaningful life than he could ever offer her, and she was probably right. Many in her position would have simply acquired the billionaire's lifestyle but she had used it to create something heroic and useful, and she cared enough about each individual's life to sacrifice herself on that road.

Zillah called him. 'This film is from her phone? Why didn't you tell me you had it when we saw each other?'

'I didn't know until I charged the phone. I thought it belonged to the second victim, Louis. She slipped it to him before he ran.'

'Where are you now?'

'On the way back to the hotel. I left a note on your car. I looked for you and both your numbers were busy. She took a lot of film – it's all there.'

'You've got access to the phone! How?'

'It doesn't matter – there are clear pictures of the two kidnappers.'

'Samson, I'm afraid that's not as important as it was. Anastasia escaped and managed to fire off an email to Denis. She's on a boat headed to the Black Sea. We're trying to get an interception in international waters. The Israelis have a naval vessel in that area, but we're probably too late. We're taking the plane there. Jonathan, Pete and I are on the way to the airport now. Sorry, we can't wait for you.'

'Understood. Let me know where and when you land and I'll find a way of joining you.'

He looked up the flights on his phone. There was no direct service from Naples to Odessa. He would have a ten-hour journey via Vienna and that flight wouldn't leave Naples until noon the next day. Hendricks Harp made the booking for him. He set off for the hotel, having left a message for Macy to call him.

When he arrived, he took a beer on to his balcony, which faced not out to sea but inland to the mountains, a hazy blue in the late-afternoon light and threaded with the smoke of autumn bonfires. The town came to life in the streets below him with the whine of mopeds and young Italians calling out to each other. He took out Anastasia's phone and began to go through the photo album. The most recent images were from Italy and had plainly been taken for professional reasons, or possibly to show Hisami the work that half a dozen Aysel centres across Southern Europe were doing. There were offices and therapy rooms, staff meetings and several groups of people in T-shirts bearing the organisation's logo and a run of photographs from a voyage on a rescue boat in the southern Mediterranean.

He found more evidence of her commitment further back, a big fundraiser at a San Francisco hotel for the Foundation and visits to Europe. He flashed through the months, pausing to look at a series with Hisami, who seemed rarely to be without papers or a laptop in front of him, even when they were at their pool or tennis court. This was an album with a few friends and no evidence of family on either side, although it was lightened by Anastasia's obsession with garden flowers, close-ups of which there were many, and the arrival of a puppy. Hisami was seen lying in the grass, the puppy asleep on his chest and a cocktail beside him.

He found the photographs of Venice, about three dozen of them, starting with shots from the *Maria Redan* as they chugged into the lagoon. But they weren't just of the city. There were some of him, lying on the bed in the hotel, gazing from the window, shivering in a gondola, and in one of the grand cafés on the main square drinking brandy, none of which he knew she had taken. There were a couple of them together in the cloister of a monastery, which he recalled being posed for by her friend Gianni. She wore sunglasses and the coat she'd bought at an expensive store. She insisted that if you see something that's truly perfect for you, it's imperative to get it, no matter what the expense. His eye was still puffy from the beating he had received in Macedonia and he looked tired yet also happy, so much so that he almost didn't recognise himself. There was nothing from the rest of their time together except one of his mother in profile sitting in the filtered light of her kitchen in her flat. It showed that Anastasia had an eye for composition, and he made a note to forward the photograph to himself at some stage.

Had Denis seen all the evidence of their closeness, he wondered, and why hadn't Anastasia deleted the record of those few days in Venice? Their infatuation was plain to see. Maybe she hadn't forgotten that time altogether. Perhaps she'd scrolled through them smiling, as he had just found himself doing. He closed the album and moved to search the email account.

Starting with recent emails she'd received, he found a timeline of her arrangements in Italy, the five days at sea with the rescue boat and the four days divided between the two centres in Sicily where migrants were offered emergency psychotherapy. It was easy to distil the information because Anastasia always wrote sparingly and to the point. He got a good idea of the last fourteen days, but there was nothing that was going to help him, no chance encounters, nothing out of the ordinary.

He moved to the emails in her 'Sent' file and found little to interest him except a recent one to her husband, whom she addressed as 'Hash'. This was confirming her return date, which she had broken. She added that they would talk everything through when she got back. He put Hisami's address into the search bar of sent emails and found dozens, again mostly discussing their schedules, but there were two longer ones from the previous year when she was in Germany and had visited Naji's family for a second time – this time without Samson. He noted that Naji hadn't mentioned this to him. She was concerned about an issue that she didn't specify.

'What's the problem with backing off, Hash?' she wrote. 'These people – whoever they are – have the power to hurt you. And to what end? What are you going to gain? Why don't you let it go? It's not important to your life. And it's not important to *our* life, and yet this thing is taking us over. That is REALLY unlike you, Hash. You've always got the big picture in front of you, which is why I love and admire you. I know you have to win, but is this worth your time? Do you really want them to dig up all those things in your past? I don't know much – I guess that's for a reason. But you are a fine and good man, and the therapy centres are doing great work. Why don't you move on? As ever, all my love, A.'

Her second email on this subject included his reply, which Samson read first.

'Ana, what you say is right, but I took a legitimate stake in this company and built my investment, while offering support to the management. So, yes, I feel really sore about their treatment of me. I will consider what you ask.'

Anastasia's reply thanked him profusely and referred to the phone call they'd had since she received the email. Apparently, they kept missing each other because of the time difference between the West Coast and Germany.

'It was lovely to speak just now, and I was so touched that you would consider this for me. You must know I hold you in great esteem and that I value your wisdom and intelligence above all things. You spoke of calling out the corruption, but why is that for you to do? Why not leave it to the authorities? This is your world. I guess you know best, but I want to understand why you're doing this. It's crazy to take them on.'

It was like overhearing a rather formal marital spat in the next room. There was respect between them and she expressed admiration for him, but there was no sign of passion, or of Anastasia's humour. When she and Samson were together, they'd laughed and fooled around and teased each other remorselessly, but this seemed more like a business partnership, where the parties were bound by a memorandum of understanding. Is that what she had left him for? She wanted to influence her world for the better and Hisami's money and connections gave her that, but did she really have to accept bloodless formality? But this was all incidental to the revelation that Hisami was hell-bent on 'calling out the corruption' at the new company, which must be TangKi.

He finished the beer and rose. It was nearly two hours since Zillah had taken off. She must be at Odessa by now, if that was where the container vessel was bound. He'd call once he had got his things together and was on the road to Naples – anything was better than sitting in the hotel. There was activity in the street as two cars drew up, some catcalls from loitering kids. He popped his head over the parapet. Two cars of Carabinieri had arrived. Fenarelli got out of one. Samson drew back, switched off Anastasia's phone and left the room. A little way down the hall there was a picture with a heavy frame – a nineteenth-century study of a mountain shepherd's hut in fake gilt. He pulled the picture a few centimetres from the wall, slipped the phone into the gap behind the canvas and let the picture fall back.

Fenarelli and two uniformed officers had taken the first flight when he bumped into them, ostensibly looking for the bar. They went back down to the lobby, where Fenarelli put his hands together. 'The phone, *signore* – the phone you found at the crime scene. This is evidence and you must give it to me now.'

Samson looked puzzled. 'Ms Dee has it. As you must know, Mrs Hisami was taken out of Italy on a boat and Ms Dee is on a plane to Ukraine. She said she was going to send you the film. Has she not done that?'

'Yes, but we need the phone.'

Samson smiled politely. 'You misunderstand me, sir. Zillah Dee has it.'

'Why did you give it to her?'

'Because she's running the investigation for Mr Hisami and insisted the phone was the property of the family. How could I argue with that?'

'I am sorry, but we will have to search your room, Mr Samson.'

Samson appeared offended but handed Fenarelli the keys.

They waited awkwardly while the men were upstairs. At length, Samson said, 'Why's the phone so important? That part of the story is dead.'

Fenarelli turned to him. 'The crime was committed on Italian soil. This is a very serious affair. We are investigating three, maybe four, murders and one kidnap. We want to know who the men were working for and why they were eliminated.'

'You have the film – there's nothing else. I looked through the phone before Ms Dee took it from me.' Fenarelli glanced at the receptionist and suggested they move to a room overlooking the street, where a fat young boy sprawled in a chair between fake pot plants. Fenarelli said, '*Perdersi, ragazzino*' – 'Get lost, kid.'

'There's one thing I don't understand, Colonel,' said Samson. 'Did the Camorra sacrifice these two men, or were they double-crossed?'

Fenarelli studied him, deciding how far he should go. 'We believe this was a contract, *signore*. These men, Scorza and Bucco, they were offered €100,000 each and the organisation more than $1 million.'

'You say dollars – did this money come from the States?'

Fenarelli just looked at Samson, which was as good as a yes.

'So you have a source in the organisation and they told you this, right? You do know that her trip to Italy was only planned just sixteen days ago when she got confirmation on a place in the migrant rescue ship. Only four people knew where she was.'

'The contract was issued even more recently.'

'After she arrived here in Italy?'

He nodded slowly.

'That's a hell of an operation to put together so fast. The boat is headed for the Black Sea, but the money came from America. Does that make sense to you?'

'It does not.'

Samson returned to the subject of the kidnappers. 'Did the Camorra know their people were going to be killed? That's important, right? I mean, if they didn't know, we're dealing with someone who is not afraid of a major international crime organisation.'

Fenarelli didn't answer. His attention had turned to his officers in the lobby. One shook his head. He turned to Samson. 'I need to see what you are carrying with you, *signore*. I'm sorry.'

'I have two phones – both are mine. You can check by dialling the numbers.' He pulled out two Samsungs, his wallet and passport.

Fenarelli glanced at them and shook his head. 'Not her model, *signore*. But we need to check the car.'

'It's the Audi right outside,' said Samson, handing the fob to Fenarelli, who tossed it to one of his officers.

'I came because I wanted to see you personally and ask you something.'

'Go ahead.'

'This investigation started in Italy, but it will not end here. Perhaps you will keep me informed of developments? It will be helpful to me personally, you understand.' Samson understood perfectly. Fenarelli was ambitious and knowledge was the way to the top.

'I have no problem with that. None at all.'

The officers returned, having found nothing in the Audi. Fenarelli offered his hand to Samson.

'You have my card?' Samson nodded. 'Good luck. I appreciate it is important for you personally to find Mrs Hisami.'

He was letting Samson know that he was well informed and was not the average provincial commander in the Carabinieri.

CHAPTER 12

In that moment when they found her and men were scrambling up the stack of containers to seize hold of her, she had no thought for her own safety. She had jumped up and used the length of wood against the men, hammering their hands as they clung to the side of the container, swinging at them as they crawled towards her and connecting with one man's head, sending him toppling unconscious to the container below. She'd fought hard to suppress the aggression her father had warned her about, to the point that she was always known among colleagues as the calmest person in the room. But now, overwhelmed by a blind rage, she didn't give a damn about her safety or who she hurt, and as she was backed into a corner she yelled out that she would kill with the knife the first man who laid hands on her. It was clear they had understood her and they backed off. Then a voice speaking in English hailed her from below, the same voice she had heard on the PA system.

'You cannot escape. There's no place for you to hide. Come down. You will be treated well.'

This confirmed what she had suspected since she'd found the dead kidnappers lying in the dark of the container with her. They were prepared to kill as many people as was necessary, but they needed her alive. She had value. She felt the gap between the two highest containers to her right, stuffed the wooden bat into the jacket and the knife into the pocket, then slipped between the containers and shimmied up between them with the skill she had perfected over the previous thirty-six hours. The three men on top of the container lunged after her, but she was too quick for them and in no time at all was standing on the topmost container against the full force of the wind. She looked over the edge and called down, 'I'll kill myself, then what have you got?'

'There is no point.'

'There is to me!' she yelled wildly. 'I will never allow you to take me prisoner again. Do you understand? Never!' Some part of her knew this was untrue, for she wanted very much to survive, but she could not go back into the dark of the container.

'We can work this out. What do you want?' came the voice, now through a loudhailer.

'A shower, food, light.' This, too, was hopelessly unrealistic. The ship's crew had already dumped two murdered men in the ocean. They were hardly going to give her a shower and a hot meal.

She kept her captors at bay by threatening to run across the containers and jump into the sea, so the stand-off continued for an hour or more, until dawn, when she noticed clusters of lights in the distance either side of the bow of the ship. She had seen this view before, when she was a child, and realised they were approaching the Dardanelles and these were the lights of Asia and Europe converging on the straits through which they would pass into the Sea of Marmara. Lights meant mobile-phone coverage. Now she had a chance. She took the phone out and frantically began to dial, but in her panic couldn't recall Denis's number. She went back into the phone's log to find the numbers she had dialled as they slipped past the island earlier, but these didn't work either. Then the fog cleared and she managed to dial the right number. She got through and the call went straight to voicemail. She didn't need his fucking voicemail. She wanted her husband on the other end telling her what she should do and ready to organise her rescue. She left a crazy, incoherent message, hung up and crouched, knowing that the crew would soon reach her. Then she dialled a number she was absolutely certain of and, after three rings, the call was answered.

Samson had driven the four and a half hours to Naples International Airport the evening before and parked in front of the terminal. Early next morning, unable to sleep he had gone in search of coffee and was now waiting outside the terminal on a bench, smoking a cigarette and trying to get hold of Zillah Dee when one of his phones started to vibrate. He took it out and answered.

'Samson, it's me,' Anastasia said. 'I'm on a boat . . . we're going through the Dardanelles . . . the boat is called the *Black Sea Star* . . . you got that?'

He suppressed his astonishment. 'Where are you now?'

'I'm on top of a container . . . they're about to lock me up again . . . you've got to get me off this fucking ship . . . please . . . I can't do it any more . . . please.'

'We're sending people. Which port are you going to – Odessa, Burgas? Which port?'

'Don't know. You have to track the ship. Get it searched.' And then she began to break down. This was anger rather than self-pity or fear and he told her calmly to keep talking to him. How big was the boat? Where was she, exactly? What could she see? Who were they? Russian? Ukrainian? She answered as best she could but kept on losing her voice. She was speaking in gasps, breathing rapidly.

'Listen, Anastasia,' he said. 'There are people looking for that boat now. They are coming to find you. Whatever happens, I promise I'll free you. I promise. Do you understand? I will find you wherever you are, no matter what it takes. I *will* find you. Stay alive. I'm coming for you.' In the background there were sounds of men's voices and he sensed that she was about to be seized because the sobs of frustration and anger had stopped and her breathing had become more rapid. She uttered just three more words before the call dropped. 'Please, Samson! Please.' Then the line went dead. Samson was left with a phone in his hand, staring at the row of buses waiting for the early flights from the United States.

He dialled Zillah. 'She got hold of a phone. She just called.

She's entering the Dardanelles. Have you tracked the ship yet?'

'There's no trace of any vessel of that name.'

'Have you checked the ships leaving the ports of the eastern seaboard of Italy?'

'Doing that now.'

'We have an accurate position, so the ship could be intercepted any place from the Dardanelles through the Sea of Marmara and the Black Sea. How are you doing on that?'

'Not good – the Israelis won't play.'

'It's in Turkish waters – does that work?'

'I have to get through to DC, and it's late at night there. Can't get hold of anyone.'

'Where are you?'

'Odessa, but we're on the plane and we can take off when we need to.'

'We don't have long. That boat will head for Russian waters as soon as it reaches the Black Sea. I'm going to call Macy and see what he can do. I'll keep this phone free.'

He hung up and cursed himself for failing to give Zillah the number used by Anastasia. He wrote a text instead, which he sent to Macy as well.

Then he called Macy, who awoke after two rings and answered with his usual unflappable good nature. Samson told him about the call from the ship and his conversation with Zillah.

'I sent you a text. Can you get anyone at GCHQ to locate that number? It's from the phone Anastasia used on board. We can get an exact position for her. Maybe the phone is still on and we can track it.'

Macy murmured doubt about the speed with which this would have to be done. 'Okay, so what else do we need to do here?' he said. 'I'll find out if we have any naval assets in the area. There may be something we can do with NATO, but this will probably mean that the kidnapping is made public and with Denis in jail that will become a big story.'

Samson's other phone went. It was Zillah. He laid the phones side by side on the bench, wishing he'd had the sense to have these conversations in the car because of the background noise of the airport, and put them on speaker so Macy and Zillah could hear each other. 'We believe the vessel left Taranto container port six hours after her kidnap,' she said. 'It was once called *Black Sea Star* but was renamed CS *Grigori II* and it's registered to a Russian company.'

'Very hard to intercept a bloody Russian boat. NATO won't touch it,' said Macy.

'The Turkish government is a possibility,' said Zillah. 'It's just a question of getting to the right people in the States.'

'How long have we got?' asked Samson.

'The boat will head straight for Russian territorial waters once it enters the Black Sea – something like twelve to fifteen hours, maybe a little more. If they caught Mrs Hisami with the phone, they'll assume that her presence on board is known. That means she will be in much greater danger than she was – they may be tempted to dispose of her. If they keep her alive, they will likely go to great pains to conceal her presence. This is a goddamn big boat and there are a lot of places to hide a person.'

'I'll talk to my contacts here and try to get a trace on that phone,' said Macy. 'And you deal with the American side. By the way, does Denis know any of this?'

'He's in lockdown. He has no idea what's happening,' said Zillah.

'That seems harsh,' said Macy.

'Tulliver and Castell are up to date with all the developments. And one or other of them will see him today. But there's . . .' She stopped.

'What were you going to say?' asked Samson.

'Mr Hisami hasn't given Tulliver access to his phone, so even if Anastasia manages to send a message or makes a call, they'll miss it.'

Samson realised that she had failed to get through to Hisami and then called him, but was relieved that she had remembered his number. The call had left him with a sense of powerlessness – there was nothing he could do. He bent down to the pair of phones. 'There's no point me flying to Odessa until you've got news about the boat. I'll stay put until I hear from either of you. Just be in touch as soon as you can. Oh yes! Zillah, I was going to ask about the package I gave you?'

'I had it sent from Italy. Should be there by now, and the collection of the other materials was carried out yesterday. We're in good shape on that.'

She hung up and he was left with Macy on one line. 'Paul, I should warn you that Nyman was round here last night. SIS is obsessed by all this. They've got good relations with their Italian counterparts and the wires are fairly humming about Anastasia's abduction. Nyman's trying to work out the connection between Crane, Hisami and the kidnap.'

'Like we all are,' said Samson.

'Equally, he could be simply trying to find out how much you know. But this is plainly not a matter of only academic interest to them. I'm sure they're not just gathering intelligence for the hell of it.'

'What was he asking about?'

'He's particularly interested in the American end, and for some reason he can't get what he wants through his usual channels to the CIA and FBI. Of course, things aren't as easy as they used to be in that way.' Samson caught a note of regret and remembered that Macy loved America and revered its intelligence agencies, with whom he had worked on so many operations during the Cold War. Macy wasn't happy with the way things were going in the US, or anywhere else, for that matter. 'Keep your end up. I know this is rough for you, Paul,' he said.

'Thanks, old pal,' said Samson, and hung up. Things were back to normal between them.

He got in the car, which had begun to attract the attention of two traffic cops; it was parked illegally. He drove to the half-empty short-stay car park and found a place on the top storey where he wouldn't be disturbed. He climbed into the back seat and, using his backpack as a pillow and with a spare sweater draped over his shoulders, he crashed for an hour. When he woke he checked his phone for messages and emails but found nothing important, so lay back, sipping from a bottle of water and eating an energy bar he'd bought on the road. He kept Anastasia from his mind. Hearing her voice again, and hearing her in such distress, upset him profoundly, but he knew from searching for Aysel Hisami in Syria that nothing was gained by obsessively imagining the circumstances of the victim.

His eyes were closed when there was a tap on the window above his head. He snapped up and saw a man in a T-shirt and jacket beckoning to him. The man stepped away from the car and held his hands up so that Samson could see that they were empty. Samson got out using the far door to the man. There were five of them – two of them bodyguards with hands on guns in their waistbands, who stood a few metres away; one in a grey hoodie with a purplish birthmark that ran from the side of his nose to the middle of his left cheek, who stood apart; and a short man leaning against a Maserati Quattroporte that now blocked in Samson's car. He was smoking a cigarette using a tortoiseshell holder.

'Can I help you?' asked Samson, looking at the man who'd knocked on the window and seemed to be the person designated to speak.

'Signor Samson, this is the father-in-law of Salvatore Bucco.' He gestured to the man by the Maserati. The speaker was young, no more than thirty, and his voice was soft and lazy. 'He wants to speak with you, but he must do this through me because he does not have English.'

The Camorra had found Samson, and he had no doubt who

had told them where he was going to be – Colonel Fenarelli. But whether as payback for keeping Anastasia's phone from him, or simply as part of a hidden relationship between the Carabinieri and the Neapolitan underworld, Samson had no idea.

'Go ahead,' he said.

'Niccolo Scorza is dead. We believe that Salvatore has been murdered also.'

'A reasonable assumption, I'm afraid,' said Samson.

'Signor Esposito is afraid, too,' said their interpreter. 'He is afraid for his daughter and his two young grandchildren, and he is afraid for Salvatore, who is a good father and friend to us all.'

'I understand,' said Samson looking at Esposito. 'But there's very little I can do.'

The younger man translated for Esposito and there followed a few murmured sentences. 'Signor Esposito says you can lead him to the people responsible for this.'

Samson looked at him incredulously. 'Surely Mr Esposito knows much more about this thing than I do. Your organisation was paid to carry out the kidnap of an innocent charity worker. You know who paid you – I don't. You know who told you to take her to a container vessel named *Grigori* at Taranto – I don't. What can I tell you?'

'Nothing was said about killing our two friends.'

'Forgive me if I don't show a lot of sympathy,' said Samson slowly. 'Bucco and Scorza murdered two migrants on that road – executed them like dogs. Then they took Mrs Hisami, presumably drugged her, and put her in a container. Did they give a damn about what they were doing? Did they think of the suffering they would cause? No, because they were paid a lot of money. And now they wind up dead. I cannot help you.'

Esposito took his cigarette holder from his lips and held it about six inches from his face, squinting through the smoke. He was utterly unexceptional – jowly, thinning hair that was cropped short, bags under his eyes, a white shirt buttoned to the neck, a gold ring and bracelet. Except for the deadly, contemptuous expression in his eyes, there was very little to distinguish him from a cab driver in any European city. He spoke a few more sentences then replaced the cigarette holder between his lips and puffed.

'Signor Esposito wonders why you have this attitude. He is suggesting an exchange of information – that is all. He does not threaten you. He wants only to help you.'

'What information does he want from me?'

'He says you do not have it now, but that you will have it soon.'

'And what will he give me in exchange?'

'He is going to tell you how to find the people responsible for your girlfriend's kidnap.' He smiled. 'You see, we know a lot about you, Signor Samson.'

'You talked to Fenarelli, right? I guess you also know that I'm employed by Mr Hisami to find his wife.' His anger was rising, partly from lack of sleep but mostly from the revulsion he felt for these men. 'You people organised the kidnapping and now you come to me complaining that your friends are dead. Why would I trust any information that you give me? Why would I feel any need to help you?'

Esposito made an impatient motion to his interpreter, who handed him an envelope. 'He gives you this and asks you to look at it now.'

Samson opened the envelope and pulled out a picture of Adam Crane and the copy of an electronic transfer form for €2.2 million made out to a construction company called Arco di Ferro Cavallo in Turin and paid by Valge Kuubik, apparently an engineering firm based in Tallinn, Estonia.

'You know this man?' asked the interpreter.

Samson shook his head. He wasn't going to tell them anything. 'This is dated two weeks ago. Why are you giving me evidence that will put you in prison?'

'We are allowing you to see it. That's all.'

'Why?'

'The man in the photograph is called Shepherd – an English name – but we know he is from Ukraine. He is from our world. We want to know who he is and who is behind him. He is also – how do you say? – political.'

'Did he arrange this payment personally?'

Esposito understood what was being said and nodded.

'Did he come to Napoli?'

They shook their heads. 'Signor Esposito met with this man in Austria.'

'How did he get to you? People don't just call up your organisation.'

'A lawyer in Napoli who works with us. He knows nothing of this man, except that he has connections.'

'So you didn't check him out – you didn't bother to find out if you were being set up. You didn't think to wonder why you were delivering the woman you kidnapped to a Russian ship. You just wanted the money, so you asked no questions, right?'

A car came up the ramp then reversed the moment the driver saw their group. Esposito took no notice but launched into a stream of invective, gesticulating with his cigarette. Samson knew enough Italian to understand that he was telling the younger man to give him something.

This was a piece of paper with several numbers printed on it. 'What is this?' asked Samson.

'Bank-account numbers.'

'Where did you get this?'

'You say we don't check people out, but we do. Mr Shepherd was followed after his meeting with Mr Esposito to a club called the Erotische Palast. This came from his wallet.'

'I take it I can keep these?'

'But you must tell us what you find out from them, or we will find you. I give you this card. You can call anytime.'

'Don't threaten me,' said Samson sharply. He took a couple of paces towards Esposito. The two bodyguards moved quickly to intercept him, their guns aimed at his head. Esposito smiled and muttered something that the young man translated. 'He says you are not a good investigator because you have not even asked him where to find your girlfriend.'

Samson stepped back to lean on his car. The bodyguards lowered their weapons. 'Okay, where the hell do I find her?'

'Russia. And they will keep her there as long as they want – until Mr Hisami does what they say.'

'You know what they are demanding in exchange for her freedom?'

'Shepherd, he said that they want something from Hisami. And they have many secrets about Hisami. But we do not know what this is.'

'Why did he tell you so much? You were just contractors.'

'A man talks when his wine has a little extra something,' said the young translator. He gave Samson a card with a telephone number scrawled in biro at the bottom. 'The lawyer – he will find us.' They climbed into the Maserati and unhurriedly turned to take the ramp down. As the car passed Samson, Esposito gave him one last pitiless look.

CHAPTER 13

She was lying down in a long box. Her hands were tied in front of her and her mouth was sealed with tape. She could rock sideways and touch the sides of the box with her elbows and the top with her head. The confinement horrified her. She began to breathe rapidly but told herself to calm down. They hadn't killed her so they obviously wanted her alive. However, they had hurt her as they hauled her from the top of the container, tearing muscles in her left arm and shoulder, and these now burned with pain. She blinked and realised that her right eye was nearly closed with a swelling. She remembered that one of the men had slapped her across the face as she struggled to keep hold of the phone, only relinquishing her grasp to hurl it between the containers so they'd never see the numbers she had dialled. But she had no idea where it landed.

Now she kept telling herself, 'Cool it, Anastasia. Control yourself!' She tried to distract herself by thinking of Samson, his voice steady and calm, and his promise to come for her whatever it took. That gave her something to hold on to. He would do it! This is what he was good at, and he never gave up. He was like a tracker dog. And she knew he still loved her. She had heard it in his voice in those few seconds on the phone. He always spoke to her like that, as though they were in bed. She consciously summoned up images of their time in Venice, their love-making and the pleasure they took from the same things – sweet wine from the Veneto, with biscotti on the coldest day of their trip, the sound of a child practising the piano in an upstairs room overlooking a bridge, that sunlight through the mist which made them both gasp. Samson had said that, if he lived in Venice, he would have to try to be an artist, however hopeless. She had laughed. She hadn't expected him to be quite so sensitive to everything they were seeing. In one gallery, where they were almost alone, they stood in front of a painting of the Flight into Egypt and he had wondered out loud if this was the first picture of a refugee crisis. He was attracted to the details of paintings – the line of laundry in a Canaletto, the columbines and lilies in the foreground of a hunting study, the goldfinch on the Virgin's hand. He was very observant and rarely missed anything, in life or in art. It was so unusual that his appreciation of a painting was sparked by minute details rather than grandiose themes, and she had loved that in him.

She trawled through these memories again and again for new details, but she kept on coming back to their extraordinary closeness in bed, something she'd never experienced with anyone else before or since. Samson was at ease with himself physically, unself-conscious and undemanding. She didn't feel guilty about thinking of those times, in the same way as she hadn't felt remorse – merely a sense of loss – when she dumped him for Denis. The images of Samson were what she needed right now and she would hold on to whatever kept her panic at bay. Damn Denis. Where the hell was he when she needed him?

They'd given her a shot when they took her down from the containers. She had the same chemical blur in her brain as she'd had when she woke in the container, and her stomach churned, though that was possibly the motion of the ship. She dozed, but halfway between consciousness and sleep, her mind filled with terrifying thoughts of being left in the box for months, like the British hostages in the Lebanon she had read about. She forced herself to stay awake and tried to interpret the sounds that occasionally came to her, yet these never included the voices of the crew she found herself yearning for.

It was impossible to tell how much time had passed – maybe twelve or fifteen hours. Maybe more. She became aware of things quietening down. She sensed less motion in the box, and the ship's engines, which seemed to have been going flat out since she had come round, created less vibration.

She waited. If they wanted her alive, they would have to feed her and give her water, so they must come. And they couldn't leave her lying in her pee. Nobody does that. She waited and waited, then, much later, she heard footsteps reverberating in the space around the box. Before she knew it the lid was lifted and the beam of a torch was run over her face and she had to screw her eyes shut. 'Please,' she said. 'Please get me out. I won't run. Please!' Two men grabbed her by the shoulders, but she screamed so loudly when they wrenched her injured arm that they let her go. They consulted, put their hands under her back and legs, lifted her up and swung her round so that her bottom rested on the side of the box and her feet touched the ground. She slumped forward, determined not to faint from the pain. 'Just hold on. I need to get my breath. I'm feeling sick.' The throb of the engine was much louder and there was a smell of machinery and urine. She looked around. There were three of them. They didn't speak, but from their few words she already knew they were Russian. She looked down. The box she had been held in was labelled 'Safety Equipment'.

They frogmarched her up a companionway – her legs were still numb and she could barely walk – and then up two more flights of stairs until they were out in the open. It was night – a whole day had passed. She gulped in air and begged them for water, but they didn't seem to understand and kept her moving until they reached the light flooding from the open door of a cabin. They pushed her in and forced her on to the bed. Expecting the worst, she began to shake her head and shout, 'No!', but one of the men cut the rope that bound her wrists and gestured to food and water on the table. Another picked up a heavy wrench that was propped up just outside the cabin and hit the handle on the inside of the door until it sheered off. They left without a word, slamming the door and locking it behind them. Something heavy was dragged to block the doorway and a man was left on guard outside. She heard him muttering and smelled his cigarette smoke for the rest of the night.

She ate the bread, sausage and apple that had been left for her and sipped the water, while revolving her shoulder. It was not until she stood under the dribble of warm water in the tiny shower room that she realised that she was in Zhao's cabin. All his possessions had been cleared away and there was nothing to say that he had ever been there, but the mirror in his shower room had been missing the bottom-right-hand corner and so was the one she stood in front of. She had completely forgotten about the strange little chef and begging him to send an email to Denis's account. Did he manage to send it? Had he been caught and murdered and his body heaved over the side, like the others? She considered the possibility that they had chosen his empty cabin to make a point – attempting to suborn any member of the crew would result in death.

She dried herself and washed some of her clothes in the sink, kneading suds from the tiny bar of soap while looking at her scratched and battered face. She barely recognised the haunted reflection that stared back at her. But she was alive and she had talked to Samson and he was going to find her.

It was six in the morning when Denis Hisami was brought from his cell in the Manhattan Correctional Center, which he shared with a notorious author of a pyramid scheme for whom he had formed an abiding dislike, and another man, who claimed he had been wrongly identified by Immigration and Customs Enforcement as an illegal Jamaican immigrant.

Jim Tulliver and Sam Castell were already there when he was led into the interview room and placed in the chair opposite them with what seemed like unnecessary force.

Castell went first. 'We've got another hearing – not sure when but I expect you to be released with a tracker. I'm sorry, but we had to tell the judge about Anastasia because that was the only thing that made her reconsider. ICE still says you are a risk, but they won't specify what kind – a flight risk or a terror risk – so it's hard to argue with them. Both are ridiculous, and the judge has lost patience with ICE because they won't produce their evidence. But I think you'll be out of here in about thirty-six hours.'

'Make sure it happens,' said Hisami. 'Who did you talk to?'

'Senator Shelley Magee.'

'And what did she say?'

'She is concerned, naturally, but she asked where all this is coming from. Why has it happened to you? She's, like, anxious about the stuff going on below the surface. She wants to know who's involved before tangling with it.'

'Shelley always was a shrewd politician.'

'But she wants to help. She really does.'

Hisami shrugged and shifted his attention to Tulliver. 'Okay, so tell me about Anastasia. You obviously have news.'

'She somehow managed to make a call to Samson from the vessel. She tried you first, we suspect, but we don't have access to your phone so there's no way of telling.' He let that hang in the air and gave his boss a look. Hisami wasn't going to react. He'd never give Tulliver access to his phone. 'So they were able to identify the vessel and get an exact fix on its position, and they tracked it through yesterday,' continued Tulliver, watching Hisami carefully. We tried our damnedest to get the boat intercepted. But the State Department didn't lift a finger. They said there was no proof that Anastasia was on the boat, despite the phone call and Zillah getting all the evidence together about the boat, its departure from Taranto, intercepts and satellite imagery. Without their backing, the Pentagon wouldn't help. The boat passed through European waters into the Black Sea, but the only way we could get the Europeans to act was with the help of the US Ambassador to the EU, and of course she wouldn't move without instructions from State. And it didn't help that your wife is no longer a European citizen. The British offered help, but the nearest Royal Navy vessel was five hours away, and by the time the captain was ordered to intercept it was night and the *Grigori* was practically in Russian territorial waters.'

'And she made no more calls?'

'Not to Samson. I don't know about your phone. We weren't allowed to bring any mobile devices in here, so we can't look at yours now. We do need to do that, at some point.'

'I'll be out tomorrow.' Hisami thought for a few seconds. 'If they've taken her to Russia, there is, of course, little hope of getting her out.' He looked down, feeling more helpless than he could ever remember. His failure to take Anastasia's advice in the first place had preyed on his mind all night, and now, finding himself incapable of helping her, even to the extent of picking up the phone when she had no doubt fought with all she had to make the call, he questioned his fitness as a man and as her husband. He should offer protection and security but had been found wanting.

'So we can expect some kind of demand,' said Tulliver. 'Do you have any idea what that will be?'

Hisami sucked in air, making a hiss with his lips. 'That won't come, Jim. They won't make contact. Forget it.'

'How do you know that?' demanded Castell, eyes darting between the two men.

'Just accept that there won't be a demand, if Denis says so,' said Tulliver sharply.

'But Russia!' said Castell. 'What the fuck is going on, Denis? Why Russia?' He shook his head idiotically and looked to Tulliver for help. Tulliver ignored him.

'All you have to worry about is getting me out of here, Sam. Just stick to that, and leave the rest to me and Jim.'

'And TangKi?' asked Castell. 'What do I do about that? The board doesn't know Crane is dead yet. The London media has mentioned a guy called Shepherd, that's all.'

'You do nothing about TangKi, Sam. You have no status with the company. We warned its major shareholders, and we have done our duty. Anastasia is the only thing that matters. Getting me out and Anastasia home – that's what we have to focus on.'

Tulliver brought his hand up to his mouth and coughed. 'Meanwhile, I'm afraid I have some further bad news.'

'Go ahead,' said Hisami calmly.

'The website – newsJip – that ran the original story about

you which started all this contacted the office last night and sent some images by email, and they want your reaction . . .'

'Go on.'

'They aren't good.'

'Show them to me.'

Tulliver took out a file of legal papers and parted them. He withdrew three printouts and spread them in front of Hisami. They showed a group of armed men standing around a ditch in which bodies were piled. Hisami, a gun over his shoulder and a pistol in his hand, was clearly visible in all three shots. The same flying jacket, the same beard and the same commanding presence.

'They say you supervised the massacre of these Iraqi soldiers.'

'Do they?' said Hisami. He picked one up and squinted at it then nodded to himself. 'I remember this well. These were indeed Iraqis, but Saddam's forces executed them because their commander was about to come over to our side in the 1995 uprising.'

'Can you prove that?'

He let the photograph drop from his hand so it landed in front of Tulliver. 'See the man in dark glasses – the one without a uniform and just a side arm?' Tulliver bent down and searched the photograph. 'That's Bob Baker of the CIA. He writes books now and is on CNN. I see him when he comes out to San Francisco.'

'I'm lost,' said Castell.

'I imagine you are,' said Hisami.

'So, he can testify to that fact?' asked Tulliver.

'Put it this way,' said Hisami. 'If they publish that photograph and say the men standing round that ditch are responsible for the massacre, Bob will sue them for libel. In fact, I recommend we give them no response whatsoever and let them go ahead and publish. Bob could use the money.'

'You sure?'

'Yes. We saw a lot of terrible things, some of them done by my side, but this was not one of them. Don't worry about it.'

'Are you sure?'

'Yes. This is their first mistake, and it proves something to me.'

'What?'

'This didn't come from the CIA or from any other US agency. I was worried about that. Anyone who had access to this photograph in an American agency would know exactly what was going on in it. So it came from someone else who didn't know that one of the CIA's most talented agents to work in the Middle East was in the photograph. The Agency would know that.'

Tulliver looked concerned. 'You're saying go ahead and let them publish without saying anything. That seems like an awful risk.'

'Why not? My reputation has been shredded. If Bob comes out and says what this photograph is really about, people are far more likely to believe him than me. He will be totally convincing.'

'So where did this happen? What were you doing?' asked Castell.

'Long story, but it involved an American attempt to bring forces together to overthrow Saddam Hussein. Baker was let down by the Clinton administration, even though this was an American operation to combine the PUK, the Patriotic Union of Kurdistan, of which I was a part, Shi'ite forces and some Sunni officers.'

'There's something else. They say you lied on your immigration form and gave a false name.'

'A different name, actually. My sister, Aysel, and I legally changed our names. It was necessary.'

'You want to tell us about that?' said Castell.

'Another time.'

'We need your help on this, Denis,' pleaded the lawyer.

'It's not relevant,' said Hisami firmly. Castell looked at Tulliver for backup, but again he didn't get it.

'I appreciate that you have some kind of secret past, Denis. But at some stage you're going to have to cough.'

That wasn't going to happen and, besides, Hisami knew his past was of interest only in as much as it was being used to pile pressure on him. He gave the smallest shake of his head and retreated into his white-hot silence until the guard walked in and, in a curiously high voice, given his size, told Hisami to get up. He thought for a second or two longer, which caused the guard to take a couple of paces towards him, then he rose. 'I may need to see Samson,' he said to Tulliver.

CHAPTER 14

Doing nothing when nothing was to be done was a discipline Samson had learned as a young intelligence officer, and it had come in useful when Denis Hisami had hired him to find Aysel in the ISIS caliphate and he endured the scorching Turkish summer in a flyblown hotel, waiting for a man to cross the border from Syria. He'd hunkered down, put his mind in neutral and read, among other things, *Anna Karenina* on a tablet. He did much the same thing after the Camorra had left the car park. Hour after hour passed, with occasional trips to get food and something to read in the airport terminal, but mostly he sat in the car, waiting for phone calls. Macy Harp and Zillah Dee kept him up to date with the ship's movements, but as the day progressed it became clear that there would be no interception before it entered Russian territorial waters.

He didn't think about Anastasia – not for one second – because it never helped. Instead, he methodically sifted all the facts and came to the only conclusion there was. Everything pointed back to Denis Hisami, and that meant he had to talk to him. If Anastasia had been taken to Russia, there was virtually no hope of locating her or extracting her. Hisami had to make the deal.

He booked the first flight to London the next morning, returned the car and checked into the hotel nearest the airport. All this he could have done earlier, but while there was a possibility that he might have to fly somewhere in the east, he preferred to be near the terminal. He did not undress in the hotel room but took a beer and a packet of crisps from the mini bar and lay down on the bed. The call from Zillah came at 1 a.m.

'So, we're done here,' she said. 'The ship is likely headed for Crimea, but which port we have no idea. It's going to be tough to get anyone there in time. I need far more people to cover the ground. But I do have some news for you. The DNA results came through.' She paused to read something. 'Says here that the samples taken from Crane's house in California do not match the blood sample. I repeat: do *not* match the blood sample from the balcony of the apartment in London. They do, however, match the samples taken from the shower drain in the apartment. Seems like you got the result you expected. The body with the face blown off isn't Crane.'

'Can you send that to me?'

'It's already in your inbox. Unless there's anything else, I should go. I'll see how things develop here, but my instinct is to head back to the States and figure out with Mr Hisami what we should do next. They hope to have him out tomorrow. I'll stay in touch.'

Samson reached London Heathrow by 11.30 a.m. after changing planes in Frankfurt. As he left the plane he switched on the phone he was using and glanced through his messages. There was a one-word text from Zillah – 'Sevastopol'. The *Grigori* had indeed docked in Crimea, since the 2014 annexation part of Putin's Russia. He headed for Immigration and found himself waiting in an unusually long line of business people snaking round the hall. At some point he became aware of two men wearing lanyards scanning the crowd from the other side of the immigration desk. He got through passport control and was moving in the direction of the escalator down to the baggage hall when they approached him from behind.

'Mr Samson, would you come with us?' said one.

'Depends why.'

'We want to ask you some questions.'

'Are you arresting me?'

'Not at the moment, sir.'

He followed them through a door and was led into a room, where Peter Nyman was seated, reading a copy of *Flight International* with his arm crooked around the back of his neck.

'Ah, there you are, Samson. I thought you'd be on that flight. So glad the old intuition hasn't quite deserted me yet.' He dropped the magazine on the table and produced his more-in-sorrow-than-in-anger look. 'Knowing we are old colleagues, our friends at the Metropolitan Police here wanted my help in tracking you down. And I decided to make the journey out here to ensure that they did in fact *collar* you.'

Samson sat down and placed his backpack beside him. 'As you no doubt know, I am investigating the abduction of an American subject who has been taken to Russian territory on a container ship. Time is of the essence, so I would appreciate it if you could keep this as brief as possible.'

'We are aware of what is going on,' said Nyman.

The officers gave their names as Sergeant James Christie and Detective Inspector Kevin McDowell.

McDowell – Samson noted the beginnings of a paunch and thick, black Celtic hair cropped to a brush – began. 'This is not a formal interview, so we are not recording the conversation. Just a few questions, but arrest and a formal interview may follow and, after that, charges.'

Samson gestured indifference.

'We believe that you entered an apartment at the Wardour Park Tower in Knightsbridge three days ago and interfered with a designated crime scene. As you will be aware, this is a serious offence. There is CCTV footage of you entering the building that day.'

'Yes, I did enter the building.' Samson knew there was no CCTV in the flat to prove he had been there, and he was also sure that Jo Hayes wouldn't have admitted to anything. That was always the deal – total denial – and he wasn't going to compromise her by saying he had been in the apartment.

'What was your intention?'

'To check that the apartment where the body was found did

in fact belong to Ray Shepherd, which is one of the aliases of Adam Crane, an individual I was investigating for an American client.'

'What were you doing with Detective Inspector Hayes?'

'No doubt you have asked her, but it's very simple. She's an old contact of mine and she suggested that, in the course of my inquiries about Crane, I might be able to help the Metropolitan Police with information about him. As Mr Nyman must have told you, I am investigating the possible theft of millions of dollars from a company named TangKi. Given Crane's many identities, I just wanted to make sure that the body had been found in one of the flats I had under observation. And the only way to establish that was to get into the building.'

'But all you would need for that was an apartment number.'

'I had an apartment number, it is true, but I wanted to make sure this tallied with the apartment that I had watched from the park.'

'And so you entered the apartment with Detective Inspector Hayes.'

'No.'

'You are saying that you didn't go into the apartment?'

'Yes,' said Samson confidently. He was certain that the forensics officer in there when they arrived would not have jeopardised his job by admitting he'd let them in. And Jo would have seen him straight.

'I find it hard to believe that you went up there just to check a number,' said Sergeant Christie.

Samson turned to the officer, a peevish-looking blond of

about forty with ear piercings but no rings or studs. 'There was something else, but I didn't tell Jo at first.'

'And what was that?' said the officer.

'One aspect of the case I was investigating was the use of artworks to launder money. Mr Crane collected valuable pictures and it seemed likely that he had developed his interest in the art market because it is still one of the best ways of laundering money and keeping assets hidden from tax authorities and crime-fighting agencies. Often these works of art are held in secure warehouses in freeport zones, but I believe that Mr Crane kept much of his collection on his walls, at least temporarily, before they were shipped.'

'Yes,' said McDowell.

'I wanted to get a glimpse of the apartment through the door. I saw that all the paintings that I knew had been there had been removed. Even from the doorway it is possible to see marks on the wall where a big work has been.'

'And what did that suggest to you?' continued McDowell.

'It's obvious, isn't it?' said Samson.

'Explain.'

'I asked Jo whether the police had removed the paintings because of their value. She didn't know, but thought not. So I suggested the first thing the police needed to do was to go back into the CCTV recordings and see when they were taken out of the building, because clearly that might have relevance to your investigation – it could provide a motive for the murder.' Samson glanced at Nyman, who had his eyes firmly fixed on a loose ceiling tile. 'I did suggest to Jo that CCTV was checked to establish the date when those artworks were removed. She will confirm that.'

'We'll definitely ask her,' said McDowell.

'If you have nothing else, I'll be getting along.'

The two policemen consulted and then McDowell stood and said, 'We're arresting you on suspicion of perverting the course of justice, Mr Samson. I must warn you that anything you say . . .'

Samson raised his hand from the desk. 'Stop right there.' He put his hand down to snatch his backpack from Christie's grasp. 'First, you do not have reasonable suspicion that I have committed a crime, because you know that Jo Hayes has confirmed everything I have just told you. And the second point is, if you go ahead, there will be consequences that no one in this room desires. I will speak to Mr Nyman alone.'

McDowell protested that it wasn't up to Samson to dictate to police officers whether he was about to be charged with a serious offence.

'I will talk to Mr Nyman – the rest of you can leave.' He looked at the officers. 'I bloody well mean it.'

They didn't move.

'Maybe,' said Nyman, 'I should hear what Samson has to say. He's not going anywhere.' He made an imperceptible jerk towards the door with his head. 'Just a few minutes.'

They left. Nyman looked down at the magazine. 'What do you want to tell me?'

'I know exactly what you're doing.'

'Oh, really! Do tell.'

'You want to get me charged so you can all have a good look at my phone.'

'I believe the police do indeed have powers to seize a phone or any other device after a person has been charged.'

'And that is why you're here. Even for these strange times, it's unusual for a member of the intelligence services to be present in a police interview, however informal that interview is said to be. A lawyer would make a lot of that in court because it looks like you're putting pressure on the police, the suspect, or both. But this case won't get to court. Once you have looked at my phone, the charges will be dropped – right, Peter?'

Nyman just gazed at him.

'But that's not going to happen, and you know why. You and I know that Crane is still alive. You've known all along, and I can prove that.' He couldn't, but Nyman had no idea of that. 'Two things follow from this fact, Peter. The first is that you are withholding information from a police investigation, which is a far greater crime than anything you can hope to pin on me, but the second, bigger problem for you is that you don't want anyone to know that Crane is still alive, do you? You need Adam Crane to be dead because he's the centre of an operation.'

Nyman blew his cheeks out and shook his head vigorously. 'You're groping in the dark, Paul. This won't save you.'

Samson leaned forward so he could look straight into Nyman's eyes. 'Let me tell you this. If I'm charged, this will go straight to the media. Not only will that embarrass you, it will screw your operation. So do not fuck with me on this, Peter.

I am not in the mood for it. I'm not interested in your spook games with Crane – I just want to see Anastasia released.' He stopped, rose and hooked his backpack over one shouder. 'I'll let you tell them that they aren't going to arrest me. They'll have to agree, because this was all your bloody idea in the first place.'

Nyman looked up at him. 'Are you really going to take us on, Paul?'

He rested the pack on the table. 'The only thing I give a damn about is Anastasia's freedom. If you obstruct me and endanger her life, there is simply nothing I won't do to hurt you and your operation. Nothing. Please understand that.' Samson straightened and turned to the door.

Nyman grunted. 'Have it your own way, Paul, but you have no idea what you are dealing with. No idea whatsoever.'

CHAPTER 15

When the boat docked, a man came into the cabin, where Anastasia waited. He was short, with fine Slavic hair brushed forward into a point and the air of a busy official. He sat down on the only chair in the cabin, clasped his hands over his belly and regarded her through rimless glasses that were tinted blue, which he then took off. Her hands and feet had been bound just before he entered by the men who had lifted her out of the box and she had shrunk from this man when the door had opened, but he had told her in good English with a Russian accent to relax and listen to him.

'We do not want to harm you, Mrs Hisami. The captain is fool and treated you badly. There was no need to keep you in container – he should have given you cabin like this, then you would not have wanted to escape. But you have made things very difficult for us because you told others where you were. The crew found the phone you used and we know that you called a friend and gave him all information you had. That phone call identified ship, which is why we were shadowed until we reached our Russian waters. Our plans have been disrupted and we must make certain adjustments for the new situation, you understand.' She tried to speak but he cut her off, chopping the air with his hand several times. 'Do not interrupt me, Mrs Hisami. Just listen. Naturally, one option is to dispose of you, and we have considered this, but that would be waste of all our hard work and we still do not have what we want.'

'What do you want?' she asked quietly.

He took no notice but looked around. 'You recognise cabin, no? This is cabin of Chinaman. He sent email to Denis Hisami – email you wrote. Do you see Chinaman now? Do you see Chinaman's possessions?' She shook her head. 'He no longer exists. He is gone. Everything is gone. And no one will ever ask where. A life lost – that is the result of what you did.'

She was appalled. Five people were now dead, but this death was all her fault. The strange little man, so lonely and idiosyncratic, had sent the email, and they killed him. She shook her head, looked down and let out one guttural sob.

'There are always consequences,' the man said, examining the palm of each hand in turn. 'If you attempt to escape or try to communicate with your friends again, be assured, I will kill you. It is not problem for me – you mean nothing to me. You understand? If you behave, you may live to see your husband.'

'What do you want?' she asked again.

'I cannot say that, Mrs Hisami. But I will say to you that things have gone in some ways more easily than we expected, and in some ways worse. It is good that your husband has been put in jail.'

'He's not in jail. You're lying.'

'If you knew me, you would know that I have come this far in life by telling truth. I repeat so you understand – your husband is in jail in New York, which was reason you could not reach him when you called. Then you called your lover Paul Samson and told him where you were and we assume he alerted Western authorities – NATO, EU, etcetera, etcetera – and ship was followed. That was certainly inconvenient.'

'He can't be in jail. He hasn't done anything wrong.' Only then did she realise that the man had mentioned Samson. How did he know she had spoken to him?

'Your husband was arrested on immigration fraud – he lied on citizen application form and did not disclose past as war criminal. I am sure he told you his real name is Karim Qasim. He took the name of his hero, the Kurdish writer Hisami, for the purposes of moving to the United States with his sister, Aysel. They were both involved in the cover-up of the murder of thirty-four Iraqi soldiers in 1995.'

'I don't believe you.'

'That does not worry me, Mrs Hisami. American authorities are in possession of photographs that prove presence at the scene of crime, and Denis Hisami, or I should say Karim Qasim, is now in jail because they know he is war criminal and liar. You see, Mrs Hisami, we have followed your husband's career since our agents came across him when he was a young man fighting for the PUK. He was brilliant commander but very violent man.' He looked at her with contentment as she tried to absorb all this. 'Surely you knew of these things in your husband's past? A person who witnessed the elimination of IS unit in Macedonia must ask how a man like Hisami, a Californian billionaire, was able to shoot four terrorists – bang, bang, bang, bang – in few minutes: three in barn and one in farmhouse. When we learned your husband was in Macedonia, we knew he was the one to carry out killings. Macedonian security forces, they took credit, but we knew true story, Mrs Hisami. And that is story you know also because you were there, and so was Paul Samson, the man who became your lover in Venice. Yes, we are aware of all these things.'

'How do you know I called Samson?'

'You just told me. Now we have his number, which may be useful one day.'

She shook her head.

'Ah, I see you do not question these things any longer, and that is because you suspect they are true. Good. We are getting somewhere. How do we know all this? That is easy. We watched Karim Qasim's climb through American society because we knew he was very smart man. We admired his financial abilities and way he learned how to work system to his advantage, and so quickly, too. But we knew one day we would have reason to disclose what we know about him. His personality and his politics dictated that there would be conflict between his interests and ours. It was written in stars and we were prepared.'

'Denis is a good person, as his sister was. They would never cover up a war crime. It's against everything he believes in. Aysel was known for her humanitarian work, her love of humanity.'

'You believe this, yet you see him cover up the killing of the terrorists in Macedonia. You know your husband covered up killings in Macedonia. This is the way he operates, and his sister went back to front line to fight. She had to be there.'

'She was a doctor. She was helping the wounded. That's why she was there.'

'Believe what you like, Mrs Hisami, but does it occur to you she was atoning for sins in past?'

'Our organisation is named after her because of her humanity and the sacrifices she made to help others,' she said with sudden vehemence. 'I know my husband. He is not a war criminal – he was a soldier.'

He drew a gun from inside his jacket. 'Lean forward,' he commanded, and placed the gun at the nape of her neck. 'Here is where I shoot you. The bullet enters skull here.' He screwed the muzzle into her hair. 'Your death will come with no warning. You will know nothing.'

She jerked her head up and strained back to look into his eyes. 'You enjoy this?'

He shook his head. 'I just tell you how things are. I am civilised man and I will treat you well while you are with me, but you should know that I will end your life if it is required. Simple as that.' He stopped. 'I forgot – my name is Kirill.'

He replaced the gun and went to open the door to the men waiting outside. One of them carried a huge blue bag.

'We give you shot now,' he said. 'Then we have long journey but you will be unconscious for that – your beauty sleep.'

They assembled in Macy Harp's London office, but without a word Macy beckoned Samson and Zillah Dee to follow him along several corridors to a room in another building. 'Leave your phones in the wall safe,' he said, opening a panel outside the room which hid a small green safe. 'Better to be on the safe side.'

Samson and Zillah decanted their numerous devices into the safe and Macy placed his smartphone alongside them. 'I thought you didn't use a mobile phone,' said Samson.

'For my bookie and my wife,' said Macy with a routine twinkle. A woman that Samson hadn't seen before appeared and settled at a desk beside the panel. They went inside and Macy closed the door firmly. The room had no natural light and Samson noticed there were no desk lights, no electrical or telephone sockets – nothing that could be used to eavesdrop on the conversation. The air-conditioning had chilled the room to an uncomfortable level.

Samson poured three mugs of coffee from a flask. Macy nodded on receipt of his mug, folded his hands under the usually beaming red face and thought for a few moments.

'The first thing we need to do is to decide what the hell SIS are up to. They know Crane isn't dead. They probably knew from the moment the body was found. They must have suppressed that knowledge because they have an interest in Crane. Now what could that be?'

'He's their man?' offered Zillah.

'Doesn't make sense. He's the bad hat, surely. He was the one channelling money into London, washing it by various means – including the art market – and moving it to Europe. What do they want with him?'

'Well, they've got to be watching him,' said Zillah. 'Then Samson here comes along and spoils it by spooking Crane. So Crane has the poor sap on the balcony murdered and does a vanishing act.'

'Seems clumsy,' said Samson. 'Anyone in that situation would know that the police would eventually identify the body by means of DNA. If I thought of recovering hairs from the shower, so would the police. It's an obvious thing to do.'

'Indeed,' said Macy, 'and I suspect they did precisely that, or established in some other way that the body wasn't Crane's. That means the Security Service and MI6 leaned on them to keep it quiet. So, yes, Zillah, they are watching something unfold, something current and important. The reason they hauled you in this morning, Paul, was to find out how much you knew and what was on your phones. They weren't in the least bit interested in Anastasia – right? Then Nyman had to let you go because you threatened his entire operation by promising to go to the media, right? So that means he would rather have you running around with this information than jeopardise his operation, right again? And that leads me to conclude that Nyman is what I believe the experts term fucking desperate.'

'You understand this?' Zillah said, turning to Samson.

'No, but I'm sure Denis Hisami does, and I think I should go to see him.'

'You okay with that?' she asked.

'Sure, he's employing me, and we both want Anastasia free.' He studied them in turn. 'Looks like Crane organised the kidnapping.'

'How do you know this?' said Macy quickly.

'I was paid a visit by the Camorra in the car park at the airport. I guess they were told where to find me by the Carabinieri. They're angry about two of their men being killed on the ship – the police now assume both kidnappers were eliminated. They wanted any information that I could provide in the future and in return they showed me a photograph of Crane, whom they knew as Shepherd. They said he was connected to the eastern Mafia – part of their world.' He fished the paper with the numbers, together with the card they had given him, from his top pocket. 'They put something in his drink and went through his things. These are bank-account numbers he kept on his phone. They want to know what's in the accounts and who has access to them.'

'Maybe these are the accounts where the money from TangKi is ending up,' Zillah said, taking hold of the paper. 'Can I see what we're able to find out about them? I think I'll need to show these to Mr Hisami and Jim Tulliver – you okay with that?'

'Why don't you let me do that?' said Samson. 'I'll leave in the next twenty-four hours, so I can ask him.' He took back the paper.

'You may have to see him in jail – the outcome of the hearing is not certain,' she said.

'Why not?'

'The authorities are taking their time to prepare their case and the judge said she doesn't want to see either side until she has some evidence to assess. This is to determine whether Mr Hisami is a risk out of jail. It's not a trial.'

Macy waited for this exchange to end before clearing his throat. 'Okay?'

'Sorry,' said Samson, 'Go ahead.'

'We have to think of the whole picture. What's going on here? What's the end point?'

Zillah folded her arms and focused. 'By end point,' she said, 'you mean what is Crane actually doing? What's the purpose and why was everything so urgent? Why was the man on the balcony killed? Why are they in such a heck of a hurry?'

'Exactly,' said Macy, taking the role of the tutorial supervisor. 'Peter Nyman came to visit while you were in Italy, and he said something that interested me. He asked me, apropos of nothing, whether I had any interest in certain European extremist political groups. His remark followed some discussion of the money. He was sounding me out to see how much we know, because he basically finds Samson here such a bloody nightmare to deal with.'

'Likewise,' said Samson.

'I wondered about the connection in his mind and whether he thought this money was destined for these extremist groups in Europe. It's not like Nyman to give away his thinking, but I did note the connection.'

Zillah looked at her smart watch and frowned. 'I need to make a call to my people in Sevastapol. Is there somewhere I can do that?'

Macy told her to ask Maureen, who was sitting on the other side of the door. 'Oh, and you can leave that watch in the safe before you come back in,' he said.

After she had left, he turned to Samson. 'How are you?'

'Fine,' Samson replied.

He frowned a doubt. 'That call from the ship didn't bother you?'

'Yeah, it bothered me because I didn't like hearing her in distress, but she's another man's wife now and I'm working for him and I have it all straight in my head.'

'There's always the chance it may not end well. You know that, don't you?'

This was the unsentimental intelligence officer who had seen dozens of operations collapse and who knew the consequences of failure. To Macy, failure was to be expected.

Samson nodded.

'If it goes wrong, you're never going to forgive yourself,' said Macy sympathetically. 'I hate to say this, but you have to look after yourself in this affair.'

'Which is why we have to get her back.' Samson paused to think. 'Can I summarise? You think we have American money trying to illicitly influence European politics, is that right?' Macy nodded. 'Yet we also have a smooth-talking Ukrainian mafioso – aka Crane – who does deep cover very well. Then we have the obvious Russian connection with the boat and its destination. None of this conceivably adds up, does it?'

Macy rocked back and placed his fingertips together. 'Well, obviously, these days, there's less of a gap between the Russian and American regimes than there is, for example, between the two political tribes in America. And, if I read Nyman right, that's what's eating him.'

'"Snow on his boots" is what he said about Crane.'

Macy smiled. 'Indeed, "snow on his boots". I'd forgotten that phrase. Nyman is certainly obsessed with Crane's Russian connections, but I think his attention is focused on the States.'

'Hisami has all the answers,' Samson murmured.

'Yes, he probably does. Look, I should mention something before Zillah comes back. Denis hasn't paid us yet. He has a liquidity problem, which has nothing to do with this situation. Our friend Denis is a gambler at heart, just like you. I gather he got caught up in a speculative riptide earlier this year, which made a dent in his fortune. He's not broke but he has temporary cashflow difficulties that he's finding it hard to address from a prison cell. Of course, he's very, very rich and we will be paid, but I felt I ought to warn you, given the situation with the restaurant.'

Samson remembered Anastasia asking what he would do with Cedar when his mother had gone. He'd told her he would run it in his parents' memory. But that was before he knew of the debts his mother had taken on and the way the finances of the restaurant were set up – it was virtually impossible to cover the costs. A payment of £45,000 was outstanding. 'When do you think we'll get it?' he asked.

'As soon as he's out of jail. I talked to Tulliver last night. Denis is worth a lot, so there isn't a problem, but I guess Zillah won't be using that plane for much longer. Must be costing forty to fifty grand a week.'

Samson was thinking about his own liabilities and made a mental note to call his sister, Leila, after the meeting. Leila had a chaotic emotional life but when she concentrated she was good with figures and far better than Samson at talking with their bank manager, who, after their mother's death, told them flat out that the only course was to close Cedar. Leila and he had decided that wasn't going to happen, though, in truth, it would have been far easier for both of them if it had.

Zillah came back with some notes and sat down. 'So, I have some news. It seems Anastasia was taken off the ship last night, because the *Grigori* has already set sail for a shipyard at Kerch in Eastern Crimea, where it will be *repaired*. I have two of my guys there, but the conditions are challenging. They arrived too late to do anything and they weren't able to get to any of the crew. Jonathan established that a handful of containers were taken off the boat and one was loaded on to a truck almost immediately. He got the registration of that truck and the name of the freight forwarder that operates out of St Petersburg.' She looked up from her notes. 'Basically, she's gone and we have no goddam idea where they've taken her, but we start by working on the freight agent.'

Samson shook his head at the hopelessness of the situation.

Macy absorbed the news. 'My concern is that the Russian government is in on this. If it is, we're properly jiggered.'

Zillah shook her head. 'Everything we know about the FSR or the GRU – they're the only state agencies that would undertake an operation like this – suggests they would have gotten her into Russia far more efficiently. She wouldn't have been allowed to escape and roam that vessel, stealing phones and persuading the crew to send emails. These people are, relatively speaking, amateurs. This is all about organised crime.'

'What are you two going to do?' asked Samson.

'I'm going back to the States right now,' said Zillah. 'Need a ride?'

Samson shook his head. 'I'd like that, but I've got a few things to sort out here. I'll take the first flight tomorrow.'

They left the room and collected their phones from the safe. Samson's immediately pinged with a text from Jo Hayes. 'You owe me dinner – 8 p.m. tonight your place?'

He could do without this, but he owed Jo and he wanted to sound her out.

Samson would have asked Jo up to the office above Cedar for a drink so they could talk in private, but he was sure that it had been bugged when he was away. Everything seemed to be in place, but when he phoned Leila to talk about the money, he noticed a slight popping on the landline and moments of interference when she spoke. If the phone was bugged, so were the room and the computer he used for the business. He would eventually have it all swept, but it certainly wasn't safe to have a frank conversation there with Detective Inspector Hayes.

Jo had the presence of a performer. When she arrived, the eyes of both male and female customers followed her to the table. She wore a dark grey business suit, black shirt and silver necklace and she'd had three or four inches cut from her hair, which made her seem less like the amateur nightclub singer. 'What do you think?' she said, flipping it with the back of her fingers, first one side then the other. 'It's all in honour of our date, Samson.'

'Well, I am indeed honoured,' he said. 'It looks great – sexier.'

'It's meant to make men take me seriously.'

'They already do,' said Samson. 'You're the smartest person in the Met and they know that.'

'Thank you! I will have the best chilled white wine that Lebanon has to offer.'

'Then you shall have the Ixsir Altitudes 2015. It is grown at a thousand metres and goes very well with seafood.' He nodded to the waiter, who was hovering.

'How's it going?' she asked.

'She's in Russia.'

'Russia – why? What's this all about, Samson?'

'Your guess is as good as mine.'

'And not a peep in the media?'

'If it gets out that she's been kidnapped at the same time as her husband was thrown into jail, it will be a big story and make it much harder to get her back. I pray that doesn't happen.'

'How are you managing? Must be tough.'

'Like any other job.'

She looked sceptical while the waiter poured the wine for Samson to taste.

'So, thanks for not dropping me in it at the airport,' she started. 'They had nothing, as you guessed. But you're a rascal, sneaking DNA samples from the apartment. That's how you knew it wasn't Adam Crane on the balcony.' She put up her hand. 'No, I don't want you to say anything. I'm just telling you that I know you're a dirty rotten little shit.'

'Agreed,' said Samson.

She smiled. 'The name is Daniel Misak.'

'Whose name?'

'Keep up. The man on the balcony.'

'Right, and who is he?'

'Well, this is the interesting part. He was a US citizen – from the West Coast. Been in London just a few days when he was abducted and killed. He was tortured in a lock-up down at the rough end of Fulham. Then he was brought back to the flat alive in a chest.'

'CCTV?'

'You were right about the artwork. Crane's people took a lot of pictures out of the apartment and one or two things went in. Misak must have been in one of the larger crates. He was placed on the balcony, probably unconscious, and shot in the face at close range with a silenced weapon that was loaded with expanding bullets. He was shot three times. There was nothing left of his face to identify.'

'And Crane is the chief suspect for organising the killing, if not actually doing it himself?'

'I assume so, but I'm not on the investigation.' She picked up the glass of wine and gave him a sly look over the rim. 'You're going to have to work harder for the next bit.'

Samson grinned. 'Who was Misak?'

'You tell me.'

'I've never heard of him.'

'Well, start thinking about what he was doing with Crane.'

'Was he a friend?'

'Kind of.'

'Did he work with him? Did he work at TangKi – Crane's company in California?'

She smiled. 'Warmer.'

'What did he do? Was he something on the money side?'

'I would love some more of that flatbread with this delicious cheesy thing,' she said, turning and searching for a waiter.

'Shanklish,' said Samson. And then it fell into place. Misak was Hisami's source at TangKi. Crane had suspected him, summoned him to London on an urgent pretext and tortured him to find out what he'd told Hisami. When it became clear how much Hisami knew, Crane had decamped with all his artworks.

'Is there CCTV of Crane leaving?' he asked, signalling for more bread.

'Interesting you should think of that. The answer is no.'

'So he came out the same way Misak went in, immediately after Misak was dumped there?'

'Could be.'

'Was Misak drugged?'

'GHB and a drug called scopolamine – known in Colombia as the Devil's Breath. You blow it into someone's face from your hand and they become a zombie. He wouldn't have known where he was. When the place had been cleaned out someone came back, propped him up on the balcony and shot him.'

'Why the display?'

'Maybe for your man in prison. They were sending a message to him, as if he needed it after his wife had been kidnapped.'

'Crane organised the kidnap.'

Her eyes shone. 'How do you know that?'

He told her briefly about his encounter with Camorra but left out the piece of paper with account numbers on it.

'You get about,' she said.

'They found me – your counterparts in the Carabinieri. They want me to help them identify the person who ordered the death of the two kidnappers.'

'A lot of bodies are piling up – one here, two in Italy, two in the sea. There's a kind of desperation about it.'

Jo was smart and could look after herself, but she was also a natural companion and Samson found he was enjoying himself, even though the obsession with freeing Anastasia was not far beneath the surface. He asked her about her life, and she told him, without fuss, that she had just been 'given the heave-ho', as she put it, by an architect from Sussex whom she had met on a dating site. 'In point of fact, he saved me the trouble – he needed looking after too much, but it was annoying that he got in first. This bloody job! I didn't have time to phone and tell him, and then the bastard dumps me in a text.'

'Miss him?'

'Nah. It's nice to have someone to do things with, though. In this line, you've never got time to organise things, so you end up dating colleagues, who are just as dull and unreliable as you are.'

'What about your friends in the Security Service?'

'To go out with! You have to be joking.'

He smiled. 'No, what do they think about this story?'

'They're interested and they want to know what you know.'

'Yes, I believe I had a visit when I was away in Italy – the office upstairs. Doesn't feel right.'

'Are they here now?'

'No, Ivan always knows who's here.' With business and embassy people from the Middle East dining at Cedar every night, the table plan was a complicated part of running the restaurant. Ivan kept a list of people who could not be placed next to each other and those who required one of the three booths along the side. He was familiar with all the customers and those who tried to book that he didn't know were either put in the Siberia at the rear of the restaurant or found they couldn't get a table.

'It runs pretty smoothly,' she said.

'I've changed a few things – painted it, lowered the lighting, took down the pictures my dad bought and introduced these,' he said, tapping the little oil lamp on the table. 'And those green cushions were my idea.'

'Your feminine side,' she said.

He studied her. 'Have you got anything else to tell me, Jo? Seems like you might.'

'I'm not sure what you mean.'

'You have something, I can feel it.' He topped up her glass.

'You're trying to get me sloshed. You should know that I can drink the whole of West End Central under the table.'

'Didn't enter my mind.' He grinned.

'You asked me, so I'm going to ask you. Did you miss her when she went off and married Hisami?'

'Yes, but you get used to it.'

'Any girlfriends since?'

'Yep, a couple, but you know . . .'

'They weren't what you were looking for.'

'Other way round, plus, I have all this to worry about,' he said, sweeping the restaurant with his gaze. 'I hadn't realised what a lot of work my mother did every day.'

'And she was . . .'

'A terrific person,' said Samson. 'Always wanting me to get married, though. But the place got on top of her, and that's probably why she had the stroke that killed her. The problem was that she didn't share her worries – didn't want to burden us, and I suppose there was some pride involved. She wanted to make it work and had just about got control of the cash flow and, well, it ran away from her.'

'You've had a rough couple of years.' She touched him on the arm.

'I guess,' he said, and put his hand on hers. 'Is there something

I should know? Nyman warned me off. Why? After all, I'm just investigating a kidnapping in Italy, and they've successfully suppressed the identity of the murder victim for the time being. So, what's he so worried about? All I had to say was that I knew Crane wasn't dead and he let me go.'

She said nothing but withdrew her hand and continued to eat while flashing him a smile. She waved her knife in his direction. 'You nearly got me into a heap of trouble in that apartment. How can I trust you?'

'I'm sorry. I . . .'

'You were fucking with my career, Samson, and that isn't funny.'

He filled his own glass and decided to leave it at that. The more you asked at these moments, the less likely you were to get the answer. She would tell him if she wanted to. No point pushing it.

'When are you going to the States?' she said eventually.

'How do you know I'm going?'

'You aren't in Russia, so you have to be going to the States.' She turned away from customers. 'And leave the phone behind.'

'My phone?'

'Not your phone, you idiot! Her phone! And hide it!'

He said nothing and she returned to pick a few bones out of the sea bass.

'They didn't know you had it when you came through Heathrow this morning,' she said, with rather too much in her mouth. 'But the Italian police tipped them off just afterwards. I know because I tracked down the guy in charge in Italy because I wanted to find out a few things, and he assumed I was working with Nyman, so I did nothing to disabuse him of that idea.'

'You seem to know an awful lot about all this.'

'I've made it my business,' she said, finally giving up on the fish and leaning close to him, 'because I want to know what I'm getting into here. You see, the dinner was their idea. They want me to find out if you have the phone and when they can lay their hands on it.'

'I don't. It's on a plane to America right now, so it can be returned to Hisami when he gets out of jail. Whose idea was this?'

'My old colleagues.'

'I'm sorry you can't go back to them with anything.'

It was plain she didn't believe him, and also that she wasn't going to push him.

They had Cedar's famous mint sorbet and a glass of dessert wine. 'There's something else,' she said, 'but I'm going to have to tell you somewhere very safe.' She moved closer and whispered to his sleeve. 'By which I mean in bed.'

Samson smiled. 'Were you told to seduce me, too?'

'No, that part was my idea. And anyway, you're seducing me to find out what I know, in case you didn't realise. Unless, of course, you've sworn a vow of chastity?'

'She's another man's wife and he's a client. I have that straight in my mind,' he said for the second time that day, not sure what he was going to do.

'Liar, but I'll choose to believe you because, to be honest, Samson, I want you even if it's only a one-night stand.'

'I don't do one-night stands.'

'All the better,' she said.

Later, they made love in Samson's big first-floor flat in Maida Vale. Jo had none of Anastasia's playfulness in bed. She considered sex a serious subject and at one stage told him to stop smiling and concentrate. He replied that he was smiling because he had not expected a senior police officer to be quite so beautiful without clothes. This made her relent and kiss his eyes. 'Yes, you will do fine,' she said, as though concluding a rental agreement, and pulled him on top of her and held his face between the palms of her hands as they began to move together.

'You were going to say,' he murmured afterwards.

'Yes, I was. They know where he is. They're on to him.'

'Crane?'

'For Christ's sake – are you slow, Samson? Yes, Crane, you fucking bozo!'

'How do you know?'

'Simple. They have the number of one of his phones.' She paused and yawned then kissed him. 'I like you, Samson, but I'm not expecting anything – understand?'

'This is a speech I'm getting used to,' he said, the back of his hand brushing her breast. 'Anything else?'

'He used the phone to call Misak when he landed in London, and they found Misak's phone in the lock-up and scrolled through the recent calls. People always fuck up. Crane fucked up.'

'How did they find the lock-up?'

'That I don't know.'

He waited until she was asleep then left the bed.

They gave her another shot during the night, at least they thought they had. The needle entered her buttock through her filthy chinos then exited a couple of centimetres away and she felt the liquid shoot down the back of her leg. But she wished that they'd knocked her out. Though no longer trussed up in the bag in which she had been removed from the ship, she was bound and blindfolded and gagged with tape. In her previous enforced confinements – in the container and the box – she had done everything she could to keep track of time and to work out where she was, but now she existed in a state of resigned dread which no thought penetrated, apart from the awareness that it was very cold and she couldn't feel her hands and feet.

She understood that she was in a truck because she heard the gear changes and the engine labouring as they ground up a hill, but that was all she took in. Like a torture victim, she had got used to the routine of abuse, expected no release from the discomfort and pain, and now could not imagine a future without it. She told herself they wanted to keep her alive, but the appalling Russian creep who called himself Kirill was evidently as happy to snuff out her life as keep her alive, and the realisation of her worthlessness to them had somehow filled her being. She did not think of Samson to distract herself, or of her husband, who seemed a weirdly distant memory. She could not even summon his face, and all the experiences they'd shared in the last two years seemed like a fantasy. The work she had done with his money seemed suddenly futile, ridiculous.

This third incarceration delivered a profound depressive shock, as well as much physical pain. She could not bring herself to acknowledge that she was starving and desperately thirsty. They clearly didn't believe she needed food and water so she concluded she probably wasn't worthy of them. Only when she asked herself if the drug they had given had caused the terrible blackness in her mind as well as the toxic feeling all over did she begin to think that it was reasonable to expect food and water. She had long given up trying to hold her bladder, yet urinating did little to relieve the persistent ache in her stomach, which she realised must be constipation, possibly brought on by the terror and anxiety. She didn't know, she didn't care – she supposed she couldn't give a shit. That joke to herself generated a tiny light in her mind, and she tried desperately to think of other humorous things, but she was soon back in the deathly trance, lying there for mile after mile, hour after hour.

She was asleep when the brakes screeched and the truck pulled up. The whole vehicle shuddered then bounced a little with the sudden halt in momentum. She expected nothing. They were getting fuel, she told herself, but a moment later there was some clanking and she smelled food – she was certain of it, a kind of sausage smell, onions maybe. Her empty stomach began to rumble. Then she felt hands all over her. She was pulled upright and the blindfold was removed. She saw three figures in the dim overhead light. A man took hold of her head and ripped the tape from her mouth. He forced the nozzle of a water bottle between her teeth and squirted a jet so she had to jerk her head away to avoid choking. He kept doing this until she had finished the bottle. In the background she recognised Kirill's voice murmuring instructions to the man in Russian. Kirill came forward, bent down and cut the plastic tie from around her wrists. He picked up a tray that he had placed on the floor of the trailer. 'You will eat hot dog – make you feel at home.'

She rubbed her hands and tried to knead the blood back into her fingers. 'I can't feel anything I'm so cold. Why are you doing this?'

He guided her hands to the oblong tray, in which lay a spiral-cut sausage covered in sauce inside a bun.

'We have microwave on truck,' he said. 'Best hot dog in Russia.'

She bit into it and looked up. 'Why are you treating me like this? What have I done to you?' she said, her mouth full.

He didn't answer.

She felt the warmth spread through her hands and her stomach, and some of her strength returned. 'I can't escape. Look at me. I'm too weak and I don't know where I am. For God's sake, don't tie me up again.'

'It is necessary. You bang side of truck and make noise and people think migrants are inside and police come and find you.'

She shook her head. 'Please! It's too cold and I'm sick.' It was true she felt so lousy she wondered if she was coming down with an infection. She looked up at his portly profile and his breath smoking in the cold of the truck. 'You need to treat me better if you are going to get what you want from my husband.'

'Eat, or I will take hot dog,' he snapped.

The only thing she had control over was the speed of her consumption. She ate slowly, chewing every mouthful far more than necessary. He grew impatient, stamped on the floor of the trailer and in the end tried to seize the tray from her, but she was too quick for him and clasped it to herself so he couldn't get it without a struggle. She knew that Kirill probably thought it was beneath his dignity to wrestle with a woman over a half-eaten hot dog. He walked the few paces to the tailgate and exchanged some words with the men, then let himself down into the dark and lit a cigarette, which made him cough in the cold air.

She had eaten as much as she wanted and let the tray slip to the floor, and then, quite suddenly, she found herself silently crying with anger at her powerlessness.

One of the men came towards her and held her arms together while he slipped and tightened a plastic tie around her wrists. 'Four hours,' he murmured. 'Four hours max.' He pushed her down gently on her side and covered her with an unzipped sleeping bag, then left the trailer and closed the doors. She might have a friend among the people who held her, at least someone whose heart could be moved by her plight.

CHAPTER 16

With his bare feet up on a coffee table piled with exhibition catalogues bought by Anastasia that he couldn't bring himself to throw away, Samson picked up with her phone where he'd left off when Leila had called the previous afternoon to go through Cedar's figures. With Jo asleep next door, he wondered if he should feel more discomfort than he did, but he swiftly put the thought out of his mind because there was nothing to be gained from it, and Jo had given him some distance and helped him see things more clearly, particularly with the information about Daniel Misak, the man without a face.

He sipped from a mug of tea and went through the photographs. He found a series taken in Germany when they had both gone to visit Naji Touma, the young boy – now young man – that he had been hired to find among tens of thousands of refugees on the road to northern Europe three years before. The family was struggling with the practicalities of life, as well as with the growing hostility to refugees. Naji's sisters had been bullied at their school and his mother was experiencing a greater sense of isolation and despair than she had in the Turkish refugee camp. A film of Naji being roughed up had appeared on the Web.

Anastasia was at her best. She found a new apartment for the family and put a bomb under the social workers that were meant to be looking after their welfare. She contacted local refugee associations; liaised with the German officials who had brought Naji to Germany; and eventually made the connections which won Naji a handsome scholarship in Latvia, where the family subsequently moved. There was a photo of them all, Naji, standing between his mother and two sisters, and behind them Samson and Anastasia, who was wearing a determined expression, as though she had just walked from a meeting with the welfare people. The growing distance between Anastasia and him seemed obvious now.

He moved on to the Notes section of the phone, where he found a cache of Anastasia's most private thoughts about Denis Hisami and himself, which he supposed were either jottings for a journal or a means of working through her options. Full of abbreviations and half-formed sentences, they were obviously not intended for anyone else, and he imagined that, after all this time, she might have forgotten they were there. There was something girlish about them, but also something hard-headed.

D called again. Embarrassing because am with Samson, and had to lie. Once Denis wants something he never lets up . . . I feel a little like a company he's taking over . . . so much more rounded than Samson . . . he can give everything I want for my career. The good we could do! Real improvement for refugees' lives. But I love S. for myself. That's the me part satisfied, not the good part that wants to help people. Leave him when we have so much? Samson's faults 1. Gambling addiction/ likes risk 2. Remote even when tries not to be. 3) sister, pain in the neck 4) obstinate 5) irresponsible with himself and his money. Qualities – funny, bed wonderful, generous, and he reads and knows a lot, likes food. CAN COOK. Sexy and doesn't know it. TOUGH. OMG so TOUGH!

There were no dates to any of the entries, but he had an idea when they were made because of occasional references to things they had been doing together – a movie at the British Film Institute; a race meeting at Newmarket, which he knew she'd loathed and about which she'd written: 'Red-faced English people. All drunk. Horses beautiful'; and a weekend in Prague where they had failed to rekindle the magic of Venice and which came very near the end of their relationship. Anastasia wrote:

He doesn't understand me, or what I need to do in life. We are like bad teenagers. There is no future with Samson. Denis called. Said he wanted to make a Foundation with me to remember his sister. He already had business plan and structure. When he flew to Lesbos and told me of his plans, I didn't believe him. Now I do.

Samson noted that she hadn't told him about Hisami's visit to Lesbos, but then he wasn't surprised and had known they were seeing each other, or at least that they were in touch regularly. He moved on to a list, which was evidently Anastasia trying to order the arguments for leaving him.

> 1 He will be happier without me. 2 No more arguments 3. S. wants children – I don't 4. Pressure from mother to have grandchildren 5. I cannot be happy in London and he doesn't want to live anywhere else. 6. I need to follow my career.

There was a postscript.

> Must say, I love S. and my heart breaks with all this. We have been through a lot together and he will always be special to me. No one has made me laugh as much or enjoy simple things. He is a GOOD man and I love him!!!

As far as he could recall, this was exactly the way her speech had gone, and almost in the order she'd sketched out. He hadn't bothered to argue his case because by that time he knew all about Hisami and she was adamant, but he did know, or thought he knew, that she still loved him. He saw that particular softness in her eyes, though she tried to hide it. And, absurdly, he had banked on her coming back to him eventually.

He moved on through the notes, which described the new life she had found in California, with guest lists, possible members of committees, notes from meetings, memos to herself, must-do lists before big occasions, all of which seemed to be events arranged around the new foundation. She was much more organised than Samson had ever imagined. She collected her thoughts before meetings, wrote down ideas for presents, even listed the things she needed to bring up with her new husband. Samson groaned inwardly. It seemed like they were the type of couple who set aside time to go over each other's schedules. She was right. This was not a life that he could ever have given her. Samson did not possess a diary.

In the later notes, he noticed that Denis was always referred to and signed himself as Hash, and it occurred to Samson to search her emails with just that name. In her inbox he came up with a series of laconic messages from an email address, DH1Spoleto@spoletomix.com, which he assumed came from a private server, though they were notoriously easy to hack. Hisami said nothing of note in them, but then he began to read the emails Anastasia had sent to him and his replies.

Nine months before, she had written from Germany.

I just called. I don't want you to make this investment, Hash, darling. I think it will turn out badly for you, because you are not allowing yourself to make the judgement with your usual criteria. I don't get back for another week and by that time I know it will be too late. I love you and I don't want you to waste your life on an unnecessary fight. You are too big for that. XXXX

He replied:

In a meeting. We'll speak in the morning. Don't get this out of proportion. I send my love. Sleep well. Hash X

Samson was sure that the disagreement was over the investment in TangKi but, frustratingly, there wasn't any more on this. He combed the later emails and found nothing until some exchanges within the last month.

She wrote:

Up here in the State of Washington, things seem clearer, Hash. I couldn't say it last night, but I did want to tell you how much I admire you. It's something people should say to their partner more often. I also wanted to say this – sell your stake and let things be.

Again, a short reply:

It's a matter of principle. I can't back off. Anyway, my sweet, with patience and good thinking, I will win.

And then Anastasia showed her mettle:

Hash, accept you are wrong. You need to think about your motives and realise what you stand to lose. I've decided to go to Italy from Seattle. Saves time and I know

I won't miss the boat I am hoping to meet. And you can handle that reception without me, right!!!

This was the Anastasia he knew, and he was momentarily pleased to find that this part of her personality – truculent and really difficult – hadn't been altered by all Hisami's money. She was as capable of having a row with Hisami as she was with him. Samson was now certain that TangKi was the issue between them. He thought for about five minutes and briefly considered taking a cigarette from the unopened packet that lay beneath the framed photograph of his mother, but her gaze deterred him. She hated smoking and blamed it for her husband's premature death – that, and the stress of his gambling.

He got up and started for the bedroom, but then had a thought and sat down again with one of his own phones and tapped out an email.

Naji, Hope you and your family are doing well. I need your help urgently. If you call me tomorrow morning early, will explain everything. Can you get into this email – DH1Spoleto@spoletomix.com? I need to see it all. It belongs to Denis Hisami – Samson.

He rose and went into the kitchen where he and Anastasia had spent so many hours cooking, dining and, of course, sparring – part of the fun of dinner for her – and made for the stove. He reached up and with two index fingers pulled away the stainless-steel splash-plate behind the cooker to reveal a tiled surface, a remnant of his old kitchen decoration. Then he levered out a section of four tiles, which came away with some difficulty. Behind it lay the wall safe he had installed when he was gambling and had kept large amounts of cash in the flat. He punched the eight-digit code into the pad and the safe door popped open. He placed Anastasia's phone inside, on top of some documents he'd gathered while researching Adam Crane.

He paused before returning to the bedroom. Reading the exchanges between Anastasia and her husband had certainly convinced him that they had a close and equal relationship, but it had also put her voice in his thoughts again and it seemed strange to be returning to his bed where another woman lay – a woman he liked and very much wanted to sleep with, but another woman nonetheless. He grimaced to himself, more from irritation at Anastasia's continued hold over him than actual remorse, and went into the bedroom. He slid in beside the unconscious form of Jo Hayes, who stirred and a few seconds later murmured. 'What've you been up to, Samson?'

'Doing the crossword,' he replied.

'Such a bloody liar,' she said.

CHAPTER 17

Hisami never managed more than a few hours' sleep at a time in the detention centre, and on the night before his hearing he did not sleep at all but instead lay thinking about the events of the last few weeks, not sparing himself in the process. The guards had removed the fraudster from the cell and he was left alone with Nelson, a fifty-five-year-old father of four who had been snatched on the street by officers of ICE who were convinced he was in fact an individual named Aldane Coombes, an illegal immigrant from Jamaica. Nelson had never lived anywhere but Queens, New York, but it seemed he bore a striking resemblance to Coombes and he was, at the moment, unable to prove his real identity.

Nelson's plight struck Hisami and listening to the man's tale not only convinced him of the raw injustices that occurred in America without anyone ever hearing about them but gave him distance from his own problems. In the small hours, Nelson sat up on his bunk, leaned over and touched Hisami on the shoulder. 'You're not sleeping Denis. I know you're just lying there beating up on yourself. I got no idea why, but you just gotta straighten yourself out. You have a powerful rage inside of you, sir, and it don't do no good in a situation like this.'

Hisami crooked an arm under his head and turned to him. 'You're right. Thank you. My wife calls it my white-hot silence: she mistakes concentration for anger.'

'Which is it now, friend?'

'Some of both: I'm thinking through a problem. I have a few urgent issues that can't be addressed until I get out of here, plus, I've got an enemy and I don't know who it is.'

'Tell me about your foe, brother?'

Hisami didn't go into any detail, but he sketched the characters of Micky Gehrig, Martin Reid, Gil Leppo and Larry Valentine. He saw each one in Castell's conference room as he described them, and that process made him think more deeply about their characters.

Reid was not someone he had ever warmed to. Too definite for Hisami's tastes, and he never showed the slightest sign of self-doubt, or empathy for that matter. A hard, obsessive man was the gravel-washer, but he had his own code of honour and, no matter what the pressure, he would not sit in front of Hisami and look him in the eye, knowing that he was orchestrating the abduction of his wife. The same applied to Larry Valentine, who was simply too rich to reach into this particular gutter. Rocket-boy Gehrig was basically a ruthless attention-seeker. His trip into space would ensure that he could talk about himself for the rest of his life, but Gehrig – unlike Martin Reid and Larry Valentine – was a Democrat and had been a big donor to the Clinton campaign in 2016. Going by what Daniel Misak had told him, the money was leaving TangKi to finance right-wing groups in Europe. So, this wasn't Gehrig. That left his friend, Gil Leppo. It was inconceivable that Gil, who had brought them a gift of a puppy at Thanksgiving, would do anything to harm Anastasia. They had become so close that Hisami suspected Gil came over more to talk to Anastasia than to him. He almost seemed dependent on her.

'You've got a lot of rich friends,' said Nelson when Hisami paused. 'How come you're in here?'

'I miscalculated.'

'I miscalculated my first wife. And she miscalculated me, too.'

'How so?'

'I knew maybe something was going on behind my back so I get myself one of them tiny little cameras from RadioShack and I rig it in the bedroom right there, then I have the pleasure of seeing my wife's huge fat ass being screwed by a man from across the street. And that's how I lose my wife, who is also my soulmate.'

'I'm sorry. Do you regret it?'

'I regret it – yeah. I regret it. All I'm saying is that your best friend is the person who can trick you most easy. Think about that, Denis. If you're close to someone, that treachery thing is always a possibility, and some people, they really can't help it.'

Hisami did think about that.

★

When Samson arrived at the Immigration Court on Federal Plaza in lower Manhattan, it was crowded with media. Hisami was evidently now a big story and the absence of his wife from these proceedings the subject of much speculation. But Hisami had hired the best publicist in New York City, who had spun the line that while the billionaire was defending himself against a politically motivated attack on his reputation, Anastasia had travelled abroad to view the Aysel centres and had been unavoidably detained, which was certainly true.

He had read versions of this statement, going through news sites in the cab from JFK. When he switched on his phone he'd hoped to pick up a message or email from Naji, but there was nothing from him. He sent another email, saying it was vital they speak before the end of the day.

He went straight to Federal Plaza, took the lift to the twelfth floor and found the noticeboard he had been directed to by a guard. Hisami's hearing was listed at the bottom, under several other cases, and by the time he had worked out which courtroom it was in and had threaded his way through the supporters of those whose cases were being heard, the judge – a crow-like woman in her mid-fifties with a sharp, impatient manner – was already speaking to the lawyers representing Hisami and ICE and Homeland Security. Tulliver caught sight of him and did a kind of salute then sat down in the front bench. The last time they had seen each other was when Samson was being deported from Macedonia and Tulliver had swapped places with him at Skopje airport, so leaving Samson to pursue young Naji in the mountains of northern Macedonia.

Journalists were already writing stories on their devices; they could insert detail and quotes as the hearing progressed. Samson watched the young woman next to him type, 'Billionaire Denis Hisami, who faces allegations that he lied on his immigration application, did not notify the authorities of his change of name and concealed a past that included war crimes and terror-related offences, was returned to prison after Judge Jean Simon concluded that he was a risk to the public. Judge Simon said . . .'

Hisami was brought in wearing civilian clothes, not the prison uniform Tulliver had warned Samson about on the phone. He looked exhausted but also oddly removed from his surroundings. Samson knew Hisami had spotted him but there was no acknowledgement and he simply turned his back to the public and sat down while the two guards who had brought him from the prison moved to the side of the courtroom and watched him as though he represented a major threat to national security.

The judge tapped the microphone then looked down at some papers. 'The purpose of a Reasonable Cause hearing is to decide just one thing – whether Mr Hisami's continued detention is justified. That, ladies and gentlemen, is the only thing we are here for. We are not here to determine the merits of the case against Mr Hisami, or order a removal or any other action. And in this narrow context ICE and the Homeland Security – and I quote – "has the burden of proving clear and convincing evidence that the alien should remain in custody because the alien's release would pose a special danger to the public".' She removed her glasses and looked at the government lawyers. 'The evidence you have produced so far is unimpressive. You will need to up your game, sirs, if you are to continue to hold Mr Hisami.'

A rather sinister lawyer with a shaven head, button-down collar, club tie and a drab suit rose and assured her that he was in possession of a very considerable amount of evidence.

'Then let's hear it, Mr Balstad.'

But before he could begin, Hisami's lawyer got to his feet. He was in his sixties, wore a bow-tie and had the woebegone expression of someone who had just heard the words 'Brace! Brace!' over an aeroplane's intercom. His mouth hung open, his eyes darted about the court and he had a nervous tic that made him pinch the edge of his lapel. Samson assumed his appearance belied his expertise as an immigration lawyer and that he had been chosen by the two tanned lawyers next to him because he knew what he was doing. 'Judge,' he started, 'I hope we can dispense with the term "alien". Mr Hisami is a legitimate American citizen and has no other citizenship. He has contributed more than most people to the well-being and prosperity of the nation and it seems inappropriate, not to say inaccurate, to refer to him as an alien. My client is as American as you or I, Judge.'

'Does this matter, Mr Weber?' asked the judge.

'It is important that the court acknowledges that Mr Hisami has done absolutely nothing wrong. He appears here as an innocent man.'

She nodded. 'Mr Balstad, proceed, if you will, and avoid the word "alien" in recognition of Mr Weber's sensitivities.'

Balstad stood and contemplated Hisami, as though he were looking at the embodiment of evil. 'It is the department's case that Mr Hisami is a man with a secret past that includes multiple acts of terrorism and at least one war crime. In order to facilitate his entry into the United States in January 1996, and his eventual application for citizenship, Mr Hisami constructed an elaborate backstory, changing his name and covering up his role as a violent terrorist who led attacks on the Turkish state. Mr Hisami was born a Kurdish national and from an early age was an active member of several different Kurdish nationalist groups, all of them dedicated to the creation of a Kurdish state. My colleague will distribute evidence that will leave the court in little doubt about the true nature of the man who passes himself off as a law-abiding American citizen.'

A woman got up and handed a sheaf of photographs to the judge and to Hisami's lawyers, then Balstad produced enlarged photographs printed on boards and marched over to an easel. 'It may help, Your Honour, if I go through them here. These items are marked A through P – there are sixteen in all. The first four are copies of Turkish intelligence reports from 1993 to 1995 which feature a terrorist commander named Karim Qasim, who the Turkish government have connected to several attacks committed on Turkish soil. You can examine the intelligence reports at your leisure. This fifth establishes that Karim Qasim is in fact Denis Hisami.' He lifted the photograph of an ID card showing the young Hisami with a short, unruly beard and a mop of black hair brushed forward. 'This is a driver's licence from the period issued to Karim Qasim by the Iraqi government.' He let the court absorb the image of the tough young man. 'And now we'll go through some of the attacks which the Turkish government – a NATO ally and friend of America – believes that Mr Hisami was responsible for.

'In the spring of 1994 the PKK attacked a convoy of unarmed military in eastern Turkey. Thirty-five young men were killed, together with four civilians.' There were four photographs of a burnt-out bus and an SUV with bodies cremated in the wreckage of both. They were shocking images, and the last, which showed the charred body of the SUV's driver slumped across the open door of the vehicle, drew a gasp from the courtroom.

'I think you've made your point,' said the judge.

'But there are two other incidents I wish to draw to your attention,' said the lawyer, who had not missed the journalists leaning forward or rising from their seats to get a better view of the easel. 'This is what remained of the Golden Anatolia Hotel after it was firebombed by Mr Hisami's terrorist group.'

There were more charred bodies, this time lying in the lobby of the burnt-out building. In the foreground was a child's doll part melted by the flames. Samson looked over to see Hisami raise his head slowly and regard the photograph with indifference. Weber was peering at the bundle of images before him with glasses held out away from his face, like a very old man studying a rare manuscript. The two lawyers beside him, who Samson guessed were from California, exchanged glances with Tulliver then nodded to another man, who had slipped into the court and now joined them at the table.

'Finally,' said Balstad, with a melodramatic tone, 'we have

conclusive proof of Mr Hisami's involvement in one of the most disturbing war crimes of that period. I apologise for bringing this material into court, Your Honour, but the DHS believes it is relevant to our view that Mr Hisami should remain in detention while his case is being processed, and that this material graphically demonstrates the government's concerns about the man before you.'

He propped up several images at the foot of the easel, some of which were intentionally the wrong way round so the court couldn't see them. He revealed the first – the scene of a mass grave with the bodies of young soldiers piled high in a shallow ditch. They had been executed at the side of the ditch and fallen forward, but at the moment of death some had turned, and their faces, many of which had been blown apart from the bullets, could be seen. It made a truly horrifying tableau. At the other side of the ditch, where the soil had been piled, stood a group of soldiers, appearing altogether too relaxed in the face of such horror. Three, cigarettes in their mouths, were bent over a lighter held out by a companion. The others stood about, showing no visible signs of emotion, wiping their faces in the heat, checking their guns, chatting. 'This shows the summary execution site of thirty-four Iraqi army recruits in Northern Iraq in 1995. International investigators have declared this atrocity to be a war crime. The men were all in their early twenties and were shot after they surrendered and had been disarmed by the men you see standing at the side of the grave.'

There followed a shot of the same scene from another angle. Samson saw immediately what Balstad was building up to. At the centre of the group – though partly concealed – was the young Hisami, in a leather flying jacket with an AK 47 slung over one shoulder and a heavy field radio handset hanging from the other, a pistol in his hand. The beard and the cigar raised to his lips were reminiscent of Fidel Castro. His commanding presence was obvious.

The close-up of Hisami came next. 'You will recognise the commander of the execution squad as Karim Qasim, the man Denis Hisami, who sits before Your Honour and pretends to be an innocent American citizen, just like the Nazi war criminals who came to our country to escape prosecution for crimes against humanity after the Second World War. Denis Hisami is not only a terrorist but also a war criminal, and he should remain in detention until an order for deportation is made, which undoubtedly will be the outcome of this case.' He paused and gave the courtroom a satisfied look. 'That concludes our evidence, Your Honour.'

The judge nodded and turned to Hisami's lawyer. 'Mr Weber, what do you have to say on behalf of your client? You've insisted that the government had nothing to back up its argument for continued detention, but now it seems they do. We are all ears, Mr Weber.'

Weber rose and looked around, as though he were not quite sure where he was. 'We are familiar with these photographs,' he said slowly, 'because, as you know, there have been attempts by the other side to circulate them. These attempts have been unsuccessful, because these photographs, as presented, are obviously libellous of Mr Hisami's reputation. If the court allows, I will address the last allegation first, because it is the most serious levelled in this vexatious case against my client. We have our own photograph,' and he reached down to a board handed up to him by an assistant from the front bench. Weber seemed to stagger slightly then set off unsteadily towards the easel, where he placed the board.

'Here you see almost the same photograph, but the shot is wider and allows a full view of the men immediately surrounding Mr Hisami. Oh, by the way, we do not deny Mr Hisami's presence at this dreadful scene.' He paused, placed a finger on the photograph and looked around the court. 'Here you will notice a man of fair complexion who is not in uniform and who carries only a sidearm. It is clear that he has taken off his aviator sunglasses to talk to my client.' He nodded to himself and then turned to face the judge. 'We are lucky, Your Honour, to have this gentleman in court with us today and he will give the context of this photograph as well as furnish details regarding the other allegations.'

'Who is this man?' demanded Judge Simon.

'It is I,' replied the tall man who had joined the table of lawyers a few minutes before. He rose and smiled obligingly.

'And who are you, sir?'

'Bob Baker, Your Honour.'

'I said who are you, not what's your name.'

'I am the former director of field operations in Northern Iraq for the Central Intelligence Agency. I am the one in the photograph standing next to Mr Hisami. Subsequent to this event, I became director of all operations in the Middle East for the Agency and have just retired from a desk job at Langley, overseeing another aspect of the Agency's work overseas.'

'Mr Baker is too modest to tell the court that he received the Distinguished Intelligence Medal on his retirement for, and I quote here, "achievements of an exceptional nature that contributed to the Agency's mission",' said Weber.

'What do you have to say?' snapped the judge.

'Well, I have a lot to say about this incident. At the time, Mr Hisami and I were working together, and I should, at the outset, stress that Mr Hisami was one of our most important friends in Kurdistan at that time.'

'You are saying he worked for the Agency?'

'Indeed he did, and he saved my life at least once – probably twice, if you count an ambush when I was unarmed.'

'You mean Mr Hisami worked for the CIA?'

'We don't normally confirm these details, but, absolutely, yes he did. He was a very important part of our efforts in the Kurdistan theatre.' Baker glanced down at Hisami. 'He is one of the bravest and most resilient individuals I have ever had the privilege to know.' Hisami showed no more interest in this testimony than in Balstad's evidence, although he did acknowledge the compliment with a slight nod.

'Can you explain these photographs?' asked the judge.

'Sure. These men were renegade Iraqi army soldiers, part of a force led by General Mahmood Al-Samarra, who was part of a plot to overthrow Saddam Hussein in 1995. The unit was compromised before they reached the rendezvous with my team and PUK forces led by Denis. They were taken from their vehicles and murdered on the spot by Saddam's security forces. We were just too late to save them.' He stopped to compose himself. 'This was an appalling tragedy, and the greatest regret of my time in the field, without doubt.'

Balstad shot up. 'How do we know you're telling the truth?'

'I'll take an oath, if you like, but I am telling the truth,' said Baker amenably, and in a way that no one could doubt what he was saying. 'This episode is part of my book, which comes out next spring and has been passed by the Agency as suitable for publication. The Agency fully recognises the service Mr Hisami has given to our country.'

The judge looked at the photographs. 'It seems strange that such a scene of horror provokes so little reaction in the men around you in the photograph,' she observed.

'These men are battle-hardened troops, Your Honour. They'd seen many terrible things and the best way of dealing with an atrocity on this scale is to distance yourself from it, and the way you do that is by acting normally and not absorbing the horror. I know this from my own experience, I regret to say.' He stopped and held the judge's gaze. 'I look at myself in that photograph today and wonder how I was able to behave like that. Was I any less of a human being then than I am now? I don't think so – it's just what you have to do.'

'You're saying Hisami had nothing to do with this?'

'No more than I did.'

'And these other terrorist atrocities – what was Mr Hisami's involvement? The government would lead us to believe that Mr Hisami is the author of this barbarity. Do you have any information on the murder of the Turkish army recruits and the arson at the hotel in Anatolia?'

'They are well-known incidents, all of them carried out by the Kurdish Workers' Party – the PKK. That is quite distinct from the PUK – the Patriotic Union of Kurdistan – of which Mr Hisami was an important member. The PUK was an insurgency, but you could not describe it as a terrorist group. It was founded by intellectuals in the seventies and, to this day, that tradition is alive.'

'So why is it that Mr Hisami is named as Karim Qasim on the intelligence reports?'

'I believe Mr Weber is in a better position to answer that, Your Honour.'

Baker sat down and the judge swivelled to Weber, who was standing at the easel with a rather vacant look on his face.

'Mr Weber, what do you have to say?'

'Um, this is not my field and, of course, I bow to almost anyone when it comes to the technology, but it seems that the disks whence these documents came have some issues.'

'Issues, what issues? Are you suggesting they aren't real?'

'I must object,' said Balstad.

'This is not a trial, Mr Balstad. I don't want objections,' said the judge, 'I want to hear what Mr Weber has to say. Mr Weber, please proceed.'

'On Mr Baker's advice, we took the disks for forensic examination, just to make certain my client was not being unfairly maligned. The documents are said to come from 1996 to 1997 – so, more or less, contemporary with Mr Hisami's activities as a PUK commander.' He paused and consulted some notes in his hand. 'What the analysis found was that these documents were not all that they should be if they were generated in the mid-nineties. The metadata – that is, the data that summarises other data, I understand – was certainly dated to that period. But then, when they used a particular piece of equipment known as a Hex editor, which displays all the binary information in a file, they found that the metadata had been tampered with.' He looked up. 'I hope I am not losing you?'

'Go on, Mr Weber,' said the judge.

'It seems the file contains a very modern version of a font called Calibri, which was introduced by Microsoft in 2006 and is the default font of Office 2007.' He looked around the court to see if the penny had dropped. Among the young press corps, it most certainly had. 'All these documents had apparently been saved at a much earlier date, but of course they couldn't have been, because the font did not exist in the nineties. It came into use much later. That means that all or part of the documents is a fabrication.'

He clicked his fingers at the assistant, who rushed forward with another board. 'And here is the proof,' he said, revealing a large-scale copy of the code which, among other fonts, spelled out c.a.l.i.b.r.i. 'These documents are recent forgeries,' he said, and began to make his way back to the table.

'You're certain of this?' asked the judge.

'We will submit all the evidence now to the court,' said Weber, hovering uncertainly by his chair. 'And it will form part of our case in the defence of Mr Hisami.'

Samson saw that Hisami had barely moved throughout this. He didn't look up or acknowledge Weber when he at last sat down.

The judge took off her spectacles. 'If Mr Hisami is the hero that your side makes him out to be, Mr Weber, why did he need to change his name from Karim Qasim?'

Balstad rose angrily. 'Are you hearing the case now?'

She turned towards him. 'No, as I explained, we are deciding whether the ICE – that is, the DHS – is right to continue to detain Mr Hisami on the basis that he is a threat to American citizens.'

Weber leaned across Hisami to consult Baker then drew back and looked at Hisami, who gave a barely perceptible shake of the head. 'That concludes our argument,' he said.

'Well, we no doubt will hear why Mr Hisami changed his name in due course. It is not a crime to change your name, unless it has been done as part of an attempt to conceal information from the immigration authorities.'

Weber bobbed up again. 'I can say that Mr Hisami changed his name for reasons of personal security, which he would rather not speak about for the moment.'

The judge nodded and turned to Balstad. 'If you are to continue to hold Mr Hisami, you must bring more convincing evidence to this court. I am going to order Mr Hisami's release, but with an ankle monitor, which will be fitted by the New York Police Department before he leaves this building.'

Weber rose more quickly than he had done during the hearing. 'But this is nonsensical, Your Honour. Mr Hisami is not a flight risk and the government has never argued that he was. They said he was a danger to society.'

'This is the way it's going to be. The DHS will know where your client is without the necessity of locking him up.' She turned to Balstad. 'I want a complete report on the disks and photographs you have brought into this court as evidence. And the next time I see you, I will expect an explanation. The evidence that you bring then will be incontrovertible, or the case will be dismissed immediately. Do you understand?' She paused and glowered at him. 'Next case!'

The man was right. It was just a few hours before the truck reached its destination, but it felt like days to her because of the intense cold. When the truck came to a halt and the doors were flung open on a misty and frosted forest clearing, they had to pick her up bodily and carry her out of the truck. From watching people who had been rescued in the Aegean, she dimly recognised what was wrong with her – she was shivering and her teeth were chattering, her speech was slurred and she couldn't order her thoughts to tell the men about the pain in her shoulder. A few more hours of that and she knew she'd be dead of hypothermia.

But now she was out in the morning light and the sun was shining above the autumn mist and she saw Kirill standing in the glade, now sporting a tweed hunting jacket with leather shoulder pads, pockets with large flaps and a dark green Tyrolean hat which had an orange feather stuck in the hat band. She thought she was hallucinating until he bent over to examine her and she smelled the tweed jacket and the acrid aroma of a Turkish cigarette.

He spoke rapidly in Russian to the three men who held her and they carried her across the clearing to a compound surrounded by a high mesh fence and inside which was a large log cabin and several smaller outhouses. The porch of the main building was decorated with boars' tusks and antlers. One of the men caught his jacket on a set of tusks as they negotiated the door and had to be unhooked before they finally got her inside, laid her on a hard bench and covered her in a rug made from crochet squares.

Kirill barked out more instructions. A kettle was boiled and a hot-water bottle smelling of rubber was placed on her chest. Kirill cut the wrist tie, and she was able to hug the warmth from the hot-water bottle, but her teeth didn't stop chattering and violent shivers still ran through her shoulders and arms. A few minutes later, he was at her side with a cup of soup, which evidently came from a packet because there were dried bits floating in the foam on the surface. He held it to her lips. 'Best room service here.' It was too hot and burned her lips. He blew on it. She noticed that his face glistened and his lips were moist. 'Take some,' he said. 'Make you feel warm inside.'

Gradually, she was able to drink the soup and it did make her feel better. She nodded when he asked how she was feeling, but she could not yet speak.

'I put vodka in soup,' said Kirill, as though he were the host at a social event. 'Bison-grass vodka. Maybe taste not great in soup, but will do trick, eh?'

He pulled up a chair and sat back, hands across the front of the tweed suit, fingers toying with the jacket belt. He took off his hat and twirled it on his index finger. 'What do you think of hat? Good, no? Austrian hat. It will bring luck. I will kill many – I forget name of animal in English – *dikiy kaban.*' He searched round and pointed to a massive black boar's head over the fireplace. 'So, this place is where you will stay until we have agreement from Mr Hisami.'

'What do you want from him?' she murmured.

'It does not matter. But you must pray he agrees to what we want. Otherwise, it will not be good for you, Anastasia. Your Russian name will not protect you if he does not give us what we want.'

'It isn't Russian, it's a Greek name,' she said groggily. 'It comes from St Anastasia. She was a Greek saint and the name means resurrection.'

'A good name for position you are in.' Kirill liked to have the last word.

'How can Denis do anything when he's in prison? Did you have him put in prison?'

'His lies put him there.'

'But how can he do what you want?'

'He can make instructions – that is all it will require.'

'Have you told him—' She coughed and waited to regain her breath. 'Have you told him what you want?'

He shook his head. 'He knows why you were taken; he knows why his business across America is in trouble. He knew before you were seized. You suffer because of him. He took something that was not his. It is now in his hands.'

She finished the soup but kept her hands locked around the heat of the mug. 'Have you contacted him? You've got his phone number, right? Email?'

Kirill considered this then smiled to himself. 'He has one opportunity. We do not propose to extend the negotiation. He has one chance to say yes or no. One chance to save your life. But maybe I talk to Samson first because we know his number from the phone call you made.'

She peered through his glasses at his eyes. They were bland and without emotion. 'Why are you telling me this?'

'You asked me. I always tell truth, Anastasia. May I call you by your first name? What did Mr Samson call you? Maybe I call you by name he used.'

She ignored this. 'Why are you treating me so badly?'

'To bring you to dacha is not treating you badly, Anastasia. You have comfort here. Hot shower. Food. Nature. Conversation.' He stopped. 'Is my conversation boring to you?'

'If all you talk about is killing me, yes, it does get boring. Can I have some more food? I'm still hungry.'

Without turning, he shouted to the two men who were standing around watching the third lug boxes into the cabin. This man set down the box he was carrying, began to search for something then retrieved a bag of crisps and some pre-packed cheese. He brought them over and handed them to her with a lopsided, sheepish grin. She was sure this was the same man who, in the truck, had whispered in her ear that it wouldn't be long to the end of the journey.

'I can't open the packet – my hands,' she said, passing the crisps to Kirill. He shook his head and gave them to the man, who tore the bag open and cut the packaging on the cheese with a penknife.

'Good Russian cheese,' observed Kirill. 'President has brought cheese industry to life after sanctions. We destroy European shit that comes into Russia and now we have fine Russian cheese.' He called for an ashtray and lit a cigarette then studied her through a veil of smoke. 'You are strong. You already recover. We have maybe one week in this place. You will be confined except when you are in my presence. You will not speak to guards and you will not try to escape.'

She nodded her compliance.

'We spend much time together. Do you like to read?'

'Do I like reading?' she said incredulously. 'Yes, when I have the time.'

'You have time now. We make – how do you say? – we make book club in forest. And talk about a book every day. I am fast reader.'

'You want to talk about books out here!'

'Why not? It is good way to pass time while we wait for your husband to respond.'

He rose. 'Can you walk? Get up!'

'I don't know – do you have painkillers? I have a bad shoulder.'

'That won't affect legs. I show you something.'

She dragged herself to her feet but knew she couldn't stand long without help. Kirill beckoned to two of the men, who took her arms and guided her forward.

He replaced his hat, led them out of the building and turned towards the opening in the fence where four armed men waited. Kirill nodded to them as he passed and they fell in behind Anastasia and her two supporters. They all set off across the clearing behind Kirill, who had acquired a twisted walking stick from a stand inside the porch and moved with a quick, officious gait that implied ownership of everything around him. He pulled aside the bough of a larch to reveal a path then moved off again, needlessly slashing at the dead undergrowth with the stick.

At any other time, Anastasia would have noticed the delicately frosted vegetation, the mist hanging in the trees and the extraordinary quiet of the forest, where no birds sang and nothing moved. But she was aware only of the feeling restored to her legs and feet and a strange, prickly sensation in her toes.

They went about three hundred metres and she caught a glimpse of an orange object between the trees. Soon they emerged into a much smaller clearing, where there was a mini digger and a trench that had evidently just been excavated, for the earth was damp and had not been touched by the frost. Kirill ordered her to be brought to the side of the trench, whereupon he put his stick to the back of her head. 'If you try to escape, I will end your life here. Then this machine will cover your body with that pile of earth and no one will ever know what has happened to you. So, no tricks! Do what I say and do not speak to my men.' He moved from behind her so he could look into her eyes. 'We have an understanding, I believe. Yes? Now let us go and view accommodation.'

He moved away from her and she turned from the trench, knowing that in this ugly, pompous man she was confronting the same evil as she had in the Macedonian mountains with Samson and Naji. Kirill maintained a plausible veneer of civilisation and humanity but, ultimately, he was the same entity as the terrorist Almunjil.

The men turned and began to lead her back to the dacha, but she was now capable of walking without help and shook herself free of them. Kirill shouted over his shoulder to her. 'We will study Russian literature, but first you tell me about American fiction.'

'I know nothing about American books,' she said to his back. 'I am Greek.'

'Then we will learn together. We read *Huckleberry Finn*. You have read this author – Mark Twain?'

'No,' she replied.

'You will enjoy book and we will discuss later.'

CHAPTER 18

A failure of communications between the NYPD and ICE meant there was a delay in fitting the ankle monitor and Hisami was forced to spend several more hours in custody. Tulliver and Samson met in a coffee bar a block away from the Metropolitan Correctional Center, once Samson had checked into a downtown hotel near Hisami's apartment in Tribeca.

He had slept on the plane so he felt fresh. The same couldn't be said of Tulliver, who was fighting several fires at once. The media were all over Hisami, who, up until a few weeks before, had managed to maintain a low profile that bordered on the secretive. In the past, he had consented to do interviews only when publicising his sister's work with children suffering from cancer or, more recently, the Aysel centres. Though many remarked on his pleasant manner, they also noted that Hisami was reticent, elliptical. 'Delphic' was a word used a few times. Now he had even reached the pages of the *New York Times*, which had published a long profile that asked questions about his past relationship with the CIA and referred to the rumours about his part in a raid on a terrorist cell in Macedonia three years before. Hisami's publicist regarded this as helpful coverage that portrayed him as America's friend and as an action hero, but Tulliver said that none of it was good for business. The doubts about Hisami's past and the credible rumours about his involvement in the Macedonian incident were causing the banks to review their relationship with Hisami. The elaborate structure of Hisami's holdings and investments, particularly in media and biotech start-ups, already stressed by shorting the pharma stock, was beginning to rock. He was very rich, but it could all go overnight. 'His wealth relies on a perpetual forward momentum and his constant focus,' said Tulliver. 'The most important part of his life is his daily conversations with bankers, which cannot be conducted from the Metropolitan Correctional Center. He's got a long way back to rebuild those relationships and the confidence people had in him.' He looked Samson in the eye. 'He may not make it.'

Samson rubbed his neck and looked out of the window. 'What the hell is this about, Jim? I mean, what the fuck are we all dealing with? Tell me what it is, because for the life of me, I don't get it. A massive sum has gone missing and Adam Crane is responsible. Is TangKi merely the channel, or has Crane raided its reserves? Five people have been murdered and Anastasia kidnapped and held hostage in Russia without any kind of ransom demand. And now we know that Denis was working with the CIA in the 1990s and whoever is punishing him has access to detailed information about that time. Are we dealing with a vendetta? What's it all add up to?'

'I know as much as you do.'

'Crap – you know much more.'

'I have intimations.'

'What the hell are they?'

'I knew nothing of what he was doing with TangKi, but with Denis there is always a very good reason for his actions and that usually involves a principle. This is at the core of his psychology. He thinks very hard about an issue, a business opportunity or an idea, then he develops this principle which absolutely governs everything he does from then on.'

Samson shook his head. 'I don't give a damn about his fucking principles.' He picked up his cup, swirled the remains of the black coffee and knocked it back. 'Russia – it's all about Russia. Anastasia is held in Russia, Crane has Russian family and, I'm making a guess here, but I believe that the money originates in Russia.' He stopped again. 'And the provenance of those photographs from Iraq and the changes to those documents have the smell of a smear campaign that would never stand up to any kind of forensic examination. This was an intelligence operation and ICE and Homeland Security fell for it.'

'A lot of assumptions there.'

'How did Denis get involved with Crane?'

'He met him on the San Francisco charity circuit and he guessed he was suckering all those people into something or other at TangKi. Once Crane had bought the company from the founders and was bringing in all that five-star money, Denis became interested and he let Crane approach him.'

'What's the company actually do?'

'It offers a few services. Using a crypto currency, it allows people to buy real estate anywhere in the world without the usual complications of lawyers, realtors and currency exchange. It's also designed a blockchain service for owners of large developments so everything is transparent and investors can go into the records of a building and see exactly what has been done to the structure, when and who paid for it. And finally, it provides a way for people to invest in a portfolio of buildings and developments. That's the original business and where the name TangKi comes from – it's Malay for a 'tank' or 'pool'. It was set up by two realtors – one of them Malaysian – who made a lot of money when they sold it to Crane.'

'And Crane spotted it was a great way of laundering money, or his Russian masters did.'

Tulliver shook his head and looked down at his phone, which vibrated with a text message. 'That's Zillah. I'll tell her to come here.'

They sat in silence for a minute or two. At length, Samson said, 'If there's anything you think I should know, you tell me, Jim. Pick up the phone, whether Denis gives you permission or not. It may just save Anastasia's life.'

Tulliver looked at him hard.

'I mean it. He's not levelling with us about something.'

Tulliver nodded. 'Okay. Let's see what happens.'

Zillah arrived at their table with a laptop in a tote bag and a

Japanese umbrella that collapsed so that it stood on the tips of its ribs. She muttered hello, hooked her hair back and opened the laptop. 'Okay, so we tracked the vehicle four hundred miles north of the Crimea. It was hard. They had outriders and we lost it. But we have the plate and we know which company arranged the truck. It's an outfit called Arcady-Ax Logistics, which likely has Mafia connections, and it operates out of Rybatskoye industrial zone, south-east of St Petersburg. The driver must have delivered Mrs Hisami with the kidnappers at some point between the place where we lost the truck and St Petersburg, so that's, like, nine hundred miles.' She raised a finger. 'But if the truck came from the city – it has a St Petersburg plate with the number 178 – it seems possible that she's being held at the top end of that nine-hundred-mile route.'

'Maybe,' said Samson.

'Satellite imagery was our first thought, but the majority of the journey was undertaken at night and, besides, there was heavy cloud cover – the Russian winter is coming. So we figure our best line of inquiry is with the trucking company, and we aim to locate that truck and the man or men who drove it all the way from Crimea. I now have four people working on this, including one female Russian national who usually does work for us outside Russia. She has agreed to make an exception this one time. If we identify the driver, we'll launch her and she'll find out where the truck stopped, I promise you that. So we are putting all our resources into that area of the investigation.'

'And what happens if you find the place?' asked Tulliver. 'Do you go in?'

'That will be for Mr Hisami to decide. Going into a situation like that is fraught with danger for the rescuers and the kidnap victim.' She looked from one to the other. 'Have we received any kind of demand?'

'No,' said Tulliver, 'but we haven't had access to Denis's phone since he's been in jail.'

'If this is coordinated,' said Samson, 'the people holding Anastasia will know that Hisami is being released.'

Tulliver didn't reply to this but got up and pocketed his phone. 'I'm going to go down to the jail. Denis is bound to be out soon. I'll call you about the meeting later.'

'It has to happen tonight,' said Samson.

'He's got a lot of calls to make.'

Samson rose so he wouldn't be overheard. 'Tell Denis we're not going to free Anastasia sitting in New York. If he wants his wife back, he needs to see me as soon as he can and he has to be completely open.' He sat down as Tulliver turned without a word and left the café.

'We've got company,' said Zillah, without looking up. 'They're using the restaurant's wifi to hack us. You should turn off your phone.' She shut down and closed her computer and swiped the top of her phone screen.

'Where?'

'Two men behind you, four tables back. They're using a laptop. They probably picked you up in the court.'

'In earshot?'

'No, but maybe we should move.'

Samson paid and followed Zillah to the door. As she passed

the two men, who appeared to be engrossed in what they were doing, she darted over to lean on their table.

'Hi, guys. Do you have the broadband password for this place? I'm in here all the time and can't make it work.'

One of them, a man in his thirties, looked up sheepishly and said he thought the waitress could help.

'Right, so you don't have it.' She straightened and her hand knocked the glass of water standing on the table into the laptop keyboard. They both jumped up, shouting. She stepped away and announced to the restaurant. 'These two guys here, they're hacking your devices.' It took a few seconds for the café to erupt, by which time Zillah and Samson were on the way to the door.

'We'll walk, if you don't mind,' she said, beckoning to the silver SUV at the kerb to follow them.

'What made you so certain about them?' asked Samson.

'The dongle with an aerial that picks up the signals of the devices in the room and tricks them to connect with it.'

'Who was it?'

'Could be anyone – the government, Crane's people. God knows. ICE and Homeland Security are pissed about what happened in the court today.'

She stopped when they had crossed the street. 'I have news. We think Crane is in Estonia.'

Samson stopped. 'How do you know?'

'One of the numbers you got from your friends in Naples was a bank account accessed from Tallinn two days ago. My people have a way of monitoring access to the account, though we cannot tell what's in it, or what transactions take place. But we can tell where the source is.'

'I didn't give you the numbers,' said Samson.

'I've got a good memory,' she said.

'Tallinn is just a few hours from the Russian border,' he said, ignoring her slightly annoying smile.

'Four and half hours by road.'

'Does anyone else know this? Macy, for instance?'

'No.'

They walked on a few paces. 'Keep this to yourself, Zillah.'

'I have to tell Denis, but I can avoid telling anyone else. Why don't you want Macy to know?'

'I think the MI6 surveillance on Macy is pretty intense at the moment. I'm sure they know exactly where Crane is and are determined to protect that information. I don't want them to have any clue that we know his location.'

She nodded.

'Will you let me hear of any more activity?'

'Yes. Are we done now?' Zillah had a strictly transactional approach to conversation.

She turned and hopped into the back of the SUV before he could say goodbye. He kept walking in the direction of the park, but then hailed a cab to take him uptown to Union Square, where he got out and walked until he found another cab, which he asked to take him to the intersection of Varick Street and Canal, and there he went through several cleaning routines to avoid being followed, including diving into the subway and exiting on the other side of the street. It was unnecessary, because anyone could guess where he was going, but he had been aware of the minute barometric pressure exerted on the pursued by the pursuer, and he just wanted to know if he was right.

CHAPTER 19

It was late in the forest and Kirill built a fire in the compound from lengths of dead pine which had been sawn to one size, placed in a half oil drum and anointed by him with diesel. In front of this he had his men position two crude chairs, cut from the same pine long ago and pimpled with spots of hardened resin. For the purpose of Kirill's midnight literary seminar, Anastasia was wrapped in a blanket, handcuffed around one wrist and chained to a man with an automatic weapon. She was thus able to sip at a glass of vodka provided by Kirill, while looking down at *The Adventures of Huckleberry Finn*.

She'd spent so much of the day asleep in the small wooden cell at one end of the dacha that she hadn't finished the book and had tried to skim it. Yet the first part of Huck's journey on the raft down the Mississippi and the relationship between the boy and the runaway slave struck her as wonderful.

It was impossible to get her head around the strangeness of the situation now, the combination of threat and hospitality, and having to endure the literary pretensions of a man who would not hesitate to kill her and bury her in the forest. Kirill was plainly bored and felt the need to toy with her, like a cat playing with an exhausted prey, but he also seemed to crave her approval, an indication that her jailer and potential executioner was at least a man of learning and insight. She watched him, in his hunting gear and still wearing that ridiculous hat, his face glistening in the light of the fire, and wondered if she could ever loathe a human being more. And when he held out his glass of vodka and delivered the speech by Jim, the escaped slave, upbraiding Huck for his cruelty in pretending to be dead – hard for anyone not born in the South of the USA, but impossible for a Russian with a thick accent – she just snorted a laugh of contempt.

He glared at her. 'You can do it better, Anastasia?'

'I am not an American.' She looked up at the sparks shooting into the night sky. 'I can't read the dialect – it's too hard for me.'

'What is story about?' he demanded, as though her life would depend on the answer.

She waited before replying. 'I guess it's about two refugees, who, like the people I work with, are thrown together and risk everything when they try to escape terrible things in their lives. It doesn't matter whether it's the Mediterranean or the Mississippi – those waters are their fate and they are at their mercy. They've got no control over what happens to them, or where they end up; they could be drowned or saved. They have nothing and no one except each other and that makes their relationship interesting.'

'Sentimentality! Pure sentimentality. It is the sickness of the West that you do not understand what is important about Huckleberry.'

'I wasn't being sentimental,' she said fiercely. If he was going to play with her, she was going to give him a run for his money. She threw back the vodka. 'You tell me what it's about then! You tell the sentimental little Western woman how she should read this story.'

He ignored the challenge. 'Don't you see? It's about freedom. Young boy Huckleberry escapes violent drunken father but *also* rules of society he hates. The slave flees old woman owner so she cannot sell him. They are fighting for their freedom, Anastasia! Freedom!'

She let out a bitter laugh. 'You're lecturing me about freedom! The woman you've chained by the wrist like a slave!'

He ignored her. 'You in West do not understand freedoms you have and you do not value them. That is why you lose them.'

'That's bullshit. People value their freedoms – the freedom to be themselves, to express their sexuality, to defy prejudice and follow their own belief system.'

'Anastasia, those things are the reason the West has failed! You confuse identity politics with freedom.' He called for more vodka then continued. 'If you valued freedom, you would understand important message in book.'

Her glass was filled and she stared into the fire, momentarily forgetting where she was. 'Despite the differences in race and status, the boy and the slave come to see the humanity in each other,' she said. 'The boy plays a sick joke on the slave and then he apologises because he understands Jim is a person like him and he must take responsibility for his own cruelty. It's very moving.'

Kirill grinned at the fire. 'The West is failing because of this kind of thinking. Maybe it has failed already.'

'I am not a political thinker. My job is to help people.'

He placed the vodka glass by his feet, folded his hands around his stomach and looked contentedly at her. 'We are strong. Russia knows how to suffer. The West doesn't know suffering. That is why West loses freedom.'

'We were talking about a book about two people fleeing from their circumstances – two fugitives, two refugees. And now you're talking about the decline of the West. What's the connection?'

'Maybe there isn't one.' He took a cheroot out of a slim box he had withdrawn from inside his hunting jacket and tapped one end on the box. 'You know about demoralisation, Anastasia? You know that an entire country like the great United States of America can be demoralised so that no one remembers what their country stands for and democracy rots from the inside? That is what has happened in United States. It required a few years, but we see results now we could not anticipate.'

She shook her head and looked away. 'That's bullshit. The United States is still strong. It has bad times but, deep down, it is resilient. The people are decent.'

He looked at her as though she were a child. 'In book boy and Jim perceive reality as it is and they see inequality and hateful conformity of America. They have no delusions. But now Americans have lost their ability to see good or bad. They've turned on their country, their greatest enemies are their fellow citizens – imagine that! They are fearful, they see plots where there are none, their information is corrupted and no one is able to form a sensible conclusion about best interests of people.' He rubbed his hands. 'And now we watch them abandon principles of Constitution. It's like dream for us.'

She yawned. 'You really think that's all true?'

'It is fact. It is greatest victory ever won without a war – no bomb exploded, no guns fired, but USA is on its knees. We achieved aims by exploiting America's ideological weakness. The people are soft and idle and now they cannot tell difference between up and down.' He bent down to retrieve his vodka, puffed furiously to fire up the cheroot and held the glass high. 'I drink to the American people, authors of their own destruction.' He tossed the glass over his shoulder and it hit the fence with a chink. 'I can see you do not believe me but, Anastasia, you should know that this is my expertise – I am professional in psychological warfare. I know what I am talking about. I am specialist. Crisis will follow, then normalisation of crisis and great American democracy is kaput for ever!'

'Are you in the intelligence services?'

He gave her another withering look. 'It was not espionage that destabilised the United States. It was the vanity and weakness of its people. We played on their weaknesses and they did the rest. Same is true in UK.'

She shrugged her disagreement. 'I doubt that people are

happier in Russia than in America or Britain. They have no freedom. There is no opposition. Democracy is a sham. Most people are poor. And a few oligarchs own and control everything.'

'Happiness! History is not won by making people happy, Anastasia. History is won by those who persuade the people that there is more to life than happiness and personal autonomy.' He picked up a long stick and stabbed at the fire, sending a column of sparks into the air.

'You speak like a fascist,' she said, and for one moment she thought he was going to hit her across the face with the stick. But he dropped it and grinned.

'"Fascist" is old-fashioned word. I prefer "realist". I am like Huckleberry Finn. I deal with reality and I have no delusions.' He paused. 'But now I have business to attend to. Maybe we have some business together later,' he added. 'I will give some thought to it.'

Samson entered a corner deli and bought a packet of cigarettes, lit up outside the store without guilt or much pleasure and thought how to play it with Hisami. His mind kept going back to the photographs on Anastasia's phone and that wrenching call from the ship. He noted that the closer he came to seeing Hisami, the more present she was in his mind and the greater his anger was towards her husband. The reason was simple: if he hadn't pursued her with his wealth and power, she would not now be held in Russia.

When Anastasia told him she was going to move to California

to work and live with Hisami – that's how she put it, with the work before the cohabitation – he'd blamed himself for his lifestyle, which she once observed consisted of equal parts risk and frivolity. Just before his mother died, she had said, in an unsparing assessment of her son's character, that if he had shown the will to change, he could have persuaded Anastasia to stay and make a go of things. 'No woman wants to commit to your kind of life,' she had said, adding, 'it took a long time for your father to grow up. Try not to be like him, son.'

It was true – he was at fault and he had lost her. But now he wished his dear old mum could see how things had turned out. Hisami tagged like a crook after a spell in jail and her son hired to find the woman who'd spurned him and who his mother knew was the only woman he'd ever loved, indeed the only woman he was ever likely to love. That would certainly give her pause, and he found himself hoping that she might think of him in a slightly more favourable light.

He looked at his phone for any message from Tulliver, took out a second cigarette, began to smoke and placed the crushed pack and the book of matches on top of a waste bin nearby. A homeless man soon scooped them up, thanked Samson and retreated to a doorway, where a wretched bundle of possessions was stowed. Samson idly watched the man light up and wondered how he'd survive the coming winter, and this reminded him of Anastasia's unfailing kindness to people on the street in London. She didn't just give them money; she stopped to talk and she made them feel valued as people.

The call came from Tulliver an hour later. 'I'm really sorry

– he has an urgent business meeting at seven and he's tied up until then. We're going to have to push it back to eight, eight fifteen?'

'Okay, Jim, but I will need his full attention then because, whatever happens, I'm going to go back to London on the first flight tomorrow. Understood?'

Denis Hisami sat waiting in a leek-green cardigan and collarless white shirt, the ankle monitor hidden beneath a pair of baggy grey trousers. He had been in the straight-backed wooden chair for half an hour, paying remarkably little attention to what was going on behind the glass screen where Tulliver and three employees worked to keep his business afloat. They had their instructions, and he'd left them to get on with it; there was nothing else he could do until the morning, when he would start a punishing round of calls with the banks.

Tulliver came over, hovered until Hisami looked up, and said, 'Martin Reid and Micky Gehrig are on their way over. Gil Leppo is already outside but is in a conference call in his car. He's going to represent Larry Valentine.'

In the event, they all exited the lift together and Hisami shook them each by the hand and offered them a drink, as though nothing had happened since they last saw each other. It was an awkward moment, which Leppo filled with a story about Valentine's marital problems. 'It turns out that old goat Larry was such a big supporter of family values he had families all over the country. The kids of his first marriage are really pissed because it affects their inheritance.'

The story fell flat. No one was interested.

Hisami showed them to one end of a bleached wood dining table that was dominated by two large canvases by Ed Ruscha and Jasper Johns, with a smaller one to the side by the British artist Patrick Heron, which was admired by Leppo, who told them he was in New York to attend a fashionably late evening show at a gallery in the Bowery.

'You called for this meeting, Marty, would you like to start?' asked Hisami.

At these moments of intense stress everything slowed – it was his battle calm.

'Are you solvent?' Reid asked, laying his scarf over an adjacent chair.

'It's going to be tough, but we've got everything covered. I'm here to reassure you that we will honour any commitments we've made on investments and collaborations.'

Reid's eyes bored into him. 'Is that the true picture, Denis? What happens if you are re-arrested by the immigration authorities, which I hear is a possibility? No one is going to support you if you go to jail again.'

'I have assets to cover everything. Cash flow is the problem, but we are working on that tonight.'

'How big a problem?'

'To be honest, a really big problem. I need about $150 million in place by the end of tomorrow morning. It's painful for me to admit it, but I've been in worse situations. We'll get through this.'

'If you're locked up again, you're fucked,' said Gehrig.

'That's not true, Micky. But I cannot disguise the fact that it'll be difficult.'

'All this material coming out about your past as a rebel commander, working with the CIA, the Macedonian incident, these things do not help confidence,' persisted Gehrig. 'Even if you aren't a goddam terrorist, it makes you look kind of wild and unreliable.'

'I agree,' said Hisami. 'But we're all, to an extent, prisoners of our past, and mine appears more colourful than most. What you have to know is that none of you will lose money.'

He was seated a little distance from the trio so that he could watch them. He saw Leppo's leg jigging. 'Is there something you want to ask, Gil?'

'I'm worried for you, Denis. It doesn't look good.'

'It doesn't – I agree. But then you may all be in the same boat.'

'How so?' demanded Gehrig, the most hostile of the three.

'Unless you want to find yourself in my position, you must order an immediate investigation into the money flow through the company. I hear that this wasn't properly discussed at the board meeting so I wanted to say, very clearly, that you all face action from the FBI if you don't take steps to investigate where this money came from and where it went. You need to place yourselves on the right side of the law.'

Gehrig pulled his exasperated face. 'Everything's fine, Denis. We have accounts. We know the money has gone to research projects and joint ventures in Europe.'

'It's up to you whether you accept my advice.' He looked at each of them in turn. 'I have some bad news. I have to tell you that a body was found in a London apartment a few days ago. The victim is likely to be Ray Shepherd, the identity that Adam Crane used in London.' He waited a beat then added, 'That leaves you guys holding the baby. I would suggest that you put your lawyers on to this immediately.'

Reid didn't need to hear anything else. He pulled out a phone and arranged a conference call with his lawyers in two hours' time. Gehrig looked doubtful then asked Reid if he could tie his lawyer into the conversation.

Leppo said he would join them. 'It was definitely Adam Crane?' he said. 'That's truly terrible!'

'Looks like it,' Hisami said.

'He was killed?' asked Reid.

Hisami nodded.

'Jesus!' said Gehrig. 'What the fuck is going on? Why isn't this in the news?'

'You're lucky it isn't and, if I were you, I wouldn't breathe a word of it to anyone. It gives you time to . . .'

'Get our shit together,' said Leppo.

'Is there something you're not telling us, Denis?' demanded Reid.

'No. Crimes have been committed – theft and/or money-laundering – and because my letter to the board is on the record, you'll need to protect yourselves.'

'Nothing more needs to be said.' Reid gathered his things and clambered to his feet. 'You coming, Micky?'

Hisami rose too. 'Jim Tulliver will stay in touch with you all about any developments.'

Leppo didn't stir. 'I think we all owe you a debt for being straight with us, right, Marty?'

Reid grunted. 'Let's see how things turn out.'

'I mean it, guys,' said Leppo. 'It's been a really tough time for you and Anastasia. I can't imagine how she has the resilience to keep working in Italy. I hope you'll send her all our best.'

Hisami turned to him slowly. 'Yes, I will be sure to do that. Thanks. She'll appreciate your thoughts.'

Gehrig and Reid left without saying goodbye, sweeping past Tulliver, who was waiting at the open lift door.

'That leaves you and me,' said Hisami pleasantly. 'Would you like a drink? I have some great scotch.'

'Yeah. Look, I have to make a few calls in the car then I'll come back. Give me an hour or so. Does that work for you?'

'I'm not going anywhere,' said Hisami.

CHAPTER 20

Samson entered the Restaurant Asolo and found himself noticing a few things he'd change – the bright overhead lighting, the tables crowded in the middle of the space and the way the maître d' had seated people randomly, creating the impression that the place was almost empty and failing. But the waitress was pleasant and welcoming. He ordered the special of veal with a salad and sautéed potatoes and a glass of La Salute, a red from the Veneto.

He had chosen a table in the corner of the restaurant with a window that looked down Hisami's street and briefly wondered if Denis and Anastasia came here on the odd night in New York. As the waitress set down the wine, his phone murmured in his pocket. It was Tulliver to tell him that he should leave it for an hour or so. They would have plenty of time later, when Denis would be able to give him his undivided attention.

Samson toyed with some antipasti offered by the waitress

and ordered another glass of wine. Then his phone sprang into life again. He answered expecting an update from Tulliver.

'Is this Paul Samson?' asked the voice.

'Yes,' he replied, straightening at the sound of the Russian accent.

'I am with your friend Anastasia.'

Samson froze. He muttered something then composed himself. 'I want to speak to her now.'

'We will do FaceTime. I call back in one second.' The man seemed excited.

The line went dead. He held the phone in his right hand and his left dived inside his jacket pocket and struggled to get hold of a second phone. He wrenched it out, ripping the lining of his pocket, and was entering the passcode with his thumb when the first phone lit up with an incoming call – again with no caller ID. He laid the second phone down on the table and answered.

The live profile of Anastasia's face filled the screen. She was shaking. She was told to stand still, look at the camera and speak the agreed words by the man that had called him moments before, going by the voice. 'Hello, Paul. You can see I am alive. Tell Denis that I'm okay and I'm being treated well . . . tell him he needs to do exactly what they say and . . .' Her voice trailed off and she hung her head. 'Tell him to do everything he can.' Then she looked straight in the camera. Her eyes were bloodshot and her hair was straggly and unkempt. He realised she was slurring some words as though drunk.

'We'll do everything they say. We will bring you home, I promise.'

She threw him a look of terrified vulnerability that he'd never seen before, even in that godforsaken barn in Macedonia. She was on the edge – at her very limit. He wanted to say how he loved her, how he would do anything to prevent her being harmed, but knew this would be too painful for her, so he just said, 'I am with you. I am with you, dear Anastasia.' And her face twitched with a shy smile, like a child who had been let off a punishment.

And then the person holding the camera began to move back and he could see that she was standing outside. Men were holding powerful torches so she and her surroundings were illuminated. The camera was unsteady but he counted four men – all armed – and saw that Anastasia had a rug over her shoulders and was swaying at the edge of a ditch and on the other side of the ditch was a mound of earth. She kept shaking her head and looking towards the camera, her eyes pleading with them not to show the horror, which, of course, was the grave they had dug for her. He recoiled from the screen and found himself staring at the waitress, who had brought a second glass of wine to his table. He waved her away angrily and looked back at the screen. The camera steadied and panned from her face down to the grave and back to Anastasia, where it lingered. They had made their point. The call ended and the screen went blank.

Samson breathed deeply, gulped some wine and reached for the second phone to call Zillah. The moment she answered he gave her the address of the restaurant and the number of the phone on which he had received the call. 'Is there any way of getting a location for the caller?' he said. 'It's the people holding Anastasia. I just did FaceTime with the bastards.'

He gave her the time of the call and its exact length just as the first phone began to vibrate again. 'I think it's them again,' he said. 'Track this call as well.'

He answered. 'You saw your lady,' came the voice.

'What are your demands?' snapped Samson.

'Her husband knows what we want. You walk down street to beautiful apartment and remind him.'

They were watching. Samson's head snapped up to look down the street. It was empty. 'He hasn't told me what you want, so you must tell me and I'll make sure that it happens.'

'Hisami has not told you? This is not good sign. Maybe he does not love wife as you love her, Mr Samson.'

His eyes were still searching the street. 'He loves her very much,' Samson replied automatically, 'and he will do anything you ask, but you have to give us time. He just got out of jail. And you have to trust me! I need to know what you want. The dossier. Is that it?' The word 'dossier' had come into his head without him thinking about it. They must want what Hisami knew – a dossier.

There was silence at the other end.

'How can I help you if you won't tell me what you want?'

'You are spy, Samson. I know you are trying to trace this call, so I go now. He must do what we want or we fill hole in ground with your girlfriend.' The phone went dead.

Samson called Zillah Dee again. 'Did you get anything?'

'Working on it. What did they say?'

'He says Denis knows what they want. They won't tell me.' He paused and looked around the restaurant. 'And they're watching us. He knew I was in the restaurant.'

'You need to talk to Denis. He has people there now, but you really need to pin him down on this.'

He consumed the wine and wolfed the veal without noticing the taste of either and went over the two calls in his mind. They had plied her with drink – that was obvious. She had that faraway look in her eyes and blinked frequently when she was speaking, which had made him laugh when he first noticed it in Venice.

He rose to signal for the bill, but the phone that had been called by the Russian started vibrating again. He answered. There were some clicks and noises off. 'Hello, this is Naji. I am speaking to Paul Samson, yes?'

'Yes, it's me. Hello, Naji! It's so good to hear you. How are you?' He sat down at the table again.

'I am doing well, and so is my family, though it is already cold in Riga. They love the sea and we are all happy here. The university is very good. The food is very good. Better than in Germany, where we also had some problems. And my professors are all my friends.'

This stream of news was typical of Naji, who tended to list things at the start of a conversation, partly out of shyness. 'I am sure they are your friends, Naji.' Despite everything, Samson found himself smiling. What he admired about Naji, apart from his playful good nature, was the combination of an incredibly simple outlook and what his professors agreed was one of the best minds of his generation. Naji had sped through a physics degree and was now studying astronomy, a dream born when he lay beside his father in the back yard of the family home in Syria and gazed up at the Milky Way. Some part of him, he told Samson when they had last met, was commemorating that moment. He believed his father would be pleased that he had devoted himself to science and wasn't selling shoes or reconditioned phones on a street corner somewhere. Naji dreamed of being rich because he and his family had known poverty, but what fired his imagination was the first time he used the Ventspils Radio Telescope on Latvia's Baltic Coast – he, Naji Touma, reaching into the depths of the universe, the ghost of his benign, broken dad by his side.

'Naji, It must be very late there.'

'Does not matter. I am pleased to talk with you.'

'I have some bad news – some very bad news – which I can't explain right now. Anastasia is in trouble and I need your help on that email account. It's really, really important.'

Naji was silent. 'I am very sorry. I owe everything to you and Anastasia. You will tell me as soon as you can.' He paused. 'Just now I looked at this problem, which is why I call you. The server is well protected. I need to send Mr Hisami an email with some code in it. He must open the email for it to work, so I want you to tell me how this is to be done.'

Samson thought quickly. 'I will send you the words to put

in the subject line in the next few minutes. Then you will let me know what you find?'

'If this works, I will.'

'I expect to need more help from you. I am coming to Estonia as soon as I leave New York.'

'Then, I will see you, I hope.'

'Let's hope so, And Naji, it's vital you keep this secret. Anastasia is in great danger. Any word that leaks out could end her life.'

'I am sorry for this. I will inform no one. Not even my sister Munira.'

'I'll send you those words. We'll speak tomorrow.'

The waitress came over and offered him another glass of wine on the house, saying that she could see he was having a bad evening. He accepted and thanked her. It was going to be a long night and he needed to settle himself after seeing Anastasia on his phone. He typed out the words, 'Subject line should read WHAT CRANE WANTS,' and sent the email to Naji, who instantly returned a dog emoji, captioned 'Moon'. Samson nodded. The dog Moon was still alive and living a blissful life in the mountains of Macedonia with Ifkar, who was now the adopted son of the old couple who ran the farm where the showdown had happened. Somehow, this ridiculous emoji gave him hope.

Before leaving the restaurant he messaged Tina at Hendricks Harp to book him on the first flight to London next morning.

Tulliver came down in the lift to meet him. 'He's got someone with him,' he said.

Samson looked him up and down as though he were crazy. 'Jim, I know you know what just happened because Zillah told you. They filmed Anastasia standing at the edge of an open grave in a Russian forest.'

'I know, but . . .'

'And he's having a damned business meeting! They're going to kill her, Jim. Are you hearing this?'

'Let me speak! I know Denis well. There's a reason he wants this meeting to overlap with yours. Keep quiet and watch – okay! Then you can talk.'

'Who's he with?'

'Gil Leppo. He's on the board of TangKi. There were two other board members here, but they've left.'

'Is Denis going to address the situation in Russia?'

'Of course.'

Samson went up and found Hisami in deep conversation with a man wearing tight black trousers, ankle boots, a leather waistcoat, several bangles and an ear stud. Gil Leppo uncoiled from the sofa and held up a soft hand to Samson. Denis got up and shook his hand, giving him a strange, loaded look at the same time.

Samson offered to wait at the other end of the enormous space.

'No, it's fine,' said Hisami, turning back to Leppo. 'Gil, I was going to get you a scotch before you go – that's what you like.'

Leppo nodded. He got up and moved to a solid, high-backed chair.

'Better for my back,' he explained to Samson, who nodded.

He guessed Leppo was in his fifties, even though he dressed like a teenager.

Hisami paused by the drinks table to consider the different brands of whisky. 'Ah, this is the one I was looking for,' he said, seizing a bottle of Aberlour.

He walked back to Leppo with a tumbler. 'I think you'll enjoy this.' He glanced at Samson and said, 'We've had some great times together. We're both outsiders. I'm from rural Kurdistan and Gil comes from Romania, via Israel. Actually, that's all we know about Gil. There are wild rumours, as there are about me. They say Gil made his first money from arms – big stuff like ground-to-air missiles, anti-tank weapons. We play tennis, and I don't think I've ever won a set against Gil, let alone a match. But at backgammon I am the undisputed champion. Right, Gil?'

Leppo grinned and raised his glass to Hisami. 'By the way, you know, that's mostly BS about the gun-running,' he said to Samson. 'He's right about the tennis, though.'

'Ah, happy times!' continued Hisami. 'You know. You're one of the few people I count as a friend in this country – a true friend. It really matters at times like this. My sister felt the same way about you.' He directed a strange look at Samson, almost regretful. 'We've spent so much time together. We have the same taste in books, the same values and political outlook. Is that going too far, Gil?'

'Democrats and liberals to the core! Your sister was a special person. You know we all miss her.'

'That's kind of you, Gil. Look, I'm afraid Paul and I have some urgent business.'

Leppo got up and gave Hisami a hug that was barely reciprocated, though he didn't seem to notice. 'You know I've got your back. Call me any time you need to. And give my best to your gal in Italy, will you?'

'I certainly will,' said Hisami, and watched him make his way to the lift with a fixed smile. When the doors were shut, he said to Samson, 'I just have a couple of emails to send. We will talk in a few minutes.'

'Did I just miss something, Denis?' said Samson. 'Were you just having a cosy chat about happy times when not an hour has passed since Anastasia was being filmed by a grave in Russia? And now you're going to catch up on your emails?'

'As I said, we will talk – give me a moment.'

He went to the dark end of the enormous space, sat down at a table and opened a laptop, where he began to work, his face illuminated by the light of the screen. Eventually, Samson's patience gave out and he went over to him. 'Either you stop what you're doing, or I leave.'

Hisami looked up then closed the laptop. 'Certainly,' he said after a moment. 'Where are we now? Where do you believe she's being held?'

Samson did a double-take.

'Where is she?' Denis repeated.

'Denis, you already know. Zillah must have told you. Our best guess is that she's in the St Petersburg or Pskov provinces of western Russia. The reason we think Pskov is important is that we have found out the firm has a big depot there. She could be close to Pskov and that would put her on the other side of the border with Estonia or Latvia. If Crane is in Estonia, that's significant, because he is obviously controlling the operation.' He stopped. 'We don't have much to work on and we've no idea what they want.' He looked Hisami in the eye. 'But you do, Denis. What do they want?'

'A dossier – a database that has a lot of information.'

'Why don't you give it to them?'

'They already have it.'

Samson thought for a moment. 'They know what you've got so they're holding Anastasia to stop you using it.'

'Correct.'

'How the hell did you get yourself into this situation, Denis?'

Hisami looked down and was silent for a long time. His eyes were very dark and his mouth hung open slightly. He rose and walked slowly to the chairs they had occupied before, as though in a trance. Samson prompted him several times but got no response. Eventually, he took him by the shoulders. 'How did they know what was in your dossier, Denis?'

'Let go of me, Paul.'

Samson stood back.

'When Crane disappeared, I pulled Daniel Misak out of the company and hid him, or rather he hid himself – badly, as it turned out. Crane somehow got to him and persuaded him to go to London. When I heard of Crane's death I somehow knew it would be Daniel's body, not Crane's, on that balcony. He was obviously tortured and told them what we had assembled. They had a very good idea what we had but they didn't know the extent of the detail.'

'And what was that exactly?'

Hisami sat with his fingertips pressed together under his nose. 'It is the entire funding programme for insurgent right-wing groups across Europe, most of them dedicated to the overthrow of democratic government by violent means. They are nationalist in nature and specifically anti-Semitic and anti-Muslim.' He stopped. 'Such operations are not uncommon in Europe, but this represents an enormous injection of funds that could turn things. That's the point. It's the scale of the ambition.'

'Where does the money come from?'

'Part was stolen from TangKi and the rest was washed through the accounts and probably originated in Russia.'

'An American company is being used to launder Russian money to disrupt and overthrow European democracies – Jesus!'

'These allegations cannot come from me – they'd have no credibility. That's why I've been encouraging the board to carry out an investigation.'

'How did you become involved, Denis?'

'I invested in TangKi because it was, primarily, a good business, though it wasn't doing as well as it should. I came to suspect Crane and made enquiries. Absolutely nothing of what we were told about his background stood up to scrutiny.' He stopped, got up and made for the drinks table. 'Bob Baker was able to establish that Crane came from Eastern Europe and was likely to be working with the Russians.' He held up an empty glass to Samson, who shook his head, then poured himself a brandy. 'The first time we met in that hotel in Skopje I had brandy.'

'Talk, Denis, we don't have time for this.'

'I owed you, and you owed me, Paul. You found my sister's killer then I saved your life in the barn. We were quits and we owed each other nothing, which is why I felt able to seek a life with Anastasia. I felt no obligation to you, but I now find that I must rely on you to find the woman I took from you. It's a strange situation, no?'

Samson shook his head impatiently. 'Anastasia is now your wife and I accept that – okay? I'm here to help you get her back. I am not going over this history.'

'Do you have anyone else? Have you found love?'

'That's irrelevant, and you have no right to ask.'

'Well, let me tell you, quite frankly, that I think there's something about you that she misses. After all, she remembered your number when she was on the boat.'

'You were in jail and your phone was locked because you won't let anyone use it.' He got up and looked down at Hisami. 'We're talking about Anastasia's *life*.'

'Do please sit down, Paul. I should explain that I cannot allow anyone access to my phone and my email because it's the kidnappers' main channel of communication to me and I have to have absolute control over that. You understand?'

'Yes, but if you're re-arrested, then there's no way we can respond if they make a demand.'

'There won't be any demand.' Samson watched as Hisami's gaze swept the enormous space. It was then that Samson noticed the Patrick Heron painting in the dining area, which he had last seen with Anastasia in the window of a gallery in St James's. She had stopped and admired it. Hisami must have bought it for her soon afterwards.

Hisami coughed. 'That individual you just met, he is Crane's man on the inside. I wasn't sure until earlier this evening, when he twice mentioned that Anastasia was in Italy. Okay, so people know she's abroad but she could have been anywhere – we have centres all over Europe and two in the Middle East. Only four people in the US knew she was there, and Gil wasn't one of them.'

Samson absorbed this. 'Does he know where she's being held?'

'I doubt it. But I'm sure he believes that I accept that Crane is dead, and that's vital.'

Samson nodded. 'You're saying you've got nothing with which to bargain for her life. What about threatening to publish what you have?'

'Don't be stupid. If I do that, I have nothing to bargain with.'

'So you're just going to sit here, trusting that a man who's already responsible for four or five deaths will agree to release Anastasia when he no longer has anything to fear from your dossier? Is that really your strategy?'

'Paul, you're not hearing me.'

'My problem is that I am.' Samson got up. 'You put her by that fucking grave – now you have no idea how to help her.' An idea came into his mind so quickly he was unaware of the logic behind what he said next. 'There's something else. They've got something else on you.'

Hisami stared up at him, eyes blazing, face like a stone. But Samson wasn't having it. 'Don't try this shit with me, Denis. What have they got on you?'

'This is not your concern,' he snapped. 'You're on my payroll, and you'll do what I say. You will continue to work with Zillah to look for Anastasia. Leave the rest to me.'

Samson moved away. 'It's not as if you've done a great job so far, is it? Remember, I was with her first and, if she'd stayed with me, she wouldn't be in the position she is now. So, let me make this plain. I'm no longer on your payroll, but I will do everything to get her back. You have my numbers,' he said over his shoulder as he headed for the lift.

He crashed at the hotel but was woken by a call from Zillah Dee. 'We've located the truck driver. He's on the road to Novosibirsk and we know his destination, just outside the city. Our agent will find him and she *will* get the information we need from him.'

'That needs to happen – we don't have long.'

'She will. We have people in western Russia to verify the information the moment she acquires it, so there shouldn't be much of a delay.' She paused.

'What?' he prompted.

'You know this operation is costing a lot of money. I'm not sure Denis can pay us what he owes. Tulliver has been dodging my questions about invoices sent two weeks back.'

'How much is he in for?'

'Approximately a million dollars. People like you are very expensive and we're burning money in Russia.'

He told her that he was no longer on the payroll and explained the reasons. 'But I'm still committed to finding and freeing her.'

'That's good, but I can't afford to do this for free, Samson. I must know that my bills will be met. Otherwise, I have to pull out.'

Samson reached over to the mini bar and pulled out a miniature Jack Daniels, unscrewed the top and took a sip.

'How much trouble is he in? A few million is short change for someone like Denis.'

'Yes, but he had a big, big loss when he bet some pharma stock would fall and it rose. He is still recovering from that.' He heard her inhale on the e-cigarette he'd seen her use discreetly a couple of times.

'I hope he pays Macy soon, for obvious reasons. And Macy won't tolerate not being paid for long.'

'Nor me,' she murmured. 'My organisation runs close-hauled. Macy most likely has more resources than we do.'

He wondered briefly if she'd been got at by the powerful forces that were bent on destroying Hisami, but then dismissed the thought.

'Can I ask you something? Why's he holding back?' It's obvious there's a lot he's not telling us.'

'Maybe they've got something else.'

'Meaning?'

'Maybe abducting Anastasia and threatening to kill her wasn't their last shot. They might have another play, which could be even more devastating to him.'

'What's that?'

'With his past, there's likely to be something. By the way, did he talk to you about his friend Leppo?'

'Yes,' she said. 'The matter is in hand.'

'And?'

'Denis is very thorough. He had us check out Leppo a few months back. That information will be released tomorrow and Mr Leppo will find out what it's like to be on the receiving end of a federal investigation. The Israeli government is going to formally raise concerns about him with the State Department. I can't tell you the details, but the allegations are firmly based in fact. It's the end for him. The Israelis will push it out in public channels once they've talked with State. He deserves it – this guy is like a tapeworm.'

Early next morning, Samson was headed to the check-in machines, thinking he would call Naji once he was through Security, when one of his phones received a call from a number he didn't recognise.

'It's me,' said Jo Hayes. 'Are you still in New York?'

'Hi, yes, I'm about to leave.'

'Don't come back to London. They know which flight you're taking and they will almost certainly arrest you.'

'On what grounds?'

'Hell knows – they'll find something. They need to take you

out of circulation for some reason, which is why I'm phoning on a friend's phone, not mine.'

'This is about Crane?'

'I guess. They're all over Hendricks Harp, which is how they knew which flight you're on. And I'm pretty sure the Security Services have searched your place.'

'Did they find anything that interested them?'

'Not as far as I'm aware.'

'How do you know all this?'

'Because they told me. I've agreed to work for them.'

'Just to be clear, is that why you slept with me?'

'No, I fancy you, and it was a great excuse. But seriously, they really are going to bang you up if you set foot back in this effing country of ours. Make yourself scarce – I would.'

'Okay. Can you call me if you hear anything else that seems important? And please use this number.'

'On the condition that we have dinner at your restaurant again.'

'It's a deal,' he said. And hung up.

He consulted flight times using the web then texted Tina with a message intended for others to read: 'New developments here. Sorry, can't make flight. Will be in NYC for next few days. Can you get refund at this late stage? Many apols again. Samson.'

He left Terminal 7 and got a ride on a shuttle bus to Terminal 8, where he bought a business-class ticket on a flight to Helsinki, which would leave in two and a half hours' time.

CHAPTER 21

Kirill had meant to cover the screen with his hand so she couldn't see Samson's face, but as he backed away from her to capture the whole scene she had fleetingly seen him and registered the outrage and dismay in his eyes. When Samson had said, 'I am with you, dear Anastasia,' she knew that he was giving her more than just support. He was coming for her, and that's why she'd tried to smile at the camera.

Kirill didn't miss that and, after he'd made another call, he caught her and her guards up on the way back to the compound, prodded her and said he'd certainly found the right man in Samson. He would make sure her husband complied with all the demands.

They had taken her watch, but she estimated it must have been two or three in the morning when they got back to the compound. Kirill had seized the bottle of vodka by the fire and now followed her into the building, behind the man who had her chained. He dismissed the guard when the chain had been unlocked and came into the room and fumbled at her breast, saying he couldn't help but be excited by the way she had handled herself. Most women would have become hysterical in those circumstances, he exclaimed, but she was strong and defiant, and that had really turned him on. She felt like hitting him, but she simply removed his hand, looked into his face and shook her head slowly.

Next morning, she noticed the room was much colder and her breath smoked in the air, and when no food arrived she realised that Kirill was punishing her. She sat shivering on the bed, wrapped in the rug from the night before and with a coverlet over her feet. But at least she wasn't trussed up in a box. Around mid-morning, a hand appeared around the door and a paperback was chucked into the room, Ivan Turgenev's *First Love*, a novella she'd read in college. Her only memory was that she had wanted to slap both protagonists and tell them to stop being so self-indulgent.

She read the book and kept her hunger at bay by rubbing toothpaste in her mouth and drinking water. Night fell and the room became colder still and the air stale. It was late when the man came to handcuff her to the chain and led her out into the open. Kirill was seated beside a roaring fire and, by the look of things, was already well into a bottle of vodka. He wore a hunting cap with earflaps, mittens, a jacket and waistcoat, breeches and lace-up ankle boots. Around his neck was a loosely tied silk scarf with a pheasant motif. She suspected he was dressing up for her.

He handed her a glass, which she refused. 'I can't drink without food. It will make me ill.'

Between them was a metal picnic table on which lay the Russian edition of the book. The cover showed a woman in a long white dress and hat standing by cheery trees in blossom. Kirill picked it up, gazed at the picture for a moment and showed it to her. 'This is very good art. Good Russian art.' Then he issued instructions in Russian and very soon a vacuum flask of soup was brought, together with some bread and smoked cheese in the shape of a sausage.

She gorged on the bread and cheese and sipped the soup while Kirill flipped through the book and very soon her blood sugar had risen and she was feeling more herself.

'You like this book we study? I chose for you.'

'I wonder why,' she murmured, looking down. 'I find the character of the boy irritating and the woman is manipulative. She is five years older than he is and she's playing with his emotions for no reason. She has many suitors and doesn't love him and, anyway, she is his father's goddamn mistress. She is deceiving everyone then she dies: end of story. What's the point?'

'Drink,' Kirill commanded.

She considered the vodka and downed it all.

'This is great Russian work about love,' said Kirill.

'And disappointment,' she said. 'But my main problem is that people don't behave like that.'

Kirill let out a guffaw. 'This happened to writer. Turgenev fell in love with his father's mistress! There was good reason I chose this book – because of your situation. You remind me of Princess Zinaida, and Samson is young boy Vladimir.'

'You have me as the flirtatious bimbo! And Samson as the lovesick youth! Jesus! Then I guess my husband, Denis, takes the role of the father. It doesn't add up.'

'But Hisami is father figure to replace your father.'

'How do you know my father is dead?'

He gave her a weary look. 'We researched you, Anastasia. And Denis is older than you. He is in his fifties and you are thirty-five years of age.'

She shook her head and looked away.

'Read to me in English the passage where the son discovers the truth.' He took her book from her, found it quickly and handed it back with a finger placed at the spot.

'It's ridiculous – I can't read this.' But he threatened to take her shoes away and keep her without food the following day so she read, with a tone of sarcastic melodrama, the scene where the father of the smitten boy Vladimir takes his riding crop to his mistress. '"Zinaida shuddered, looked at my father without a word, and then, slowly lifting her arm to her lips, kissed the streak of red that had appeared upon it. My father flung the whip away from him and, hastily running up the steps, dashed into the house."' She dropped the book. 'It's sentimental rubbish.'

Kirill affected shock at this. 'Maybe this is like your husband?'

'I don't understand. What do you mean?'

'Your husband is out of jail and he has met with Samson, but nothing has happened. He has not done what we want and Samson leaves New York and goes home to London. He spurns you.'

She straightened. 'But you've told my husband of your demands.'

'He knows what we want, but he plays games with us. Yet he can do nothing. He is under house arrest. They put tracker on his leg and he cannot leave apartment. So Samson went to New York and he was unable to persuade Denis to help you. We were watching.'

'Let me talk to Denis. I can tell him what he needs to do. Please, Kirill! I'm sure he will help when he hears from me. Call him.'

'No!' He stabbed the fire with a long stick and sparks flew into the night. 'Did you know your husband was CIA agent and so was his sister?'

'They went through difficult times in Kurdistan. Working with the CIA would be part of that, I guess. But he doesn't talk about it and I never knew his sister.'

'Professional killers.'

'You have that wrong. She was a doctor who helped children with cancer.'

'Your husband killed four men in Macedonia and saved your life. Where do you imagine he learned that kind of skill? With CIA, of course.'

'No,' she said firmly, although she had always had her suspicions, which stemmed from his relationship with the polite Bob Baker and their occasional huddles in the pool house in Mesopotamia.

'Men like your husband will do everything to save themselves,' mused Kirill. 'They have different psychology. They are very cold, very strong. That is now problem for you because he will try to win and that means you may die in process.'

'There's something I don't understand about you, Kirill. How can you sit here and drink with me and talk about books at the same time as threatening me with a bullet in my head? How many people have died? Five people, including the poor chef? Why?' She felt light-headed and bold, and she knew that she should be flattering her jailer rather than challenging him. She stopped and glanced at him, then decided to press on, knowing that the drink was talking. 'Please explain to me what is so important to you and your associates that you are prepared to kill so many people?'

'There are many casualties in these times, but your husband is responsible for deaths. Remember that.'

'Denis didn't kill them – your organisation did.' She sprang forward but the man holding the other end of the chain yanked her back and wrenched the shoulder that had been injured on the boat.

'Why?' she shouted as the pain flooded her mind. 'What do you damn well want?'

Kirill smiled. 'What is ours – nothing else.'

He kept her by the fire another two hours, drinking and making rambling speeches on the decline of civilisation and the Russian soul, all of it tinged with a sentimental fascist longing. She feigned interest, indulged him by arguing with him and once – more out of boredom than anything else – launched an attack on the corruption of his country. 'Russia is run by men for men, gangsters who do not understand the meaning of work or community, because they've only ever stolen from the people, so please don't preach to me about the values of the goddamn Motherland.' He enjoyed this and countered with a sharp analysis of the United States, but she couldn't be bothered to reply and yearned for the solitude of her room. Eventually, he tired, staggered to his feet and ordered her to be taken into the building.

But this was not where things ended. Later, he came to her room and felt his way to her bed in the half-light, tripping at the last moment on the leg of the table – the only furniture in the room – so that he sprawled over her and breathed alcohol in her face. He groped her breasts, saying something about admiring a woman with her spirit, though it was hard to tell because he was so drunk, and fumbled at the fastener on her trousers. For one moment she wondered if she should let him do what he wanted, but that thought soon vanished when his hand slipped inside her pants. She struggled upright and brought her knees to her chest. 'No!' she said. He stopped and raised his head. 'Kirill, these are not the actions of a civilised man.'

'But . . . I want you.' He could barely get these few words out. He lay motionless on the bed and mumbled something in Russian to himself. She saw that his fly was open and penis was out.

'Oh, Jesus,' she said. 'Kirill, you have to decide whether you want to be my executioner or my lover, because you sure as hell can't be both.'

He muttered something in Russian, yet she could tell that

he was thinking about this. She put out a hand and touched his forehead – he was perspiring and his hair was damp from sitting by the fire in the hunting hat. She stroked his temple. 'This is not right for people who respect each other,' she said quietly.

'I want you.' He let out a sigh before managing to say, 'And I know you want me.'

'But not like this, when you've had too much to drink.'

'I saw it in your eyes. You want me.'

'That's smart of you, Kirill. When I saw you first, I thought – this is a shrewd man, an observant man, a man of learning.'

He nodded and she kept stroking his head and speaking to him in a soft voice about his intelligence and manly virtues. Once or twice she overdid it and his face jerked up to search her eyes for insincerity, but she reassured him that she meant what she was saying, although she had to admit to him that she found it odd to be expressing such feelings in these circumstances, and in due course he relaxed.

She noticed his breathing change. 'Why don't you get more comfortable and lie down with me,' she said, shifting to one side. She encouraged him to lift his legs on to the narrow bed, then she lay, exactly as she had with Zhao on the boat, but this time she did not sleep. She waited without moving and, soon enough, Kirill rolled on to his back and began to snore gently, his arm occasionally flopping across her stomach.

CHAPTER 22

Samson turned on a phone when he landed at Helsinki and found an email from Naji Touma, which stated simply, 'I'm in.' He called him immediately but got his voicemail. Then he texted saying, 'Let's speak as soon as possible,' and got the reply: 'In observatory – we talk later.'

There was also a message from Macy Harp telling him to call him on a new number.

'I'd prefer to have this conversation face to face,' said Harp. 'Where are you, exactly?'

Samson told him that he was about to pass through Customs at Helsinki airport.

'Well, don't. There's a welcoming party. Nyman has been tracking you.'

'How do you know they're in Helsinki?'

'You have a friend. She left a message with Ivan at the restaurant to be in touch with me.' Jo! That was smart of her. Nyman must have realised early that Samson hadn't boarded the London flight and got hold of his itinerary by means of a standard request to the Department of Homeland Security.

'And you're using a new number,' said Samson.

'Yes, they're all over us like bloody maggots.'

'Are they protecting Crane?'

'Hard to say,' said Harp. 'Could be that they're watching what's going on. On the other hand, some pretty shady characters have risen in the British establishment. Might be that they're on his side. But that's not the point – what are you up to, Samson? Why are you in Finland? Tulliver sent me a message to say you'd told Hisami to get lost. Can't blame you, but where does that leave you?'

'If Hisami won't help free Anastasia, the only option is to take Crane. We know he's in Estonia. I'm crossing to Tallinn tonight.'

'Who's going to help you in this lunatic scheme?'

'Things are at the planning stage,' said Samson, now noticing a very large party of tourists, suntanned and still wearing holiday gear, enter the baggage hall and assemble around the carousel for a flight from Tenerife. He moved to join the crowd and started looking for a non-existent suitcase. 'I'll need money,' he continued. 'So can you put fifty k into my account? And I'll top it up with money from my deposit account. If we get her out, we'll charge it all to Hisami.'

'That's all very well, but Zillah told me she's having difficulty extracting money from him.'

'It's a cash-flow problem.'

'Hope you're right. Look, there's an old friend of mine in

Tallinn. He has a German wife, who I believe runs a restaurant, so you'll have plenty to talk about. He was in SIS with me during the eighties and nineties. He's in his late sixties now, but very sound. Did some work for us recently. I'll send you the coordinates and fill him in.'

The baggage from Tenerife had nearly all been collected but the tourists all remained in a group. 'Okay,' said Samson absently. 'I'll be glad to have that contact. And send the money soonest.'

He hung up and sidled over to a short, elderly woman with a large suitcase and numerous bits of hand luggage. He offered her a hand and, as the party moved off en masse towards Customs, insisted on wheeling her suitcase beside her. He also relieved her of some of her hand luggage, including a wide-brimmed straw hat, which he placed on his head to make her laugh. None of this escaped the notice of two young Finnish customs officers, who moved quickly to separate him from his new friend and took him to a small office for a search, which is exactly what he'd anticipated. They were polite enough, looked at his passport and the stub of his JFK boarding pass and asked why he had been waiting at the carousel when he had nothing apart from his backpack. Was he picking up someone else's bags? They had seen him on the phone while at the carousel, and he seemed to be waiting for the Tenerife flight. Had he arranged to collect a package from the Canary Islands? And why had he been so keen to merge with the party of tourists as they exited?

He answered no to the first two questions and seemed

suddenly embarrassed about the last. They searched him meticulously, asking him to take off his shoes and most of his clothes, and decanted his rucksack, remarking on the number of phones he carried with him, and he told them he was in the kind of business that needed a lot of numbers. What was that business? they asked. He replied that he was a professional gambler. What kind of gambling? Only horses, he replied. Tell me about your last big win, said one. And Samson told them about a horse named Pearl's Legend – a seasoned steeplechaser and a great trier – which had won at Huntingdon by twenty lengths, at odds of four to one. 'That's four hundred per cent profit,' he said to the older of the two customs officers, who asked how to spell the relevant names and looked up the race on the Web. He nodded when he found it and showed it to his companion. They bought the story – as well they should. It was indeed Samson's last big win.

While he dressed and returned his possessions to the back-pack, they asked him why he had been acting so suspiciously. Eventually, he let them extract the fact that he was being met by a woman he didn't want to see. There had never been anything between them, he added, but he was desperate to avoid her while he was in Finland for this short time to see some harness racing. She had a drink problem and she imagined things, said Samson, now more than embarrassed. He asked if they could possibly show him a way he could leave without being noticed. The customs officers exchanged looks and grinned. They led him up a flight of stairs to a door, which opened with a security tag, and showed him into Departures.

There was an escalator that led down to the arrivals hall and, as he passed it, he caught a glimpse of Peter Nyman, dressed in a charcoal-grey Loden coat and a trilby, consulting with two men and his usual sidekick, Sonia Fell, whom Samson had not seen since Macedonia. Nyman was gesturing impatiently to them. Samson was gone before they could look up, and he hurried through the exit to the back door of a bus that had just let off some passengers. His luck held and the bus went straight to the port, having circled to collect a few passengers at Arrivals. From low down in his seat, he glanced through the rain-streaked window and spotted Nyman on the phone.

He just made the last boat across the Gulf of Finland that evening and went with a beer and a couple of sandwiches to a sheltered spot on the port side of the highest open deck, away from the drunks and the noise from the cabaret and karaoke bars. The crossing was rough and, apart from a few passengers who shot from the bars to retch over the side, he was alone. He loved the sea and thought of Venice emerging from the gloom as Anastasia steered the *Maria Redan* the last few miles, insisting all the while that Greeks were the world's most natural sailors. He smiled.

He spotted the lights of Tallinn to the south and it wasn't long after that he found his phone had a signal. He called Naji, who answered on the second ring.

'What've you got?' he said, without using Naji's name.

'Everything, I believe, but only you will understand it. There is money. Companies. Groups where money goes. It means little to me.'

'You have access to all his emails?'

'Plus deleted emails and attachments. Plus sent emails and drafts. Everything, but it was hard. This is a dedicated server – not shared with other parties. Very hard to get into it.'

'Can you send me some of it, my friend?'

There was a pause. 'How secure are you? I think you should see this yourself on my laptop. Where are you?'

'Let me call you back on another number.'

They both jumped phones. 'I'm about to arrive in Tallinn,' continued Samson.

'Good, then I will come to you,' said Naji. 'My sister will drive me. It is only four hours from Riga. We have a car!'

'A car – that's fantastic.' It was a big deal for a refugee family which, three years before, had nothing. 'I hope you're keeping off the roads,' said Samson.

Naji laughed. 'You are remembering the policeman's car when I was running from everyone. I am still expert driver!'

'No, you're not,' said Samson, laughing. 'I'll text you when I know where I'm going to be.'

Samson was among the last to leave the ferry and decided to walk the half-mile to the old city because he needed the exercise and also because he wanted to make sure he hadn't been picked up in the ferry terminal. He passed through the city walls by a squat round tower and followed an utterly still cobbled street to St Olaf's Church, opposite which he located the small hotel he'd booked from the ferry. He paid for two nights in cash and gave the receptionist a Hungarian ID card in the name of Norbert Soltesz, which had lain tucked in his wallet, lightly glued to the reverse of a British Automobile Association membership card.

By the time he had slung his bag on to the bed and washed his face his phone had vibrated twice with the same message. 'Macy said you'd like a nightcap. Bar Viktor close to your hotel. Table on the right.'

A dozen determined young drinkers and a quartet of pool players populated the large, gloomy basement. Music by Keith Jarrett was on in the background. As Samson looked round, a tall man, a little stooped and with weather-beaten skin, rose and offered his hand. 'Robert Harland – Macy's chum.'

Samson took off his jacket, hung it on the back of the chair and ordered a beer from the waitress. 'How'd you know where I'd be?'

My wife spotted you at the terminal and saw that you had decided to walk. It wasn't hard to work out that you were going to the nearest hotel in the old town. Any further and you would have taken a cab. Besides, I wanted to know if you were followed from the boat. And, no, Mr Samson – you weren't.' He raised his glass. 'Cheers.'

'It's Paul, but Macy's taken to calling me by my second name.'

He acknowledged this and set down his glass. 'My wife, Ulrike, and I are Estonian citizens. We have both renounced the citizenship of our countries and we have made our home here. We have a sailing boat, a place in the sticks and have picnics with the Estonian elite, so what we don't need is someone screwing that up for us. Understood? Good.'

'Weren't you the guy in . . .'

'In Berlin, yes. I hear it's become an object lesson in SIS training of what not to do, the emphasis now being on obedience and lines of authority. But the operation was a success and we got everyone out. The Office always forgets that part.' His eyes smiled.

'You know why I'm here?'

'Macy told me all he knows. Is there any update as to the victim's location? I know you were hoping for some more information on that.' Samson shook his head. 'And there's no movement from her husband on meeting the demands – in fact, you don't even know what they are?'

'There's a complete ledger of transfers from the company throughout this year, detailing where the money is destined for. I haven't seen it but, obviously, it's one of the things tied to her kidnap. There's also the money itself – a lot of it. Maybe over two hundred million US. The accounts are being accessed from Tallinn. I believe Crane is here.'

Harland leaned into Samson's face and aimed his words at the wall. 'And your plan, which is at least as crazy as anything I cooked up behind the Iron Curtain, is to snatch him and exchange him for Hisami's wife, who happens to be your former girlfriend and great love. Is that right?'

'I see Macy did tell you everything. Hisami hired me because I'm good at my job, so it's not what it seems.'

'Yes, he said that, too, but you are the first to know that these things require planning and back-up. You're going to need people. And Zillah Dee's outfit won't supply them, not for something as illegal and dangerous as this. You need somewhere to hold him if, indeed, you manage to seize him, and then you have to contact the kidnappers and propose the exchange. I imagine you have no means of doing that. They simply phone you or Hisami – is that right?' Samson shrugged. 'And then there is the puzzling interest of our former colleagues who tried to nab you at Helsinki, presumably because they knew you were on your way here. I remember the lugubrious Nyman well. Is he now an apostle for the far right?'

'I can't answer any of that. But I can tell you that they filmed Anastasia by the side of an open grave last night. That's the only thing that matters.'

'My hunch,' continued Harland, 'is that the Office is waiting for something to happen and they are interested to watch it.' He put on his glasses, took out an old Nokia phone and started working the button keyboard with his index finger. 'This is my address – it's not far from here. Come to the house whenever you need to. Better than the phone.' He winced and suddenly lurched to his feet. 'My back gives me jip when it's damp. Walking helps. Let's take a stroll, if you're not too tired.'

They left the bar and moved through the shadows of St Olaf's, then walked towards the centre of the town through a wet mist that haloed the lights. 'It's a beautiful place,' said Harland, still moving gingerly. 'We've been very happy here.' A couple passed, one wheeling a bike. Both raised a hand and said, 'Hi!'

'And you know everyone?'

'Neighbours,' he said. 'I helped put some security in place

for the government. They don't want to lose their democracy again. They're good people. I like them a lot.'

Harland had stopped and was looking up at an ancient building with Gothic windows. Samson turned to him. 'Can you help me find Crane? I think it may be Anastasia's only chance.'

'I'll see what I can do.' He laid a hand on Samson's shoulder. 'If there are expenses, I take it you and Macy are good for them?'

'Of course.'

'I've heard that before.' He pointed down a narrow street. 'This is my turning. Come round tomorrow. It's the pretty green house set back from the road with a tree in the garden. You can't miss it.'

'So you can find Crane?' said Samson, knowing that he was probably pushing too hard.

A trace of irritation flickered in the old spy's face. 'I said I'll try for you. I'll do my best – all right!' Then he walked stiffly away.

CHAPTER 23

She waited, staring at the door because she was certain she had not heard the sound of the lock turning after he entered. About an hour later, she rolled away from him and on to her stomach so that she could let one foot drop to the ground then the other and push up from the bed causing as little disturbance as possible. Not even the wire stretched on the bedframe protested. She had kept her trainers on because of the cold and, though they made one tiny squeak on the wooden floor, she moved silently the rest of the way to the door, grasped the handle and pulled it open on to the dark passageway. She stepped out and listened before pulling the door to, rather than closing it. Then she slipped down the passage that led into the largest room in the dacha, where she had been given soup on her arrival. The building creaked a little and, outside, the rain pounded on the tin roof of an extension and drainpipes gushed water, but there was no sound inside the building.

At every step she stopped and listened. There were bound

to be men on guard – there were so many of them. She had noticed a one-storey building inside the compound, a little distance from the dacha, and during her two evenings outside with Kirill by the fire she had seen lights on and a door being opened. Maybe that was where most of them slept. Kirill maintained his distance from the men, so there seemed a possibility that there were no guards in the main building, but she was sure there'd be someone on the gate. For the moment, she had no realistic thought of escape. She would recce the place and look for opportunities – that was all. And she hadn't ruled out returning to her room and to Kirill's side.

There was a very dim light in what she guessed was a kitchen. She crossed the main room and saw that it came from the display panel of a freezer. The light was enough to see by and she made out a pile of groceries just dumped on a sideboard. She took what came to hand and stuffed some items in her pockets, not knowing what they were. This would be an explanation if she were caught; she would say she had been driven by hunger to raid the kitchen. To take one of the knives in the drawer below the work surface would destroy that alibi, so she left them. But she did pick up a long oven lighter and pulled its trigger to see if the flame worked. This, she could use.

She kept exploring, growing more confident that she was the only person awake in the building. The place was cluttered with hunting paraphernalia and possessed the musty smell of somewhere that hadn't been occupied for a long time before Kirill's men arrived. There were shelves of books and crockery, a few paintings and one or two framed photographs of men with slaughtered deer and boar. Kirill was not among them.

The flame from the lighter illuminated a staircase, which, after testing the stairs for creaking floorboards, she climbed. There was just one large suite at the top, with windows that faced in three directions and a large shower and bathroom on one side. This was where Kirill slept. His ridiculous hats were lined up on the dresser. She could see that he'd emptied his pockets in preparation for bed – a wallet, a leather key holder, a penknife, his cheroots, a lighter and some kind of ID were on the bedside table. But then his drunken libido had plainly got the better of him and he'd gone from the room in his socks, leaving his boots on their side by the dresser. She searched around for his phone but found nothing and began her descent, occasionally clicking the lighter to see where she was going. Halfway down she noticed a flash reflected back from a metal cabinet tucked into a recess that she hadn't noticed on her way up. She reached the bottom and went over and tried the handle. It wouldn't shift. Maybe he locked his phone away; maybe there was a computer in there. She listened. Nothing stirred in the building. She went back up to the bedroom, took the key holder and returned to the cabinet. Only two of the many keys were candidates for the small lock. The second worked the mechanism and the door opened with a metallic scraping noise. She froze and waited before holding the flame of the lighter inside the locker. 'Jesus!' she whispered. Three hunting rifles stood in a rack; two had scopes. Several boxes of different-sized shells and an ammunition belt lay below them, together with a spouted tin of oil and some cleaning rags. An open padlock hung at one end of a bar that secured the guns into the rack. She removed the padlock from the hole in the bar and swung it towards her.

She had never in her life touched a gun, was instinctively afraid of them and had no concept of how heavy a gun was or how to carry one. She selected the smallest rifle, which had a strap but no scope, eased it from the slot made for the stock and gently lifted it out of the cabinet. It was much lighter than she'd expected. She didn't know how to open the breach and, anyway, she couldn't manage the gun while holding the lighter to see what she was doing. She took a handful of different-length shells from the cartons and stuffed them in the inside pockets of her jacket. Then she stepped back and carefully replaced the padlock and secured the cabinet.

Even as she did so, it seemed bizarre to return the keys to the place beside Kirill's bed, but she was keeping her options open. In her mind, she was still not committed to any course of action. She needed to think things through. She sat on Kirill's bed for five minutes and breathed deeply, calming herself and going through the options, none of which seemed very practical, even with a gun in her hands. She worked the bolt distractedly and eventually managed to open the breach. It turned out that all three lengths of shell were the same calibre and slotted neatly into it. She left one in and pocketed the rest.

One option was to return to the room, leave the gun and the shells under her bed – they never searched the room – and wait for a good opportunity. But what was the point of that? They would certainly be found when her captors discovered the gun was missing and she would never have a better chance of escaping than now. Emboldened by the gun, she stole back to her room. Kirill was in the same position but, as she pulled bits of clothing from the towel hanger by the basin, he stirred and all thought of patting down his pockets for his phone deserted her. She backed from the room and eased the door shut, turned the key in the lock and removed it. The noise stirred him. She heard him murmur something then call out, but this was just Kirill talking in his sleep.

She had no thought of killing him, but she knew that if his bedroom was empty and the door of the room where she was kept locked and the key nowhere to be found, it would cause a delay that might be vital for her. She put on the T-shirt she'd washed, the patterned jumper they had given her and a scarf that was in the room – and then went to look through the windows towards the gate. She could see very little, but someone was out there because a cigarette lighter flared.

She was now committed to a course of action. She moved quickly to the kitchen, scooped up the cooking oil, turned on the gas rings without lighting them and closed the door. She went to the corner of the large room furthest from the kitchen. Behind a heavy upholstered armchair she formed a pile from magazines, kindling wood from the log basket by the fire, books and a plastic table cover, on to which she placed any combustible ornament she could find. She poured cooking oil over the top and set light to the paper at the bottom. At first, the flames didn't take. She crouched down and blew softly. The paper caught light, followed by the kindling. She stepped back, willing the flames on, and at length the fire took hold at the top of the heap and the back of the armchair began to smoke. The light from the flames now danced on the ceiling, but she wasn't done yet. She dragged an ornamental bamboo table over to the fire and toppled it on to the flames.

In a state of pure flow and almost unaware of herself, she moved behind the main door and waited. The whole room was now illuminated and smoke billowed beneath the ceiling. She shut her eyes and covered her mouth and nose with the scarf. Seconds later, the door bust open and two men rushed in, their arms shielding their faces from the flames. One dashed to the stairs, the other to the back room where she had been held. She slipped out behind them and ran along the front of the building and into the dark. She tore over the damp grass and reached the gates. They were chained and padlocked. She looked back to see if there was a vehicle she could use to ram them but then some part of her mind told her she was being ridiculous: she must scale the fence. She strapped the rifle across her back, gripped the wire either side of the metal gatepost and began to climb, placing one foot in front of the other on the post, causing the gate to rattle. The pain in her shoulder burned each time she hauled herself up with her left arm. At the top, she had to hang with her right arm so that she could unwrap the scarf from her face and neck and place it over the loops of razor wire that were strung haphazardly along the line of the fence. There was a lot of shouting behind her and she knew that if anyone looked towards the fence they would undoubtedly spot her. It took two or three agonising minutes for her to get enough of the wire covered, but even then her hands were cut as she swung one leg over and lifted herself clear of a big hoop of barbs. Her trousers caught and she had to wrench them free, ripping the material and giving herself a long scratch on the back of her calf. But she had managed the fence – just – and she hung there, panting in the rain, to give her arms and shoulder a rest before descending to within a metre of the ground then letting go and landing squarely on both feet to face the compound.

The fire had taken hold of the front of the building and the part nearest to her. Men darted about, silhouetted against the glow. She couldn't make out much of what was happening but she found herself hoping that no one had been killed or injured in the flames. Too many people had died already.

But that concern was short-lived. A loud bang came from the dacha and reverberated around the forest. The gas in the kitchen had ignited and blown out part of the ground floor. She couldn't escape the truth that she had done something that might have killed or injured people. She turned and followed the track away from the building into the vast, dripping forest and, gradually, the glow of the fire diminished and her eyes became accustomed to the dark. 'I am with you,' Samson had said, and she prayed he was.

Because of the house arrest, the only way Denis Hisami could take some air in New York was on the roof of the apartment building. He went up regularly during his house arrest, lit a cigar that mostly smouldered in an ashtray, and stood in the shadow of the building's water tank to gaze up at the towers of Midtown. The fresh air made him think clearly and it was good for him to spend time away from his computer and talking to his bankers.

Tulliver's head appeared around the metal fire-escape door and he called out. 'He's here. I've given him a whisky. Zillah's waiting.'

Hisami found Gil Leppo sitting at his dining table, hair still damp from the gym, bangles clinking as he leafed through that morning's *New York Times*, which had lain unopened all day. 'Hey,' he said, jumping up to give Denis another hug, which again was barely returned.

'How good of you to come over,' Denis said, moving away to the other side of the table, where two dark red Moroccan folders lay ready. He brushed the tips of his fingers over one folder, briefly enjoying the smoothness of the leather. 'I'm glad you stayed in town.'

'The place has great vibe in the fall – always the best time to be in New York.' He sat down. 'You're certainly causing the shit to go airborne at TangKi.'

'It's good to hear they're taking it seriously, Gil, because this is not just my problem.'

'Yeah, everyone agrees with you now.'

'Have you everything you need?' Leppo nodded and glanced at Tulliver. 'And you have some whisky – I forgot to ask, what do you think of Aberlour?'

'Fantastic,' said Gil, now picking up the tension in the room. 'So how can I help?'

'I hope you can help me. I really do.' Hisami stretched and walked to the far end of the table, where he rested for a second, leaning on the back of a chair, then continued towards Leppo. 'For both our sakes' – he patted Leppo on the shoulder – 'I hope you can help me.'

Leppo looked up, and Hisami knew he'd seen something in his eyes because his face instantly drained of its usual eager charm.

'Sure, name it – tell me what you want.'

'My wife – I want her back,' said Hisami. Then he fastened his hand around Leppo's neck and started pressing into the back of the solid dining-room chair. Leppo's arm lashed out, sending the tumbler skidding across the table and on to the floor with a clink. 'You fucking snake! Just four people knew she was visiting the centres in Italy, and you weren't one of them. We were exceptionally careful about who we told because we've had many threats from your fascist friends.' He was aware of Tulliver shouting for him to stop, but he braced his arm with his left hand and bent down to Leppo's face. 'You are going to get her back, Gil. Understand?' He gave him a jerk upwards, with half a mind to kill him there and then. Leppo managed to gurgle an affirmative.

Tulliver bellowed, 'Let him go now!'

Hisami released him and watched him fall forward, holding his throat and gasping for breath. When at last he could speak, he said, 'Jesus, have you gone crazy?'

'Shut the hell up. That's a fraction of the pain and terror Anastasia's experienced over the last few days.' He looked away towards the painting he had bought for her. 'She welcomed you into our home. She cooked for you, listened to you, indulged your self-obsession, empathised with you. And now they film her by her own grave in some fucking Russian forest. My wife! This is my wife you used against me. My wife!' He was shouting, spittle projecting from his mouth.

Leppo looked up and shook his head. Tulliver appeared at his side with a glass of water, now the imperturbable butler. Leppo took it and swallowed some.

'How long have you been involved?' demanded Hisami.

'You've got it wrong. You need help with that temper of yours, Denis.' He looked up, rubbing his neck. 'You can't treat me like this. I'm more than your fucking equal.'

'Don't tempt me, Gil. In other circumstances, I would have killed you and, frankly, it almost seems worth it right now.' He meant it, so took himself to the other side of the table and sat down in front of the folders that Zillah Dee had prepared for him. 'Quite apart from Anastasia's kidnap, have you any idea what this money will do in Europe? Did you even think of the mayhem Crane plans to cause?'

Leppo was silent. Hisami changed his position so he could look into his eyes. 'Don't go on denying it, Gil. It's all here.' He tapped one of the two folders.

'I knew nothing about Anastasia.'

'Maybe that's true, but then Crane told you just so you were up to your neck in it and you couldn't back out when things got rough, right? My guess is he had something on you. Actually, I think I have a lot more, but we'll talk about that in a moment. You got one of those emails from an account without a name with the documentary evidence attached. And in that email was the information you dreaded people knowing – the thing that could destroy you, if, as happened to me, it appeared on one of those far-right news sites Crane has connections with. And then one of his proxies – a lawyer, a politician, a business associate – or maybe even Crane himself tells you what to do, and you do it because you have no option. In your case, I guess it was something recent, like the shipment of arms to the Central African Republic that you brokered a couple of years ago.'

He picked up the first folder and drew out several documents and some photographs and pushed them over to Leppo. 'It's all there. Orders, end-user certificates, money transfers, even clear photographs of you doing the deal in a café in Tel Aviv. See, the Israelis don't like people doing arms deals in their country without their knowledge.'

Leppo looked dumbly at the papers in front of him.

'Gil, throughout our friendship' – he put air quotes around the last word – 'I never quite trusted you. I kept my ears open and I heard about this kid in Antioch. What age was she at the time that scumbag paedophile Griffin Bluett brought her to your home for a fee – fourteen, fifteen years of age? How much did you pay her family – $2 million plus her college fees? That was a nice touch. But you gave her pills – she didn't know what they were – and alcohol to wash them down, and for the next ten hours you abused her. All this was in Griffin Bluett's testimony, but you avoided prosecution because neither the girl nor her parents were prepared to testify.' The second folder opened on a high-school portrait of a pretty young girl with light brown hair cut into a bob. He turned it round to face Leppo. 'Nancy Milsum is her name and today she is nineteen years old. She never went to college because she had a breakdown. You weren't her only abuser. She was handed around five or six men – those are the ones she can remember – by Bluett, who was feeding her drug habit. Bluett destroyed Nancy Milsum's life, and you have your part in that. Just imagine what this is going to do to your reputation, Gil. And that's to say nothing about the risk of prosecution, which must now be high.'

Leppo looked at him, now totally beaten and compliant. 'What do you want?'

'Let's forget the pretence that Crane is dead, okay? We both know he's alive and that he arranged the kidnap and is holding Anastasia somewhere in Russia. We both know that he's trying to stop me using the information that Daniel Misak gave me. By the way, I also figured out that you were the go-between who persuaded Daniel to fly to London, where he was tortured and killed by Crane. He trusted you because you were a friend of mine.' He paused. 'And it was you, Gil, who passed the information on my years in Kurdistan, provided by Crane's Russian masters, to the authorities here, which is why I've spent most of the last week in jail.' He inhaled heavily and was silent.

'What do you need me to do?'

Hisami waited a little longer before answering. 'I'm prepared to forget everything if you go to Crane and have him release my wife. You have seventy-two hours. If you negotiate her freedom, none of this will be used. Now get the fuck out of my home, and of course I never want to see you again. If I do, be sure that I will kill you.'

A clock tolled some way off in the city of Tallinn. It was four in the morning and Samson had given up all hope of sleep. He got up, thinking about Anastasia, and found one of two cigarettes that he'd kept from another packet he'd thrown away and, shaking his head with mild self-disgust, lit up and opened the window to let the smoke out. It was no good thinking about her, so he set his mind on Hisami's strange reluctance to act to save his wife's life. He considered phoning Tulliver to see if there had been any developments and took out the phone, but then he noticed a movement down in the street. Someone had stepped back as he exhaled a plume of smoke into the rain. He drew back, turned off the light and stubbed out the cigarette so he could relight it, if needs be. He shut the window and angled his face so as not to be seen from the street. Someone was staking out the hotel and that person was no professional – the entrance could be watched from much further off. Then he saw there was another man, short and dressed in a parka, who was apparently unconcerned about being seen. With these two men on his doorstep, Samson didn't want Naji turning up, so he texted him with Robert Harland's address and sent Harland a message to explain that a young man would be showing up at his house, in all likelihood with his sister.

He watched the two men for a while. Unless Nyman had managed to locate the hotel then hired particularly useless local hoods to watch him, he had acquired some other interest. Did Adam Crane already know of the presence of a Hungarian national named Norbert Soltesz in Tallinn, a few hours from the Russian border? He decided to test them, picked up the cigarette butt and went down to the lobby, where the night porter, a young man with a textbook open in front of him, was serenely asleep with his chin resting in his hand. He woke up with a start, almost snapped to attention and made a move to the door. Samson said he'd get it himself, eased it open and stepped smartly into the street. He made for the men, holding up the cigarette. He called out in English for a light, but the two men immediately shot off in opposite directions. At least he had confirmed that he was being watched.

His phone rang – no caller ID. 'Yes,' he said.

'It's Jim Tulliver.'

'How can I help?' said Samson stiffly.

'You're still working on Anastasia?' Tulliver sounded exhausted.

'I told him I would, yes.'

'Right.'

'Has he decided to help me?'

'It's complicated – can we speak off the record?'

'Go ahead.'

'This is where I think we are. First, the dossier on the money and how it was to be used to stir up trouble across European democracies was devastating to the parties concerned, both in the US and Europe. Once they had found out what Misak had done for Denis and the extent of Denis's knowledge, they realised they had to change absolutely everything about their operation – the bank accounts, the signatories on those accounts, the shell companies they were using to distribute the money. That's complicated when banks are so wary of money-laundering. So they had to buy time, and they did that by kidnapping Anastasia and having Denis thrown in jail. Follow me?'

'So you're saying all they require him to do is sit on that dossier until they've made it obsolete. Once they've completed their task, they can let Anastasia go. Is that it?'

'Effectively, yes. But on the day of his release Denis received another threat, and this is what put him in such a bitch of a mood and why he was so damned difficult to deal with.'

'What could be worse than Anastasia's death? What was that threat?'

'I don't know.'

'So Anastasia's safety is secondary to this new threat.'

'No. He's desperately worried about her.'

Samson looked up and down the deserted street. 'I'm sure he is. So where does that leave us?'

'I'm going to be brutally honest with you, Samson. Anything you do to upset things right now could damage the chances of getting her back.'

'You're warning me off?'

'Not exactly. I just want you to know everything that I know.'

'Is that why Denis hasn't paid Zillah, to stop her working on the case? Or is he broke?'

'He's got money, but it's true he's got a lot of problems with finance,' said Tulliver wearily. 'Zillah will be paid in full.'

'But she has no guarantee and is pulling her people.'

'She will be paid.' He paused. 'What are you going to do?'

'This new threat has no meaning for me, Jim. That's Denis's business. Getting Anastasia back is the only thing I give a damn about.'

'You won't hold off for a few days? You see, he's got another play, another strategy he thinks is promising.'

'What kind of play?'

'I can't tell you.'

'You need to spit it out, Jim.'

There was silence the other end.

'Have it your own way,' said Samson. 'I know Denis told you to call me. Just say to him that I'm not prepared to back off, and it's for this reason: there's no guarantee they won't kill her when they've done everything they need to to cover their tracks. They're keeping her alive so they can film her on FaceTime just as long as they need to stop Denis publishing his dossier. Whatever else he's doing, you tell him I'm not backing off.' He hung up and walked slowly up and down the street, thinking, until he heard the chimes for five o'clock. Then he returned to the hotel for an hour of fitful sleep.

At first light, he got up and left the hotel, omitting to tell them that he wouldn't be back, and went to the far side of the old town to a café, where he bought coffee and a kind of cheese pastry. Tulliver had cleared things in his mind. Snatching Crane was the only solution. If Crane were suddenly taken out of circulation, they would remain exposed to Hisami's dossier, and that would keep Anastasia alive.

The new threat against Hisami was irrelevant. If Hisami was damaged, too fucking bad. He had stolen Anastasia from him, put her in appalling jeopardy and then, despite all his wealth and power, was incapable of helping her.

He consciously moved on to think about the challenge of seizing a well-protected Ukrainian gangster. He would need people and probably more money than he had allowed for. He made a list on his phone, went through it several times, committed it to memory and deleted it. Just past eight, he left the café, bought a smart card and boarded a tram that took him through suburbs of a very Nordic character bearing little trace of the country's communist past. He alighted at a stop on the east of the city, where no one else got off, waited and watched, then headed into the old city.

Harland's place was indeed pretty: a low white wall topped by ironwork from the twenties, a pale green building with shutters painted in a darker green and a doorway with a carved porch. He pulled the metal rod that operated the doorbell and waited. After a minute or two and another tug at the bell, Harland appeared, his glasses on top of his head.

'We have some former colleagues here,' he said, ushering him in with pained look. 'They expected you to make contact with me because of the Macy connection. So they invited themselves to breakfast.'

Samson followed him down a bare wooden corridor of white panelling and minimal furniture into a large kitchen and living area which opened on to a conservatory. Peter Nyman and Sonia Fell were sitting together on a sofa. Fell gave him one of her prim looks.

Nyman nodded and said, 'I was just complimenting Robert on his paintings – they really are very good indeed.' He gestured to a wall of marine paintings, executed in oil and watercolour. 'Did you know that our host was now a respected artist, Samson? Second act. Gives us all hope. They're marvellous, aren't they?'

An elegant woman in her sixties – grey hair cut into a bob with side-swept bangs, and dressed in beige and cream – appeared with a jug of coffee and a mug for Samson and flashed him a generous smile.

'This is my wife – Ulrike,' said Harland.

Samson greeted her, dropped his bag and sat down. Harland lowered himself cautiously into an upright Windsor armchair and drained his mug. 'I'll let Mr Nyman explain,' he said unenthusiastically.

'Peter – please call me Peter,' said Nyman. Harland sniffed. 'It's quite an honour to be in the presence of such a luminary of our trade. I hope you appreciate Robert's heroic past, Samson, and of course, Ulrike's.' He darted an ingratiating look in her direction.

Samson shrugged. 'What do you want?'

'As I have explained, we are here in an official capacity, representing the British government, and our message is quite simple. We have come to tell you to desist in all your efforts to contact, monitor or otherwise engage with Ray Shepherd, also known as Adam Crane, while you are in Estonia.'

'The man who you and the British police maintain is dead,' said Samson quickly.

Nyman gave him a weary look. 'That's as may be. But we will not allow you to sabotage an operation that has taken months to put together and on which our national interest depends.'

'In what way does the national interest depend on a Ukrainian gangster and murderer?'

'I am not at liberty to say,' said Nyman. He moved forward. 'Be very clear, Samson, that we will brook no opposition in this matter. The UK government is resolved. And that, as far as you are concerned, is an end to it. Go home and look after your restaurant. I hear it needs your full attention.'

Samson looked from Nyman to Fell but said nothing.

'Do I have your assurance?' said Nyman.

'You always forget that I'm not working for you, or for the British government. And we're not in London and you have no authority here.'

'But we do have the power to cause you considerable inconvenience,' said Sonia. 'Be reasonable. There's so much you don't understand about all of this.'

'I was hired to find Anastasia by her husband, and that is what I am going to do. Now you come to me and talk about Crane. Is this because you have knowledge of his involvement in her abduction? If so, you'll be covering up not only a murder but also a kidnap. You want that made public, Peter?'

Nyman shook his head. 'You're emotionally involved, Samson. We understand that, but you must not let these feelings interfere in matters of national security. We're asking for a few days. That's all.'

'For what?'

'Look, everyone in this room has been in the intelligence business.' Samson glanced at Ulrike and wondered about her. 'We all know how delicate these things are. You've got to allow us to complete an immensely complex intelligence operation, of which you have not the slightest notion.'

'What is there to fear from me if I don't have the slightest notion about this?'

Nyman's temper snapped. 'Take it from me that I will personally see that you are destroyed if you mess with me on this.' He stopped and controlled himself. 'You will not – I repeat *not* – get in our way.'

'Is that because you support the aims of a Ukrainian gangster? Because it very much looks like that from where I'm standing, and I'm sure it will to the media on both sides of the Atlantic.'

Nyman looked exasperated. Fell glanced at him and took over. 'You know us better than that, Paul.'

'Do I? Frankly, I don't rule out anything these days. But it doesn't matter one way or another. I am here to find and free

Anastasia. You both know her and of the work she does. She was abducted while trying to help people. If there is anyone in this room who has done more for their fellow human beings, I'd be very surprised.'

Ulrike had appeared from the far end of the room and perched on the long dining-room table. 'I'd be interested to hear about her work,' she said, with a slight German accent.

'She runs several centres for the psychological rehabilitation of migrants with trauma – mostly people from the Middle East and northern Africa. The centres were financed by her husband, Denis Hisami, in the memory of his sister, who was killed by ISIS. There's nothing else to say. They do a very good job. I saw for myself in Italy a few days ago.' He stopped, realising that he was sounding too passionate.

'This is not relevant,' said Nyman.

'On the contrary,' started Ulrike. 'I think it's very relevant that—'

'Let me assure you it isn't,' said Nyman rudely.

Harland shifted and said, 'I'd very much like to hear what my wife was going to say.'

Ulrike nodded to him. 'It seems to me you're placing the interests of an intelligence operation involving a very bad man and with uncertain outcomes – these things are never certain, are they? – above helping someone who is evidently a very good person.'

'I am not here to debate the issue,' said Nyman rattily. 'I am here to represent the British government and tell Samson to cease and desist.'

Harland cleared his throat. 'Just as it escaped your notice that Mr Samson is no longer in SIS, you also failed to comprehend that we are Estonian citizens and that our interest in what the British government is demanding tends to be on the low side.'

Samson's attention wandered while this was going on. He looked around and saw how elegant the place was. A door led from the conservatory to an enclosed garden, at the end of which stood a Gothic gateway set in an ancient wall. Pot plants in the conservatory were still blooming among off-white and blue garden furniture. Books were piled high and neatly; jars of brushes and pencils were lined up on a table in the corner where the morning light flooded in. Anastasia would like it.

Nyman was looking appalled. 'You're no longer a British citizen, Robert! How can that be?'

'The only thing I took from England is my language and this chair, which belonged to my father. When we got married and moved here we both decided to leave our citizenships behind.' Ulrike aimed a smile at him from across the room. 'You two coming into my house and trying to bully your way doesn't cut any bloody ice. Is that clear?'

Nyman looked down at his shoes then up at Harland. 'My apologies. You must forgive me. These are difficult times and this is a very important operation.' He glanced at Samson. 'And I believe Samson has some idea how important it is.'

Samson said nothing.

'Come on, you know what this means,' said Nyman.

'Maybe, Peter, but my task is to save Anastasia.' He got up in order to leave, but Harland gestured impatiently for him to sit down.

'Look, I'm going to be frank with you,' said Nyman. 'We're not some fascist cabal. We're genuinely concerned to map what is going on and to prepare for the undoubted tumult that will occur if this all goes through. You have referred to the American origin of the money. Please understand that this is what concerns us most. I want you to see that we are on the same side, but that I can't have my operation interfered with.'

'Well, we know where we both stand,' said Samson, not giving an inch.

'I think this conversation is at an end,' said Harland quietly. Nyman worked his way to the front of the sofa and got up, followed by Fell. At this point there was a crash from upstairs. They both looked up.

'The lodger,' said Ulrike. 'A student. He must have dropped something.'

Harland's eyes danced for a fraction of a second before he rose to show Nyman and Fell to the door.

When he came back he said, 'He's a pompous ass, but I think he's telling the truth about his motives and he makes a good point about his operation. I'd feel pretty much the same way if I were running it. I hear about these threats from the far right all the time from our friends in the government here. It's no bloody joke. They have to stay on top of it.'

'I know,' said Samson. 'But with every day that Crane has to reorganise it becomes less likely that we will see Anastasia again. Once he's done what he needs to do, he will have her killed. Taking Crane is the only way to save her.'

Harland looked at Ulrike and something seemed to pass between them. She said, 'Now, let's get our lodger down here. I am sure you'll want to talk to him.'

CHAPTER 24

Anastasia woke with the gun in her lap. She had been forced off the track when she saw headlights coming from the compound and had plunged into the forest, thinking that she could make her way back easily. But she soon became lost and wandered around in the dark, occasionally clicking the lighter to see her way through the dense pine trees. She took many tumbles and when she tripped over a stump and went flying, the gun went off. The recoil drove the stock into her ribs and the report and muzzle flash left her trembling. It was then she looked for and found the safety slide, just where her thumb came to rest when aiming the gun. Pushed back, the slide made the gun safe.

She had no experience of being in the wild, and no taste for it. She remembered Naji talking about his journey through the mountains of Macedonia and how he and the Yazidi boy Ifkar always made sure they were dry. Cold was a deadly enemy, Naji advised her gravely – it was much better always to sit out a storm and conserve your strength. He took pride in telling her about making fires and heating stones that would keep you warm through the night and using food cans as saucepans. In a dripping forest without a torch, it was impossible to follow his advice, but beneath one of the bigger pines she found a bed of pine needles and dead leaves that was almost entirely dry, and she lay with her back propped against a tree and massaged her injured shoulder against its smooth trunk. She longed to make a fire but feared it would be seen.

When she woke up, she guessed by the angle of the sun that it was between eight and nine o'clock. She examined the bruises and cuts she'd acquired during the night and told herself that she couldn't do another night in the forest. Most of the food she had grabbed in the kitchen had fallen from her pockets as she climbed the fence, or when she scrambled away from the track to avoid the pursuing vehicles. She was left with a small jar of pickles, a tin of some kind of fish and a packet of dried biscuits. What she craved was water. She got up and moved stiffly to the outer boughs of the trees and stroked the moisture on the needles into her open mouth. It helped a little. She ripped back the ring pull on the tin of fish and ate the entire contents with her fingers then poured the oil into her mouth, believing it would contain much-needed calories. The biscuits, which were like an infant's rusk, were dry, but she softened one with her saliva and managed to get it down her parched throat. She felt better and began to think about which way to go. There were no clues and the position of the sun told her nothing because she didn't know which direction she'd come from. Kirill had obviously chosen the hunting lodge because of its isolation, and she might go for many miles without hope of hitting the track or seeing any other signs of civilisation. But remaining under the tree was not an option. With the rifle slung over her shoulder and a stick in her left hand to help her through the patches of mossy bog, she headed south towards the sun because, that way, she at least knew she wouldn't be walking in circles.

Nothing stirred around her until, about half an hour into her walk, she thought she heard something moving off to her right. She stopped and, remembering Naji's story about his encounter with a bear in Macedonia, listened intently. Everything was still for a few moments, but then whatever the creature was started moving again, plodding determinedly in her direction. She raised the rifle, pushed the catch forward and waited for what seemed like an age, aware only of her breathing and the approaching sound. The animal – she could hear it snorting now – was very close and she considered firing a warning shot into the bushes but realised she would have to reload. There was a series of crashes as the creature raced ahead of her, then a black boar with massive shoulders and small, curved tusks trotted into the open twenty metres in front of her, stopped and glanced in her direction before barrelling into the undergrowth to her left. Amazed by the size of the thing and its turn of speed, she lowered the rifle with a smile, the first genuine sign of joy that had crossed her face in – God, she had no idea how long it was. She looked up at the tops of the trees and smiled again.

The sight of the boar, its flanks steaming with exertion,

gave her a lift. There was something else that occurred to her a little later, the certainty that she would pull the trigger on whatever threatened her. When she took the gun and shells from the cabinet she had had her doubts, but now she was sure she'd shoot to kill if her survival depended on it. Once, on the terrace of Mesopotamia, when, unusually, Denis and she had opened a second bottle of wine and talked late into a warm night, he told her that the only reason he'd managed to stay alive as a young man was because he had resolved he would always 'make it out'. That attitude saved him countless times, he'd said. Now Anastasia told herself the same. She'd seen two men murdered and woken up to find a pair of bodies in that container, but she wasn't damn well going to join them.

Finding the track was a piece of luck, which came to her because she'd decided to look around and notice where she was, rather than moving blindly through the forest. When she happened to glance at the sunlight on some brilliant, pale yellow leaves that were clinging to a sapling's lower branches she noticed that beyond the tree was a flat brown surface. This was a bend in the track and, if she hadn't looked at the tree, she would have missed it because this was the only point where her route going south came close to it. After checking the track was empty both ways, she stepped out into the open and made for a puddle, where she scooped up water, taking care not to disturb the mud at the bottom. She wasn't enjoying any part of this, but she felt alive and free.

Which direction? She had no idea but decided to head south. She walked for five or six kilometres, keeping to the side so that she could dive for cover if one of the cars from the compound came along. She ate some biscuits and a few of the mixed pickles – small onions and slices of carrot – and sometimes she hummed to herself.

In the middle of the afternoon she spotted a thin male figure in a black anorak, about three hundred metres ahead of her. She slowed and watched. He seemed to be moving with difficulty. She quickened her pace and came within shouting distance, but instead of calling out she kept walking towards him. When she got close she said, 'Hello.' He turned round, and she saw the haunted, white, elfin face of a young man of about nineteen or twenty. He looked puzzled and fearful, but then smiled and nodded. He uttered something and she shook her head to say that she didn't understand. He was saying, 'Igor! Igor!' That was his name. She said it with a smile, and he grinned and his fingers danced in front of his mouth, perhaps as a kind of substitute for the words he could not speak, for it was clear he had the mental age of a young child. He got close and peered at her to check she really meant him no harm, and she smiled again and he clapped his hands and clasped them together by his heart to say that he liked her, then she did the same, which delighted him. She touched him on the shoulder and pointed ahead of them. She was asking whether they should continue on their way together. And he got the point and smiled and his fingers fluttered his joy. So they walked together, Igor dragging his left foot and shyly sneaking looks at her.

This boy must be going somewhere, she thought. Someone must look after him, someone who might have a phone and possibly a place she could sleep. These thoughts were uppermost in her mind, yet she responded to Igor as she had to the damaged young people she saw in the camps in Lesbos during the mass migration from Syria. She found herself making jokes with him and pointing things out, even though there was not much to see in the unchanging forest on either side of them. In his own way, the boy was beautiful, and she began to feel there was more character locked up in him than she had first thought. After a little while, she tapped him on the shoulder again and handed him the stick she no longer needed. He looked down then tried it and his eyes lit up because it did make things easier. Why hadn't anyone thought to give him a stick? And why was he alone on this long road in the middle of nowhere and without food?

The 'lodger' making a noise upstairs in Harland's house turned out to be Naji. He had arrived with his older sister, Munira, half an hour before Nyman and Fell appeared on Harland's doorstep. Harland had got them upstairs, while Ulrike kept Nyman waiting at the door with questions about the purpose of their visit. In the time Harland had spent with Naji before Nyman arrived, he'd told him everything concerning Anastasia's situation, which he later explained to Samson was because Naji already knew she was in trouble and he was obviously capable of dealing with the news. That was certainly true: Naji's foremost traits, which had taken him all the way through the Balkans as a boy, were resilience and unrealistic optimism.

He seemed to have grown even taller since Samson last saw

him as he came in behind Munira, gave Samson an awkward hug and immediately sat down at the table and asked for the Wifi password, which Ulrike read out. Munira, without the hijab she had worn when Samson saw the family in Germany, took him aside and made him promise to look after Naji. She had to return to Riga for a part-time job she was doing alongside her maths degree, so she couldn't stay to make sure he stayed safe. She left, wagging her finger at Naji and telling him in Arabic to remember he had responsibilities, which he took no notice of, although Samson nodded to reassure her.

He sat down beside Harland, facing Naji. 'So, what've you got, my friend?'

Naji looked sheepish and mumbled that he felt a little weird hacking Hisami's email account when he'd been so generous to the family. He spun the computer around so they could both see. Samson examined the strangely configured inbox and shook his head. 'What am I looking at?'

'These are the emails from Kasim08@Kasim.com. This is the man who gave information to Mr Hisami many weeks ago. Three were deleted.' Naji spun the computer towards him and pulled one up. Samson went round to his side of the table and began reading.

'Kasim is Misak in reverse,' said Samson. 'That's Daniel Misak, whose body was found on Crane's balcony. He was Hisami's source in TangKi.'

He began reading, summarizing as he did so. 'A total of $146.7 million US has been transferred through the company since April last year. Over an eighteen-month period, 123 different accounts were used – never the same one twice. The money is entered as loans as well as payment for consultation and a lot of vaguely defined services – tax advice, legal fees, research, export facilitation . . . that kind of BS. There's a shitload of shell companies involved, here and in Europe. Lists follow. There is no trace of any of the US companies trading, with the exception of a chain of realtors in the Pacific Northwest. It's impossible for me to follow the money trail beyond the wall of phoney outfits in the US, but the government would have no difficulty doing this. Right now, we don't have access to the crypto records which will tell the rest of the story. All you need to make a case is attached.'

Samson looked down the list of US companies and the list for those in Europe, many of which were either registered by Companies House in London or in Cyprus. The attachments were screenshots of TangKi's accounts and statements from its several bank accounts showing transfers abroad.

He read out parts of the email while Ulrike poured coffee and gave Naji a glass of water. Then he opened the next email, which was more recent.

> Transfers have ceased. The operation is over and accounts are being sanitised – you had better move on this soon, or there won't be anything to see. Also, I made progress on the artworks aspect. Before the accounts were altered, there were payments to three art dealers in London for art delivered in Europe and London. The artworks were sent to two destinations

in Europe (see attachment) plus the Geneva Freeport facility where most are held in the names of shell companies. Payments total $62 million, but I am sure I didn't get all of them.

Crypto. $14.7 million invested in building via crypto. Dates and real estate portfolios are all listed in 2nd attachment – 'Ledger'. This was done through TangKi's normal operations, the money coming from accounts that are attached to suspicious-looking companies.

Samson looked through the attachments and, at length, said, 'So, we know how the money left the States, but there's nothing to say where it came from or who will be the beneficiaries.'

Naji turned the laptop without a word and worked the touchpad. 'Here!' he said, in a tone that suggested Samson was an idiot. There was a third email which didn't answer these questions, however it was dated four weeks before Anastasia was kidnapped.

Hi, here it is. Now you have what you want, I'm leaving town for a few weeks – maybe longer. Thanks for the package. It's a huge help. By the way, I'm pretty sure he is skimming most of the value of the artwork. Once the money has left the country, the donors – whoever they are – have to trust that our friend will get it to the parties he intends it for. Big mistake. This is the last time you will hear from me – over and out.

Misak's final report was another attachment and contained all the information in the previous emails. The key part was a list of political organisations which Misak must have prised out of Crane's personal computer. The groups were listed alongside the financial requests they had made, each making its pitch for staff, office space, social media, website advertising costs and concluding with a statement that, without exception, referred to a mission that combined racial purity and the forcible return of migrants to their place of origin, to be supported by other actions, which Samson took to mean violence. The statements were so similar that Crane must have helped write them. The important part was that each one was named with its country of origin, as were the companies that were to receive the money, their bank details and the amount they were to be given.

All followed the same pattern. The name of the organisation – such as Zászló Testvérei (Brothers of the Flag) – came first, followed by the country where it was based, in this case Hungary, followed by shell-company names and bank-account numbers.

There were, in all, twenty-five organisations from across Europe and each was associated with three or four companies. By using the web translation service, they established that many of the organisations had the same name. There were four groups called Our Land – Naše země (Czech Republic), Vårt Land (Sweden), A Mi Földünk (Hungary), Vores Land (Denmark); three with the name People's Voice – Glas Naroda (Croatia), Die Stimme der Leute (Germany), La Voce del Popolo

(Italy); and two called White Nation – Białe Barody (Poland) Valkoiset Valtiot (Finland).

Harland said he'd heard of almost none of them, although he was familiar with Metsa Sõbrad – Friends of the Forest – a shadowy Estonian group usually known as MS which he said was more like a masonic club than a political group. He would make a call to a friend in KaPo, the Estonian domestic intelligence service – Kaitsepolitseiamet – and see what they had on them.

Samson ran through the list again and looked up to meet Naji's expectant eyes. 'This is really important, Naji. You've done a great job. We've got the dossier.' He squeezed him on the shoulder. 'My goodness, you're a clever guy.'

'Is it possible to exchange for Anastasia?' Naji asked.

Samson shook his head and explained that they were holding her to give them time to cover their tracks by changing all the shell companies and bank accounts and making everything that he had discovered irrelevant.

Harland folded his arms and looked over his reading glasses. 'They can cover up what happens from now on, but they can't go back and erase everything that happened in the US. You may not have got that information now, but the US authorities would be able to get it.'

'Which is dangerous to Crane,' said Samson. 'Another reason for them not to let Anastasia go. But if we get Crane, that's a very different matter. They have to exchange her for him.' Harland looked at him sceptically. Naji was nodding furiously.

'You both have a lot of emotional investment in this, but

think of the practicalities,' said Harland. 'First, you have to find him. Second, you have to kidnap and hold him until they contact you, because you can't phone them, can you? Third, you have no one to help you, because my days of putting bags over people's heads are long gone. Fourth, you will be breaking the law here and, if you are caught, you will go to jail for a very long time.'

When confronted with unyielding opposition, Samson generally changed the subject. 'There's something I really don't understand. The Russians have caused all the trouble they wanted in the European Union. Far-right groups are really well financed. Why is an American pushing money at them now?'

'It's obvious they'll take it further. They're almost certainly proposing violence. But there's a lot of money going into online activity. That's the tool they're concentrating on – the kind of crap we saw in the US and across Europe, but much worse.'

'Exactly,' said Samson. 'So wouldn't it be good if we could publish the dossier while it's still relevant?'

Harland had seen the argument coming. 'And you suggest the only way to do that is to kidnap Crane, swap him for Anastasia and publish the moment you've got her safe and sound?'

'Precisely. These are bad people and they need to be exposed.'

Harland sniffed. 'You're sounding like an idealistic journalist.'

'It's the only way we can save her life.'

'And her husband's efforts – you think they have ceased entirely?'

'That's why I need your help to find Crane. It's all I'm asking. And, hell, the Estonians won't want this man in their country, organising racist insurrection across Europe. You look at the dossier. Crane and his backers have built a network. They've probably set up some of these groups.'

Harland was unmoved. 'You mentioned last night that you thought Crane had something else over Hisami. Do you have any idea what it is?' He glanced at Ulrike. 'I mean, what could be worse than someone holding a gun to your wife's head and threatening to kill her if you don't do what they say?'

Naji's fingers scurried over the keyboard. 'There are emails here with numeric addresses.'

There were three brief messages. Samson looked at the first, which was from 50527121Z@beatface.org and dated two days after Anastasia's kidnap. It read, 'Keep quiet and she will stay alive.'

The second, from 58975a576@troubadawk.com, read, 'Now you're out of jail, don't screw up. Stay quiet and you'll get her back. A word or any action will put her in that pit.'

Then came a message from a third email address, 476df476@ conspie.com. It read, 'The vid of the little bomber girl is ready to fly. With your troubles, there'll be a big market for that one. Don't fuck up, Denis.'

'These are direct threats from Crane.' Samson looked at the time and date of the last one. 'Hisami must have seen this when I was in his apartment in New York.'

'Interesting to know what he means by "little bomber girl",' said Harland. He got up and put on his coat and a black flat cap and left through the conservatory door. Samson expected him to make for the Gothic door in the old stone wall, but he crossed to the opposite side of the garden and disappeared behind a shrub, where there was evidently another exit. Ulrike watched him go then suggested Naji take a nap.

Samson agreed. 'There's nothing for us to do at the moment, Naji. Grab it when you can.'

Naji went upstairs, clutching his computer and a pastry in a paper napkin.

Samson texted Zillah Dee. 'Has Denis talked to you? Any news on the truck driver? Has anyone accessed those accounts?' He put down his phone and turned to Ulrike.

'I'm sure Bobby will help you,' she said, sitting down opposite him. 'He's incapable of refusing when there's so much at stake. And, of course, he's a romantic, though he would be very angry if he heard me say that.'

'How did you meet?' asked Samson.

'During an operation not unlike this one.' She wrapped her hands around her coffee and smiled. 'It was thirty years ago and we were both involved in the abduction of an Arab terrorist who carried out attacks in the West with the help of the Stasi. Classic state-sponsored terrorism.'

'This story I know well,' said Samson. 'What part did you play?'

'I was the SIS contact in Leipzig, where Abu Jemal visited.'

'You were their East German source? You were Kafka? Jesus! I had no idea.'

'Yes, a silly name, but I didn't choose it. There was another

East German involved, a man named Rudi Rosenharte. Bobby was running the operation for London. It's a long story, but Rudi and I fell in love in those few weeks.' She leaned forward and grinned at him, almost coquettishly. 'He was devastatingly handsome, an aesthete, a roué with a thrilling intellect. They were the best of times – for Europe, for us, for everyone – and we had no option but to fall in love.' She stopped and dabbed the corner of one eye with her knuckle. 'Forgive me. Remembering that time and seeing what's occurring today in Europe makes me emotional.'

'And Bobby – where does he come in?'

'Bobby helped Rudi get me out of Hohenschönhausen jail in Berlin, where I was being held and questioned by the Stasi. Then Rudi, Bobby and I crossed into the West on that same night, which was when the Wall came down. It was a miracle.' She clapped her hands together and repeated the word 'miracle' several times.

'I know about this – he defied orders to get you out. They still use this case to teach the new intelligence officer intake *not* to become involved with agents.'

She laughed and clapped her hands again. 'That's so funny. Of course, Bobby never took any notice of his superiors. You saw his reaction to your Mr Nyman.'

'But then what happened to Rudi?'

Her face clouded. 'We were married and I became pregnant. Before the birth we decided to drive to Spain. Rudi was an art historian, one of the top scholars in the whole of Germany. He had never visited the Prado – Velásquez, Goya, El Greco and of course Hieronymus Bosch, about whom he was writing a monograph. They were wonderful days. We were free. We were part of a free, democratic Europe and we were deeply in love. I never saw him so happy as in those weeks we spent in Madrid.' She stopped. 'Then they killed him. They shot up the car as we drove back to Germany. It was in the Pyrenees. Ex-Stasi officers. They missed me but they killed Rudi. Our car crashed. I was injured. But my baby survived.'

'I'm so sorry,' said Samson. 'I had no idea.'

'Why should you? I am sure it isn't part of the SIS training manual.' She got up and went to a small box of inlaid wood on the side. 'Do you smoke, Samson?'

'Occasionally.'

'I thought you looked like a smoker.'

'Is that good or bad?'

'Mostly good,' she said.

They went through the conservatory and stepped out into the weak autumn sunlight and smoked in silence. 'In our line of work,' she said presently, 'we experience the extremes of life.'

'Yes, we do,' he said, his mind filled with images of Syria.

'You want to hear the rest of the story?' He nodded. 'I was devastated, of course. I went back to Berlin and Bobby helped me find a place and a new identity for the time being. I had my baby boy and I called him Rudi. So there is still a Rudi Rosenharte in the world. He is twenty-five years old now and he lives with his girlfriend in Berlin. He makes films.'

'And you and Bobby?'

'Bobby left SIS after the war in Bosnia and went to find those people who shot up the car. They were all Stasi – the leader was named Zank. He was the man responsible for Rudi's brother's death in Hohenschönhausen and he put me in that hellhole, then years later he tracked us to Spain and killed Rudi. He was responsible for the deaths of two brilliant men who were never able to fulfil their potential in the free world.' She stubbed out the cigarette.

'And?'

'Bobby settled the account.'

'Meaning?'

'He settled the account.' She shrugged and looked at him hard.

Samson wasn't going any further.

'I was a mother by then,' she continued, 'and living a very isolated life because there were still Stasi who wanted me dead so I couldn't be in Leipzig with my mother and friends. Bobby helped out with things – found me a new apartment, paid some bills. We went out, though there was nothing between us. I was still in grief for Rudi.' She let out a stream of smoke and looked around her garden critically. 'And then things changed. Bobby found work with the Estonian government, helping them improve their intelligence service and suggesting ways of defending their brand-new democracy. He liked it here. Loved the people. I visited him with my son. Over the next year, we found love. It was slow and neither of us noticed it was happening and then Bobby asked me to move here with him and I realised it was exactly what I wanted, and this is where we brought up young Rudi. We married and we've been very happy.'

'That's a hell of a story,' said Samson.

'Yes, it is.' She tugged the conservatory door open. 'And that's why I believe Bobby will try to help you if he can. That's what he's doing now. He just has to be careful not to break the law. You have to understand that.'

CHAPTER 25

A pine had fallen and blocked the track. It was tall and bushy but the trunk was relatively slender. Anastasia assumed it wouldn't take long to cut it up with a chainsaw and clear the way, but the last vehicles to pass had swerved off the road and ploughed across the grass verge and over the crown of the tree, pressing the uppermost branches into the earth. Igor looked at the tree uncomprehendingly then laughed and followed the tyre tracks around it, but he became unsteady and she took his hand, which made him shriek with pleasure. They continued on their way, she feeling more and more silly with the gun slung over her shoulder. She wanted to toss it away but, just a few minutes on, she heard the noise of a vehicle approaching from behind. It might have been someone she could flag down for a ride, but she couldn't risk that without seeing the vehicle first. She tried to drag Igor into hiding, pretending it was a game, but he tugged his arm free and kept walking. The vehicle slowed and began to move to the side of the road to pass around the tree. She saw the roofs of what looked like two SUVs. It was now or never. She put her finger to her lips. Igor seemed to understand and nodded, and she dived into the bushes lining the track and ran up a slight mound among the pines, flattened herself against the bare soil and laid a handful of shells in front of her.

She had been here before – on the mountain road in Calabria. But now she had a gun and it was aimed at the dark SUV, which drifted to a stop by Igor, who turned and made wild movements with his hands as though fending off an attack by birds. She had a clean shot of the driver and she could see three men in the second car. There was no doubt who they were when Kirill, apparently unharmed by the fire and still bristling with self-importance, got out in one of his damned hunting hats, grabbed Igor's shoulder and spun him round. Igor waved his arms in protest and tried to look away. Kirill was saying something. She guessed he was demanding to know if he had seen her, but what he got in response was an even wilder fluttering of hands. He took hold of the boy by both shoulders, shook him and cuffed him across the side of his head. One more blow from Kirill and she would shoot, but then reason kicked in. She might hit the boy, and even if she winged Kirill – the best she could hope for, since she had never fired a gun – there were at least four other men in the cars and they'd all be armed and would soon overwhelm and kill her. So, she waited one more agonising minute while Kirill hit Igor some more and pushed him over. The driver laughed. Kirill climbed back in and both vehicles moved off.

Igor did not get up, but she left it a little while before hurrying down to the road. The boy was all right but shaken and plainly terrified. She put her arms around him and hugged him and kissed him lightly on the forehead. 'It's going to be okay,' she said. 'Come on, let's go.' She helped him up, brushed the mud and grass from his clothes and looked into his face and smiled. 'We've got to find somewhere to sleep.'

They walked on for another half-hour or so before Igor stopped suddenly and examined the side of the road. His mind seemed to settle on something. He parted two saplings and led her through the gap, one hand gesturing chaotically ahead of them. He was telling her he knew the way.

It began to rain. The forest became dark and it was hard to see, but Igor pressed on and she noticed that stretches of the earth had been beaten into a path. He knew exactly where he was going. Another half-hour passed before they came to a clearing surrounded by very tall trees in the middle of which was a large shack built with horizontally aligned planks of wood at the lower level and vertical planks above, all painted in a green wash. Drainpipes had become detached from both sides of the building and the window shutters hung loose. She saw there had been a flower garden once – a solitary marigold bloomed – but now only the vegetable patch showed signs of care; there were a few cabbages left. She slung the gun around her back so it was less obvious and followed Igor to the door. He pushed it open with the side of his body and flung her a strange look as they entered the dark interior.

The smell of wood burning hit her. The room was warm

but there was no electric light or movement in the shack. She saw heaps of paper and clothes and, as her eyes became accustomed to the gloom, a figure seated by a wood-burning stove – an old woman asleep. Igor went to her side and dropped something from inside his jacket into her lap. She woke and clawed the air to take hold of him. She murmured something – it sounded like gratitude – and Igor brought a lantern over between the heels of his hands. He set it down unsteadily on the table and stepped back. She pulled the glass flap open, lit the wick then examined the packets in the light – a box of medicine and a pack of batteries. The woman was engrossed in these items but Anastasia thought it was time to introduce herself and moved forward with her hand out. 'Anastasia,' she said. The woman looked up, unsurprised, and said something to Igor, who writhed with embarrassment. It seemed she thought Anastasia was his girlfriend. Well, why not for the moment? She nodded, sat down and moved her gun as discreetly as possible to the side. The old woman opened her hands and exclaimed, 'Pristrastnyy!' which Anastasia thought might mean girlfriend, or simply friend, so she nodded vigorously.

The old lady must have been in her nineties, but she was still quite nimble and seemed to have all her faculties. Five minutes later Anastasia wondered about this when she got up with the lantern and moved towards a rudimentary kitchen, where there was a basin, a washboard, one gas ring and some large pots and saucepans. She clutched at Anastasia's jacket and tugged her towards an old black-and-white framed photograph of men and women standing in the forest with machine guns, rifles and ammunition belts. '*Pristrastnyy! Pristrastnyy!*' she said. Anastasia took the photograph from the old women and saw it was dated 1944. '*Pristrastnyy!*' The old woman tapped her chest with both index fingers and said, 'Olga,' then carefully placed a crooked finger on a young girl of seventeen or eighteen in the photo, exclaiming, 'Olga – *pristrastnyy!*' She touched the rifle and made a shooting motion. Anastasia suddenly understood. Olga had been a partisan during the war. Either she thought Anastasia looked like one or that she was one. After all, she was armed and wearing almost exactly the same leather jacket as Olga in the photograph.

She smiled at the old lady, remembering that in his wallet Denis kept a photograph of him and his sister in fatigues in Kurdistan during the 1990s. Then she performed an elaborate mime of dialling and speaking on a phone. The old lady looked at her as though she were utterly mad, shook her head and shooed her from the kitchen.

Outside, there was still some light. She wondered how long the old lady would allow her to stay. She went over to the wood stove and took off some clothes to dry them, then sat cross-legged as close as she could, to warm herself. Igor watched her. At length, he clambered up and brought another lantern to her, this one made of pieces of brown and yellowish glass, lifted the top and lit the candle. Inside there was a tiny mirrored fan which, when heated, made the lights swirl around the room. She smiled, noticing that now he was home and free of stress his movements were less involuntary and his face more composed. He was extraordinary-looking – quite beautiful in his absorption with the coloured lantern.

The old lady gave them all bowls of lumpy onion, beetroot and potato soup. Anastasia ate two bowls while the old lady nagged Igor to finish his first. He sat at her feet and she stroked his hair and talked to him, possibly telling stories; Anastasia had no way of knowing. But she found herself being lulled by the sound of the ancient, cracked voice and, within a few minutes, she'd laid the gun on the floor and her head had fallen back on a pile of papers and she was asleep.

Ulrike passed her phone to Samson. It was Harland. 'You need to get out of the house.' His voice was hoarse, his tone urgent. 'We have an infestation. Ulrike will show you how. What about the boy? Do you need him, or should he go back home?'

'Not sure,' said Samson, looking over at Naji, who was monitoring a burst of activity on Hisami's email account.

'You need me for this and for the bank accounts,' said Naji, who had heard what was being said on the mobile phone, though it wasn't on speaker.

'To be discussed,' said Samson.

'No discussion,' Naji said truculently, without looking up. 'My decision.'

'On the other thing,' said Harland, 'you're going to have to move fast. Crane's here in the city and making very rapid progress. We may be able to exchange our information for his coordinates. You okay with that?'

'Of course,' replied Samson. To swap a dossier with a fast-approaching expiration date for accurate details about Crane's whereabouts was a deal he didn't have to think twice about.

'You're going to need people, and they can't be local,' said Harland.

'I know.'

'Now, get out of the house.'

'What type of pests? Ours? The opposition?' asked Samson, thumbing through the contacts list on his phone.

'Not sure, we'll worry about that later. I need that material fast. Get it to me via Ulrike – she knows what to do.'

Samson hung up and handed the phone to Ulrike. Within a couple of minutes, they had copied the dossier into a file, Ulrike had encrypted it and had dispatched it to her husband's phone. In the meantime, Samson had found and composed a text to the number that he hadn't used since Macedonia. He wrote, 'I have a job for 2/3. Estonia. Now. Good money. Big bonus. Call me. Samson.' He had little hope of getting a response but saw it had been delivered.

Before they had crossed the garden to the hidden exit a call came on Samson's phone from Zillah Dee.

'We've got the driver,' she said. 'We know where they took her. It's western Russia – forests north of Pskov.'

He stopped in his tracks. 'How are you going to play it?'

'I told Denis, but the truth of the matter is he hasn't paid us.'

'But you won't let that get in the way.'

'Of course not, and he's good for the money eventually, but

I'm burning through it right now with five people in the field. So we're going to take a look at the place and report back. If there's an exfiltration, he needs to find the money. Sorry, but that's the way it has to be.'

'I'm sure he will. How does this work? Do you take the driver with you?'

'No, he's out cold and in a secure location. We'll hold him until we confirm the site. Don't feel sorry for him. He's a scumbag. He tried to rape my operative. Then he discovered that she has certain skills and he got badly hurt. By the way, the haulage company is Mafia-run.' Samson started walking towards Ulrike, who was waiting with Naji at the end of the garden. 'There's one other matter. The story about Anastasia is about to break. That won't matter if we get her out, but it could be a big factor if we don't. The Italian police seem the likely source, however the reporter who contacted Denis's office didn't know much and the office issued a flat denial. We probably have a few hours on that.'

'But it adds to the time pressure.'

'Look, I have to go. I'll be in contact as soon as we've located and recced the site.'

'Hold on! Can you see if there's been any activity around those bank accounts over the last twenty-four hours? I hear things are moving fast.'

'Sure, I'll have someone get back to you.'

The call ended. Samson jogged over to Ulrike and Naji at the far end of the garden.

★

Ulrike drove them to the car-hire place in the port area, where Samson rented an enclosed pick-up truck then followed her for a little over an hour to their seaside cottage. Naji elected to go with Samson, though during the first twenty minutes he said nothing and looked around the car, occasionally glancing at his phone.

'You've seen a bit of Anastasia since she married?' Samson ventured.

'Yes.'

'And Denis?'

'Not so much.'

Samson glanced over to him and caught a worried look.

'We'll get her back, Naji. We three went through a lot together in Macedonia, and we will come through this, too.'

Naji nodded but didn't say anything.

'Are you doing okay? I mean, with the work and everything in Riga?'

'Yes, it's good.' A silence followed, then he said, 'We are happier. In Germany we had many problems. My sister's hijab was ripped off. It was hard. I was attacked in the street.'

'Yeah, I'm sorry about all that, Naji.'

'Anastasia, she helped me . . . about my father . . . she talked to me. It was very good for me.'

Samson knew something of this. She had stuck with Naji and helped him come to terms with the death of his father, the appalling fact that he would not acknowledge while fleeing from IS through Macedonia. It struck him that her behaviour mirrored Harland's care during Ulrike's darkest hour. He hadn't let her go, and nor had Anastasia forgotten the Touma family.

'Well, I'll do everything I can to get her back, but I don't want you involved,' he said. 'I promised Munira that I wouldn't place you in any danger.'

Naji again gave him that look that said he was a fool. 'I killed the man who was going to kill you in Macedonia. It is I who must protect you always, Mr Samson.' There wasn't much Samson could say to that, although it was a moot point whether Naji or Denis Hisami had delivered the *coup de grâce* to Almunjil.

'Nevertheless,' he said, 'you are the head of the family and they depend on you.'

'If I am head of family, why do you take orders from Munira?' He grinned at Samson, who sometimes felt slow-witted in Naji's presence.

'I gave my word,' said Samson, 'and that's an end to it.'

'But I didn't give my word,' said Naji, and grinned again.

They arrived at a village on the northern tip of a peninsula jutting into the Gulf of Finland. Ulrike pulled up beside a long white house with a red roof set behind a row of fishing shacks and boathouses. Beyond these, large boulders lay in a calm sea that was dimpled by the rain. The light was fading and the village seemed deserted.

But there were some lights on in the house and Samson was surprised to find Harland already there, sitting with his coat on at a table, waiting for the place to warm up.

'Any idea who was watching your house?' said Samson.

'They aren't Nyman's people, and the intelligence service doesn't believe it was Crane. Some tourists you picked up along the way, no doubt. The answer is, we don't know.'

Samson told him that the truck driver had been traced.

'So we may be able to forget the whole damn thing if they rescue her,' said Harland.

'Not sure about that – there's still the dossier to think about.'

'Oh Christ,' said Harland. 'Save me from bloody crusading liberals.' Ulrike smiled at him. 'You know the worst thing about our profession, Samson?' he said.

'Yes. Waiting.'

'Spot on. It's the bloody waiting. My man hasn't come back to me. I'm not sure we're going to get a result on Crane.'

'Let's hope we don't need one.'

Just after seven, Harland and Samson's phones began to ring at the same time. Samson answered first and moved away so he could hear. 'My name is Kelly,' said a woman's voice. 'Zillah Dee asked me to be in touch on the bank accounts. There's been a lot of activity over the past several days.'

'In Tallinn?'

'Yes, sir, maybe forty different connections today, though it is impossible to say what these were. The party could just be checking the balance.'

'Can you say from where in the city these communications originated?'

'No, though it's probable that the person was moving about and using a phone, or a tablet connected to the mobile phone network. That's all we know.'

'And on all four accounts?'

'Limited activity on three, a lot on the fourth.'

She read out the account number and said she would confirm by email. Samson hung up.

Harland's call went on for five more minutes. When he finished, Samson told him, 'He's definitely in Tallinn.'

'Indeed,' said Harland. 'My contact suggests a visit to the MS bar between 11 p.m. and 3 a.m. any evening – that's the Friends of the Forest bunch, Metsa Sõbrad. Crane is there every evening after dinner at one of the city's restaurants. He's known by his real name, Chumak. They didn't know he was here, but got wind of something happening because of the number of unpleasant characters turning up in their capital city.'

'Is Nyman on to this?'

'KaPo are aware of his interest but, if I'm reading the situation correctly, they don't know what he's doing here and they're pretty sure he doesn't either. He's way behind what you and young Naji have got. By the way, they are grateful for the dossier.'

'So what's the deal at the bar?'

'Crane holds court there, receiving foreign visitors. Now they have the dossier, KaPo conclude that all these people are coming to finalise things. The anti-money-laundering regulations are pretty tight across Europe and they'll have to have done their stuff on IDs, home addresses, company directors, etcetera. So maybe Crane needs to see them in person and check the paperwork before he makes the transfers.'

Samson told him about the intense activity on one of the four bank accounts.

'If you want to make yourself popular with KaPo,' said Harland, 'you'll give them all the details.'

Samson thought about this. 'Maybe later. The important thing is that it seems like Crane has gone a long way in adapting and changing everything in the Misak dossier, and we know what that means for Anastasia.'

The MS bar in Tallinn occupied a building on the inside of the old town wall, fifty metres away from one of the defensive towers that ringed the city. The bar did not announce itself, apart from a small illuminated cocktail menu by the door and a metal relief that showed figures emerging from a forest under which were the letters MS in an art nouveau script. Samson walked past the place at nine. The street was deserted and the bar appeared empty. He returned to the pick-up to watch. By 10.15, about thirty men had entered the bar, then a large rowdy group came along the street. He slid from the pick-up, walked across the damp cobbles and joined the back of the group. They were a mix of Estonian- and Russian-speakers, mostly in their thirties and very drunk. Samson latched on to one man, who was staggering, and took his right arm around his neck. By the time they had reached the desk where two bouncers were checking names, they were already firm friends. The drunk did the talking while Samson good-naturedly kept him upright. They were waved into a long, dark room with a bar on the far side staffed by three women with identical bobbed ice-blonde hair and waistcoats. A drinking game was in progress. The noise was deafening.

He wasn't going to risk being drawn into the game. He'd already attracted one or two glances, so he acted as affably drunk as his companion, steered him to the far end of the bar and gestured for a couple of beers. He deposited the drunk at a table and went to join a group who were not taking part in the game. If Samson had a talent, it was to reduce the weight of his presence in any given situation, whether in a bombed-out market place in Syria or a people-smugglers' dive in Greece. He moved little. His expression became neutral, with no hint of attention or threat. He was just there, a face in the crowd: a nobody.

He nursed his beer and watched. He had never seen Crane in the flesh but had a good idea of what he looked like from the few photos of him on social media, mostly at charity fund-raisers. The man was always at the edge of the group and in the process of turning or moving out of the frame. He could merge into the background as well as Samson could. However, there was one clear photograph of him, which showed a man of average height in his mid-forties with sporty good looks and receding light brown hair, brushed forward. The corners of his eyes slanted down, and the eyes themselves were unequal in strength, the left eye overwhelming the right. Macy Harp's assistant, Tina, had blocked one half of the photo with a piece of paper to show that Crane's real personality could be seen in his left eye. The right side of his face, particularly the eye, projected trustworthiness and warmth, and there was a slight lift to his mouth that suggested humour. Cover all this and a distant and ruthless killer emerged. 'One fellow you'd play golf with,' said Macy, 'the other would chuck you from the top floor.'

The drinking game disintegrated and some of the men peeled off and began to show interest in Samson, trying to draw him into their conversations. A blond man wearing a tight suit and a thin tie approached him; he had a small MS tattoo on the back of his hand. Samson explained he spoke only German and English, badly. In good German, the man asked where Samson was from and which group he represented. He replied Chemnitz and that he was a member of a group founded in support of anti-migrant riots in the city a year before. The man studied him with a sly grin and said, '*Aber du magst einen Araber oder einen Juden*' – but you look like an Arab or a Jew. Samson coolly told the man he should be careful whom he insulted. But the man wasn't put off and dragged a friend over to discuss Samson's race. This one breathed beer over him, smirked and said he resembled a fucking Roma pickpocket.

Samson briefly considered breaking his nose with a palm strike and kneeing the other one in the groin. But at that moment he saw a disturbance in the centre of the room. It was if an invisible wave had parted the crowd. His two tormentors tried to see what was going on, and Samson grinned at them, exclaiming, '*Ah, hier ist Herr Chumak!*' He pushed past them and started making for the space around Crane, but something stopped him. No one was approaching Crane: it was as though he had some kind of force field around him. Crane removed his tinted spectacles and Samson saw the face he'd got to know so well in the photographs, yet in an instant he grasped that the side of his face that had suggested qualities of reliability and candour to the trusting society of the West Coast had vanished and Crane's entire face now expressed all that once lurked only in the shadows on his left. This was unambiguously the man who could order the murder and torture of anyone that stood in his way, who would, without a second thought, organise insurrection that focused hatred on millions of migrants, Arabs and Jews and who was responsible for the kidnap of Anastasia.

The two thugs were prodding him aggressively from behind so there was nothing else for him to do but approach Crane. He grabbed his hand and, speaking in German, told him that he was indeed the saviour of Europe. Crane looked a little puzzled but smiled then turned away, to the others who were coming up to him. Samson wheeled to face the two men who were still pressing up against him and said through gritted teeth, '*Fick nich micht, Jungs*,' which he hoped meant something like 'Don't screw with me, lads!' then darted into the crowd to his right and began moving towards the heavy wooden door without turning his back on the room. The two men were still showing interest and he saw the fine brush of blond hair bobbing up to search for him in the throng that now surrounded Crane. He reached the door, which opened as more people came in, and glanced back to see his two pursuers moving towards him. He passed through the door, raised a friendly hand to the bouncers and left. Outside, he sprinted to the pick-up, got in and ducked down just before the two men exited the club and began scanning the street. They peered through the windows of a few cars on the other side of the street but seemed to lose heart. Then one spotted a man moving from the shadows of a buttress and walking away. They called out and began to chase him. He seemed unconcerned and didn't quicken his pace. Samson straightened to see what was happening. The two men reached their quarry, spun him round to confront him, but were stopped in their tracks as he held something up and thrust it beneath the chin of the suited blond man. A gun. Samson was baffled. Who else was watching the bar? He felt for the Zeiss binoculars in his backpack and trained them on the group. The man they had waylaid gestured for them to turn round and, as they did so, he struck them both with devastating accuracy on the back of the head. The blond man fell where he was standing; the shorter of the two stumbled, got up and sprawled over the cobblestones. His assailant moved to straddle him, the gun pointing at his head. He stood there for a few seconds to impress upon his victim that any resistance would result in more pain, possibly death, then calmly tucked the gun into his waistband and, without haste, continued on his way through the silent street.

It was some minutes before the pair began to recover and haul themselves to their feet. The savage blow each had received had plainly drawn blood because both held their hands to the back of their heads. Samson watched to see if they would return to the bar and was relieved when they went in the opposite direction. The last thing he needed was anything that would spook Crane, but who the hell was meting out this violence? It certainly wasn't MI6's style, and it seemed unlikely that it would be an officer employed by KaPo.

He was there for another hour and a half, during which time two more distinct groups of men arrived; he assumed they were delegations of some kind. The more he watched, the more he understood that Crane had probably completed his work and was finalising arrangements, perhaps raising a glass with groups that had come from all over the continent. As the bar began to empty, Samson slid over to the passenger seat to be completely in the shadows. At length, a white Porsche SUV pulled up and Crane exited the club. He lifted his binoculars and made a note of the number plate, black letters on a white background – 718 ALC.

The car moved off and passed Samson. He got behind the wheel again and, after a few seconds, started the engine, moved from the parking space and turned round to follow the Porsche. From his use of the tram system that morning, he knew the Porsche would have to head north and leave via a gateway in the city wall to join the peripheral road. He moved unhurriedly to the gateway and saw the Porsche waiting at the lights on the slip road below him. He stayed there until the Porsche moved off, then followed, speeding through the junction on a red light. But the Porsche was moving too fast on the deserted road and he couldn't keep up without being spotted. He lost it in the suburbs to the north of the old city. He circled the area for a while but saw nothing. He narrowed his search to a few streets of large Nordic-looking residences. Drifting past a building that stood out because of its clapboard and shutters, he saw two men struggling with the electronic door of an underground garage. Beyond them, in the garage, was a white Porsche. One part of his plan might just be in place.

CHAPTER 26

Anastasia woke up to feel the old woman prodding her with her stick. She was stiff and cold and it was hard to open her eyes. When she did open them she thought there must be something wrong with her vision because the room was swimming with slow-moving coloured lights. She blinked and blinked again then spotted Igor at the far end of the room setting down a lantern and realised the lights came from about twenty other lanterns, all rather crudely made and with the same delicate propeller mechanism driven by a candle's heat. Realising that the lanterns must be his and were perhaps even made by him, she smiled and clapped. He was delighted and so was Olga, who proffered an old metal flask and jerked her chin up to tell Anastasia to drink. She took two mouthfuls of a thick dark liqueur, possibly made from plums or apricots. It was delicious and warmed her and made her head spin. She lay back on the pile of rugs and old curtains to watch the lights, which reminded her of a childhood experience at an aquarium.

Igor came over to take a stool by Olga's feet and she stroked his hair. She wished she could talk to them and find out why they were out in the middle of the forest living such a strange life on their own. Igor looked so happy at that moment and she wondered what would become of him when Olga was gone.

The candles began to burn down and the lights stopped moving. Olga found a musty-smelling quilt, which Anastasia spread on the floor then wrapped around her to protect against draughts. The old woman disappeared to another room with Igor following. The last candle flickered and died and she was left in darkness, listening to the wind tearing through the pines at the back of the house. She slept.

She became aware of someone shouting. The stream of angry Russian continued and then there was a gunshot. She sat bolt upright, untangled her legs from the quilt and felt for the gun. It had gone. The pockets of her jacket had been emptied and nothing but a few smaller shells were left. She stuffed them back in, put the jacket on and crab-walked towards the two windows at the front of the house. It was getting light but the sun had not yet risen. She edged to the side of the window and peeped out. Her heart was thumping. The shouting was coming from the old lady, although Anastasia couldn't see her. She slipped to the second window and saw two men standing in front of a car. They were laughing, but she noted they also had their hands in the air. One she recognised from the compound. She went to the other side of the window and saw Olga, in a red patterned shawl and green baseball cap, standing squarely on the wooden terrace with the gun pointed at the men. Igor was nowhere to be seen. Her diatribe did not cease, which the men thought was a huge joke. The one Anastasia recognised looked as if he were about to corpse. The old lady took the short flight of steps down from the terrace to an area of wild dead grass and began to walk towards the men. She looked crazy but her step did not falter and the gun in her hand remained quite steady. She went a few paces then spread her feet, threw back her head and let out a cry that pierced the forest's quiet like nothing Anastasia had heard before. It was the scream of a banshee and, if she'd heard it out in the woods, she would have been terrified. It seemed to go on, circling the trees for seconds, and some of the fairy-tale dread that Anastasia momentarily felt seemed to affect the two men. But the smirk soon returned to their faces and they continued mocking the old lady.

With a throaty growl she now ordered them to do something – probably to get back into their car and return to wherever they'd come from. One shook his head and replied defiantly, at which Olga fired two shots, hitting both headlights without even bringing the gun up to aim. This accuracy was remarkable, but Anastasia was more surprised that Olga didn't have to reload. Only then did it occur to her that the protrusion under the gun might be a magazine.

The young woman in the photograph was back in action and handling the weapon with relish. The men, even though they were probably armed, now understood that she would be able to shoot them before they could use their weapons and began to back away to their car. Olga let off another shot that made the driver's wing mirror explode. They scrambled into the car, started it and, not being able to turn on the track, which was almost completely overgrown, began to reverse erratically. Olga's fun was not over yet. She fired three more times and brought the gun up for a final shot to shatter the windscreen.

When she returned, looking wild and flushed, there was no question in Anastasia's mind that the men had been there because of her. She realised she had to go, but she must first find out where the nearest civilisation was, a place where someone owned a phone. It was impossible to describe by gesture and she ended up drawing a picture of a row of houses and a man holding up a phone. It wasn't much better than the drawings done by the refugee children in the camp at Lesbos. Olga, who had by now lost the exhilaration of battle, looked bored and shouted for Igor, who appeared from the kitchen and came over to tug at Anastasia's jacket. She was being told to go. She made to take the gun but Olga raised it and said firmly, '*Nyet!*' There wasn't anything Anastasia could do and, besides, Olga made a good point by gesturing in the direction of the track that the men might return and she'd need protection. Anastasia took the rest of the shells from her jacket and held them out but then withdrew her hand and made an eating motion – she would exchange bullets for food to take with her. The old lady nodded and said something to Igor, who returned to the kitchen, and very soon she was given a plastic bag containing bread, water in an old water bottle and a pot holding some of the previous evening's soup, and ushered from the door.

She made one last attempt to find the way to a village by showing her drawing to Igor, but he just smiled and shook his head uncomprehendingly. He led her a little way into the woods, to the path they'd used the day before, then took his leave regretfully. Her only choice now was to return to the road.

In the seaside cottage, before his hosts were up, Samson made Naji coffee and found some bread in Harland's freezer that he warmed in the oven. Naji then took up a position by the window; he said the wifi was best there. He looked up when Samson handed him the toast and jam. 'It's beautiful here.'

'Very,' said Samson, looking out on the pristine morning and the glassy sea. 'I'd like to own one of those little boats down there – the blue one.' Naji nodded. 'What are you doing?'

'Looking at groups he gives money. Is possible to divert money, maybe?'

'Not even you can hack a bank, Naji.'

Naji grinned. 'Possible other way. I work on this today.'

'You okay?'

Naji nodded, now fully absorbed in what he was doing. A few minutes later he looked up. 'Mr Hisami has a lot of emails overnight. If I open, he will know he is being watched. But this one he has read.' He brought the laptop over to Samson and set it down. It was from another numeric email address. There was no message, just a black-and-white photograph of a woman in a dark shirt speaking into a microphone on the desk in front of her. In the foreground some men were seated, their heads turned to the woman, their backs to the camera. A digital clock on the wall above the woman's head showed the time as 02.24. Along the bottom of what was evidently a video still, the time was shown as 2.28.53 and the date as 03.23.95. It was impossible to identify the woman or the men, but Samson knew that Hisami would understand what the scene meant, and he was almost certain that the woman in the photograph was Denis's dead sister, Aysel. There was something so familiar about the way she wore her hair – she never lost the parting on the left side.

Samson ignored one of his phones vibrating on the table for a few seconds more while he looked at the photograph, then answered. A familiar voice rasped at the other end – Vuk Divjak, the man he'd texted earlier without expecting a response. Vuk was a Serb who had helped in the search for Naji in Macedonia and was connected to a range of Balkan low-life. 'I come now with disco pussies – Lupcho and Simeon. We driving into the night-time without the stopping and we are now in goddam, bastard country Litvanija.'

'Lithuania.'

'Yes, that is that which I am saying – Litvanija.'

'So you're five or six hours away from Tallinn?'

'Fewer hours in Simeon's car.' Samson was aware of the hum of a powerful engine in the background.

'I'll send the map reference for a rendezvous from another phone. Keep me up to date with your progress. My guess is that you'll be here by about two.'

'I speaking to you when we enter Estonija in few hours,' said Vuk, and hung up with a grunt. Samson wasn't encouraged by the news that he was bringing Lupcho and Simeon, who were both involved in the early stages of the search for Naji. They were basically hired killers. Their shady appearance was grounds enough for ejection by any alert border police, though in the last twenty hours they'd crossed Hungary, Austria, the Czech Republic and Poland without trouble. He sent the rendezvous to Vuk and returned to look at the photograph on Naji's screen.

Another call came in on one of his other phones. It was Zillah Dee. Samson put up a hand to stop Naji making noise at the coffee machine.

'The truck driver's information checked out. The place was exactly as he described – a hundred and seventy kilometres north of the city of Pskov in dense forest, with very little human habitation anywhere nearby. We got there at 3 a.m. local. It was burned down. The main building was levelled by fire and the place was deserted. The ruins were still smouldering.'

'Were they destroying evidence?'

'No, another building was left untouched, a guard hut with eight bunks. That was vacated – no sign of possessions but a lot of food and fresh milk.'

'What happened?'

'No telling. It's wild country. No towns, no locals, no witnesses. We did find the grave they dug for her, which complies with your description of what you saw on your phone. It was full of water and they left a new excavator right there in the middle of the forest. But there's no sign of her. Nothing. My people have searched the area thoroughly in the last few hours. I don't know what to say. It's a big goddamn mystery. There's another thing. I just got off the phone with Jonathan – my top guy out there. They heard gunfire an hour ago, maybe six shots in the space of a minute or two. Might be a hunter. They got a fix and they're investigating that right now.'

'How are you going to proceed?'

'I'll keep two of my people there – that's on the house. But the whole situation with Denis isn't good. His plane's been grounded. He's way overleveraged, got a lot of debt that no one knew about – not even Jim Tulliver – and it looks like he's going to lose a real big slice of his empire. In addition to those problems, he's got another court appearance today and it isn't looking good. They're going after him with new evidence.'

Samson was silent for a few moments. 'Look, I'll get you the money if we need to keep your people there. I'll find a way.'

'As I say, this is on me. And I know how much it means to you. But after a couple of days, I have to pull out. It's not just that we can't afford to pay for this ourselves. I have other work for them, so it's a double loss to the company.'

'I'll go the distance for a few days.'

'Thanks.'

'One other thing,' he said. 'Can you have someone look at the bank-account activity?'

'That costs a lot of money, but I'll see what I can do.' Then she rang off.

Without looking up, Naji said, 'I heard what she said.'

Samson didn't respond. He went through a sliding door to the patio, lit up and looked out across the bay at the small boats that hadn't been brought ashore and chocked up for the winter. There was no guarantee Anastasia was alive. She might have escaped, but she couldn't survive in that forest for very long, even if Crane's people hadn't yet hunted her down. The silence from the kidnappers could mean anything. She was already dead; they'd lost her and were in no position to make demands; or they didn't have to continue with the pretence that she would be returned, because they knew Crane had completed his business in Tallinn. But the video still of Aysel, whatever that meant for Hisami, didn't fit with the last solution because they clearly still needed to threaten Hisami. There would be no purpose to this if they had achieved all they wanted in Tallinn.

As he stubbed his cigarette out, Samson warned himself that he might have to accept he'd never see her again, even though there was another part of him that was still convinced she would survive.

He phoned the car-hire company to ask about the white Porsche like Crane's he'd seen there the previous day, and it turned out to be available. He booked it and paid with a card. 'Have we got a printer here?' he said when he went back inside. Naji looked blank. 'Maybe in the studio,' said Samson. They found one, connected it to Naji's laptop through the wifi and checked it worked.

Samson showed him a photograph he'd taken on his phone outside the bar. 'Can you see if you can reproduce this?'

'Maybe with best paper,' he said.

Samson caught the expression on his face. He sat down, reached over and patted the top of his hand. 'I am going to do everything I can, Naji. She's as important to me as she is to you – believe me.'

'Best person I meet in my life,' he said, looking away to the sea. 'In Lesbos she helped me and in Macedonia she helped me. In Germany she helps all my family. I am not here without her.'

Samson smiled, got up and squeezed his shoulder.

'It's an odd way of saying it, but I agree – I am not here without her either.'

Harland came in looking less than happy but he brightened when Naji offered to make him coffee.

'There's something I need,' said Samson.

'I imagine there is.'

'You didn't go into Leipzig to lift Abu Jemal all those years ago without this particular item.'

'We were fighting the Cold War. It was an officially sanctioned operation by Western intelligence services, for Christ's sake.'

'We're fighting a war now. It's a war against the subversion of Western democracies, which is more dangerous than anything the communists pulled off.'

Harland groaned. 'Oh God! I don't need a bloody lecture from you, Samson. You're doing this for your friend.'

'Still, I need at least three guns, maybe four,' he said quietly.

'I have to go to town. Meet me at the back of the house in Tallinn in two or three hours. And bloody well phone before you arrive.'

Samson left instructions about the second Porsche that was about to arrive from the rental company with a tip for the driver, then departed for Tallinn.

It was less than an hour before he spotted a hardware and camping store in the northern outskirts. There he bought rope, duct tape, glue, black paint spray, two short lengths of heavy steel piping, a shovel, a hunting knife, torches and a sleeping bag, not knowing whether he'd need any or all of it. He charged it all on his card and went to collect money wired by Tina to the Danske Bank. He called Harland at ten thirty, at ten forty-five and got an answer only at eleven, whereupon he went to meet him at the rear of his house. Harland appeared in the street in an anorak with a spiked mountain walking stick, having left by the front entrance of his house. He was in a better mood than he had seemed to be on the phone and Samson wondered if the old spy was actually enjoying his return to the business. He gave Samson a crooked smile. 'I've had that bloody tick Nyman there for the last three quarters of an hour. Couldn't get rid of him.'

'What did he want? Were you followed?'

'Of course I bloody wasn't. Nyman thinks that Crane still has much to do and he doesn't want him disturbed. He's told me to tell you to lay off. He was appealing to my patriotism and invoked the British Foreign Secretary. He forgets that, these days, no one gives a solitary shit what the Foreign Secretary or what Her Britannic Majesty's government think about anything. He wanted to know where you were. Said I hadn't seen you and you'd gone east, possibly crossed over to Russia.

He's struggling to keep up and he's got no help from the locals.' Harland seemed pleased about this. 'Where's your car?' Samson pointed downhill and they moved off, Harland using his stick to spear the gaps between the cobbles.

'I've got help coming from the south,' said Samson. 'Three Balkan ruffians. I've used them before and they'll only be here a very short while. I don't imagine they've attempted to smuggle weapons across the six or seven different borders, so I'll have to provide them with some.'

They drove to the southern suburbs and parked outside a house with a white picket fence, an impressive cord of wood under a shelter and an old camper van in the yard. Johannes, the Dutchman living in the house with a number of dogs and a young Sri Lankan wife, was a licensed dealer of hunting weapons with a sideline in fly rods, which was legal, and handguns and automatic pistols, which wasn't. Samson bought two Glock Compacts and a Sig Sauer, plus ammunition, for €2,250. After a beer and having listened to a number of fishing stories, he and Harland left with the guns in a supermarket bag.

'Odd character,' said Samson as they got into the pick-up.

'You can say that again. His main business is renting out fishing lodges with women. It's a great business. Very little fishing is done, except by the women, one or two of whom have become excellent with a trout rod.'

On the way back to the city centre, he told Samson to make a couple of sudden detours. 'What's up?' asked Samson, searching his wing mirror.

Harland took his time to answer. 'You should know that

someone is interested in what you're up to, and I'm not talking about Nyman. My pal at KaPo says you've been followed while you've been here. A third party, they think. They don't know who.' That made sense, Samson thought, with the men at the hotel and the armed individual who gave the two amateur thugs a beating outside the bar. 'Could be the Russians,' Harland said slowly. 'Might be the Americans, though I doubt it, and I suppose you can't rule out your friend Crane.'

Samson spent the next few hours recceing the streets around the bar and timing the ride from Crane's villa to the restaurant he habitually ate at and then to the bar. He received a call from Zillah Dee as he finished the final run and stopped to speak to her.

'She got out and she's in the woods somewhere. My two guys traced the gunfire I told you about to a house in the back of beyond where she stayed the night. They aren't certain what happened because the old woman was crazy and threatened them with a hunting rifle. But they talked her down. Seems she fired at two men looking for Anastasia, which gave her a chance to escape. So we are actively looking in that area.'

'You'll tell me immediately if they find her.'

'Of course.'

'But I'm going to assume you won't find her and I will proceed with my operation.'

'I'm with Denis. He doesn't want you to do anything until we have definite news.'

'Zillah, you've got a couple of people searching for her in terrain they don't know. You said there was a guardhouse with several bunks. That means they'll have a lot of men looking for her. And Anastasia's going to be in pretty bad shape.'

'We'll find her.'

'I'm glad to hear that, but what if you don't? What's the back-up plan? There isn't one, right? I hear Denis has another play – what is it?'

'You can ask him.'

'I will, because I know he's praying they keep their word and let her go. Does that sound a reasonable expectation, after what they've done? Does it? No, it fucking doesn't, Zillah. It sounds like the same shit that got her into this mess.'

'Can you stop yelling at me for one second? Denis wants to talk to you. It looks like he may go back to jail for a few days. And that's a problem in more ways than one. Samson, I know this means a lot to you but, for Christ's sake, keep your cool.'

He took no notice. 'Did you have any luck with the bank accounts?'

'Yes, I'll send you the data.'

As she walked the phone to Hisami, Samson heard New York's soundtrack, the *whoop-whoop* of a patrol car, people leaning on their horns, the crash of a dumpster being lowered on to the street.

Hisami came on. 'Hello, Paul.'

'Denis.'

'We need you to sit on your hands. We think we're going to find her. And if we don't and they do, I have an alternative plan. Do nothing to endanger my wife's life. That's what I am telling you.'

'Denis, I didn't put her where she is. You did. If she doesn't come out of that forest, I'll continue with my operation and it'll all be on me.'

'You have no idea what you're dealing with.'

'Crane is stalling for time. They don't give a damn about honouring an agreement with you because there isn't one. They'll keep her alive just so long as they need to. If Zillah's men get to her first, there's nothing to worry about, but if Crane's people find her out in the woods, you can forget your back-up plan.' He remembered the video still in Hisami's email inbox. 'They've got something else, haven't they? And you're afraid they'll use it?'

Hisami didn't answer.

'It's your sister,' said Samson. 'They're threatening to reveal something about her past?'

At length, he said, 'Yes, but it's really not the point. Anastasia is what I care about.'

'And you think we'd be raising the stakes by taking Crane.'

'Yes, and they will respond,' said Hisami.

'It's a paradox, Denis. If you don't raise the stakes, you'll be gambling with your wife's life. It's as simple as that. These people have killed multiple times. Crane is our insurance policy. If we've got him, they can't kill her if they find her.'

'This is not something you can gamble on.'

'But that's the game you joined, Denis, a game of the highest stakes. So let's hope Zillah gets to her first.' There was nothing more to say and he hung up.

CHAPTER 27

She walked parallel to the road, never straying into the open but never losing sight of it. A lumber truck roared past but she was too slow to break cover and flag it down. Eventually, she decided it was pointless walking in either direction, because there was no hope of reaching a town: far better to sit it out at a spot where she could dash from the trees on to the road when she heard a vehicle coming. She built a screen from thick boughs of pine, which she cut using the serrated meat knife she had stolen from under Igor's nose. If the old lady was keeping her gun, she was going to have their knife. She lay quite comfortably for a while, listening for a vehicle, but soon began to drift off. No! She couldn't sleep. She must do everything she could to stay awake. This included fifteen minutes of yoga exercises she remembered from a course designed to relieve stress among aid workers in the camp on Lesbos, watching some ants carrying food to a mound of pine needles and thinking of her life with Denis and with Samson. 'I am with you, I am with you, dear Anastasia.' Samson had said it with such intensity that she knew he still loved her. Looking up at the goddamn trees – she was sick of trees – she supposed these words meant something to her but, really, what the hell good were they out here? Samson wasn't with her. Nobody was. Even from herself she seemed absent.

She hadn't been moving for an hour or so and she became cold. She worried how she would survive the night and decided to build a fire. This she approached methodically, digging out a hole and surrounding it with stones so the flames could not be seen from the road. She excavated two channels so the fire would have enough air. Then she piled pine needles and twigs in a wigwam and surrounded these with pointed pine cones that oozed resin. These made a lot of smoke and she realised that more flames meant less smoke. She flicked the cones away, broke some dead branches and laid them against the fire. Once the fire was properly alight and there were glowing embers at its base, she set more stones around the flames and these began to heat up satisfactorily, just as Naji had described to her. Now there was virtually no smoke.

She ate some of the congealed soup from the pot; she would heat the rest when it was dark. She followed the soup with some bread and washed them down with the well water from an old plastic bottle they'd given her. She felt herself nodding off and forced herself to sit in a less comfortable position, but this didn't work and she finally succumbed to a deep, days-long exhaustion and slept.

What woke her a little later was the smoke. Raindrops

falling through the branches above her had extinguished the flames and sent up a cloud of smoke around her so she could barely see. She coughed and fanned the air furiously.

'The woman who likes fire,' said a voice to her right. 'The woman who was released by fire is now trapped by fire. An irony, no?'

She shot up and reached for the knife, but a boot stamped on her hand. There were four men around her. Kirill was crouching by the fire, warming his hands. He smiled at her surprise. 'I should kill you now because you left me to die. You wanted Kirill to burn.'

She didn't speak.

'You locked door. You wanted me to burn. But Yuri and Timur here, they saved me. I owe my life to them, Anastasia.'

'Tell them what you were doing in that room.'

He smirked and poked the fire with his stick. 'They knew. It does not matter to them. They don't give a shit for you. They will be the ones that bury you.'

He rose and gestured to the four men, and they picked her up and bore her down the short slope to the road, leaving the knife and the remnants of her meal beside the smouldering fire, and pushed her into one of two vehicles that had slewed to a halt when the smoke had been spotted.

When Samson arrived at Harland's cottage by the sea, Vuk was lounging by a black BMW coupé with low-profile tyres, flared exhaust pipes and bonnet vents. He remembered Simeon and Lupcho appearing in a similar car on the Greece–Macedonia border when he had first encountered Vuk, but this was much larger and could doubtless outrun any police vehicle in the six or seven states they had flashed through to reach Estonia in just under eighteen hours.

Vuk wore the same large khaki jacket with bulging pockets as he had three years before, a black cap, a fleece of great age and a red jersey with a zigzag motif. He held a cigarette in one hand and a bottle in the other and was staring into the distance. When he saw Samson, he flung his arms around him and gave him a bristly, smoke-laden kiss on both cheeks. 'Magnificent cunt! How you are doing?'

Samson smiled weakly. 'Where are the others?'

'Looking at ocean. Disco pussies never see sea in Macedonia.' He roared with laughter and proffered the bottle. Samson shook his head and took him by the elbow to the beach, where Simeon and Lupcho were skimming stones. He spent five minutes explaining the situation; anger and outrage flickered in Vuk's face. They settled on a price for the operation – €5,000 in cash each for Lupcho and Simeon and €8,000 for Vuk.

'Anastasia best woman in the world. We get her for Samson to make babies.'

'I told you, she's married to Denis.'

Vuk shrugged and spat out a piece of tobacco. 'Samson love this woman and that not fucking detail.'

'Follow me and we'll go through the plan at the house. By the way, Naji is there.'

'Little Syrian bastard?'

'He's a grown man now and you can't go round calling people "little Syrian bastard", Vuk.'

'Smart little bastard,' said Vuk, seeking compromise. He gave a piercing wolf whistle. Lupcho appeared from the beach in a long leather coat with headphones horseshoed around his neck and lifted a hand. Simeon, sporting a new tattoo beneath his Adam's apple, shaven hair, ripped jeans and a red hoodie, followed and aimed a finger with a cocked thumb in Samson's direction. Just as he registered that both of them were probably high, his phone vibrated in his hand and he answered a call from Zillah.

'It isn't good news,' she said. 'They found the place where she'd been – the fire was still warm. There was some food and a knife, which sounds like the one the old lady said Anastasia stole from her kitchen.'

'Maybe she abandoned camp?'

'There are two sets of tyre tracks on the side of the road. Those vehicles braked in a hurry. They're ninety per cent sure she's been recaptured.'

'You've told Denis?'

'He's in court right now – not a good moment.'

'What about his plan B?'

'I have no idea what it is.'

'No?'

'No.'

'Has there been activity on the bank accounts?'

'I sent an email,' she said. 'This comes from within an *agency* so it's accurate.'

'What's going on?'

'It's all in the email.' She was losing patience with him.

'Okay, thanks. Keep me in touch with what's happening on the other side of the border.'

'We'll look for the rest of today, but after that I have to pull them out.'

He hung up, went into the house and called for Naji, who was nowhere to be seen. Nor was Harland, whose Volvo estate was parked beside the rented white Porsche. He shouted again and returned to Vuk, who was giving his two assistants a dressing-down. Samson took in the scene. 'They're out of their heads,' he said. 'I'm sorry, but I can't use them.'

'They take too much drugs to drive in night.'

'I'm not having them anywhere near this operation. They're out. I'll pay their expenses and a thousand each for driving you here.'

'Make it fifteen hundred,' said Vuk.

'Okay, but they should leave now,' he said, counting out the money and adding €500 as a generous fuel allowance. 'Now you wait here,' he told Vuk. 'I'm going to see our host.'

He found Naji inside and sent him the email from Zillah. 'Have a look at the email I just sent you – there's a lot of information which may be useful. Something might strike you.' Naji slipped the laptop under his arm and tugged a ring pull on a tin of Coke.

Harland was out at the back, standing over a chopping block with a hand axe, looking out to a mass of birds that had appeared over the bay. 'Starlings,' he said. 'They're migrating to Western Europe.'

'They think she's been recaptured,' said Samson.

Harland turned to look at him. 'I'm sorry to hear that, but it's not surprising.' He flipped the axe into the chopping block and took off his gloves. 'So that means you're going ahead.' He moved towards Samson and gripped his shoulders. 'How on earth do you expect this to work? Think about it. You've spent precisely five minutes in that bar. You've got no one on the inside. You know nothing about Crane's schedule. No idea if he has bodyguards, what kind of back-up they can summon. And if, by some undeserved miracle, you do manage to grab Crane, you don't know how to contact the people holding Anastasia and you haven't even thought of where you're going to put the bastard until you do. Unless you've got something seriously good up your sleeve, I would suggest that you abandon the whole thing.'

'I have to go ahead. This is her only chance.' He glanced at his phone, which had just vibrated with a message from Zillah Dee. 'Looks like he's going down,' he said. 'And a story is breaking about Anastasia.' He read the text out to Harland.

'Publicity is not what we need,' said Harland. 'Look. I'll help, but when I say I won't do something, please don't argue. We'll use Johannes's fishing cabin. There's a key, but we'll have to break in because he can't be implicated. I'll make good the repairs afterwards and add something for the inconvenience.' He held out his hand. 'A thousand will do the trick.'

Samson handed him the money.

'You can never breathe a word of this to Ulrike. She's gone back to the city and thinks I'm just keeping an eye on you here. Okay?'

'Yes, of course. Thanks, I'm grateful.'

'You can thank me when we've got her out,' said Harland. He glanced at the wind chime, which had suddenly become agitated on a low bough. 'Bad weather's coming in. That could be to our advantage.'

Samson explained about the loss of Simeon and Lupcho.

'Don't worry about that,' said Harland. 'I've had an idea, and I'm going talk to some people now.'

'Look at sunset, Anastasia,' Kirill said, and wrenched her chin towards the orange slash in the clouds to the west. 'Look, because this is your last.'

Kirill had changed. He no longer pretended to be anything but a sadistic killer and he was as rough with her as the men who threw her into the car had been. She had changed, too. She accepted that she was going to die and just prayed that he wouldn't rape her before ending her life.

She looked dully at the sunset. She had never liked clichéd sunsets and, besides, this one wasn't especially beautiful – just a sign that the day was ending. She wouldn't see another. So what? She didn't matter. She had had her time.

'You like sunset?'

'It's hard to appreciate when you are in pain,' she said. They were in the open and all around were concrete buildings without windows. It looked like an abandoned military facility, a place that could withstand bombs. Her hands were bound behind her back and plastic ties cut into her ankles. She had lost the circulation in her left foot and her shoulder was in spasm, and when the pain overwhelmed her, as it did in the car, she gave up all pretence of bravery and just cried.

Kirill may have let the mask slip, but he was no less ridiculous strutting around, barking orders and trying to provoke her with needless insults.

'Why have you done this to me? What did I do to you?' she asked.

'You tried to kill me.'

'I had to get away. You were drunk. You wanted sex.'

That earned a vicious kick on her thigh, which made her topple over and bang her head. One of the men picked her up and placed her against a wall.

'If I'm going to die, I want to know why,' she pleaded through fresh tears. 'Why don't you kill me now?'

He hooked his thumbs into the armholes of a gilet under his jacket and stomped around some more. 'We wait. I will receive word, then you will be no more.'

'But why?'

'Because your husband causes trouble to my organisation and we must rectify certain matters.'

'What organisation? What matters?'

'Political matters. Matters of great importance that you would not understand.'

'Try me,' she said.

'Husband infiltrated network in United States and used a spy to gather information and disrupt operation.'

'He's a businessman, for Christ sake! He's not interested in politics.'

'You do not know your husband well.'

'Just have the good manners to explain why you're going to kill me.'

He smiled and sat down beside her with his back to the wall. She smelled some kind of hair product. Clearly, not everything had burned in the fire, as he claimed. Though it was cold, she noticed a fine sheen of sweat across his forehead and a trickle ran from his temple. His face shone when he lit a cheroot. He turned to her, smoke dribbling from the corners of his mouth. 'You hear noise, Anastasia? That's my men digging new hole for you! First hole we could not use because people are looking for you. They found dacha and hole. They were very smart to find dacha. Truck driver told them, I think.' His face creased with a smile and he laughed – not a real laugh, of course, because she doubted Kirill was capable of genuine emotion. But he wheezed and slapped his thighs and made as though the joke had suddenly just struck him. 'If you didn't make fire at dacha, they would have found you. Maybe they rescue you.'

'Well, I avoided having sex with you. That makes it worth it.'

'We can still have sex.'

She knew he was playing with her. 'You couldn't get it up last time.' A muscle moved in his cheek but he didn't strike her. 'You can't even rise to that,' she added.

'You are not serious person, Anastasia.'

'Maybe, but I know the difference between serious and pompous.'

He shook his head, as if to say that she did not even have the power to provoke him now, and puffed furiously on his cheroot. 'I now explain everything to you. When Soviet Union fell, people in West believed Russia would become a liberal democracy. But Russia was still Russia and West was still West. We hated you just the same, but we were weak because economy was shit and we lost Soviet Empire. Yet we kept our hatred of West and we knew one day we would triumph over complacent liberal democracies. You know how we do that?'

She looked away and muttered, 'I may die of boredom before you have the chance to kill me.'

'You are brave to make such joke, Anastasia. But it is good joke.' He raised a finger. 'I finish now without interruption. We destabilise West with two things. First, we use social media, invented by Americans, and we kill their truth and Americans don't know what is true and what is false, what is up and what is down. Second, we use fault in human nature, and you know what this is? Racism. Hatred for migrants, for blacks, Arabs, Jews, Roma, for Pakistanis, for any fucking person who is not same as you. And we do just little to inflame hatred with Internet. Political elite sees hatred and fear everywhere in their own societies and illusion of Western superiority dies, morale is fatally undermined. When enemy does not believe in himself, he loses his power.'

'And you're saying Russia did all this as a planned strategy?'

'No. West helped us by taking bad decisions. Bringing million migrants into Europe was like dream for us. But there was one other thing. Instead of protecting liberal democratic system, Westerners became obsessed with themselves. Identity politics. Gender politics. Personal fulfilment – all that shit. Me fucking Too. No one is serious about anything if it's not their own pain or their personal journey. This is the decadence communists predicted.'

'That's all such a cliché. Anyway, if the West is already doomed, what's the point of what you're doing?'

He pulled out a flask. 'The sun is down. I drink now.'

'Are you going to give me some? I'm cold.' The forlorn point of the remark was to remind Kirill that he was dealing with a human being who felt the same things as he did. 'I'm really cold.'

He ignored her. 'You know what pressure point is, where nerve lies close to surface in human body? We use far-right action all over Europe's pressure points. We give them money and they execute certain tasks for us.'

'Violent fascists.'

He smiled. 'Insurgents.'

'You're financing terrorism. They're no different from ISIS.'

'Both serve our purpose to weaken West. In my lifetime, we will see the Russian Empire strong again.' He swept his hand across the massive concrete towers and bunkers which glowed faintly in the last of the daylight. 'In my lifetime, but not in yours, Anastasia.'

He put the flask to her lips and tipped brandy into her

mouth. She choked but managed to keep some in her mouth so she could swallow it slowly and take what pleasure she could from it.

'I regret that you must die. You have good spirit, Anastasia.'

'And I regret that my last conversation on this earth is going to be with an impotent, fascist hypocrite. Don't pretend you're not enjoying this, because you're loving it.'

He chuckled to himself and looked at his phone. 'We have not got long now,' he said, as though they were waiting for a supermarket to open.

Naji saw a pattern of transactions in the four bank accounts, although he had no figures. The email address of the man who generated the data had survived being forwarded through three parties, including Samson. Naji replied to the email, suggesting they moved to an encrypted messaging service. For Naji, it was standard to imply he was much older than his actual age and, in this case, that he was an experienced investigator. He soon won this individual's confidence. His name was Jamie, and he explained he was no longer at the office, having finished an early shift at some kind of financial monitoring agency, which Naji took to be a branch of the US government. Since he was twelve, Naji had been used to corresponding with young men and women in science and tech forums – it helped his English. Sometimes he realised their expertise could only have been gained in government service. Also, they liked to show off. Jamie was no exception. He had an expert understanding of SWIFT, the highly protected network that allowed financial institutions to exchange information about transactions. Most laypersons wouldn't know that the architecture of the SWIFT network was divided between European and transatlantic transactions. Jamie volunteered that the transactions of all data centres in the Netherlands and the underground facility in Switzerland weren't mirrored in the US data centre. The transactions they watched all took place late at night, between 11 p.m. and 1 a.m., Estonia time, every working day, and in the last ten days, millions of dollars had flowed between the four principal accounts and hundreds of accounts across the world. Jamie couldn't swear to it, but most seemed to be new because they were associated with freshly minted shell companies. He confirmed that these entities were mainly registered in London and Cyprus.

Naji kept an ear on what Samson, Harland and Vuk were planning. He noticed that Harland did not seem to like Vuk at all, but the exchange with Jamie went quickly. Soon he realised that Jamie was telling him a lot and he began to experience the thrill he'd had when hacking into IS systems as a boy. All the transactions came from the same location and were apparently made on the same device. And the pattern was the same every night. First, the bank account of the new shell company would transfer funds – usually between $250,000 and $350,000 – to one of Crane's four principal bank accounts. Then another would transfer a much larger sum, in the millions of dollars, to the shell company's bank account. Jamie wrote: 'Maybe the kickback is being paid up front. That's why your Joe is using multiple accounts. He is skimming!!!!'

Naji realised that the faster Jamie responded, the more he gave away.

'What device is he using?' he typed.

'Looks like a new iPad Mini – the compact version of iPad.'

'Would that remember passwords?'

'If he allowed it, but most people don't when using it for banking. Palm prints, iris or face recognition are most often used.'

'Have you got a list of new shell companies and accounts?'

'It'll take a while. Hey, are you kosher? Which agency did you say you're with?'

'I didn't. British SIS.'

'Respect! Okay, so this is going to take a little while. We were doing this for a former colleague and have not bundled up the data. But it would be my pleasure.'

'Thanks,' Naji replied, punching the air.

'Do you mind telling me what you're working on?'

Naji considered the risk. The guy seemed cool, so he gambled. 'Money is being supplied to far-right violent groups in Europe,' he typed.

'You got it, brother. Give me an hour.'

They signed off.

Naji focused on what was happening with Samson and Harland. Harland had just hung up on a call, which had lasted almost as long as Naji's interaction with Jamie. He was smiling and his eyes were watering.

'So?' said Samson.

'Nyman's people are going to work for us tonight,' said Harland. He paused and laughed. 'But they don't know that.'

'How do you mean?' said Samson.

'My friend at KaPo wants to get them off his back, so he's offered Nyman the old dossier in exchange for surveillance help. Nyman accepted with alacrity. His people will cover Crane's home, the restaurant where he dines and the bar. When they see Crane's white Porsche move, they'll phone him and he'll let me know immediately.'

Samson smiled. 'And they have no idea?'

'No. But there's a price. KaPo want everything we have.'

'There's some good stuff in the email,' said Samson, looking over to Naji.

Naji nodded but said nothing. He was aware of Samson's gaze lingering on him with suspicion.

'Send it to me and I'll put it their way,' said Harland.

'But you didn't tell them what we're planning?' said Samson, turning back to Harland with one final penetrating glance at Naji.

'Of course not! They suspect he's preparing to leave, anyway. There's been activity at the house to indicate that. If he goes missing, I believe they won't be overly concerned. They're angry that he's been running his operation here because of the problems they've had in the past with Russian money-laundering.' He sat down and dabbed his eyes with a tissue. 'There's something else. They inserted surveillance devices into Crane's house. A rushed job: two or three needle microphones, which they got in overnight. Seems KaPo independently located the house yesterday. They need help on something and they've sent an email with a transcript which' – he looked down at his phone – 'should be here any moment. Yes, here it is. I'll send it to you.'

The transcript was of two individuals talking in English, one of whom was Crane, identified as Chumak. There were occasional interruptions from a third individual who spoke in Russian, and these were redacted. KaPo wanted explanations and an ID for Chumak's main interlocutor.

CHUMAK: I asked you not to come but you came anyway. That was unwise.

AMERICAN MALE: I had to – what else could I do?

CHUMAK: You came on your own plane, landed at the airport in Tallinn. You think the authorities won't register this? They pay attention to private jets.

AMERICAN MALE: I couldn't email or send a message. I needed to see you personally. You have to understand that he's in possession of more information that Daniel gave him. Much more.

CHUMAK: What makes you think that?

AMERICAN MALE: Things he said to me after the meeting a couple of days ago.

CHUMAK: It doesn't matter – the operation will be completed by the end of the day. There are just a few things to tie up. (Pause.) Now you are here you should celebrate with us. You'll meet some of the people we are working with and then . . .

AMERICAN MALE: Then what?

CHUMAK: We go our separate ways, of course.

AMERICAN MALE: What about the hostage? You're going to let her go, right? That was the deal. We agreed that you would do this. Just a few days while he was in jail and you got things straight, you said.

CHUMAK: Her husband is still a danger to us.

AMERICAN MALE: He's in jail. His business is fucked. He can't hurt you. You got everything you wanted, Adam. And now you're going to disappear . . . (inaudible)

CHUMAK: Why are you so concerned?

AMERICAN MALE: She's a good woman. She has nothing to do with this.

CHUMAK: You like her?

AMERICAN MALE: Sure, I like her.

CHUMAK: This is the reason you're here – to plead for her life.

AMERICAN MALE: What's the point of another death? Let her go, Adam. That's what you agreed to.

CHUMAK: I'll see what I can do, but you have to understand this is a very complex matter now. (Pause.) I'm surprised by your sudden interest in her welfare. Has he got to you? Has he told you to come here?

AMERICAN MALE: No, of course not. I'm here of my own volition. I came because I wanted to make sure you knew what was going on in the States.

CHUMAK: Thank you. But you shouldn't have come here.

AMERICAN MALE: I understand, but you owe me, Adam. I've helped you to do what you wanted. Now I'm asking you for something in return. Let her go and . . .

CHUMAK: We'll talk about it later.

Samson skimmed it again, then looked up. 'The American male is a man named Gil Leppo. Anastasia's husband identified him as Crane's man and sent him to plead for her life. This is his back-up plan – definitely not working. Crane is going to have her killed, that's plain.'

'What do I tell KaPo?' asked Harland.

'Say it means nothing to us.'

'They're not stupid.'

'Find a way of stalling them.'

A few minutes later, they gathered round a laptop, opened Google Earth and went through the plan. The snatch was ludicrously simple and would involve just Samson and Vuk. It could only work if the timing was perfect and they had more luck than they deserved. Harland said he would run the communications from near the Soviet-era Olympic yachting centre at the port, where they would dump the Porsche and transfer Crane to the pick-up.

'Where I will be?' asked Naji.

'You're staying here,' said Harland.

Naji picked up his laptop and walked to their end of the room then faced them. 'I have new information on all bank accounts. I must be with you to look at his iPad.'

'How do you know he has an iPad?' asked Samson.

'My source. In one hour he will tell me everything about Crane's operation. I must be with you.'

'I promised your sister,' said Samson. 'What source?'

Naji remembered the moment in the Macedonian border town when he had implored a group of migrants to take him with them on the road north. He placed his laptop on the table. 'You can tell me nothing about fear, nothing about danger,' he said quietly. 'I have seen more in my life than any of you – men killed for smoking cigarette, women beaten for wrong ringtone. I saw barrel bombs fall from sky and destroy a school. I see what security forces did to my father. I was nearly drowned. I survived. Perverts and terrorists tried to murder me. I lived. And when Almunjil was going to kill you, Samson, I saved your life.' He stopped. 'Even then I was not a boy.'

Harland cleared his throat and said, 'He can wait with me in my car at the port. He'll be fine. Then we will lead you to Johannes's place.'

'I'm against it,' said Samson, 'but I agree, on the understanding that you do not place yourself in danger.' Naji nodded. 'So I have a few things to say,' he continued. 'I and Vuk will be armed, but these weapons will not be used.' He looked at Vuk. 'I repeat, they will not be fired. I don't want a bloody shoot-out. This has to be quick and clean. Talking of which, Vuk, you need to shave and get yourself a jacket and put on a bloody tie and clean shirt for the first time in your life so you can pass as Crane's driver.' Vuk looked aggrieved; Harland said he could help. 'As soon as they know we've got Crane they'll contact us. They won't call Hisami because they know he's back in jail, so the call must come on this phone.' He held up one of the several phones lying on charge. 'Then we'll make arrangements to swap Crane for Anastasia. This will take place somewhere along the Russian border.'

Harland's face betrayed his many doubts, but in response to a less than friendly look from Samson, he said, 'It is what it is. We'd better get on with it.'

The storm rolled in at 9.15 p.m. with strong winds that forced two ferries trying to dock in the port of Tallinn to retreat to the open sea. The downpour halted traffic and sent the few people still on the streets running for shelter. Torrents coursed in the roads; the tram system was paralysed because of fallen trees that had taken overhead lines with them; and a section of the city was plunged into darkness when the Ranna substation, undergoing an upgrade, was inundated.

By the time the storm hit, several messages had passed from Harland to Samson relaying the movements of Crane's white Porsche, which had departed the Russian-style residence at 8.35 p.m. and at 8.57 p.m. arrived at the restaurant Gogol, where it dropped off Crane and male and female companions. One of Nyman's people had booked a table, so was able to relay to KaPo the descriptions of Crane's party for dinner. Harland's friend at KaPo passed much of this information to him, but only essential details were relayed by an encrypted message service to Samson and Vuk, who waited in the white Porsche identical to Crane's in a back street three minutes' drive from Bar MS. The sending of these messages had been taken over by Naji, who had put all the phones in a group on an app and was quicker at typing than Harland, who, with eyebrows raised and glasses at the end of his nose, tended to stab at the phone's screen with his index finger.

Naji and Harland watched the storm in silence while waiting for news from the restaurant. When the wind died Harland got out and dashed to the pick-up to make sure it would still start.

To Naji, Harland seemed something like the model Englishman conjured up by his father, who had almost certainly had inaccurate ideas about such things from his reading of the English classics. He was polite, listened intently and asked many interesting questions about Syria and Naji's escape through the mountains.

Their conversation came to an end when messages began to pour into Harland's phone. Naji relayed them to Samson via the app.

'Party about to leave restaurant.'

'Two cars outside restaurant.'

'Crane and companions get into white Porsche.'

'Four men get into Black Mercedes SUV, German plates.'

'Crane's car now on way to Bar MS.'

'Second car waiting at Gogol. Passenger has forgotten something.'

Harland looked at his watch. 'Now we'll see what happens. If that bloody Porsche stays outside the bar for the duration of Crane's time there, we're . . .'

'Screwed,' said Naji.

'Just so.'

Fifteen minutes passed before the white Porsche appeared at the bar. It took much longer than Harland had expected and he assumed there had been some kind of hold-up because of the storm.

A message from Samson asked, 'Has Porsche left the bar with Crane's woman?'

'No word,' replied Harland.

Another few minutes elapsed. Harland tapped the steering wheel. Naji consulted the message app he was using to talk to Jamie. As yet, there was nothing from him.

Another message came in from KaPo. 'Both cars outside bar.'

Harland waited, his eyes locked on to the screen.

A new message read, 'Three people are out of white Porsche. Four men out of black Mercedes. They are saying goodbye to the woman.'

Harland held his breath.

'Woman returned to white Porsche with driver. Both vehicles leaving now.'

Harland nodded and patted the steering wheel a couple of times.

Naji sent the message on to Samson and got the reply, 'Thanx.'

'We have a bit of a wait now, maybe two hours. I want to hear about your music. Samson tells me you have talent,' said Harland.

Naji looked mystified.

'I'm interested,' said Harland.

But before Naji could respond Harland received a call from Rasmus, his source in KaPo, who spoke for thirty seconds, during which Harland said nothing apart from a grunted goodbye. He dictated a message for Samson. 'One unidentified male – not ours – watching bar.'

The white Porsche rented by and containing Samson and Vuk had moved closer to the street with the bar in it and was now parked just two minutes away, in the shadow of a church. On reading the latest message from Harland and having replied, Samson got out and moved along the side of the church so he could drop down into the street about a hundred metres from the Metsa Sõbrad bar. It was still raining and there was much debris in the street, but evidently the main body of the storm had passed on its journey eastwards. Samson waited in the lee of the church, quite well sheltered from the rain, watching for any movement. There were more cars parked opposite the bar than on the previous evening, but nothing stirred until ten thirty, when three vehicles arrived in quick succession, followed by two Mercedes people-carriers, and dropped off men at the entrance of the bar. Several more cars drew up. Samson estimated that about twenty-five men had gone into the bar. He lifted his binoculars and watched them as they hurried to the door. They were a less rowdy bunch than before, and most wore suits. There was certainly a sense of occasion and formality.

Three quarters of an hour passed during which he became aware of an uneven bump in an otherwise regular shadow on the other side of the street, cast by one of two streetlights between him and the bar. There was no movement, of course, yet the shadow could conceivably have been the back of a man's head. A glance through the binoculars wasn't conclusive, but Samson remembered this was more or less the spot from which an armed man had emerged to beat up the two drunken thugs.

A dog appeared, trotting from the direction of the bar, stopped, lifted its leg against a tyre and seemed to do a double-take by the driver's door, as though it had picked up a scent or a movement in the car. It soon lost interest and continued on its way. Samson trained the binoculars on the car and saw mist on the inside of the windscreen – the breath of perhaps two occupants rather than one condensed on the rain-chilled glass. The car was facing away from the bar, which meant that the driver could observe the entrance in his wing mirror. It had to be Nyman's team.

Muffled by the rain, the clocks of Tallinn began to chime eleven. Samson folded the binoculars and put them inside his jacket then made his way back to the Porsche. When he opened the door, Vuk thrust a mobile in his face. 'You fucking idiot who does not look at fucking phone.'

Samson read that Crane's white Porsche had left the residence four minutes before.

'Go! You know what to do,' he said, scrambling into the back and reaching for the gun on the floor. 'When we get into the street, slow down until you see people at the door. Don't arrive there too early. Then pull up beyond the door so they don't see you.'

'Numbers fucked with water. I take away.'

Samson processed this. The registration plates Naji had mocked up were unusable because of the storm. 'They won't notice – they'll still think it's Crane's car.'

They entered the street. 'Slow down!' hissed Samson.

'I know this. Don't tell me fucking story again.' The car coasted across the cobbles and stopped. 'They come now,' said Vuk, moving off.

'Okay . . . Just ease it beyond the doorway.'

As the car moved towards the bar's entrance, Samson looked between the seats and saw the doorman recognise the car as Crane's and move into the street with an umbrella.

They glided past the entrance. Crane was standing in the doorway. He looked up crossly from a leather folder he held in both hands then back into the doorway. Vuk stopped.

'Damn! He's waiting for someone,' said Samson under his breath. 'Fuck, fuck, fuck!' And he knew who that might be. The doorman moved to the car. Crane glanced behind him then followed and arrived at the passenger door just as it was opened. At that moment, Samson saw Gil Leppo, in a long black raincoat, dive towards the car. Crane was halfway in. Leppo opened the back door, saw Samson with the gun and let out a kind of yelp, which made Crane hesitate. At this point, there was a soft explosion behind Samson as the back windshield shattered. More bullets clipped the roof of the Porsche and thudded into the back door. The doorman, who was midway between the car and the entrance to the bar, was hit and fell sideways. Samson saw Crane rooted to the spot, looking astonished. The only thought in his mind was that, if Crane were killed, Anastasia would certainly die. He flung open the back door on the driver's side and rolled on to the street, loosing off three shots blindly into the shadows, where he had seen the immobile shape of a man. But the man was no longer hidden. He was in the centre of the road holding a silenced automatic weapon that produced a series of muzzle flashes not much brighter than a Christmas-tree light.

Samson rolled again and fired and at the same time became dimly aware of Nyman, who had appeared out of nowhere and was dithering between two parked cars to Samson's right. The gunfire continued and he heard a yell from the direction of the car. Now Nyman was looking at him aghast, trying to compute what his former colleague was doing in Crane's car and why he was now carrying out the duties of a seasoned bodyguard. Samson also took in Sonia Fell, crouching by the wall of the building on the other side of the line of parked cars. Next thing he knew, Crane's white Porsche had materialised in the street and Crane's driver, comprehending at least part of what was happening, had opened fire on the gunman.

Samson rolled once more, scrambled up and went round to the front of the Porsche to seize Crane, who had taken shelter behind the back door, which had been wedged open by Gil Leppo, who had been wounded in the stomach but was still moving. Crane searched Samson's face, not knowing whether he was friend or foe, and rightly decided that the man he vaguely recognised from twenty-four hours before was trying to save his life. He let himself be hauled over the wounded

Leppo and bundled into the back of the car. As Samson gave him a final shove, he noticed the leather iPad case lying on the cobblestones by the doorman. He picked it up and leapt in with Crane, dropping the case on to the front passenger seat without another glance at Leppo, who looked as though he was about to die.

'Go!' he shouted. Vuk hit the accelerator, but the wheels of the Porsche spun wildly on the damp cobbles and the car began to drift sideways into the body of the doorman. Then Vuk took his foot off the gas, tried again and the Porsche lurched forward and over the man's lifeless body. They passed rapidly through the old gateway and down the slip road, crossed the ring road, crashing three sets of lights, and entered the avenue of modern commercial buildings that led to the ferry terminal. It was only when Vuk swung left towards the dark, concrete mass of the Linnahall – the V. I. Lenin Place of Culture and Sport – that it dawned on Crane that these men were far from his saviours. He scrabbled with the locked door. Samson placed the gun to his chest and said, 'Shush! We just saved your life, pal.'

They made for wasteland near the Linnahall, much of it under water, and skidded to a halt between Harland's Volvo and the pick-up. Harland was already out of his car. Samson pulled Crane out of the Porsche and held the gun at his chest while Harland bound his hands behind his back with tape. Holding the Glock Compact with one hand, Samson opened the bullet-pocked door, reached in, picked up the iPad folder and held it aloft, which prompted Naji to dash from the Volvo.

They both knew that, if Crane hadn't switched off the device before the gunman opened fire, it could still be accessed without a passcode. Naji opened it and gave Samson a thumbs-up. He'd now be able to change the auto-lock setting to 'Never'.

They left the Porsche on the wasteland, and with Samson now at the wheel of the pick-up, they followed Harland's car at a sedate pace on to the road that circled the old town to the south. Vuk was in the back with a gun pressed to Crane's temple, a length of pipe in his right hand.

Several police cars passed them going in the opposite direction with flashing lights and sirens, but very soon they left the lights of the city for the motorway. Apart from one or two trucks toiling eastwards, there was very little traffic. Samson glanced in the rear-view mirror. 'Who's trying to kill you, Crane?'

'I'm not Crane,' he said.

'Right, you're Aleksis Chumak. You kept the same initials for the all-American Adam Crane. And by the way, if you're not the man known as Adam Crane, what the hell were you doing with Gil Leppo – the guy who was pleading with you for Anastasia's life earlier today?'

There was no answer.

'A lot of people must want you dead,' continued Samson. 'Who was that in the street?'

'I assumed you had arranged the attack to get me into the car?'

'I don't go round killing innocent people like that doorman. That gunman wanted you dead. He was after you. Who was it? Maybe it was your Russian masters, who knew you were skimming their money and decided to do away with you now that your operation is over – huh?'

Crane looked sourly out of the window and said nothing. Samson examined him in the glow of the light from the footwell. Gone was the swagger of the previous evening, and now Samson noticed he looked heavier than in recent photographs and his hair was much shorter. He had the pallor and edginess of the all-night gamblers his father used to mix with. It looked like he'd been drinking a lot.

He prodded Crane again. 'If we don't get what we want tonight, we're going to kill you.'

'Don't be ridiculous,' he said. The accent was corporate America with no hint of the Ukraine.

'You kidnapped Hisami's wife in Italy to stop him publishing what he knew about your operation, giving you time to clean up your books and cover your tracks. But he wants her back. If that doesn't happen in the next twelve hours, Vuk here is going to put a bullet in the back of your head. Before that he'll make sure you suffer, just like you made Daniel Misak suffer in London.'

Crane shrugged and glared at Samson's reflection in the mirror. 'I've no idea what you're talking about.'

Samson engaged his eyes. 'Well, whatever happens with you tonight, you should know that tomorrow we will publish everything we have – the bank-account numbers, the phoney shell companies in London who you're giving money to and what they are going to do with it.'

'What do you want?' he said.

Samson had his attention. 'I told you. We want Anastasia back, and you're going to make the call to save your life. Otherwise, I'm going to let Vuk here get to work on you. Vuk comes from Serbia and is currently being hunted for war crimes. He likes to keep his hand in.' Vuk snarled, perhaps a little too theatrically to have effect.

The Volvo was slowing and had its indicator on. Samson cursed, followed Harland into the motorway service area and saw Naji leap from the Volvo and disappear into the shop. 'What the fuck are they doing?' murmured Samson, and went to park on the far side of the forecourt. A few seconds later, the phone reserved for Macy Harp started vibrating.

Macy's first words were, 'You know what to do with the phone after this call?'

'Yep,' said Samson, getting out of the vehicle and into the rain.

'Our former employers are hopping mad. They're saying you wrecked their operation.'

'Bollocks! They didn't have an operation, and we saved Crane's life from an attack by an unidentified gunman. The only thing they had was the intelligence they'd got from us, and that's out of date.'

'Take Crane back right now, or there's a risk they'll charge you with weapons offences, endangering life, armed kidnap, and so forth.'

'Sorry – no.'

'They'll find a way of prosecuting you in the UK as well.'

'On what grounds? Making SIS look stupid?'

'Nyman was hit.'

'Badly?'

'No, he'll pull through, but Fell's saying you shot him.'

'Wrong. There was a hitman with a silenced automatic spraying the street with bullets, at least forty rounds. By the way, was the gunman hit?'

'No, there's no sign of him now, which means they can pin all this on you, Samson. Take Crane back to Tallinn and they might just let you off.'

'Not going to happen. You know Anastasia's life depends on it.'

'Well, I've delivered their message to you,' Macy said regretfully. 'Now it's on you. They mean business.'

'Fuck them.' Samson hung up and saw Harland moving rapidly towards him, holding his hand up against the rain. 'What's going on?'

'Naji has to keep that iPad powered up. It's nearly out of battery. He's making a lead out of something he's bought in the shop and the cigarette lighter from my car. God knows! Says it won't take long.' The rain was dripping down his face.

They moved towards the pick-up. Samson checked on Crane and Vuk in the back. 'Just got word from Macy that all hell's breaking loose,' he said to Harland. 'They want Crane. If you need to bail out, now's the time.'

Harland shook his head. 'I suppose I'm bloody well in now. Did you find a phone on Crane?'

'No, Vuk checked.'

'So I guess we may need that iPad.'

'That reminds me,' said Samson. He handed Harland the phone he'd just used and pointed to a flatbed van that had driven into the service area for fuel. 'Can you toss this into the back as you pass?' Harland nodded. If the phone Macy had called on was being monitored by GCHQ, they'd end up tracking an old van carrying two pneumatic drills and dozens of traffic cones.

They turned to see Naji burst from the shop triumphantly holding up a piece of wire.

'Right, we'd better get going,' said Harland. 'It's a long drive.'

Samson climbed into the pick-up and noted Crane's deadly, indifferent expression. The gangster in Crane smelled the weakness of his position. There wasn't a plan and Crane damn well knew it. They were about to head into the vast darkness of eastern Estonia and they didn't have a clue how to reach the people holding Anastasia, or what they would do if they failed to make contact. They didn't even know if Anastasia was alive. But Crane knew. Samson switched on the interior light and turned round. 'Have you given the order to kill her? Is that what's going on here? Is she dead?' To ask this straightforward question seemed wholly unreal to him, but the words were out and he needed an answer.

Crane met his eyes and it appeared for one moment as though he were about to smile. 'I have no idea what you are talking about.'

'Is she dead?' said Samson.

Without warning, Vuk brought the pipe across Crane's right knee then hammered the kneecap two or three times more, causing Crane to scream. Samson ordered Vuk to stop.

'If you've got a way of contacting your friends, you'd better tell me about it now, because this guy really wants to kill you.'

Crane said, 'I don't know what you're . . .'

'How would you give the order?'

Vuk made as though he was about to start beating Crane about the face.

'There's a number on my phone. I don't have it. I lost it in the street.'

Samson waited a beat. 'Did you contact them before you left the bar?' he asked. 'A text, an email, a call – how was it done?'

Crane rocked with pain and shook his head. Harland's car shot past them. Samson started the pick-up and followed. 'You'd better fucking well pray she's not dead, pal.'

He phoned Harland as he drove. Naji picked up. 'Look on the iPad for any messages or texts sent in the last few hours.'

CHAPTER 28

She was sure the storm had kept her alive for a few hours more. They had been talking, almost normally, and she had asked Kirill about his life, especially his childhood, which, in her experience, was a sure way of inducing someone to talk. Kirill was reluctant at first but then she asked about his mother and he began to loosen up, however not before observing, with his usual casual brutality, that he knew she was only trying to make herself seem more human to him and therefore less easy to kill.

'No,' she fired back, 'I am trying to make *you* more human, Kirill.'

They had lived on the outskirts of St Petersburg. Kirill was the eldest of three. His father was mostly absent then vanished for good when he was thirteen. His mother was pretty but, unlike many of the women in the huge apartment blocks around them, she didn't seek to supplement the family's income by selling herself, although she had many offers. She had worked in a government office and was of an austere nature that became cold and punitive as the years went by. Kirill's youth was spent outside the apartment with young thugs on the street. Reading between the lines, Anastasia guessed he hadn't been a particularly impressive boy to look at and that he had learned to survive with brains as well as cunning, qualities that after a few brushes with the law eventually recommended him to a nameless secret agency. The pleasure of Kirill's boyhood was in outsmarting his peers, seeing the strong boys bend unwittingly to his will, manipulating everyone around him. It became a game at which he excelled. And of course, Kirill told her with some pride, he had always known that he was destined for great things, which his contemporaries didn't have the capacity to imagine, let alone achieve.

They talked on, and he gave her brandy and she hinted that sex with him was not out of the question, but he curled his lip and said she looked like a diseased hooker and, besides, she smelled like a pig.

He kept checking his phone while stamping about on the concrete. Around midnight, he received the text he had been expecting and issued orders to two men in parkas who had been hanging around in the dark smoking. He became distant and removed himself from her. Then the rain came and the wind tore through the massive structures around them. Kirill ordered the men to break the padlocks on a sliding steel door to the building nearest them. They cut the ties that bound her leg, marched her inside and at the entrance made a fire out of old tables and chairs, for it was clear the storm was going to last some time. Trying to rekindle the conversation, she asked if he might get into trouble breaking into a state facility, and Kirill replied, 'I am the state.'

The rain eased off a couple of hours later. The fire was put out and the embers kicked from the doorway to fizzle in the water still gushing from the buildings. No one said anything. They dragged her from the shelter and she began to weep. They went about three hundred metres into the trees, where arc lights had been set up around a pit. She struggled to escape but the men held her fast and placed her at the side of a deep grave that had been dug with shovels which now lay on a mound of earth ready to fill the hole. She was shaking and weeping and pleading with them. Kirill took out a gun and held it to her head.

'Ah!' he said. 'Now I have better idea.' And he brought out his phone and gave it to one of the men with some instructions. 'We show Samson how you die,' he said.

The only things Anastasia was now aware of was her utter disbelief that this was happening and an awful, crushing sorrow. She was barely conscious of Kirill fussing about the angle of the camera shot and insisting that only his hand must be in the frame. He kept going over to the man to look at the screen and check for himself that he would be able to see Samson's face when he made the call on FaceTime. Finally, he was satisfied and ordered the man to dial the number.

Harland's Volvo and Samson's pick-up had pulled up on a grassy track that led to Johannes's cabin. The ground was sodden and they decided not to push their luck by parking right by the cabin, because Harland said there was every chance they would get stuck. Beyond the cabin, they heard the roar of a river in full spate; water was everywhere. Vuk threaded his way between large pools with a torch to break into the cabin while Samson got Crane out and stood him against the pick-up with a gun to his chest.

Samson's phone sounded with the FaceTime ringtone, but he didn't immediately register it. He pulled the phone awkwardly out of his pocket with his left hand, pressed to answer and was bringing it up to his face when he saw the pathetic image of Anastasia with a gun at the back of her head.

A voice said, 'Now you must say goodbye, Anastasia.' For a second, Samson didn't react. 'Say goodbye to lover!' demanded the voice.

'Wait!' shouted Samson. He dragged Crane into the headlights, forced him to the ground and held the gun to his temple in front of the phone. Harland didn't see what was happening but Naji understood straight away and rushed over to take the phone from Samson.

Samson yanked Crane's head up. 'You know who this is. If you harm her, I will execute this man.' He thrust the gun into Crane's eye and said, 'Talk!'

Crane looked into the camera and said, 'He will kill me.' Then he mumbled something in Russian.

'Speak English,' Samson ordered.

He placed himself in the frame with Crane and looked at the phone. 'Get her out of the damn mud! Pick her up! Help her up!'

Nothing happened for a few seconds then two pairs of hands seized Anastasia under her arms and lifted her from her kneeling position in the mud. 'Now, keep the phone trained on her so I know she's all right. And show yourself or I will kill him. Now!'

A man wearing a hat and a cravat appeared next to Anastasia and raised a gun to her head.

Samson allowed himself no emotion. He had to control the situation. 'If you do everything I say, Chumak, or Crane, or whatever you call this bastard, may live. Now, give her something to cover herself – she's cold.' The face vanished. And someone put a jacket around her shoulders. 'Show her my face and let her hear what I say. One false move and I will kill this man.'

Anastasia stared blankly at the phone. She looked as though she hadn't eaten for days. Her face was drained of life, her lower lip trembled and her eyes did not focus, but she began to free herself from the dread and, in a few seconds, recognition dawned. 'Is that you?' she asked.

'Yes, it's me. I want you to keep it together and we'll get through this.'

'I'm here,' she said. What that meant to him was that the woman who had fought so hard to survive was still there.

'I want to speak to the man with you,' Samson said.

'What do you want?' asked Anastasia's executioner.

'You will give her food and warm clothing. That is to happen now. Any divergence from my instructions and I will kill Crane. You are in Russia. We are in Estonia. We will exchange Crane for Anastasia at the border.'

Crane said something rapidly in Russian. Samson cuffed him on the side of the face. 'What did he say?' he shouted to Harland, a fluent Russian-speaker.

'The iPad has to be included in the swap,' replied Harland.

'We want device also. No device, no deal,' added the Russian in the hat, who had now passed out of the frame.

'Okay,' said Samson. 'Where on the border?'

'Narva,' suggested Harland. 'The bridge at Narva.'

'You hear that? The bridge at Narva in two hours.'

'Two bridges at Narva – we will go to bridge for trains.'

'Right, the rail bridge at Narva,' said Samson. Harland nodded.

'Now you're going to give me a number and I will call you to arrange the exchange. If you don't text me, he dies.'

'Then beautiful girlfriend dies also.'

'Text me the number,' said Samson.

'Three hours. You bring my friend and his device. Then we talk,' said the Russian.

'Two and a half hours – a hundred and fifty minutes. If I don't have Anastasia alive with me on the Estonian side of the border by that time, I will execute this man and throw his body into the river.' He hung up and, a few seconds later, a text message arrived with a number.

It was on.

Samson moved quickly to put Crane in the pick-up and was joined by Vuk, who had returned to fetch a tyre iron to break into the shed. As they took Crane to the open rear door, Samson said in his ear, 'That was dumb, to mention the iPad. Now we know how important it is to you. If things go wrong and I have to kill you, I get to walk away with valuable material. British intelligence will be grateful.'

Crane looked up as they bundled him into the back seat. 'You'll never win. The world is . . .'

'Shut the fuck up,' said Samson, slamming the door shut before he could finish. He went round to stand by Harland, who was looking out into the night. A pair of headlights was moving slowly along the road they'd taken from the motorway and which passed the end of the track. They turned off the lights of the pick-up and the Volvo and watched. The vehicle paused at the junction with the track then continued along the road until the lights vanished to the south. 'Could be someone wondering about Johannes's place, but I'm not confident of that,' said Harland. 'We need to recce the bridge at Narva as soon as we can. They may call for help on this side of the border, which will be inconvenient, to say the least. This isn't going to be easy.'

Samson called out to Naji, who was standing in the same spot, engrossed in his phone. He stirred and came over, holding the phone up to show Samson that the CNN news site was leading with a story headlined, JAILED BILLIONAIRE'S WIFE KIDNAPPED IN ITALY. The piece was short and had little information but carried a quotation from the State Department which confirmed that State officials were coordinating efforts with the Italian authorities to find Mrs Hisami.

Then Naji handed Samson his own phone. 'Look, the kidnapper!'

While holding the phone up to Samson and Crane during the FaceTime exchange, he had had the presence of mind to take video grabs and had captured two images of the Russian with Anastasia in the frame as well as a series of close-ups of the man on his own.

Samson laid a hand across his shoulder. 'That's great, Naji! We can probably identify the bastard. He's almost certainly on a database somewhere.'

He emailed an image of the Russian to Zillah Dee. 'Can you ID this Russian hood?'

Robbed of the pleasure of killing her in front of Samson, Kirill replaced sadism with a display of high dudgeon and strode off up the incline towards the buildings to make several phone calls in Russian. She assumed he was consulting his masters about what to do with her but, judging by his gestures, he was also defending himself. That call to Samson would have to be explained to his superiors. She was cold and terrified, yet alert enough to recognise that the iPad was probably more important to Kirill and his friends than any single life, even that of the man whom Samson had taken hostage. This might just save her.

She stared down into the hole and, for the first time, she noticed that the pungent chemical smell she'd noticed clinging to the buildings was much sharper here. It occurred to her that the whole facility had been abandoned because of some sort of contamination.

She moved away, aiming a defiant look at the three men

who, just minutes before, had been content to watch her murdered then fill her grave. The sudden reprieve seemed to embarrass them. They had written her off as good as dead but now she had acquired a little agency and they avoided meeting her eyes. She took a few more steps before one of them lazily waved a gun at her and she stopped. But when they weren't paying attention a few seconds later she shuffled a few more steps. The further away she got from that stinking ditch, the better chance she had of surviving.

She knew her life depended on the outcome of Kirill's calls. They seemed to take for ever, but at length he returned and made a scene about her not being ready for execution. She squared up to him. 'How dare you treat me like this! How dare you!' He grabbed her by her arm, but then the man who had waved the gun at her and also, she thought, had whispered to her in the truck that the journey would not take much longer, protested. From his tone, it was obvious he was telling him to let her be and wait for instructions. A ray of decency had shown itself – so rare in the men who, in the history of Eastern Europe, had executed hundreds of thousands of innocent people at the edge of hurriedly dug trenches like this. Tiny though the gesture was, it stayed Kirill's hand and she remained rooted to the spot.

Eventually, a text pinged on Kirill's phone and he walked off up the incline towards the buildings and the vehicles. She was saved! The men seemed relieved. One even took her arm to help her on the slippery ground, and when they arrived at the cars to find Kirill with a cheroot in his hand and his flask being shaken empty into his mouth, they quietly supported her next display of defiance. As she was manhandled towards the rear of one of the SUVs, she told Kirill that she would not be bundled into the boot. She demanded a seat in the back of the car.

He shook his head.

'If you think about it for one moment, escape is the last thing on my mind. I need you like you need me, you fucking moron.' She spat the words out.

The men around her understood quite enough English to find this highly amusing and, without asking Kirill's permission, one of them steered her to the rear door and helped her into the seat, his eyes never leaving Kirill's indignant face. If Kirill hadn't lost all their respect when he was found locked in her room as fire ripped through the hunting lodge, he had with that business of trying to film her death. Besides being cruel and unnecessary, it was also a security risk. She read it in their faces and she knew they loathed him almost as much as she did.

CHAPTER 29

Harland looked out on to the bridge that carried the Tallinn to St Petersburg rail line through the Estonian city of Narva then on to the Russian city of Ivangorod on the other side of the river. He had been here before, though not at this exact bridge, which, like most examples of Soviet post-war reconstruction, was no beauty. He recalled a similar bridge in Berlin, where agents had escaped with false IDs and spy swaps between the West and the Soviet bloc were conducted at the same deathly hour and in the same perishing conditions as these – a vigil by a bridge between one universe and another, where sometimes you waited through the night for men and women who didn't make it and were never heard of again.

Thirty years on, he was back at a similar bridge, chilled to the bone with his eyes watering and nose running, smoking one of Samson's cigarettes as though he were still a young man. He wasn't. He felt old and tired and faintly absurd, and he wondered how he came to be standing there at this hour.

He would see it through, of course, because Samson was right and his love for this woman was right. In a world of bad actors and liars, that counted for a lot.

The storm they had pursued eastwards had lost its fury when it met with a bank of cold air over Russia. At the demarcation between East and West, the rain was turning to snow, which haloed the few lights in this deserted part of Narva and smeared the lens of the binoculars he had borrowed from Samson, who had gone off to recce the bridge. He searched for him now through the murk.

Harland had to hand it to Samson. He moved with impressive stealth and, even though a CCTV camera was trained down the line of the track into the mouth of the bridge, he was sure Samson hadn't been spotted. A small guardhouse stood on the other side of the track, not fifty metres away from where he was standing. No doubt it was full of eager young men protecting the easternmost border of Europe. But there was no sign of alarm, nothing stirred.

He turned to see Naji in his car, his face illuminated by one of the devices. The boy was a wonder. He had downloaded pictures of the bridge, which he informed them was a classic truss design that relied on Newton's Law of Motion and had been cheap to build because of the efficient use of materials. The images allowed Samson to think about the distances involved and what to do in the event of a train passing over the bridge. Two had crossed over while they had been there.

The pick-up containing Crane and Vuk Divjak was about two hundred metres away, parked on a grassy bank under some trees and beside the rickety site fence that protected the railway. The position of the vehicle meant that Samson would approach the bridge with Crane from an angle, not directly along the track. Harland looked around. The city of Narva was still. Apart from the trucks crawling along the official crossing downstream, there was little sign of life. There was certainly no traffic on Raudsilla, the road named after the iron bridge that had spanned the river until the war brought ferocious battles between the Soviet army and the SS division around the Narva bridgehead in the winter of 1944.

As he raised the binoculars again, he was aware of a scraping noise to his left. Samson had squeezed between two sections of a temporary site fence that had become permanent and within a few seconds was beside him.

'See anything?' asked Harland.

'No, but we now know who we're dealing with. He held up his phone and quietly read out the email from Zillah Dee.

> My contact in the Agency would be very interested to know how you came across this man. He is Nikita Bukov, forty-seven, a talented mid-ranking officer in FSR – the successor to the First Chief Directorate of the KGB. An expert in psychological warfare, Bukov has been a key mover in operations throughout the Balkans and Eastern Europe aimed at destabilising political institutions, amplifying local disputes and maximising sentiment against migrants and migration. A fluent English- and German-speaker, he served in

both the London and Berlin embassies. A posting in Athens was terminated in 2012 after Bukov hospitalised a local prostitute when drunk. British Intelligence planned to use his issues with women as an angle, but he was sent back to Moscow before they could get their hooks into him.

Samson stopped.

Harland looked at the screenshots of Bukov that Samson was now in the process of sending him for safekeeping. 'He isn't the usual thug. Probably doesn't know how to handle this, and that'll make him more dangerous. But he's a killer, remember that.' He sniffed and dabbed his eyes with a tissue.

Without either of them realising, Naji had left the Volvo and scrambled up the incline to where they stood. He held the iPad. 'I can go into the bank account where his money is.'

'How?'

'Passcode and print of hand. I have passcode – my friend can . . .'

'The iPad is part of the deal,' Samson cut in. 'I have to take it with me.'

Naji shrugged. 'Okay. Just saying.'

Samson's phone vibrated. 'Yes!' he said.

'Ten minutes on bridge,' came the voice. 'Alone with Mr Crane.'

'Agreed. But if you fuck with me, I will kill your man.'

Bukov laughed. 'You are real tough guy, Samson.'

Samson hung up. 'We're on. Naji, go back to the car and stay there until one of us comes. Got that?' Naji handed the iPad to Samson and retreated. Samson stuffed the device down the back of his trousers and pulled the black woollen beanie over his ears.

They took Crane out of the pick-up. Samson prised the fence apart, pushed him through and followed. Harland returned to his position under the tree and Vuk walked along the road to pass under the concrete bridge that carried the rail track to Narva station. It would be a few minutes before he slipped through a gap in the fence they'd made earlier, entered the guardhouse with his gun and told the guards to turn off the CCTV monitors for the few minutes it would take to swap Crane for Anastasia. Once he had things under control, he would send a text to Samson and Harland, which Samson had taken the precaution of writing, due to Vuk's incompetence on a keypad.

Samson prodded Crane across the open area towards a low concrete projection that was part of the bridge's structure. He glanced at the guardhouse but didn't expect to see much movement in the slight glow coming from the observation windows. Eight minutes passed and there was still no text from Vuk. Crane's mouth was taped, but he was complaining about the pain in his knee by dipping his head in the direction of his right leg. Samson told him to sit in the slushy grass. Crane declined. Another minute passed. Then he got a call from Bukov. 'I am on bridge. Where are you?'

'Nearly there,' said Samson calmly. 'It's all going to be fine. I have Mr Crane and his iPad with me.'

He called Harland. 'What's happened with Vuk?' he hissed.

'On my way now,' said Harland. 'I'll let you know.'

Harland clambered up the embankment on the other side of the rail line, cursing to himself, negotiated the fence as quietly as his bad back allowed and covered the short distance to the door of the guardhouse, where he listened for a few seconds before sensing a rush of air behind him. It was followed by a sharp blow on the side of his head. He slid unconscious down the cold metal door.

Samson rang Harland several times and got no answer. Something must be wrong. His mind raced. Had the Russians brought in people on the Estonian side? They would certainly have had enough time to field their agents in Estonia.

Bukov called again. 'You have thirty seconds to show Mr Crane.'

He was breathless and edgy. Samson stalled. 'I'm alone with him now. We're just making sure that there's no one else with you.'

'I am alone with Anastasia. This is true.'

Samson thought he could hear Bukov moving on the rocky ballast by the tracks and possibly the tread of another, much lighter person, but he couldn't be sure.

He called Vuk and Harland once more but got no response. Then he phoned Naji and asked him if he had seen anything. 'Mr Harland has gone to the hut and I have not seen him since then.'

'Jesus! Okay, you stay there. Whatever happens, don't leave the car.'

He prodded Crane on to the rail track and pushed him towards the towering, square proscenium of the rail bridge. He moved slowly, stopping to listen for sounds coming from the other end. Crane made noises of protest behind the masking tape. Samson told him to shut up. The last thing he was going to do was take the tape from his mouth and let him blurt out that Samson had no back-up. They went a little further and the sounds of people walking carried through the swirls of sleet. He knew from Naji that the bridge was a hundred and fifty metres long and the Russian border sliced through it about ninety metres from the Estonian bank. He estimated they had gone thirty. He'd have to make damn sure not to go too far and stray into Russian territory.

Now he called the number, just to see where Bukov was. He knew the Russian would have the sound off but had guessed correctly that the phone would be in his hand and saw a brief glow in the dark as he whipped it up to his face.

Samson said, 'I see where you are. Walk twenty metres and I will do the same. That should put us at the border. Then we will make the exchange.'

Bukov swore and hung up.

Samson jabbed the gun into Crane's back and said, 'Understand that, if you try anything, I will certainly kill you.' Crane jerked his head down the line. Samson saw what he was looking at. Three powerful lights of a locomotive had rounded the gentle bend out of Ivangorod, on the Russian side, and would be upon them in no time. He didn't bother with the phone. 'There's a train!' he yelled. 'Wait until it's passed.'

Silence.

'A train's coming!'

A couple of beats later a man's voice responded. 'Yes!' he shouted back.

A minute passed and the massive diesel locomotive thundered on to the bridge, making the seventy-year-old structure groan and shudder. The lights from the engine briefly illuminated a man and woman on the other side of the track, about forty metres away, then they vanished behind a procession of silver gas-tanker carriages. Samson felt Crane tense up and knew in an instant that he planned to dive in front of the engine to the other side of the tracks, leaving Samson with nothing to exchange for Anastasia but the iPad. He seized Crane by the collar of his jacket, but Crane was powerful and easily wrenched himself free. He might have made it across the line if Vuk hadn't set about his knee with such savagery, yet that was debatable. Before he even reached the first rail, the man's head was knocked sideways by some unseen force, as though an invisible heavyweight boxer had landed a punch at his temple. Samson caught sight of a face suddenly emptied of expression before Crane fell back on to him, utterly dead, as the locomotive stormed past them.

Samson knew what he had seen – a bullet had smashed into the side of Crane's head at the moment he was going to dive in front of the train – but he couldn't process it; couldn't work out where it had been fired from or who the shooter was. He staggered backwards, aware of the warm blood coming from the side of Crane's head, and dragged the body away from the track and propped it against the safety fence. One thought was in his mind. The moment Bukov discovered Crane was dead he'd kill Anastasia. He moved away a few paces then stopped and took out his phone, switched on the sound and placed the phone head-high on a ledge on one of the bridge's vertical supports. Then he ran eastwards, against the endless flow of tanker carriages that *clank-clank*ed past him. He went two thirds of the way across the bridge, into Russian territory, waited for the last carriage to pass and dived over to the other side, where he crouched in the shadow of the bridge supports, ears straining into the night.

On this side, the sound of the river was louder but, once the train had cleared the bridge, he heard movement on the stone ballast about twenty metres away. He glanced behind him to see if there were any others on the bridge. He thought he saw a man with a headlamp some distance away on the Russian bank and maybe some shadows of two or three more; he wasn't sure. He looked ahead and saw the glimmer of a mobile phone. Bukov was calling him.

Within a second or two, the silence of the bridge was broken by the sound of his phone's ringtone from the ledge where he had placed it – the first bars of Piero Toso's violin solo from Vivaldi's concerto in B-flat major, the music they'd heard together in the deserted church in Venice, which, despite Anastasia's withering disapproval, he'd put on his phone that day.

The distraction worked. The shape of a man silhouetted against the nightglow over Narva moved towards the phone. Having decided that he couldn't risk using the gun for fear of hitting Anastasia, Samson rushed forward and hit the man hard in the small of his back and heard a kind of crunch in his spine before he sprawled forward. Samson was aware of the gun flying from his grasp and clattering across the metal deck, then silence as it shot over the side and down into the river. Then he heard Anastasia's voice. He took the man's phone and used the torch to find her. She was cowering by the safety fence. Her hands were tied. He took the knife from his jeans, cut the tape and raised her to her feet. 'It's okay,' he said, 'I'm with you, Anastasia. I'm here.'

If she smiled, he could not see it. She leaned into his body and murmured something. She was very weak.

'I need to see this bastard,' said Samson, waving the phone screen at the face of the man lying unconscious on the stones. 'This is not Bukov!' he exclaimed.

'Who's Bukov?' she asked.

'The man in charge, the man I've been talking to. Where the fuck is he?'

'You mean Kirill,' she said. 'He stayed back there.'

'This man had his phone.'

'Yes, Kirill gave it to him. He wouldn't risk himself out here.'

He took hold of her around her waist. 'We're going to walk to the other side. Everything's good. You're going to be okay.' He felt her nod against his chest and they started walking. They were doing fine, keeping close to the side and moving steadily, then Samson guided her across the tracks to collect his phone. As he reached for it, he heard a crack behind him and instantly felt a scalding pain in the arm that held her so tightly, lurched forward and fell, taking her with him. Both of them cried out. There had been only one shot but she had been hit, too, and he realised the bullet must have passed clean through him and torn into her shoulder. They lay face down on the stones, entangled and helpless. 'Shit! Shit!' he gasped with the pain. 'Shit.' But Anastasia didn't make a sound. Right there, on that old creaking skeleton of a bridge between West and East, Samson felt her reserves finally give out. When Kirill appeared in his hunting hat and casually kicked her in the ribs, she didn't even cry out. She could not react, because she wanted him to get it done: she'd had enough.

Samson had his face in the ballast stones but he knew it was Bukov who had approached them from behind and shot him because the man was already muttering his usual sadistic crap about killing her in front of him. Now he told them that he had considered reversing the original plan so that Anastasia would watch him die. It was a finely balanced question, he said. Which of them loved the other the most? He was tempted to say it must be Samson because of all the trouble he had taken to free her, and yet he must give her credit for having put up such a decent fight these past few days. The spirit she had shown was fired by love for Samson, not by the hope of seeing again her war-criminal husband, he was quite sure of that.

He discovered the iPad at the back of Samson's jeans and pulled it out with a chuckle. He poked them with his stick a few more times, rammed the gun into their backs, circling them, and talked and talked. This all seemed to go on for a very long time, but in fact it was only a few minutes, at the end of which Samson raised his head and saw something move at the portal to the bridge on the Estonian side.

Bukov was oblivious. He told them that Crane's death did not matter in the least because he now held the device in his hands. And right then and there he, bizarrely, turned to politics, briefly outlining the stupidity of the Western public and telling them about Russia's coming glory. He was enjoying himself and so caught up in his flow that he didn't notice a tiny red light dance among the stones on the braces and struts behind him. Samson, turning his head as much as he dared, saw it land on Bukov and the Russian furiously trying to brush it off. When he realised what it was he jumped and fired his gun, a crazy shot that zinged into the steel structure above them. This provoked several flashes in the dark about twenty metres away from them. Nikita Bukov, known as Kirill, fell hatless and dead on to the stones in front of them.

And now a short man wearing a parka with a hoodie underneath it was with them. Holding the gun away, he helped Samson to a sitting position with one hand then gently rolled Anastasia and brought her upright. She groaned and seemed to be trying to make sense of what was happening, staring wildly at Samson through the damp snowflakes that fell and melted on them. Samson, his mind spinning, noticed a bar of greenish light over the town of Ivangorod in the east. Dawn was breaking. He turned back to Anastasia and flopped a hand in her direction.

The man waved a light over them. He seemed agitated about

something and uttered the word *Dio* several times. '*Devo prendere questa giacca – la giacca di mio cugino*,' he said quickly. '*Sua moglie lo vorrà*.'

Anastasia stirred and said, 'He wants the jacket. He says it belonged to his cousin – one of the dead men on the boat. He's going to take it back to his wife.'

'*Si, signora, è corretto*' – that's correct.

Although it cost her something to take off the jacket, they discovered that her wound was much less serious than Samson's, just a nasty gash on her shoulder. The bullet had lost most of its force when it passed through Samson's body. She handed the bloody jacket to the man and said, '*Mi dispiace anche*.' I am sorry, too.

The shock of being shot had slowed Samson's thinking but he now recognised the man by the birthmark that ran from his nose to his cheek. He was one of the Camorra crew who had been with Esposito in the car park at Naples airport. He'd worn a hoodie and stood slightly apart from the others.

'Ask him about our friends,' he told Anastasia. 'Are they all right?'

The man understood '*Amici? Stanno bene*.' Vuk and Harland were okay.

'They are fine' said a voice a little distance away. Naji was standing tentatively in the dawn light. 'They were knocked out by this man and his friend. They are with his friend now.'

'And what the hell are you doing here?'

'A deal,' said Naji. 'Where is the iPad?'

Samson gestured to Bukov's corpse. Naji felt in the man's

pockets and withdrew the device. He opened it and started tapping. 'This is good,' he said, and showed the Italian, who nodded.

Samson's mind swam. 'What's going on?'

Naji didn't reply but beckoned to the Italian. Together they walked to where Crane's body lay and crouched down. Samson pushed himself up on the bridge support to see. 'What are you doing?' he called out as Naji took Crane's lifeless hand and pressed it to the iPad's screen. He then passed the device to the Italian, who started tapping at the keyboard. They stood together and waited. Then the Italian put his hand on Naji's shoulder and said, '*Bravo, ragazzo! Bravo!*'

Naji closed the iPad cover and nodded.

'*Tutto bene!*' Everything's good. He gave them one last look, nodded as though a job had been well done and set off with the jacket of the dead Italian kidnapper tucked under his arm.

Naji returned to them and helped Anastasia to her feet. Then, with Naji between them giving both support, they began to walk towards the lights of Narva and the West.

'What the hell was that about?' said Samson when they reached the other side.

'My deal,' said Naji.

'More!' said Samson.

'He was hitman. I give them Crane's money to kill the man who shot you. That was the deal. Without this man you would not be alive.'

EPILOGUE

The events on the rail bridge didn't become clear to Samson until after he had received surgery for a bullet wound in the shoulder and the hole in his chest where the bullet had exited four inches below his clavicle on its downward path to Anastasia. Harland came into his room wearing a large square bandage at the back of his head that covered the cut he had received when he was bludgeoned at the door of the observation post. He said hello with a slightly sheepish smile and dragged a chair over to Samson's bed.

'All right, then?' he said.

'Yeah,' said Samson.

'She's still asleep,' Harland said. 'She's been out for a straight twenty-four hours. Utterly exhausted. But she's going to be fine. Hisami has been informed, but he has a fresh set of difficulties.'

Samson ignored this. He'd got Anastasia out and he didn't give much of a damn about Hisami's problems. 'Where's Naji?'

'With Ulrike. He's required to extend his stay in the country by KaPo. Ulrike, needless to say, is furious with me, so I'm rather glad of Naji's company at home. Extraordinary boy. He's been teaching her the Arab flute.' He grunted. 'Oh yes, Vuk sent this in for you.' He proffered Vuk's battered silver flask. Samson took it with his right hand and poured a little slivovitz into his mouth. 'We have a lot to get through. Where do you want to start?' Harland continued.

'I've been sitting here wondering how they traced us, but of course it was the phone – the Carabinieri gave the number to them and someone in Italian intelligence traced it. That's how they found me in the car park in Naples.' He looked out over the roofs of Narva, now lightly dusted with snow. 'Dumb of me not to realise.'

Harland's eyes twinkled agreement. In the cold winter light his skin was a ghostly white and he looked his age. 'How's your head?' asked Samson.

'It's fine, just a small cut, and I wasn't unconscious for long. It turned out that being set upon by your Italian mobster friends worked out very well for us. Because they disarmed Vuk and me and tied us up with the guards, we couldn't possibly be accused of committing any crime.'

'Except the small matter of the kidnap of Adam Crane?'

'Doesn't seem to be a priority to the police – they let Vuk go back to Serbia this morning. The intelligence services are keen to talk to Naji, as are MI6. Things have broken well for us, Samson.'

'How so?'

'Well, for one thing, no weapons found on any of us. And there was nothing to tie either of the vehicles to the kidnap and murder outside the bar.'

'But the bodies on the bridge?'

'There were none. The Russians collected their dead. And the Italians wiped the CCTV footage of the incident from the system, though they used it right up until they left. In fact, the infrared camera was the thing that saved you and Anastasia because they could see exactly what was happening – we all could. By that time, I'd come round.'

'And where the hell did Naji come in?'

Harland shook his head in amazement. 'He just walked in, bold as brass, looking for me, and they didn't know quite what to make of this lad with an open laptop in his hands. Luckily, one of them had good English.' Samson remembered the man in the car park who spoke for the Mafia boss Esposito. 'Just at that moment, we saw you had been shot and a stocky fellow – Bukov – emerge from the shadows. The Italians had got their man and weren't interested, but Naji explained that he was on the point of breaking into one of the bank accounts – all he needed was the small iPad and Crane's palm print. They knew about the bank accounts so they were inclined to believe that this might be possible, especially as Naji showed them a lot of information on his laptop that seemed authentic. He bought your lives for the whole amount in one bank account – €2.2million.' Harland waited for this to sink in. 'It was extremely fortunate that we took him along for the ride.'

'He's some piece of work,' said Samson.

'A fast talker, very persuasive and very clever – a natural for our trade.'

'And where are they now?'

'The Italians? Oh, I should imagine they've taken their friend's jacket back to Naples. Two men matching their description boarded a plane to Frankfurt early yesterday morning.'

Samson poured a little more of Vuk's slivovitz into his mouth. 'And Gil Leppo – what happened to him? Before my surgery Macy Harp told me he had lost a kidney but was expected to survive.'

'He'll wish he hadn't. He's the subject of several criminal investigations for fraud, money-laundering, wire fraud, conducting illegal arms deals from United States soil and sex with an underage girl and he'll be arrested on his return to the United States. Macy filled me in this morning. He was working with Crane from early on. The reason he was in Estonia was because Hisami had found out enough about the abuse of a minor and the arms deals to blackmail him to beg for Anastasia's life, which we now know was a hopeless endeavour. Crane had already given the order to kill her, as well as arranging the release of the video of Aysel Hisami.'

Harland took out a phone, poked at the screen and held it up so Samson could see. The still of the woman in fatigues who he'd seen in Hisami's email was now animated and in the clip she glanced up to the ceiling. Samson found himself looking at the young Aysel Hisami, as he knew he would. She was probably no more than twenty and was very striking, with a fiercely handsome face. A caption crawled across the bottom of the footage: 'Aysel Qasim – also known as Dr Aysel Hisami, sister of billionaire Denis Hisami, confesses to American investigators her part in the attack on a Turkish border post in south-eastern Turkey carried out in 1993.'

The interrogation that followed was carried out in Kurdish. Samson saw Aysel nod candidly at the two men as they asked questions. At the critical point, subtitles had been added. 'Can you explain what part you took in the action?' Onscreen, Aysel felt in her pockets for something. A man with his back to the camera leaned forward and offered her a cigarette. She lit it and blew the smoke towards the ceiling, then looked at the interrogator. 'I drove one of the vehicles.'

'And were you yourself involved in the attack?'

She shook her head and took another drag on the cigarette.

'But you were armed. Did you use your weapon?'

'When the army returned fire, yes.'

'Did you kill anyone?'

She gestured with the cigarette. 'Maybe – I cannot say for certain. This was a battle and several people were killed. There were many casualties on our side. I helped two of our wounded fighters escape.'

'And this was an action with the PKK?'

She shrugged a yes.

'So you confirm that at this period you were with the PKK, not the PUK?'

She nodded. 'Yes.'

'And your brother, was he a member of the terror group?'

She paused. 'You ask my brother about his life. You talk to Karim.'

'We have,' said the interrogator.

'What he tells you is the truth. He always tells the truth.' She stubbed out the cigarette half smoked. 'Karim is too proud to lie.'

'You confirm that you were a member of the PKK and took part in several actions, which resulted in the deaths of Turkish citizens?'

She shook her head several times and continued speaking for a few seconds longer, but there the sound and the subtitles ended. Samson said, 'It does what it was meant to do – implicates Denis and makes things much harder for him.' He paused for a beat. 'And for Anastasia, too: it's not going to be easy to run a humanitarian operation that's named after a terrorist.'

'Mandela was a terrorist at one time,' said Harland. 'And she only admits to firing back at Turkish troops. That's hardly terrorism. If they'd got anything worse, they would have used it.'

'But she was with the PKK – that matters. All those months I was looking for her, I had this sense that she'd been more closely involved in active combat than Denis ever told me. The risks she took on the front line three years ago wasn't the behaviour of someone who'd never seen action.' He stopped and looked out of the window, Syria and the knowledge of Aysel's appalling end flickering in his mind. 'Where's Denis? Still in jail?'

'Yes, and if he is released, he's not going to be allowed to leave the United States until the whole business is settled.'

'Have Anastasia and Denis talked?'

Harland shook his head. 'He's still banged up, no access to a phone.' They were silent for a few moments. Samson closed his eyes. 'You can't go to sleep yet,' said Harland. 'There's much more. There's Peter Nyman . . .'

His eyes flashed open. 'Jesus, yes! And Sonia bloody Fell said I shot him.'

'She's withdrawn that. Nyman was only grazed – a fuss about nothing. But you won't have any more trouble from him for some time, I suspect. Nyman and Fell were acting completely outside their remit. They had told SIS nothing and achieved even less. He has seriously angered his superiors by failing to give them the big picture. It's the stuff he's paid to do, but he kept all of it to himself. Now, the Kaitsepolitseiamet – an Estonian government intelligence agency – has scooped SIS and they have to beg for the material, so that's pissed them off royally.'

'You gave it all to KaPo?'

'Of course! My friends have cut us a lot of slack over the last few days. They needed a reward. Naji has agreed to share everything he's got on the groups, their finance and all the rest of it. As soon as you're out of here, we'll meet for the debrief. You should get some rest – you look bloody awful.'

He rose and did an odd thing with his shoulders and neck.

'I'll leave you Vuk's flask to see you through the night.' He stopped and laid a hand on his good arm. 'You won, Paul, you won.'

'Couldn't have done it without you.'

'It was you, Samson. You brought her back.'

Two days later at eight in the evening Samson arrived at the Harlands' seaside cottage, with a police escort, because the authorities believed he might still be at risk. Anastasia had arrived in very similar circumstances the day before.

Harland was making soup – apparently, a speciality of his – at the stove. He lowered a small silver ladle from his lips, greeted Samson with a wry smile and explained that Anastasia was upstairs sorting through clothes she could borrow during her enforced stay in Estonia, occasioned by the security services, who wanted to interview her a second time, and the need for a new US passport. Earlier in the evening she had spoken to Hisami, who was now out of detention but was still confined to his apartment. It was around that time that Samson noticed he'd missed a call from Denis, followed by a text that thanked him and wished him a speedy recovery. Samson spared himself the embarrassment of returning the call and talking to Hisami in person. As long as Hisami paid what he owed Macy Harp and Zillah Dee and all Samson's expenses, they were quits.

Naji had bobbed up from the table when he entered then seemed not to know quite what to do or say and returned to his computer. 'How're you doing, Naji?' asked Samson when he was settled with a glass of wine.

'Good,' he said, and told him about some work that he had been asked to contribute to at the university – his first job as a research assistant. He was bubbling over with it.

Samson listened and said quietly, 'Thank you, Naji.'

'It is not a problem for me to save your life. I am getting used to it.'

Anastasia came down in a big black polo-neck sweater and a grey skirt. They kissed and made oddly formal enquiries about each other's injuries, yet much more passed between them – a mute wonder that they were still alive, as well as a kind of helpless acknowledgement of their love for each other. The five of them sat down to dinner, Harland having taken soup to the armed officers who were guarding the house. Ulrike raised her glass in silence to the table, directing just a hint of reproof to her husband, who replied with a squeeze of the eyes that meant something to both of them. She smiled.

The wine, the warmth and the enormous sense of relief affected Samson, who staggered to his feet forty-five minutes later and said he must sleep, which he did in a neat white bedroom where there was a wooden half tester bed and a nightlight in a frosted glass jar.

In his dream he was with Anastasia, back on that huge black bridge slung between two worlds. The waters of the River Narva had risen impossibly high and lapped the structure, threatening to sweep them away. He couldn't move. He was calling out. Then he became aware of a hand stroking his cheek, the back of a hand, moving in a particular way. He opened his eyes and saw in the candlelight a face in shadow and the blur of a white robe. 'Thank you for being with me: thank you, dear Samson,' she said. She kissed his forehead, lingered for a few seconds, during which the scent of soap reached him, then her finger ran down to find his lips and she bent again to kiss him, saying, 'Thank you,' as her lips touched his.

'Stay,' he said. 'I'm awake now. What time is it?'

'Two. I couldn't sleep.' She kissed him again and climbed in beside him so she was lying on his right side and they did not touch each other's injuries. They held hands and looked up at the shadows on the ceiling made by the patterns in the frosted candle glass. It reminded her of Igor's lamps and she told Samson about the elfin boy and the old partisan lady out in the woods. Then they lay, more or less wordless, until she said, 'It's like we're being repeatedly shipwrecked together – only you and I know what we've been through. All that terror!'

'The ultimate nakedness,' said Samson.

'You remember I said that?'

He looked at her in the half-light and nodded. She struggled out of her nightie and stood for a moment. There was a large bandage just below her right shoulder. She was incredibly thin – she said she'd lost twelve pounds and dropped a whole size. She stripped the covers back and, holding on to the bed post for balance, straddled him and leaned forward so her breasts pressed against his chest and she was looking into his face. 'I need a gambler in my life,' she whispered.

'I've given up,' he said.

'You're still a gambler. You took so many huge risks! How can anyone just decide to kidnap a man off the street? I mean, who does that?'

'It was the only thing I could come up with.'

'I'm glad you did, and I am so, so glad to be here with you.

It's just the most perfect sensation in the world. I love the smell of you and that funny little-boy look of excitement in your eyes when you think you're going to have sex.' She straightened and moved down and let him inside her. 'I love you, Samson, but God you're infuriating. You're so obstinately you!'

'You've said all that before. Please stop talking and kiss me,' he said.

'Of course! And now I'm going to have to do all this by myself, I suppose.'

'You suppose right. I'm hardly in a position to do anything with this.' He jerked his chin towards his bandaged and bound arm. Then she began to move and they found the wonder of the first days in Venice again.

The next day, the team from KaPo – all of them, it seemed, around Samson's age, or younger – arrived, together with a whey-faced individual from British GCHQ who was just about tolerated.

Samson abruptly changed his mind about Denis Hisami's determination to expose Crane's operation. He realised he had been so focused on freeing Anastasia that he hadn't fully absorbed the implications of what lay in Misak's dossier, or the blizzard of discoveries made by Naji. Hisami had stumbled on the project to destabilise Europe with Russian money channelled through a respectable American start-up and had gone ahead and exposed it all, with the gravest consequences for himself and Anastasia. Of unprecedented scale and wickedness, the operation was now the priority of all Europe's intelligence agencies and KaPo had distributed the relevant evidence for each territory to react to the threats that faced them.

The media blackout on Crane's demise and what had come to pass on Narva's rail bridge had allowed them a little time to round up the key suspects and freeze assets before the networks were properly alerted to the implications of Crane's disappearance. As the head of the French DGSI – the General Directorate for Internal Security – later observed, the response of the European agencies to the networks of violent right-wing extremists was almost exactly the same as three years before, when a Syrian boy named Naji Touma produced a hoard of intelligence on IS. But no one appreciated Naji's vital role in this affair because, while Samson and Anastasia were being treated in hospital, Harland had ensured that his name was never mentioned.

Naji was nevertheless as irrepressible as ever and was rather enjoying himself, taking seasoned intelligence officers through his latest discoveries about the shell companies, bank accounts and many false identities used by Crane's Russian beneficiaries, as well as Crane's operation to skim millions from the money transferred from TangKi. Yet he was also modest and kept saying that his work would not have been possible without help from Jamie, his source on the other side of the Atlantic, or the digging done by Daniel Misak before he was murdered by Crane. Nearly $165 million of the $270 million was accounted for, though a good portion of that had been skimmed or invested in artworks now stored in Switzerland, Luxembourg and Italy. Through one scam or another, Crane had stolen in the region of $32 million from the Russian terror fund. Samson argued that any money that was recovered should be returned to TangKi so that the board members would have to own what had happened on their watch.

That point made, he stepped away to call Jim Tulliver in New York and gave him the bare bones of what was happening. Tulliver still had no idea that Samson had arranged for his boss's email to be hacked. He wanted to keep it that way and left a lot out but, clearly, Tulliver had now read the Misak dossier. A team of forensic accountants was already putting together the story of how the company was used to launder money and they were paying particular attention to the source of funds in America.

'There is some good news, however,' said Tulliver. The authorities are backing off on the citizenship issue. It looks like Denis will be free to move about the country in the next twenty-four hours. His passport is still suspended.'

'And the film of Aysel made no difference?'

'Denis expected much worse. He can survive that.'

'But can Anastasia? Can the Foundation survive that publicity?'

'We'll see,' said Tulliver. 'There's also now a question of funding it.' He tried to congratulate and thank Samson, but Samson brushed him off. 'Is Anastasia there? Can I speak with her?'

At that moment Anastasia entered the room with Ulrike. Everyone rose and Ulrike gestured that they should return to their seats. Anastasia's eyes met Samson's and she smiled.

'I'm afraid not,' Samson told Tulliver. 'She'll be in touch when she's feeling stronger.'

Tulliver began to thank him again.

'Jim . . .? Jim . . .? Sorry – you're breaking up,' Samson said, and hung up.

He tipped his head towards the door. Anastasia smiled and nodded enthusiastically.

Later, on the beach, he said he liked the clothes Ulrike had lent her. 'Those colours suit you.'

'Thanks,' she said, and looked down at the prints her borrowed Wellington boots had made in the wet sand. Her face had clouded. He said nothing and they walked to the great boulders at the water's edge. The sea was calm. A little way out a cormorant stood on one of the boulders, drying its outstretched wings in the weak winter sun. 'It looks like a sculpture,' she said, then moved to his other side, her hand seeking his uninjured right arm. She turned and looked into his eyes. 'I still can't believe what you did for me, Samson.'

'Don't forget what you did for yourself,' he said. 'You decided you were going to survive.'

'Yes, but you . . .'

'Don't thank me,' he said, grinning. 'Anyway, I have to admit I was in two minds until I found your phone and realised you'd kept all those photographs from Venice and that my birthday was still your passcode.'

'You found the phone! My phone! The one I put in Louis's pocket? Jesus!'

'It's a long story. The Carabinieri missed it. But for one

reason or another, it was really helpful to us. You can have it back, of course.'

'And you went through it,' she said with dawning horror.

'For professional reasons only,' he said, and she gave him a light punch on his bicep. 'Then I understood,' he continued, after a long pause in which he held her searching gaze, 'that I loved you and I had to tell you this in person, which could not be done while you were being held by those bastards in Russia. So, here I am, doing precisely that. I love you, Anastasia.'

'I know that!' she said with irritation, and stamped a boot into the sand. He waited. They looked out to the horizon in silence. 'The thing is,' she said at last, 'I'm not yet used to the idea that I'm not going to be killed at any moment. The absence of terror is weirdly hard to deal with. Somehow, I'm going to have to find my normal, fucked-up self again. Do you understand?'

'I do,' he said.

'Of course you do. You've been through it more than me.' She looked along the beach to the line of trees that ran down to a bank of grey shingle. 'Last night was so . . .'

'Wonderful,' he said.

'Yes, it was wonderful, and we are so very close like that. What are we going to do? Please tell me how this ends. What do we do now? I mean, I have to go back to Denis. You know that, don't you?'

'Yes.'

'Where does that leave us?' Tears were springing to her eyes.

'You need time,' he said. 'Denis is in real trouble and he needs you.'

'Don't be so fucking noble.'

'I'm being realistic, but at least you can never doubt what I feel for you. You are married, and that matters, and I had a kind of a sort of a thing going with someone in London, but I mean it – I love you and I always will love you.'

'I don't care who you've been to bed with. It's really not the point. What about us? How do we go on?'

He shook his head. 'I have no idea.'

'And we've got so little in common – it's just sex and Venice.'

'We shared a bullet, too. That must count for something.'

She smiled, her eyes still glistening with tears. They turned to see a figure waving from the boat sheds and starting towards them.

'And we have Naji Touma in common,' he said.

'And Naji,' she agreed, and darted a kiss to his lips. 'Thank you, Samson.'

ACKNOWLEDGEMENTS

Thanks to my editor, Jane Wood, who has done so much to bring this series of novels to life, and to my agent, Rebecca Carter, of Janklow and Nesbit, for her unflagging support. My gratitude also to Otto Penzler and Morgan Entrekin for their shrewd suggestions, and to Pamela Merritt for her first read.

Living with someone writing a book is almost certainly worse than actually having to write the book yourself so I thank Liz for enduring the process and the author.